THE AUCTION

Sadie Kincaid is a *USA TODAY* and Amazon number 1 bestselling dark romance author who loves to read and write about hot alpha males and strong, feisty females. Her backlist has sold over 4 million copies, and she lives in the UK with her husband and sons.

Sadie loves to connect with readers, so why not get in touch via social media?

sadiekincaid.com
@sadie_kincaidxx
@sadiekincaidauthor

Sign up to her newsletter for all the latest news and releases at https://www.subscribepage.com/sadiekincaidnewsletter

Join Sadie's reader group, Sadie's Ladies and Sizzling Alphas, for the latest news, book recommendations, and plenty of fun at https://www.faccbook.com/groups/3951453674941245/

Dear reader,

You are about to enter the sizzling and mysterious world of Sadie Kincaid's *The Auction*, the first book in the captivating Wages of Sin dark romance duet.

If you can't get enough Sadie Kincaid, check out her fan-favorite Chicago Ruthless series of dark mafia romances starring the infamous members of the Moretti family. The full series is available in ebook and audiobook now, with exclusive deluxe print editions releasing from Sadie Kincaid and HarperCollins through 2026.

And don't forget to preorder the enthralling conclusion to the Wages of Sin duet, *The Game*, releasing November 2026 in all formats wherever books are sold. Once you enter the spicy, romantic world of Sadie Kincaid, you'll never want to leave.

Also by Sadie Kincaid

The Wages of Sin duet
The Game (forthcoming)

The Chicago Ruthless series
Dante
Joey
Lorenzo
Keres

The Broken Bloodlines series
Forged in Blood
Promised in Blood
Bound in Blood

The Manhattan Ruthless series
Broken
Promise Me Forever
Rebound
Played
Made

The London Ruthless series
Dark Angel
Fallen Angel

The New York Ruthless series
Ryan Rule
Ryan Redemption
Ryan Retribution
Ryan Reign
Ryan Renewed
A Ryan Collection (a collection of New York Ruthless novellas)

The LA Ruthless series
Fierce King
Fierce Queen
Fierce Betrayal
Fierce Obsession

Stand-alone novels
The Perfect Fit
Heart of a Devil

A Curse of Blood and Fate series (with LJ Morrow)
Cursebound

For additional books by Sadie Kincaid, as well as updates on all of her current and upcoming releases, visit her website, sadiekincaid.com

THE AUCTION

SADIE KINCAID

HarperCollins*Publishers*

HarperCollins*Publishers* Ltd
1 London Bridge Street
London SE1 9GF

www.harpercollins.co.uk

HarperCollins*Publishers*
Macken House, 39/40 Mayor Street Upper
Dublin 1, D01 C9W8, Ireland

First published by Sadie Kincaid 2026
This edition published by HarperCollins*Publishers* Ltd 2026
1

Copyright © Sadie Kincaid 2026

Illustrations © naddya/stock.adobe.com (roses); © Christos Georghiou/stock.adobe.com (queen); © Quarta/stock.adobe.com (chess board).

Sadie Kincaid asserts the moral right to be identified as the author of this work.

A catalogue record for this book is available from the British Library.

ISBN: 978-0-00-879964-9

This novel is entirely a work of fiction. The names, characters and incidents portrayed in it are the work of the author's imagination. Any resemblance to actual persons, living or dead, events or localities is entirely coincidental.

Printed and bound in the UK using 100%
Renewable Electricity at CPI Group (UK) Ltd

All rights reserved. No part of this publication may be reproduced, stored in a retrieval system, or transmitted, in any form or by any means, electronic, mechanical, photocopying, recording or otherwise, without the prior written permission of the publishers.

Without limiting the exclusive rights of any author, contributor or the publisher of this publication, any unauthorised use of this publication to train generative artificial intelligence (AI) technologies is expressly prohibited. HarperCollins also exercise their rights under Article 4(3) of the Digital Single Market Directive 2019/790 and expressly reserve this publication from the text and data mining exception.

For all the wonderful readers, a reminder that although you might feel alone in this world, you are stronger, braver, and more courageous than any character in any book ever written.

Lincoln Knight

Content Warning

This book is intended for mature readers and contains topics and events which may be triggering for some readers. These include, but are not limited to:

Age-gap relationship
Human trafficking
Menstrual kink
Praise and punishment kink
Sexual assault (not involving the MC or FMC)
Violence

CHAPTER 1
IMOGEN

"Have you heard who's here?" The whispered question comes from the girl with brown eyes as wide as saucers. In my head, I call her Kit because she reminds me of the kitten I found hiding beneath a dumpster when I was nine.

I take a furtive look around to make sure she isn't caught speaking. The tallest guard, the one with a cobra tattoo on his neck, is staring at the exit. One lone steel door—that's the only way in or out of this room. The other two guards are watching us, eyes greedily ogling our bodies like they own us. No doubt imagining all the things they'd like to do if they only had the chance.

My skin crawls, but I refuse to let it show on the outside. Eighteen years of my life have been spent in preparation for this, and I will not break. Especially not now that I've heard the crowd's reaction when a girl breaks down onstage. It spurs them on. Drives their cruelty.

"No, who?" the girl sitting beside me asks quietly, her knees tucked up to her chest and her back to the wall. I call her Sam because she looks like a character from the kids TV show that I was occasionally permitted to watch.

While our guards observe us still, they no longer seem interested in stopping every attempt at conversation. I suppose now that we're so close to the end point, they have no need to prevent us from talking to each other. From forming bonds that would have made our time together a little less hellish. Now, it's certain that we'll never see each other again. Many of us won't make our next birthdays.

But that won't be me. I'm a survivor. Larissa taught me well.

I remain silent despite our guards' reduced interest in our conversation. I won't do anything to incur their wrath. They are no longer allowed to physically harm us, since we must be unblemished for the customers, but there are other ways to break a person's spirit.

And I will not break.

"Lincoln Knight," Kit whispers even more quietly than before.

My ears perk up.

There are seven girls left in here, and Sam waits for the guards' leery gazes to drift to the ones on the opposite side of the room before she risks responding. "No way. How do you know that?"

I stare at the door, perfecting the art of looking like I'm not paying attention to either the girls or the guards while being finely attuned to every movement happening around me. And most importantly, I don't want to reveal just how intrigued I am to hear Kit's answer. Because Lincoln Knight is . . .

Well, he's Lincoln Knight.

Billionaire. Recluse. Genius. Psycho. Depending on who's telling the story.

"I was near the door earlier, and one of the guards told the ugly one that he was here."

Sam lets out a barely audible gasp. Her legs are trembling, and I have to stop myself from resting a reassuring hand on her thigh. I figure the ugly one is the guard nearest the door who has an unfortunate overbite that makes him look like his chin has sunk into his neck. They are all equally ugly to me. Vicious. Pawing. Evil.

But Lincoln Knight. What the hell is he doing here? Of all the labels he has been given over the years, recluse is the one I know to be true. The man hasn't been seen in public in over a decade.

"You think he's here . . . here to buy?" Sam murmurs out of the corner of her mouth.

"Shut the fuck up!" Snake Tattoo bellows, causing both Sam and Kit to clamp their lips together.

Of course he's here to buy. I guess we can add sick puppy to his list of titles.

I'VE REMAINED AS DETACHED AS POSSIBLE FOR THE duration of tonight's vile proceedings. Years of conditioning can do that to a girl. I stared ahead, unblinking, as almost every girl to leave the room pleaded and begged for her life. I didn't flinch when the crowd cheered as Sam stumbled out the door with urine running down her bare legs. Or any of the times when they clamored to see more.

Each of us will leave this room in an elegant black dress, but once onstage . . . Well, then we must submit to the will of the crowd. Show off our *assets* in whatever way they demand.

But when it's Kit's turn to leave—Lot No. 50—something inside me finally cracks. She's the last to go before me. The last to be sold into a life of . . . what? A quick death at best. Years of slavery, torture, and pain at worst. I already know I cannot hope for the former, highly prized as I am. The daughter of the most infamous disgraced ex-member of the Brotherhood. Here to atone for his sins eighteen long years after his death. I suspect most of my peers are aware that the men who attend events like these aren't here for any kind of benevolent purposes, for anyone who trades in human life cannot possibly be anything other than morally bankrupt. But I'm blessed to know a little more about the kinds of men who buy women at Brotherhood auctions. They come from all walks of life, but one thing they have in common is that they are rich and powerful enough to serve the Brotherhood in some way, and to do the kinds of things that ordinary mortals could never hope to get away with, and they act with impunity. Perhaps this knowledge is not a blessing at all, but a curse.

But it's not the knowledge of my almost certain fate which nearly unravels me. It's Kit's face. Her huge brown eyes swimming with tears. The wobble of her plump lower lip.

"Move!" Ugly shoves his semiautomatic into the small of her back, and she stumbles forward. And then she lets out a strangled cry, filled with terror and despair. It has every hair on my body standing on end, but still I don't move. I don't react. Don't show weakness.

"Please! Let me go. I'll do anything," she pleads with Ugly.

"Yeah, you're gonna, little girl." He sneers at her, his face twisted with cruelty. How can anyone with a soul partake in this sick trade? How can anyone look into the face of another human being and then . . .

I blink away a single tear and hope that nobody notices, but thankfully, they're all focused on Kit. Taking twisted pleasure in her torment. In her abject terror. The girl is no more than eighteen, if that. Poor thing.

At least I had twenty-one years of my life before this. My upbringing wasn't without its hardships, but I was alive. I was always *safe*. Always untouched. I was eleven years old when I was first told how *special* I was. How my grandfather managed to spare my life by giving his sworn oath that he would prepare me for this—my ultimate penance to the Brotherhood for my father's mistakes.

THE AUCTION

Kit is shoved out of the room, still crying, and the crowd predictably jeers her for it. I imagined they would have grown smaller and quieter by now with forty-nine lots sold already, but they sound as great in number as they have all night. And even more riled up.

"They're all waiting for you, ya know?" Snake Tattoo says.

I don't look at him, keeping my eyes trained on the door.

He steps closer and trails the tip of the barrel of his semi-automatic across my cheekbone. "Lot 51." He snickers like an adolescent boy seeing a pair of breasts for the first time.

When he crouches down, his sour breath washes over my face and makes me want to retch. I fight back the instinct and stare through his disgusting face. "They all want a piece of you, uptight little bitch. Some real sick fucks looking to spend a lot of money to get their hands on your untouched cunt."

Panic swims up from my gut, fighting for a stranglehold. But I breathe through it.

In. Out.

One, two, buckle my shoe.

Three, four, knock at the door.

He leans closer, his eyes only inches from mine, and tilts his head from side to side like the cobra on his neck would—right before it strikes its prey. "And your ass, I expect. Mouth. Nose. Ears. Not a part of you will go unfucked and unused. Traitor."

I stare, unblinking. *In. Out.*

Five, six. Pick up sticks.

He leans closer still, and then he licks a trail from my cheekbone over my right eye socket to the top of my forehead. I don't flinch. Don't even blink. I leave his rancid saliva on my skin, where it sears my flesh like acid. My fingertips twitch and my limbs ache to move, to wipe him off me. Gripped by a visceral need to clean his stench from my body.

But I don't. I go on breathing.

In. Out.

Seven, eight. Lay them straight.

Mercifully, Snake Tattoo tires of trying to get a reaction from me and returns to his spot against the wall. And now we both stare at the door.

I go on breathing. Reciting the nursery rhyme over and over while I drown out the sound of the crowd as they force Kit to strip naked before some sick fuck buys her. I repeat the words like a mantra, until I unlock the safe space deep inside me, the place where nobody else can ever be. Where nobody can touch me.

"Your turn, bitch," Snake Tattoo says, yanking me out of the comfort of my trancelike state.

I jump to my feet before he has a chance to lay a finger on me, brush the creases from my black dress, and take slow, steady steps toward the door. My knees quiver with each small stride, but I go on putting one foot in front of the other. This is the end, but also the beginning. And every new beginning is an opportunity for change. Perhaps the person who buys me will not be a devil, but a lonely man—or woman—who simply wants a companion.

I immediately chide myself for such foolish thoughts. Larissa warned me that my mind would try to make bargains like this. But that is not the reality of the world I live in. Nice people do not come to auctions organized by the Brotherhood. Nice people do not buy other people from heinous events where women are paraded like slabs of meat. Every new beginning is an opportunity for revenge. For escape. For retribution.

The door is opened by Ugly, and despite my resolve, it takes a nudge from the barrel of Snake's gun to urge me through it. I stumble into the bright spotlights illuminating the stage, and I'm welcomed by a smiling emcee dressed in a smart tuxedo, looking like he's hosting a charity auction. Like all of this is in any way normal.

I walk onstage to a chorus of jeers, catcalls, and vile comments about my *pussy*.

THE AUCTION

Deep breath.
One, two, buckle my shoe.

Just a few words and I'm back in that space where they can't get to me. Can't taint me.

"Now, now, patrons," says the guy in the tux, his shark teeth glinting under the lights. "I know this one here is tonight's star prize. But we're going to behave with some decorum, gentlemen. There'll be no seeing the goods until we have some serious bids. I'm authorized to open at half a million dollars."

Gentlemen, my ass! Sick, twisted fucks.

The crowd starts up again. But through their lewd comments and their disgusting noises, one loud deep voice cuts through them all. "Ten million dollars."

The room falls silent. Tux Guy holds his gavel aloft, his mouth hanging open as he shields his eyes, trying to see where the voice came from.

I squint, trying to do the same, but the blinding stage lights mean I can only make out shadows.

"We should get to see her virgin pussy at least," a lone voice calls out, but it's met with an eerie silence as thick vines of tension begin threading their way through the room.

My still-trembling knees want to buckle, but I breathe deeply. In. Out. I need to stay focused. Need to be alert to any and every opportunity to gather any information that may be of any use to me. *Knowledge is power, Imogen.*

Yet I can't stop wondering what kind of man is capable of bringing a room so full of evil to silence. Surely only someone who is more of a devil than all of them combined.

"Any advance on ten million?" Tux Guy asks, his voice shaking with excitement.

Silence.

"Sold to Mr. Knight!"

My knees give way. I drop to the wooden stage with a thud. Panic overwhelms me.

In. Out.
One, two, buckle my shoe.
"Deliver her to my car," Lincoln Knight demands.
In. Out. Three, four, knock at the door.

The spotlights seem to grow closer, and I'm blinded by them. Then there are hands grabbing me, lifting me. Instinctively, I struggle, forgetting all my years of conditioning.

Until I hear her voice. *They may touch you. Defile you. They may take your body, my sweet child, but they can never take your spirit. Never have what's inside of you. That is yours and yours alone.*

I stop fighting, close my eyes, and breathe.
In. Out.
I will not break.

CHAPTER 2
LINCOLN

She stumbles onto the stage like a newborn foal, all long limbs and glossy dark hair, blinking in the harsh spotlights illuminating her face. Full pink lips and long lashes flutter against the olive skin of her cheeks. I can recall her striking green eyes even if I cannot see them.

Imogen DeMotta. Daughter of Luca DeMotta and tonight's most prized auction lot, which is why she has been saved until the last. No sense in selling off the most sought-after goods first. How, then, would the Brotherhood retain the attention of their most affluent customers? This isn't the first auction of its kind. The Brotherhood hold them every other year, however it's only the second one I have ever attended. The first was sixteen years ago, when my cause was a new one. I no longer attend such events, at least not in person. But I'm aware of every single one, and of every single lot that is sold.

Perhaps it's a misguided attempt at some redemption—an effort to save my blackened soul. Not that my soul is worth saving.

Nothing has changed in sixteen years. It's still a room packed full of men in custom-tailored suits, reeking of cigars and the finest Scotch money can buy. Businessmen, lawyers, supreme court justices, politicians, oil barons—they come from every walk of life. All of them linked by a common thread: They see women as a commodity to be bought and sold and have zero qualms about watching it happen. Even if they do not have the means to buy, they still like to watch the show. Men who, to the outside world, appear to be respectable gentlemen. Yet within these walls—without the disapproving eyes of their wives, their colleagues, their friends, or their family upon them—those men behave like animals.

Mob mentality has always fascinated me. How individuals can be so easily swayed by the will of the crowd. Those who are attending these events for the first time are easy to spot. They fidget uncomfortably at first, eyes shifting left and right as though they're naughty schoolboys fearing they're about to be caught doing something they shouldn't be at any moment. But after the first few women—for it is always women—are sold, they lose their inhibitions. Enthused by the new and illicit nature of it all, they lose sight of their sense of right and wrong and join in with the rest, often with even more vigor than their more seasoned counterparts.

Sex is a trade as old as time, and the Brotherhood has perfected it into an art form. The biannual auctions last an entire day and are as elaborately catered as the wedding of an oil baron and a society princess.

A whole smorgasbord of women is put on display. Some are as old as their late twenties and *used*, as they're referred to in the glossy catalog that is emailed to a secure database and can only be accessed with a thirty-eight-digit passcode. Then there are the girls as young as eighteen who have been groomed for this life from a tender age. And they are always the most highly prized.

The crowd, full of lobster, Scotch, and champagne by this point in the proceedings, calls for Imogen to remove her dress as soon as they catch a glimpse of her. Someone a few feet to the left of me demands to see her virgin pussy, and I bite down on the inside of my cheek, having to physically restrain myself from crushing his skull with my bare hands.

What these sick fucks—deviant little boys who like to play-act at being very important men—don't understand is that she is mine. And I would gouge out the eyes of every single one of them before I allow them even a glimpse of what lies beneath her dress.

But I cannot do that. Not tonight. Not as Lincoln Knight at least. Instead, I do the only thing I am able to. I wait for the auctioneer to open bidding, and while these useless pricks are grabbing onto their dicks and imagining what it might be like to touch her, I make my bid. "Ten million dollars."

That sure as hell shuts them all up. The most any woman has ever sold for here is five million. And she was a Saudi princess. I would pay ten times that for this one. In fact, there is no price I wouldn't pay for Imogen DeMotta. I'd give every single goddamn cent I have.

The auctioneer tries to see who made the bid, but I'm at the back, among the shadows—the place where I'm most comfortable. I only give him a heartbeat of my attention before my focus is drawn back to her.

She blinks under the bright lights, peering out into the crowd. The same crowd who would use her up and tear her apart if they were given half a chance, yet she stands there like a warrior goddess. I notice the slight tremble in her legs but her glare is determined. Defiant. She knows she's the main event. She knows that some sick fuck is about to buy her like a piece of cattle and do who-the-fuck-knows-what to her. Yet still, she stands there, facing her demons. Facing the monsters who want nothing but to use her and hurt her—the same men who would piss themselves with terror if they were in her shoes.

Mutters and whispers of my name ripple through the crowd. It's true I don't get out much and always cause a stir when I do.

They call me a monster too. Or a freak. Absentmindedly, I trace my jaw with my fingertips, feeling only the smooth ceramic mask that covers my face. I guess they would be right.

"Any advance on ten million?" the auctioneer asks, a distinct crack in his voice. He's probably rock-hard in his tuxedo pants thinking about how he's going to spend his cut. My bid just added a hundred thousand dollars to his earnings for tonight.

He's met with silence, as I expected. Although I was prepared to up my bid if necessary. There are others in this room who have as much money as I do, and some who would buy her simply to prove that they could. But they do not speak up. Even the most arrogant of men know when they are outranked, and as far as predators go, I am very much at the top of that food chain.

"Sold to Mr. Knight!"

Imogen's knees buckle, and she drops to the stage with a thud. But nobody is paying her much attention as they file out of the ballroom. She's no longer a source of entertainment to them now that she belongs to me.

And as far as they are concerned, I am the fiercest monster of them all.

CHAPTER 3
LINCOLN

The rage is indescribable, burning through every vein and sinew of my body. It takes me seconds to reach the stage, and less time to have my hand around this pathetic fuck's throat—my fingers clamped in a bruising grip, obscuring his snake tattoo.

"What part of 'deliver her to my car' do you think gave you permission to touch her? Who gave you permission to touch what is *mine*?" I snarl, certain that the sight of his filthy hands on her delicate skin will haunt me for eternity.

I squeeze his throat tighter, until his eyes bulge in their sockets and he claws at my arm in a plea for release. Imogen remains on the floor, staring up at me like she doesn't know who to be more afraid of—the animal who just grabbed her like she was a racoon stealing trash, or me. I shake him. "Answer me!"

"Mr. Knight, sir," a soothing voice is at my ear. I recognize him as Faraday Barnes—one of the organizers of tonight's event. A snake with a smooth tongue, employed by the Brotherhood to be the *face* of such proceedings, so that they can continue to hide within the shadows like the cowards they truly are. "He can't answer you with your hand around his throat like that."

I loosen my grip just a little, enough for him to croak out a pathetic apology. I should force him to his knees and make him apologize to her, but there's a danger that my demand would reveal too much of why I'm really here tonight. They have always believed of me only what I want them to believe, and that is that I'm as sick and twisted as the rest of them. If they suspected my true motives, or who she is to me . . . the consequences would be too dangerous for both of us.

I shove the disgusting little prick away from me and wipe my hands on Faraday's jacket, desperate to remove the stench of him from my skin.

"My apologies, sir, when you requested she be delivered to your car, Alec here assumed . . ." He clears his throat and dips his head a little. "It was not intended to cause any offense."

I roll my neck and pretend that his act of deference has appeased me. It has not. "Do not touch my property again."

"Of course, sir. Would you like one of my men to escort her to your vehicle while you pay your tab?"

I glance down at her and she's still staring up at me, vivid green eyes filled with both fear and determination. I wear my mask in public, but no doubt she would also be staring at me with horror if she could see what lies beneath it. No, I do not want any of his men to escort her. I want none of their lecherous eyes on her. I want there to be no chance of them speaking to her, and allowing their vile words to wash over her skin. The truth is I don't want her out of my sight for a second longer. Not until we're away from here and in a place where another soul will never lay eyes on her ever again. "She may accompany me while I make the payment."

Faraday blinks twice, but quickly schools his face to neutral. It is unheard of to allow the *goods* to remain in this area once they are purchased, but I am no ordinary buyer. He gives a curt nod, displeased but too much of a shrewd businessman to refuse me. "Of course, sir."

I'm tempted to hold out my hand to Imogen, if only to see if she would take it. But I haven't felt the touch of another woman for so very long, to feel her skin on mine may be enough for this facade I so delicately crafted to crumble into ash. Instead I simply look her in the eyes. "Stand."

She smooths down her dress and sets her jaw in grim determination. And then she stands, all elegance and poise, her gaze still locked on mine.

"Continue to do as you're told and we will be out of here in but a few moments. Understand me?"

She nods.

"Then come this way, Lot 51."

I don't miss the way that title makes her bristle, as it's designed to do. The Brotherhood aren't the first to use numbers to dehumanize their prisoners. But I would not chance calling her by her name in front of these men and risk that the sound from my lips would be an echo of a name I have spoken many times before. In a past life.

Obediently, she follows me to the small office where payments are taken, where a dozen other buyers are paying for the souls they just stole. Rage still simmers deep in my veins and I snarl at anyone who even glances at her. They mutter about how much I paid for her, but wisely, they look away. And all the while she quietly stands among us, her head bent low and her eyes on the floor.

An angel among demons.

CHAPTER 4
IMOGEN

The leather seat is warm and soft against my bare thighs, but the climate-controlled interior of the black limousine prevents my skin from getting sticky. My hands are curled delicately in my lap and I desperately resist the urge to pick at a fingernail. To do anything. Movement might betray my fear, and I refuse to do that. Emotion is weakness.

So I simply stare out the window at the passing scenery, hoping for a clue as to where this devil is taking me.

Devil. The term fits him as well as his perfectly tailored suit. He sits opposite me, a laptop on his knee. The pale blue light from the screen illuminates him in the otherwise comforting dim light of the car.

He wears a mask, no doubt hiding the disfigurement people whisper of. It covers his entire face and appears to be made of something lightweight, possibly ceramic. Its surface is smooth and unnatural looking, with only subtle ridges along the cheekbones, like some attempt has been made to make it look vaguely human. But the mouth is expressionless, merely a curve indicating lips without having any.

It's devoid of humanity. Cold and untouchable.

He has dark hair, a little longer than would be considered

respectable in my grandfather's opinion. Its curls fall over his forehead and ears, as well as the pristine white collar of his shirt. All that can be clearly seen of his features are his eyes. And they are enough—certainly the eyes of a devil. Dark, brooding, and so intense I'm convinced they could see inside a person's soul.

Not mine though. Everything inside of me is locked down tight. Lincoln Knight will only ever see what I want him to.

He looks up from his computer screen and finds me watching him. Instinct almost makes me flinch at being caught, but I fight it, remaining still. We must have been driving for an hour, and there's little else to look at, given that the scenery has morphed from the twinkling lights of the city buildings to a seemingly endless stretch of night and highway. I can't help but feel as we get farther and farther away from the lights, we get farther from civilization. Farther away from people who could potentially help a girl who was just bought by a monster.

"Are you thirsty?" His deep smooth voice almost catches me off guard. I can't remember the last time I ate or drank anything. Subconsciously, I swallow. My throat feels scratchy and dry.

"Yes."

He opens up the center console beside him and pulls out a glass bottle of water. Condensation runs down the side of the bottle and suddenly it's the most appealing-looking drink I've ever seen before in my life. I watch him intently while he slowly closes the compartment, still holding on to the bottle of liquid nirvana. He takes out his pocket square and carefully wipes the glass down before unscrewing the metal cap. Still, he doesn't hand it over. He replaces his pocket square and palms the cap.

Is this some kind of power play? Is he going to drink the water himself after asking if I'm thirsty? It wouldn't surprise me if he were to do something so cruel, but surely it's in his interest not to let me die from dehydration after he paid ten million dollars for me?

My instincts are confirmed correct when he finally hands

me the bottle. I take it with slightly trembling fingers, annoyed at myself for the one physical reaction I cannot seem to control. No matter how many tests and punishments I endured, I couldn't always fully control the trembling. There were times when I could, but in others the slightest tremor would give me away, and it was always when I was facing something new and unknown.

"Thank you," I say, my tone as cold and detached as I can manage.

Then I take a swig of the water, ice-cold and soothing. It floods my mouth with sweet relief, washing down my throat and almost making me want to groan with pleasure. I close my eyes and commit this simple experience to memory, having learned from an early age to find happiness in the smallest of things. And this, I will savor. Because I have no idea when I'll experience anything close to happiness next.

When I open my eyes again, Lincoln is watching me intently. Those inscrutably dark eyes narrowed on my face, almost like he's enjoying my pleasure—or more likely he's enjoying my torment. Does he think me so easily rattled that I cannot endure his scrutiny? He may be used to that from the other women he has purchased like cattle, but he won't get any such reaction from me. Unlike those others, I'm prepared. I, Imogen DeMotta, am not like other women, and I am ready for anything.

WHEN THE CAR FINALLY ROLLS TO A STOP IT'S still dark outside and I have no idea of the time. I think the auction started around noon, given that we left the *safe house* a little after sunrise and we drove for a few hours to get to the venue. Then we were given some food and water before it started. The whole day felt like it lasted for an eternity, but I do some mental math and figure even if every lot sale took ten minutes, and accounting for the time between sales, it must have lasted at least ten hours. Then I had to wait around for a short time while Lincoln *paid* for me, so I would guess it's already after midnight.

Lincoln opens the door and holds out a hand to me, offering to help me climb out. Because it would be impolite to refuse, I take it and allow him to assist me. In contrast to his cold exterior, his fingers are warm against mine. His grip is firm yet somehow tender. The gesture could almost be described as chivalrous . . . if he hadn't just bought me like a piece of meat at some sick, twisted auction. If the man wasn't a devil who's in league with the Brotherhood.

He drops my hand as soon as I'm out of the car and turns his attention to his driver, who's standing beside the open door, staring at his boss intently, his bright blue eyes unblinking. The driver's tall, over six feet, and almost as broad as the brute beside me. My eyes scan the area quickly, always alert for any potential opportunities for escape, but there are none here.

Lincoln signs something and then his driver signs back. I wonder if he's actually deaf, or if Lincoln just doesn't want me to hear whatever it is they're speaking about. However, I know a little sign language, and all I can decipher is that his driver is telling Lincoln to call him when he's needed next.

With a respectful nod, the driver grabs a large flashlight from the car and hands it to his boss. Then he climbs back into the car and the sleek black limousine pulls smoothly away, leaving Lincoln and I standing on the side of a long deserted road lined with dense forest on either side.

"This way." He flicks on the flashlight and jerks his head in the direction of the trees.

I walk beside him obediently, following the white arc of the flashlight as it bobs through the trees. I try not to think of what manner of wild animals or insects might be scurrying through this undergrowth and instead take in as much information about where we are and where we're headed as possible. But there's not much to go on at all. Just darkness, trees and more trees. Why are we even headed into the woods? I suppose it does make sense for Lincoln to live in the middle of nowhere, given his reclusive reputation. And the man has just paid ten million dollars for the pleasure of my company, so I figure even if he is a serial killer with a fetish for tracking his prey in the woods, he'll at least want to keep me alive until he gets his money's worth. If he was merely intending to kill me on the side of the road, surely he wouldn't have gone to such expense. Still, my fear of whatever unknown I'm walking into is keeping my nervous system teetering on a knife's edge, and I'm sure my body is being powered solely on adrenaline right now.

We only walk a few hundred yards before coming to a square concrete building. It looks so out of place here in the middle of so much nature, but it's deep enough into the forest to not be seen by passing cars. The structure is bigger than a house, but from what I can see from the beam of the flashlight, it has no windows and only one steel door. And now my survival instinct is kicking in. Panic curls in my chest, its icy fingers squeezing my heart so tightly that I struggle to breathe normally. Is this some kind of torture chamber set up in the middle of nowhere where nobody will hear me scream? Bile surges up in my stomach, burning my throat.

I swallow it down and remember how to breathe.

In. Out.

One, two, buckle my shoe.

Lincoln obviously senses my panic, because he takes hold of my wrist and pulls me along with him. Despite the building looking like an abandoned warehouse, the door is controlled by a fingerprint and retina scan system, and I'm not sure if the high-tech security makes me feel better or worse about what I'm going to find inside.

Lincoln walks in first, keeping me behind him. Sensors immediately flood the space with light and I'm filled with surprise, and relief, to find the building is housing nothing but two vehicles. A black motorcycle and a giant black car that looks part SUV and part tank. He closes the door behind us and then releases his grip on me. After he crosses to the other side of the room, he presses a few buttons on a digital panel and the wall directly opposite us begins to slide open.

Again, I contemplate an escape. If I ran now, could I use the deep forest as cover to hide even if I couldn't outrun him?

I'm still considering that option when he opens the door of the SUV and indicates I should get in. Running right now would be futile. I'm sure he knows these woods much better than I do, so I choose survival and obediently climb into the car. The door locks behind me as soon as he closes it. When he gets into the vehicle, he buckles me in securely. It's a three-point seat belt—the kind I once saw in a racing car on a TV show for kids. He double-checks I'm securely fastened and I'm struck by how caring that gesture appears, at least on the surface. I'm sure he simply doesn't want me unclipping the thing and throwing myself out of his moving tank—which I have already considered.

My stomach swirls with nervous anxiety as the wall slides open in front of us, revealing a dirt track into the woods, which he proceeds to drive down for a few minutes, until we eventually pull onto an actual road again. I peer out the window the whole time, staring into the pitch-black night, and trying and failing to pick out any landmarks. I still see nothing but trees for miles and try to count as many as I can as the headlights from the car illuminate them one after the other. I imagine them falling like dominoes behind us as we pass, and it works somewhat to keep my mind from spiraling out of control. I have no idea where we are, and even less of an idea of where we're going.

It feels like we've been driving for hours already. How much longer is this journey going to take? I'm tired and hungry. Not to mention thirsty. And terrified. But lack of sleep and water are my most pressing concerns. My brain isn't as sharp when I'm tired. Up ahead I see the first glimpse of the sun's first morning rays—a faint ribbon of pink on the horizon. It's no wonder I'm tired when I've been awake for almost twenty-four hours now.

When Lincoln speaks, his deep voice startles me, pulling me from lamenting my lack of sleep. "We'll be there soon. And you can get some sustenance. And some rest."

I dart out my tongue to wet my dry lips. It feels very wrong to thank someone who has bought you against your will. And also he doesn't deserve an ounce of gratitude from me. But this is a game, and until I know the rules, I'll be polite and respectful. "Thank you."

He doesn't reply, keeping his eyes fixed firmly on the road ahead. And when the trees grow too thick to see through around us, he turns down another long dirt road.

Ahead, a dilapidated old Gothic mansion looms against the faint light in the sky. It looks less like a home and more like a lonely old ruin. We drive through a set of black iron gates, one of them sagging on its hinges and bearing a tired Danger: Keep Out sign. Beyond is the house itself, two stories of gray stone complete with fearsome-looking gargoyles, half obscured by creeping ivy.

At first glance it appears haunted, or perhaps condemned. All of the windows are dark, some boarded up and others broken. It's hard to believe that a billionaire who has warehouses full of luxury vehicles lives in such a run-down place.

Or perhaps he doesn't. Maybe this is simply where he likes to imprison the women he buys. Because every so often, a security light blinks on in the distance and then immediately winks out again. Why have security lights if there's nothing worth keeping secure?

Lincoln stops the car at the end of the long driveway, outside of the wide double doors that appear to be the main entrance which are now illuminated by the headlights of the SUV.

They're a solid bank of gray metal amidst the crumbling masonry, and carved into the stone beside them is a single word, what I assume to be the house's name—*RooksBlood*. It's clear now that these doors are different from the mansion around them. They're certainly newer and appear to be made of some kind of steel.

Yes, this is most definitely a prison.

When the headlights of the car switch off, the shadow of the mansion plunges the area into almost darkness. I step out of the car on shaky legs, which I tell myself is from lack of food and not because I'm allowing my fear to show so openly. I was taught better than that. Lincoln beckons me to follow him up the three stone steps that lead to the house and I do so, obediently. There's no security light here, which strikes me as odd. Why have them scattered around the perimeter of the property and not here where they are needed? The same fingerprint and retina scan system is in place here too, another indication that this place is definitely not what it seems.

When the door opens, we are bathed in a soft amber light. Peering inside feels like looking back in time. The vast floor opens up in front of us, squares of black and white marble, which seem to stretch on endlessly before swooping around the sides of a grand staircase. Flickering lamps line the enormous hallway, illuminating at least six doors on either side. Where do they all lead to? I rein in my awe and don't gasp upon seeing the historic suit of armor, complete with broadsword, standing guard at one of the doorways. Perhaps there are more rooms, and more timeless guards at their entry, but I cannot see much beyond the staircase. The grand opulence of the interior doesn't meet the expectations set by the decaying exterior at all, and when I step onto the tiled floor, there's a faint hum underfoot, a vibration that is in disaccord with the antique decor.

Tentatively, I take a few more steps into the hallway, evaluating as much of my surroundings as possible without making it appear obvious I'm looking for a way out. Thick bloodred velvet drapes line the leaded windows, and from the inside it seems like the boards are simply for show, because I don't see any cracks or breaks. They are made of solid panes of glass surrounded by solid walls of stone and wood paneling. Nothing inside the building seems to be crumbling at all.

"You appear surprised." Lincoln's voice again, deep and gruff.

"The outside doesn't quite match the inside," I reply politely.

"Appearances can be deceptive."

"People see only what they choose to see, or what Mr. Knight wants them to see, isn't that right, sir?" A different voice now, one with a French accent.

I spin in the direction of the sound to see a man approaching from the hallway. He's wearing faded jeans and a navy shirt open at the collar, and I don't know why his informal attire offers me a modicum of comfort. Out of years of habit, I take a quick appraisal. He's a little shorter than Lincoln, maybe six feet. Late fifties. A thick crop of tawny brown hair, peppered with gray. A full goatee and mustache. A kind face, but something is different about him. It's only when he draws closer that I notice something unusual about his eyes. He doesn't appear to have any eyeballs behind his almost-closed lids. Is that a trick of the light, or my overtired brain, or is he blind?

"Pierre, would you show our guest to her room and provide her with some sustenance?" Lincoln asks.

Pierre smiles and nods in Lincoln's direction. He is blind. "Of course, sir," he says.

Sir? Is he the butler or some other kind of house servant?

Lincoln turns to me, his dark eyes raking over me intently. "Before you leave, Miss DeMotta, there are some things you should know. Do not spend energy looking for an escape because there is none. Exterior doors are accessible only by me, except for the kitchen which leads to the garden. The garden is walled and unscalable. Cameras will record your every move and alert me should you even try. If you noticed the retina scan and are considering gouging out one of my eyes to get out of here, they are biometrically enhanced and only work on living tissue with a blood flow."

Gouge out his eyes? Is that what he did to poor Pierre? And cameras will alert him if I try to scale the walls? My gaze darts to the corners of the hallway, checking for cameras that I don't find. And if the doors can only be controlled by him, is Pierre a prisoner here too? I bite my tongue and don't ask any of those questions, even though they tumble around my head. I'll discover the answers by myself. I wouldn't trust either of these men to be honest with me anyway.

"You'll find clothes and toiletries in your room. The kitchen is well stocked. If a door is locked, then it is not for your use. Aside from the rooms at the very end of the east wing of the house, both upstairs and downstairs, which belong to Pierre, you may roam the rest of the house freely and use any of the facilities as you wish. Now eat, drink, and rest." I have no idea which is the east wing and which is the west, but I don't tell him that. His tone is so cold and detached; he's less brute and more robot now.

Without another word, he walks down the hallway, disappearing from sight.

"Would you like to follow me, mademoiselle?" Pierre's voice is soft and gentle. Kindly even. Perhaps it's his French accent that makes him sound much more human and approachable than his employer, or maybe it's his overall aura. Even his footsteps are soft as he heads toward the staircase, and I fall into step behind him. He's clearly very familiar with this house and moves through it with ease despite his lack of sight. I have a billion more questions whizzing around my head, but they can wait—

for now anyway. My body is telling me that my tiredness and hunger are much more pressing matters.

Pierre shows me to a bedroom. It has the same lead windows and thick drapes as the hallway downstairs. None of these windows are falsely boarded up, which I'm grateful for, because at least I can see the world outside even if I can't live in it. It's furnished with what appears to be vintage wooden furniture, but my eyes are drawn to the large bed in the center of the room, complete with a pristine white duvet and pillows. Despite the circumstances, and it being first thing in the morning, it actually looks incredibly comfortable and inviting and I want nothing more than to curl into a ball beneath the duvet and sleep.

"I took the liberty of preparing you a tray, mademoiselle. I'm sure you'll find something to your liking. And you'll find some clothes in the closet and dresser and toiletries in the restroom."

I spin around, noticing a tray on the dresser, which holds a plate covered with a silver dome and a large glass bottle of water. My stomach rumbles at the idea of food.

"Will there be anything else, mademoiselle?"

Yes! So much. But I keep hold of the questions racing around my head, only asking the most pressing one. "Is there a lock on the door?"

"No, mademoiselle, and you will not require one. Only Mr. Knight and I live here. My room is at the end of the hallway on the opposite side of the house."

So, I'm in the west wing, then?

"And Mr. Knight's is directly across the hall from yours," he adds.

And that's why I need a lock on my door, Pierre. Of course his room is close to mine. He'll want easy access to his new toy, won't he? I'm sure the guy didn't buy me from a vile auction for just my company. I swallow down the panic that swells up inside me. Emotions are weakness. And they do me no good here. Information and a clear mind are my only weapons right now.

I peer at the open doorway, half expecting his boss to walk through it, unbuckling his belt as he does. I push down another swell of panic. "So Mr. Knight sleeps right across the hallway?" I ask, wondering if I can glean how much time he spends here. Maybe this is one of his many houses and he's rarely here?

"Yes, mademoiselle. Or in his basement."

"His basement?" Of course he has a basement. It's probably a dungeon. A creepy as hell dungeon full of torture devices, or perhaps where he keeps some of his other prisoners. Why else would he have a basement? Terror winds its way up my throat.

I suck in a deep breath.

One, two, buckle my shoe.

"Will that be all?" Pierre asks, pulling me from my spiral and also clearly steering me away from asking any further questions about his employer.

Unable to ignore the torrent of them spinning in my head and clamoring to be asked, I take a chance and ask just one more. "What do I do now, Pierre?"

"Eat. Drink. Rest. Those were Mr. Knight's instructions."

They were, but why? Does he simply want me at my best before he . . . before he *what*?

My stomach rolls at the thought of what he might do. There's only one reason a man buys a woman, isn't there? That thought is inescapable now. Larissa prepared me as much as she could for sex, and for what men like him will want after they buy a woman. But I'm not sure any amount of talking it through or watching the online videos that she showed me would be suitable preparation for what's actually going to happen.

I steel myself for whatever's to come, rolling back my shoulders and holding my head high. Even though it changes nothing of my reality, the simple act of altering my body language still makes me feel more in control. "Thank you."

"Good day, mademoiselle."

Pierre leaves the room, closing the door behind him.

I LIE IN THE COMFORTABLE BED, PROPPED UP against the fluffy pillows. Pierre's tray consisted of two sandwiches, one peanut butter and a purple sticky substance and one ham and swiss cheese, as well as some potato chips. I ate the ham and cheese one quickly while I rummaged around the room. As he said, I found clothes in the dresser and closet. All with their tags still on. Seven pairs of white panties. A bra which is close enough to my size that I can make it work. Three pink tank tops. Four white T-shirts—two regular size and two large, which I assume are to be worn as nightwear. One pink sweater. One pair of pink shorts. Two pairs of black leggings, like the kind you might wear to the gym, and seven sundresses—one white, two pink and the other four with various fruit and flower patterns, as though the person who chose them had no idea what to choose so simply asked what a young woman might like to wear. Pink is very much a feature, and I don't dislike the color, in fact the items picked are nice, and they at least feel like they're of high quality, but most of my previous clothes have been black or navy—functional. I don't know yet if I'm touched or creeped out by the thought that went into choosing these clothes. I have no idea where in the US we are, but the air was mild when we got out of the car, and the clothing items suggest a warm climate. Given that it's April, that could be a lot of places though.

I took a shower after my sandwich, using the nice-smelling shampoo and conditioner as well as the luxuriously thick shower gel. There's also toothpaste with blue and red stripes, which I've never ever seen before, and the pink theme is continued with a toothbrush of the same color. There's a hairbrush and hair dryer and some moisturizer, one for my face and a mango-scented one for my body. It's clear they were prepared for my arrival. Or if not me explicitly, then some other woman just like me. Are these Lincoln's tastes? Pink. Fruit-scented. Are those things inherently feminine to him, and is that what he's hoping I am? I recall what Larissa taught me. Be available, submissive. Acquiesce at all times. Be feminine, not a feminist. I had no idea what a feminist was when she first told me that, and I'm still not sure that I do.

I still suspect all of these things were all purchased with me in mind. Lincoln paid a high price, and he waited for the last lot. The one they were all waiting for, if the guard with the snake tattoo was speaking the truth. The traitor's daughter.

A shiver runs down my spine at the memory. Along with the other fifty women who were sold at the auction, I was kept in a house two weeks before it. It was a horrible place with twelve women to every room, except we weren't allowed to talk to each other, and any breaking of the rules would be met with punishment. Nothing that would leave a mark though. Being held underwater until you were sure you'd drown. A bucket of ice water over the head. Being forced to stand for twenty-four hours straight. Food and water denial. But their favorite was to force us to walk around naked. Then the guards would leer at us, making crude and vulgar remarks about our bodies and the unimaginable fates that were awaiting us all.

In comparison, this place is like heaven. At least right now it is. I curl my toes against the silky cotton sheets—the kind that gently caress your skin rather than scratch. I bask contentedly in the sweet relief of a bed and a fluffy pillow, the kind where your head sinks into the material and cradles your neck in a warm embrace. And the space—so much space all to myself. I spread my arms and legs wide and then bring them back in again, like I'm making a snow angel from the luxurious white cotton.

I know this won't last, but for now, it's my reality. And like the ice-cold water in the car earlier, I'm going to take pleasure in it while I can. I burrow deeper beneath the covers and pull them up to my chin, feeling cocooned, and . . . safe. How strange that I feel safe in a monster's prison. For now, I will take it and I will revel in this feeling.

There's a giant screen attached to one wall, which I assume is some kind of camera system. No doubt Lincoln Knight is watching me right now. Brute!

However, there's also a remote control on the nightstand. Out of curiosity, I grab it and flick the screen on anyway. To my complete and pleasant surprise, it's just a regular TV and it opens to the home page of something called Netflix. There are two accounts on there, labeled Pierre and Guest.

Guest! I suppress a snort at the irony and then immediately click on the profile. I was very rarely allowed to watch TV living at my grandfather's home. It was deemed *unnecessary and distracting*. However, when he used to go away for a few weeks every summer, I would be allowed to watch some in the late afternoons so long as I'd completed all my lessons, and I was good and didn't bother Larissa. It was always our secret, the only one I ever kept from my grandfather. It stopped when I turned eighteen and Larissa told me I was too old for childish television. I had more important tasks to focus on, such as learning how to sew and bake, and how to never show emotion. I can bake a delicious rabbit pie with my eyes closed, sew a stitch as neat as any seasoned dressmaker, and as for hiding my emotions . . . well, I've been told I'm pretty good at that too.

With little knowledge of current TV shows, I choose the number one pick in the US. It's a program about a maid but it could be a show about a turkey farm and I'd watch it. Something about seeing people on a screen makes me feel less alone. Less afraid.

I don't see much of it before my eyelids start fluttering closed.

CHAPTER 5
LINCOLN

It's a relief to pull off this damn mask. I toss it onto my desk, and feel like I can finally breathe again. Rarely leaving the house, at least as Lincoln Knight, I'm unaccustomed to wearing it for any long periods of time. I could have sent Edgar to the auction in my stead, my occasional driver and my connection to the outside world. But he's not me, and there's no acceptable level of chance when it comes to Imogen. She's far too precious to risk losing for a second time.

Flicking the switch on my console, I light up the bank of screens in front of me. Time to get to work. I haven't slept in over a day, but a new auction means fifty more women sold into a life of slavery and fuck knows what kind of pain and cruelty. A lot of the men who go to these auctions to actually buy them are ghosts—men like me, who live in the shadows—much like the Brotherhood they buy from. I'll be lucky if I manage to track down half of them, and that knowledge hurts me as much as it did eighteen years ago when I first discovered their sick little trade. That was also when I discovered I had an older sister, Olivia—another woman I couldn't save. She died in my arms believing I was one of the men responsible for her misery. Even after eighteen years, the rage at how badly I failed her would swallow me whole if I let it, so I push it all down, storing it away for when I can put it to better use.

Pierre's familiar footsteps draw closer as he descends the spiral staircase to my haven. Or my *lair*, as he describes it, particularly when he's berating me for spending too much time down here, which I sense he's about to do again.

I don't ask if she's okay, even though the question is the first thing that pops into my head. Of course she's not. She was just bought and sold, from one monster to another.

"What are you doing down here? Shouldn't you be seeing to your guest?" His voice drips with the sarcasm I'm accustomed to.

"Is she settled?" I ask instead, keeping my eyes on the screen in front of me while I load up a computer program that will trace the payment of ten million I recently made. Ten million is pocket change to the Brotherhood. Auctions aren't a money-making business for them, more like a loss leader. And while I hate that I gave their cause a single cent, I would have given it all for her. The truth is, I would sacrifice every soul on this earth to save Imogen's, and I would do it in a heartbeat. And if that makes me a monster, then that's what I am.

"I made her some sandwiches. Showed her to her room." He flops down onto the seat next to me.

"And what's she doing now?"

"I have no idea, sir." I hate when he calls me that, but pointing it out is futile. "I hope I'm not expected to babysit her while she's here. I have more important things to be doing."

He's such a liar. "Things like?"

He huffs indignantly rather than answering my question, before spinning idly in his chair. "Why did you lie to her?"

I'm lying to her about a lot of things, so he's going to have to be a little more specific than that. "About what?"

"You said you were the only person who could access the exterior doors."

THE AUCTION

"I thought it would be easier for you if she didn't know the doors can also be opened with your thumbprint."

He snorts. "You're worried a one-hundred-pound girl could knock me out and carry me to the door to secure her escape?"

Actually, I'd say she's more like one-thirty than one hundred, but I don't tell him that because then I might reveal to my old friend that I've spent far too much of the past twenty-four hours looking at her body and wondering how it would feel in my hands. I don't even want to admit that to myself. "How do you know how much she weighs? She could be bigger than both of us, for all you know."

He snorts again. "From the sound of her footsteps. From the way she moved. She is slight, *non*? Or she is used to having to make herself appear small. Per'aps both."

I concentrate on the screen, not wanting to think about Imogen making herself small for anyone, nor how much she weighs, because that makes me think of the curve of her hips and her long lean legs. And thinking like that is more than fucking wrong.

Pierre mutters something unintelligible in French, and disapproval is practically seeping from his pores.

"What else was I supposed to do, Pierre?"

"I have no idea what you're referring to, sir."

"I can hear you cursing me in your head. You think I made a mistake bringing her here, don't you?"

"And you do not, *non*?"

Yes, I absolutely fucking do. And not only for the reasons he's thinking about, but also because I haven't seen her for eighteen years and I did not expect her to look the way she did. She was a child when I knew her and now . . . now she's very much a woman. A beautiful one too. Although it wasn't her beauty that made my body light up with desire when she walked out onto that stage. It was her defiance. Her strength. She looked out into that room full of goddamn fucking animals and dared them to come for her. "What other choice did I have? Let one of those sick fucks buy her. I made a promise to protect her."

He huffs. "You can protect her without bringing her here. You could have sent her to one of the safe houses. Anywhere but here."

"But she's not like the others, Pierre. How would we know she was truly safe? They've kept her hidden from me and the rest of the world for all these years. You think they wouldn't find out and come for her again? How would I protect her then, Pierre?"

He shakes his head and jumps up from his chair, pacing the room. "You are letting your guilt cloud your decision-making, *mon ami*."

"I made him a promise," I snap. But it's overwhelming guilt rather than anger that has my temper so close to fraying.

With a heavy sigh he stops pacing before placing his hand on my shoulder and giving me a reassuring squeeze. "You can't keep living in the past, Lincoln, because one day soon it's going to swallow you whole. And if you think that girl upstairs is going to offer you any kind of redemption, I'm afraid you're setting yourself up for a very big fall."

I hate that he knows me too well.

He drops his hand and walks out of the room, leaving me to glare at his retreating back.

Redemption? The monster the Brotherhood made me is far beyond any kind of redemption. It doesn't matter that I believed Imogen was dead for eighteen years, because I should have known. I should have looked harder for the truth instead of believing their lies, no matter how convincing they were. God knows who that poor child was who perished in her stead, but it wasn't Imogen. Because of my carelessness I left her at the mercy of the Brotherhood, and I broke a promise to the only people who ever gave a fuck about me. My only real family, at least the only one I ever actually knew. Because I never knew about my biological family. Not until the Brotherhood had already tracked my sister down and sold her like a piece of meat.

Olivia was broken beyond repair by the time I found her. She didn't know who I was when I came for her, saw only that I was one of *them*. I'll never forget the fear in her eyes when I held her in my arms. I told her she was safe, praying that she'd believe me. Hoping that at least she would die knowing that somebody cared about her. I don't know if she did and that memory haunts me still.

I left the Brotherhood the next day, swearing I would take every single one of them down. Eighteen years later and I'm still trying.

CHAPTER 6
IMOGEN

It was noon by the time I fell asleep yesterday, and I slept surprisingly well because it was almost six the following morning when I woke. Which is pretty exceptional, considering I'm a prisoner of a reclusive billionaire who's sick and twisted enough to buy women like cattle. I half expected to wake with him standing over me, his mask removed and a lecherous grin on his face, but thankfully the room is empty.

Sunlight streams through the open drapes and the house is eerily quiet, which makes the rumbling of my stomach sound incredibly loud. I was too tired to eat more than one sandwich yesterday, and I was also a little suspicious of the purple sticky substance. I recall Lincoln declaring that the kitchen was well stocked and available to me, so I suppose I should go make myself some breakfast. Then at least I'll have a full stomach and a clear head for whatever horrors this day has in store for me.

Freshly showered and dressed in a pair of leggings and a tank top, I make my way to the kitchen, anticipating bumping into Lincoln Knight on my way there. But I see no sign of any life until I get to the kitchen where Pierre is rolling out some pastry.

"What would you like for breakfast, mademoiselle?" he asks, still concentrating on the pastry.

I cannot remember a time in my life I've ever been asked what I'd like to eat. It's a surprise to be asked it here, in the home of my captor. "Um. Do you have oatmeal?"

"Yes. How would you like it?"

"With water please."

He lifts his head for the first time. "What? No milk? No honey? Berries?"

My mouth waters at the prospect of such decadence, but I remain firm. "No thank you."

"Not even a little cinnamon?"

"Just water is fine, thank you," I say with a polite smile that I know he cannot see, yet still it feels necessary. As does my breakfast of oatmeal and water. *The body has no need for sugar or unnecessary additives, Imogen!* Larissa's words ring in my head. *Oatmeal is healthy and nutritious. A healthy body and mind is the key to strength, and strength is survival.*

"Fine," he huffs. "I will make it as soon as I am finished here."

"Can I go out into the garden?" I ask, biting on my lip.

Pierre nods, focused on his pastry once more. "Mr. Knight said you are free to roam the house and garden."

Right. Mr. Knight said so. I'm still nervous to open the door that leads me to the outside world, unsure what to expect. He said the garden was walled, so I anticipate it will be small, but I'm wrong. It must be at least half an acre, probably more—all tangled undergrowth and knotted brambles. I imagine they were once manicured gardens now lost to the ravages of time and neglect. A crumbling greenhouse juts out like an iron skyscraper in a city of green, its glass roof broken and vines spilling through the cracks. It's simply . . . the most wondrous thing I have ever seen. I resist spinning around on the spot and squealing with delight, although I do it internally. Somehow, I appear to have stepped into a world of fairy tales and secret gardens, and all the pleasant memories of my childhood are right here with me, like precious buds entwined within the knots and thorns. I am Belle dancing with her Beast. I am Mary having adventures with Colin and Dickon. I am not a lonely orphan child, unloved and unwanted.

Right beside the kitchen is a square patch of paving stones, which appear to have been scrubbed clean of the moss that crawls over the garden walls. And in the middle is a small metal table with two chairs. Their green paint is peeling and faded from the cruel sun. Still, they look inviting to me and I take a seat, tilting my face toward the sunshine and enjoying the warmth on my skin. I take a deep breath, filling my lungs with clean air and the subtle scent of jasmine. I've already decided this will be my favorite place in the world.

I have never felt so . . . unobserved? Would that be the word? Even with the threat of Lincoln's cameras watching my every move, I do not *feel* them. I feel no eyes on me. No judgment. There is no one standing guard, waiting for me to commit some minor indiscretion. I believe I could sing a very loud nursery rhyme and nobody would care to stop me. I bet I could even curse. I could scream obscenities and ruffle nothing but the long grasses, already swaying in the gentle morning breeze. I don't do any of those things though. Of course I don't. They are foolish and don't get me any closer to my goal. Finding a way out of this house.

Freedom.

I suspect what will bring me closer to those goals is unfortunately not within this beautiful garden, but inside the house. The place where I still have so much to explore. If I look hard enough, I am sure I'll find a way out. And if I don't then find an escape, surely time alone will offer me an opportunity for one. And while I wait, I'll ensure that both Pierre and Lincoln learn to trust me.

I'll make sure they never break down my walls. Never discover my secrets. I'll be a good girl and do everything they ask me to, even if those things aren't what I want to do.

Immediately, I push away those thoughts. They're too dark to sully this otherwise perfect moment. And right now, I'm not being asked to do anything. So right now is the perfect time to start looking for answers.

When I go back inside, the kitchen is filled with the aroma of apple and cinnamon. Pierre's no longer here and there's a pie on the side counter, protected with a glass dome and waiting for baking, and another in the oven. There's also a bowl of warm oatmeal on the table, covered with a dish.

I eat alone, wondering if Pierre's apple pie is supposed to be for everyone to enjoy, or just him and Lincoln. I've never tasted apple pie, at least not as far as I can recall, but the smell alone is making my mouth water, and already bland oatmeal is becoming considerably less appealing. I wonder if I'll be permitted to relax my eating habits here, if even just a little.

I can still be strong even if I eat a slice of apple pie, can't I?

AFTER MY BREAKFAST, I'M STILL ALONE IN THE kitchen and I have zero idea what I'm supposed to do now. Lincoln did say I could use the house as I wished, didn't he? So, rather than sitting here on my own with the temptation of apple pie, I should get to work and go explore this vast fortress I'm currently trapped in.

I'm bubbling with nervous anticipation as I make my way down the hall. This house is so unlike my grandfather's estate. His was much more modern. Minimalistic. All hard edges— glass and steel and marble floors, where every sound would echo through the hallways. Nothing soft, not even the beds. Everywhere was muted in color, as opposed to the vibrancy of the rich red drapes and the dark paneled wood of this house. I've never been anywhere so still and so peaceful, like the entire place is sleeping, waiting for something or someone to wake it up.

I trail my hand over an antique dresser in the hallway, half expecting dust to collect on my fingertips, but there is none. Everything feels untouched, like the inhabitants move through this place without leaving a mark. Ghosts, even in their own home. What kind of man lives in such a house? What kind of a man is Lincoln Knight? Who is the true devil behind the mask?

I wander the hallways, too cautious to venture into any rooms that I pass, at least until I come across a set of arched double doors. They appear to be made of antique oak carved with vines and flowers in eternal bloom and they are begging to be opened. What is the point of such exquisite doors if they are not to be walked through? I trace my fingertips over a carved rose petal and feel an irresistible urge to push against the door. I glance around and find I'm still alone. Is he watching me? Are there cameras hidden in every dark corner? Is he spying on his captive, waiting for me to make a mistake? Does he want me to open the doors and peek inside? Is he waiting for me to find the things he hides away so that he can punish me for any indiscretion?

My curiosity wins out, and with a hard push, I open the doors wide until the hinges creak under their heavy weight. Immediately, my nose is filled with the scent of old paper and aged wood. Perhaps I was wrong about the overgrown garden being my favorite place in this house. Stepping farther into the room, I'm unable to contain my joy and I spin around, like a ballerina in a music box, my mouth hanging open in awe. There's no need to hide my feelings when I'm alone after all, and this library is breathtaking. The ceiling rises almost two stories high, atop walls lined with shelves and row upon row of books. The same bloodred heavy drapes that hang in the rest of the house dress the high arched windows, allowing in vast swathes of sunlight that dapple and dance across the book spines. A tall ladder, almost the full height of the room, runs on a track around each of the three walls lined with books.

Beneath one of the arched windows, an old-fashioned desk

sits as though waiting to be used, and behind it, a heavy wingback chair. Beside that is a small table, containing a crystal decanter half full of dark liquor beside a tray of glass tumblers. The entire room is stunning and now I truly feel like I've stepped into a fairy tale—into the Beast's castle itself.

"I see you've found the library." His deep voice echoes in the room, reminding me this is more nightmare than fairy tale.

I school my face into neutral and turn to him. Lincoln Knight looks different today. He still wears a mask, but this one is vastly different. It only covers the lower half of his face—like a surgical mask but made of thick black fabric. On closer inspection, it appears to be fashioned from fabric and metal. There's a fine steel grille over his nose and mouth, enough to obscure his features while allowing him to speak, and to breathe—pity! Half of his right eyebrow is missing, a patch of mottled olive skin in its place.

"It's beautiful, sir," I say, adopting the same title that Pierre used for him. There's no time like the present to start pleasing him and earning his trust.

He takes a few steps closer and his black military-style boots squeak on the wooden floor. I resist the instinct to step back because I assume he's here to inspect his property, and I refuse to be intimidated. He has his hands stuffed into his black cargo pants, exposing his tattooed forearms. I don't know why his tattoos surprise me so much, but there was no hint of them when I first met him. Dressed in his finely tailored suit, he looked sharp and clean-cut. Not that tattoos alone would make him not so, but everything about his appearance is the opposite of that now. He also has a large hunting knife strapped to his thigh, and the watch he wears appears to be very high-tech. In fact, I'm sure it's also a cell phone. One of my grandfather's drivers had something very similar—a smartwatch, he called it. It would make sense for Lincoln to have one, as I haven't seen any kind of phone in the house, cell or otherwise. He wears a tight-fitted black T-shirt that appears to barely contain his muscles, making all of him seem much bigger, intimidating. I see why they call him a devil.

"It was here when I bought the house, as were most of the books." His eyes narrow on my face, so dark and intense that it makes a thrill of something shoot through me. I can't quite identify the sensation, but oddly enough, it's not fear. Lincoln Knight is dark and brooding and intense, but I'm not afraid of him. Not yet anyway. "You may use it as you please."

That makes me want to very inappropriately throw my arms around his neck in gratitude. I adore reading, but was permitted very few books as a child, and even as an adult. My battered and worn copy of *The Secret Garden* was one of my most prized possessions and I hated leaving it behind. Of course I don't hug him because that would not only be wildly inappropriate but also bizarre. I'm not a natural hugger, at least I never thought I was. I can count on my fingers the number of hugs I've had in my life, at least that I can recall. I like to imagine my parents hugged me multiple times a day, and maybe that's where this innate desire to hug comes from. But I don't hug Lincoln Knight. Even though, very strangely, I want to, all of my conditioning warns me against it. Instead I mumble a very polite thank-you.

He tilts his head to the side, scrutinizing me. His meticulous gaze raking over every inch of my flesh. Is this where he carries me off to his bed? Or will he simply take my virginity right here on the floor of his beautiful library.

I push away all thoughts of hugging and gratitude, and instead steel myself for his unwelcome touch. My skin itches. I want to scratch and fidget under the heat of his eyes, but I don't. Part of me wishes that he would just do it, if only to get it over with. Because maybe then he'll let me go back to being alone, and even better, to escaping into one of these books. Perhaps he has a copy of *The Secret Garden* hidden amongst these shelves.

His rich brown eyes never stray from me even for a fraction

THE AUCTION

of a heartbeat. Why is he staring at me like that, and what the hell is he waiting for? Is this some kind of test? I take a calming breath and recall what Larissa taught me. Show no emotion, because emotion is weakness and he will use it against you. Be passive and obedient. Most importantly, make yourself useful to him. Useful people are less dispensable. Useful people survive.

"Is there something I can do for you, sir?"

His brow furrows in a slight frown and my pulse spikes. He takes a half step closer and his scent invades my senses. Sharp and clean yet familiar, like fresh soap mixed with leather. "I'm leaving for a few days. Pierre will tend to your needs while I'm gone. If you should need any additional clothing or incidentals, then let him know and I will make arrangements to get them." He sounds detached, but there's something else too. An edge to his voice that makes shivers race up and down my spine.

But he's leaving! It'll just be me alone here with his butler. Does that mean I have a few days of freedom? I'm tempted to ask exactly how long a few days will be and where he's going, but dare not for fear of provoking his anger. *Curiosity killed the cat, Imogen. Don't ask questions. If people want you to have information, they will offer it.* So, instead, I simply say, "Enjoy your trip, sir."

He grunts something unintelligible before turning and walking out of the library. As the heavy doors close behind him, I spin around and mentally clap my hands with glee. Me and this library for a few days. Now this is a slice of happiness I definitely wasn't expecting, and I'm going to enjoy every second of it.

CHAPTER 7
IMOGEN

Last night I fell asleep watching TV again, still expecting someone to disturb me from my peaceful slumber and show me the real reason I'm here. But nobody came.

Although it's very odd being in this house with only Pierre for company. Pierre who moves through the place like a shadow, close but untouchable. He has taken care of me in so many small ways—preparing my meals, checking if I need anything, doing laundry, even though I insisted I could do that myself. But aside from that, we haven't had a lot of conversation—a situation I intend to change.

As I wander down the stairs, I hear music coming from the kitchen, and Pierre humming along to the unfamiliar song. I'm not familiar with any modern music. We had a radio at my grandfather's house, but I rarely heard it on. Certainly I was never allowed to try it for myself, and it was a source of fascination as a small child. But as I grew older, it became one of the many things that was simply not mine to touch.

The kitchen seems to be Pierre's favorite place, and he's an excellent cook. Unlike at breakfast, he didn't ask my preference for lunch or dinner yesterday, he simply served me a plate of food at each meal. They contained some of the most delicious food I've ever eaten in my life. Although his heavenly smelling apple pies remained untouched on the counter in their glass display cases, and as he seemed annoyed about something, I didn't dare ask him for a piece. Perhaps later today I will.

He's still humming softly when I walk into the room, but he stops as soon as he hears me, pressing a button on a screen on the wall that lowers the music volume a little. "Breakfast, mademoiselle?"

I perch on a stool. "Yes please."

He's peeling carrots this morning and I enjoy watching him, while listening to the male vocalist, who's currently singing about being on fire—a reference I don't understand at all.

"And what culinary delights can I fix for you on this wondrous day?" Pierre asks, and I can't determine if he's being sarcastic or genuine.

"Whatever you're having will be fine."

"Ah, I do not eat breakfast. Coffee and a cigarette is all I can stomach until lunch."

"Oh?" I can't help feeling a little deflated. If Pierre was eating with me, then I would have whatever he was having, and no doubt it would be much more pleasant than my usual oatmeal. But I do need to eat, because I feel lightheaded if I skip breakfast. *There's nothing wrong with oatmeal, child. It's healthy and nutritious!* Larissa's words are never far from me, and I take comfort in them always, even if that feels a little harder to do this morning when I'm so hungry and Pierre's suggestion of adding cream, honey or berries yesterday is so deliciously appealing. But I'm strong, and I was raised right. I won't discount all her years of teaching simply for the promise of some short-term gratification—as delicious as it might be. "I'll just take some oatmeal please."

"Ach!" He pulls a face, but then he washes his hands and prepares the food without another complaint. A few moments later, he sets the bowl down in front of me. Then he grabs the pot of coffee.

"Coffee, mademoiselle?"

The smell of coffee intrigues me, rich and smoky, so decadent that it almost feels forbidden. And Pierre seems to enjoy it, given the way he smacks his lips together in satisfaction after he takes that first sip. "I don't know. I've never tasted coffee before."

He gasps dramatically. "Never tasted coffee?"

"No." I take a spoonful of the bland paste he just served me and swallow it down.

He grabs a cup and pours me one alongside his own. "I take mine black but I would suggest a little cream for your first time. And per'aps a little sugar, *non*?"

"No sugar," I insist, not wanting to stray too far from my regular diet. "But I'll try it with the cream."

He mumbles something in French before handing me the cup. Then he sits opposite me at the table and I don't bother to hide my smile at his company. I like Pierre.

"So, take a sip and tell me what you think." He makes a hurrying gesture with his hands.

I lift the cup to my lips and the rich earthy aroma floods my sense of taste and smell before I even take a sip. It's bitter, shockingly so, dulled a little by the cream but still foreign. I swallow quickly, not knowing how to hold it in my mouth. It leaves an oily residue behind that feels unfamiliar, along with a comforting heat. I take a bigger sip and feel a little buzz of adrenaline in my chest. Wow!

"Well?" Pierre asks.

I lick my lips, still tasting the lingering bitterness in the back of my throat. "I like it."

"*Bien*." He smiles and then drinks his own.

It's hard to go back to my oatmeal after the coffee, but I force it all down anyway. Because it's good for me and it would be rude to waste food.

"Never had coffee, huh?" Pierre asks, almost to himself.

"No."

"What about tea?"

"I've had green tea," I tell him, recalling how much I disliked it. I forced it all down anyway because Larissa made it for me and she would have scolded me for wasting it had I not. I never asked for it again. I don't tell Pierre this though, not because I particularly want to keep it secret, but because I think he already thinks me fairly naive and inexperienced, which is true in a lot of ways. And if I tell him that I don't even like tea, maybe he'll stop sharing his coffee with me.

"Soda?" he asks.

I shake my head instinctively and then remember he can't see me. "No, I don't think so."

"Candy?"

Sugar is addictive. It will make you fat and rot your teeth, and it has no nutritional benefit at all. "No."

"Did your parents not allow you to eat sweet things?"

"My parents died when I was three."

"I am sorry, mademoiselle."

I swallow down the pain of having to spend almost all of my life without them. I remember so little. I recall their faces though. The dark scatter of my father's stubble and how he would tickle my hand with it. My mother's beautiful smile. The limited memories are always bittersweet, because I know for certain my parents would never have allowed me to be sold by the Brotherhood. In fact, there would have been no suggestion of it. Had they not been murdered by the one man they were supposed to be able to trust, then my grandfather wouldn't have had to make a bargain with that vile organization in order to spare my life. And I wouldn't be sitting here now telling Pierre I've never eaten candy.

"So who raised you, Imogen?" His words pull me back to our conversation and away from my melancholic musings of how my life might have turned out so very differently.

"My grandfather, and his . . ." I falter, unsure how to describe Larissa and her importance in my life. I would have surely perished in that house if it hadn't been for her.

"His what?" Pierre asks, his voice soft and soothing.

"I would guess his housekeeper, perhaps? She didn't always live there, just a few days a week. But she was much more than a housekeeper to me. She taught me everything I know. She taught me how to survive."

He arches an eyebrow. "To survive, mademoiselle?"

Have I spoken out of turn? Surely, Pierre knows how I came to be here? "Do you know why I'm here, Pierre?" I assume he doesn't know of my notoriety within the Brotherhood circles, given that he wasn't aware my parents had died, but surely he knows his boss bought me.

He hums again, the way he does when he's thinking. "That is not for me to say, mademoiselle."

"I mean, do you know how I got here?" my voice is small, a reflection of how I'm feeling right now. For a few special moments, we were simply two people enjoying a conversation, and I wasn't the daughter of a traitor, sold off to the highest bidder. And now I'm her again. Only ever her in this house.

"Ah!" He nods. "I know the circumstances of your arrival, yes. I know of the auction you were a part of."

"So, then yes, Pierre. I had a pleasant enough, if sheltered, childhood. But yes, I was taught how to survive."

"Your grandfather and his . . . Larissa, they did not . . ." He winces and flaps his hand around, like he's searching for the appropriate word. "They did not stop it? The auction?"

I bristle. Feeling defensive of the only people who have ever shown me any loyalty in this life. If it wasn't for my grandfather's intervention, I'd have died along with my parents and it's my loyalty that makes me defend him still, even after he handed me over to those monsters. "They couldn't."

"And why is that, mademoiselle? I know of your grandfather. He is Saul DeMotta. He is a very rich man, *non*? Even Pierre knows this."

How dare he assume? I take a breath and soothe my temper.

"I guess money doesn't count for a lot when you made a promise to the Brotherhood, does it? They wanted their revenge and if it wasn't for my grandfather paying them off eighteen years ago, I'd have been killed with my mother. As it was, he managed to bargain for my life, at least until I turned twenty-one."

He nods. "Ah, and then you would be returned as property of the Brotherhood, *oui*?"

"*Oui*," I murmur.

Unexpectedly, he reaches across the table, feeling for my hand. He finds it easily and gives it a gentle squeeze, and it's strangely comforting. It reminds me of the rare occasions Larissa would pat my hand reassuringly, and how even that simple contact would brighten my whole day. "You are a brave young woman, mademoiselle."

I don't feel brave, but I don't tell him that. Instead we sit in silence for a few moments before he asks, "Have you ever tasted apple pie?"

I can't help but smile, reminded of the pastry still untouched and sitting beneath its glass dome on the counter. "No. But yours does smell delicious."

"Then why haven't you taken a slice, mademoiselle?"

"I wasn't sure I was permitted to," I admit, feeling foolish for some reason.

"You are a grown woman, yes? Not a child any longer. If you want some pie, you simply take some pie."

"I was taught never to take something without asking, and this isn't my house. I'm a . . ." I want to say prisoner, but instead choose my word more carefully " . . . guest."

"Then you ask for some pie." He throws his hands into the air and then mumbles something in French again. "I understand this is an adjustment for you, mademoiselle. And Mr. Knight has left last night without per'aps explaining how this all works." His tone is softer now. He takes a deep breath. "Yes, you are a guest here but for now, this is your home. So, if there is food in the kitchen, then it is for you to eat. If I spend hours making a delicious pie, even if it is Mr. Knight's favorite apple pie with extra cinnamon, you are free to take a slice, or four."

"It's Mr. Knight's favorite?" I suppress a snicker at the thought of the huge brute in the black camo gear, with the hunting knife strapped to his thigh, and the scary-looking mask loving apple pie.

Pierre nods. "*Oui.*"

So his trip must have been unexpected, then. Or at least, Pierre must not have known about it in advance. Why else would he have spent time baking not one, but two of his favorite pies? That begs the question as to where the elusive Mr. Knight has gone and what he's about to do. He definitely didn't look like a billionaire recluse when he left. I expect Pierre wouldn't like me asking any of those questions though. "Do you enjoy cooking, Pierre?"

"*Oui*, mademoiselle. And tell me, what do you enjoy doing?"

I stare at him blankly. I don't think I've ever been asked that question before, and I'm honestly unsure. I've really enjoyed watching some TV these past two nights, but I'm not sure that's just because it's so new and exciting to have such unrestricted access to a television. "I like reading, and I like being outside."

He hums softly, like he's turning that information over in his mind. "That is all?"

"Yes. Although I did like the song you were listening to when I first came in."

"Ah, *oui*." He smacks his lips together. "The Boss."

I blink in confusion. "Your boss was on the radio."

His lips quirk in a smile. "No, mademoiselle. Not my boss. *The* Boss. Bruce Springsteen."

I'm still confused.

Pierre waggles his fingers in the air. "It is his name, *non*? His pet name. You have not heard of him?"

"No. I never really listened to a lot of radio."

THE AUCTION

"Ah, we have no radio here, but I have added you to our plan if you wish to listen to music. It is the Guest account. That way you will not be forced to listen to Mr. Knight's drivel." His nose wrinkles in disgust.

And now I'm even more confused. "You have no radio? How do you listen to music? And what is *our plan*?"

Pierre whistles softly. "*Merde!* You really have led a sheltered life, mademoiselle." Color heats my cheeks and I'm grateful he cannot witness my overt show of embarrassment. But then Pierre goes on to explain something called Bluetooth and how it connects to various speakers throughout the house, some of which are portable so I can take one into the garden. And he explains how I have my own guest account on their music subscription service, which I understand to be like Netflix, but for songs, and I will be able to choose all of my own songs from one any of the TV screens throughout the house. Then I simply link the speaker I want to use to the chosen TV, and I can listen as easily as I watch Netflix.

"That all sounds so . . ." I search for the correct word " . . . wonderful. You can really choose any song in the world just with the touch of a button?"

He nods. "*Oui.* It is that simple."

I'm awestruck. Such a world of words and feelings and connection being opened up to me—just like that. For no reason at all other than I said I'd like to listen to music. This is a strange and unfamiliar feeling, yet one that makes me feel giddy and also a little delirious with power. I try to focus on the practicality of what he just told me. "What music should I choose, Pierre?"

He tilts his head to the side. "Whichever you wish, mademoiselle."

"But I don't know what I wish. It's like being asked to search for a book in a vast library but you don't know the name of the book," I say, not sure I'm explaining myself properly.

But he nods his understanding. "I see, mademoiselle. There

will be suggestions made for you based on the information I entered—your age for instance. And then there are trends and charts too, like what you see on Netflix."

So he knew my age before I got here? I'm not sure if that creeps me out, even if Pierre is decidedly un-creepy. "Oh, I see."

"But, mademoiselle . . ." he pauses dramatically " . . . you cannot go wrong with some classic eighties rock."

"Classic eighties rock?"

"*Oui*. It is by far the most superior decade of music in the history of music," he says, full of passion and conviction.

"Then I will be sure to give it a try."

He nods. "So being outside, reading, TV and a little music? Is there anything else that you enjoy, mademoiselle?"

Does he have any idea that he just described my fantasy life? "No, I think that's it."

"Then you should be very happy here with the garden and the library, *non*?"

I take another sip of the coffee, already enjoying the warmth it leaves behind in my mouth. "Yes," I reply. It would be impolite to say no, but also, it feels like it could be the truth.

So far, this house is a much happier place to be than the place I grew up in. I've only been here for two days and yet I experience more freedom as a prisoner here than I ever did in the house I called home. And something about that doesn't sit comfortably with me, but I'm too afraid to pick at those threads right now. There's already too much I don't know, and if I start to question everything I was taught to believe, well I might just lose my mind. Because what if everything I thought I knew was wrong?

As I've been doing far too much of these past two days, I push those unwelcome thoughts away. I know this sense of peace and contentment can't last, and whatever Lincoln Knight has in mind for me will bring me back down to earth with a crash soon enough, but for right now, sitting in this kitchen with Pierre, I am as happy as I've ever been.

CHAPTER 8
LINCOLN

For a very long time I have fantasized about taking out every last one of the sick fucks who work at those auctions. And over the past eighteen years I've killed at least forty of them, maybe more. I've never actually counted. They all met *accidental* ends. From falling out of a skyscraper to jumping in front of a train—deaths that, while suspicious, were different and spaced out enough so as to not form a pattern and unintentionally leave a trail of breadcrumbs for the Brotherhood to find.

I've enjoyed every single kill, but I already know this one is going to be special. This one I'm going to take my time with. It's not often I get to inflict the kind of pain they deserve, but for this man I'll make an exception. I'll revel in watching the fear in his eyes while his life slips away from him. I only wish I could let her witness it too.

Clutching the six-pack to his chest, he walks out of the store and straight into me. He bounces off me and I put my hand on his forearm to steady him, keeping my head bent low and the hood of my sweater pulled down over my face. I mumble my apology.

"Watch where you're fucking going, fucking asshole," he yells loudly.

I murmur another apology and then go into the store, pretending to look at potato chips while I watch him through the window. Grumbling to himself, he tosses a lit cigarette into the gutter before climbing into his car—a bright green Chevy with one of those ridiculously huge exhaust pipes. Alec Brown. Twenty-eight years old. A high school dropout. Recruited by the Brotherhood at the age of sixteen, he's never risen far enough up the ranks to be anyone of significance. The Brotherhood won't miss him—which is kind of a shame. He's a mere Pawn, and I prefer to take out higher value pieces, all in pursuit of the King of course. But Pawns are aplenty and their abundance, as well as their relative insignificance to the cause, makes them much easier targets. Killing one of the Brotherhood's major players is a more difficult crime to both execute and cover up.

I follow him to his house, wait for him to walk inside and imagine him locking the dead bolt I know he has on there—like that would be enough to stop me. Alec thinks he's untouchable, but I've already been inside his house. I already know the layout and where the weakest points of entry are, such as the kitchen window with the broken lock. It's how I got in last night, when I searched his house for any information that might lead me to some of the key members of the Brotherhood. As expected, I didn't find any, but I did grab his back-door key, hanging on a hook on the refrigerator. It took less than a few minutes to make a mold, and tonight's entry will be much easier because of it.

I wait, and I watch. It's not the kind of neighborhood where anyone is likely to be suspicious of an SUV parked down the street and nobody bothers me. Light spills out onto the lawn as he moves from the den to the kitchen a few times, drinking his beer, smoking cigarette after cigarette and sometimes talking on his cell phone. It's two hours and fifty-six minutes before the downstairs lights go off and the bedroom light is switched on. Another six minutes before it goes off again. He's had a similar routine for the past two nights, and I did consider the possibility of already being inside waiting for him when he got home earlier. Pictured the look on his face when he switched on the light and saw me sitting on his sofa patiently expecting his return, or staying by the door in the shadows so that I'd be the first thing he'd see.

But something about waking him from his sleep appeals to me. I want to see the slow realization dawn on his face when he sees that he can't move. I want to watch him discover who I am and what I'm going to do to him.

When another half hour has passed, I climb out of my car and head across the dark street and through his garden, skirt around the house to the back, and let myself in. My boots are quiet on the thick carpeted floors leading straight to his bedroom.

The door creaks a little when I push it open, but he doesn't stir. He's lying flat on his bed, on top of the covers, wearing only tight black boxer briefs. From here I can see that the snake tattoo on his neck winds all the way down to his chest.

I check my watch. It's been four hours since he bumped into me outside the drugstore. Four hours since I touched him and left the pathogen on his skin.

I give him a nudge with my foot. "Wake up, asshole."

His eyes flutter open and he looks at me for a few seconds, sleep still clinging to him. I flick on the light and he sees me—the masked man dressed all in black standing at the foot of his bed. He tries to move. Can't. "Who the fuck? What the fuck?" he sputters, his head jerking up and down like somehow that will give him the momentum to move. It won't.

"No sense in wasting your energy trying to get up, Alec. Your nervous system is being attacked by a pathogen. Biochemical engineering at its finest. A company in Japan that I invested in has been developing it for over a decade. They have the vaccine too." I flex my hand, now encased in a leather glove. "Makes me immune to the effects. So I'm able to easily administer it, maybe leave it on someone's skin when they bump into me."

"You. Outside the store," he snarls. "What the fuck have you done to me?"

"I've infected you, Alec. The same way that you infect every single person around you. My kind of bacteria is much smarter than yours though. It attacks the spinal cord, disabling the body from the neck down. The good news is, you can still feel pain though. Lucky for both of us, huh?"

He shakes his head, his face red with the effort of trying to move his now-paralyzed limbs. "Untraceable in toxicology reports too. Comes in handy more times than you can imagine."

"F-fuck! Who are you?" he sputters.

I sit on the bed beside him and take off my mask, letting him see my face. "Don't you recognize me, Alec? The one they taught you all to fear? The freak, isn't that what they call me?"

His eyes widen in horror. I'm almost unidentifiable from the man he's studied pictures of. My head was shaved back then. I had no beard. But it's the scars they all recognize. The thick twisted knots that cover almost the entire right side of my face, from my cheekbone to my neck. Distinctive—that's what the surgeon who painstakingly removed the hundreds of particles of gravel and road from my face and body told me. I guess he was right.

"N-no. You're an urban legend. Not real," Alec babbles.

"Oh, I'm real. And if you know the legend, you'll know who Imogen DeMotta is to me." I trail the tip of my knife over his eye socket and down his cheek. He's pissed himself now. I can smell the urine soaking his boxers. "Or maybe you'll remember her as Lot 51?"

"I was just doing my job, man," he wails. "I only did what they told me to."

I bring my face closer to his, smell the sour stench of his breath. Beer and cigarettes. Did he breathe on my girl? Did his filth taint her? "You touched her," I snarl.

"I only—"

I slam the base of my knife handle into his teeth, causing the front ones to break and his gums to split open. No point in interrogating him because he speaks the truth about only following orders. Men like this are never given any high-level information, and they never think to ask for it either. No ambition.

He howls in pain, so I slice out his tongue while I let him know that I've barely started yet. Hardly even scratched the surface of the agony he's about to endure. I take the cloth parcel out of my bag and open it on the bed beside him. His eyes dart to it and then back to me, wild and animallike. "They're nettles." I explain, taking a handful in my gloved fist and crushing them until the sap starts to seep out. "You ever get stung by nettles, Alec?"

He shakes his head, and any sounds he makes are strangled by the blood still pouring from his mouth and down his throat.

I coat the blade of my knife in the sap. "These grow everywhere on my land. Particularly vicious little bastards. I was pushed into a patch once when I was a kid. Stung like a motherfucker all over. But, you know what was the real hell?" I press the tip of my blade against one of the thick veins on his forearm. He wails and chokes so much that I'm forced to prop his head up with another pillow. Don't want him to miss the show, or choke on his own blood before we get to the best part. "The kid who pushed me gave me a split lip beforehand and the cut was still open."

I slice the blade into his arm, not enough to rip open the vein yet, just enough to bite. Tears squeeze from the corners of his eyes, and he thrashes his head, the moans coming from him unnatural and inhuman. Fucking music to my ears. "Nettle sap in an open wound burns like hell, right?"

He makes another garbled sound. I slice another cut. And another. "This is what you get for touching her, Alec." I drag the tip of my knife over his abs before cutting through the fabric of his boxers. Every move I make accompanied by the melodic sounds of his pain, like my own personal symphony.

I coat the blade with fresh sap, and then I hold up his flaccid cock. "Were you there when they operated on her? When they stole her chance of ever having a child?"

Every woman sold at auction is sterilized to prevent any unwanted pregnancies. Not that the Brotherhood care about the women having to go through that, but a pregnancy might get in the way. The women are bought only to be used and abused until there's nothing left of them, not even their soul.

"Did you ever get hard looking at her? Thinking about what you'd like to do to her?"

He shakes his head.

"Liar!" I slice him from balls to tip, and to ensure he knows what pain really feels like, I stuff some of the crushed nettles in the open wound. His eyes roll back and just when he's about to pass out from the pain, I slap his face hard, bringing him back. "Not yet, buddy. We're not done yet."

I STARE AT MY FACE IN THE MIRROR ABOVE HIS sink, my cheeks spattered with thick welts of his blood and my clothes and gloves covered in him. I clean myself as best I can before wiping down his bathroom. I'm a ghost who doesn't exist. No fingerprints or DNA of mine will show up in any kind of system, and I don't intend to leave any behind today. The person I was is dead and buried and I intend for him to stay that way, which is why I'm usually much more careful than this.

This is the messiest kill I've carried out in a very long time, and there's no way to pass this one off as accidental, but it had to be this way. There's only so much rage I can carry inside me before I have to let a little of it out. And he *touched* her. He touched my fucking girl. Alec is the kind of man who has enough enemies so his murder won't come as a surprise. The brutal nature of it might though, and I can't help wondering if I've just alerted the Brotherhood to a threat they were previously unaware of. Maybe that's a good thing. Maybe it will flush some more of the evil scum out into the open.

And I'll go on picking them off until I find the one I'm looking for, the one they call the King. When I do eventually find him, he'll beg for mercy like the pathetic stain on humanity he truly is. And I will take even greater pleasure in exacting my revenge on him, for every single day of her life that he kept her from me. Every single second of pain she has ever endured, he will suffer one hundredfold. The Brotherhood will wish they had never heard the name Imogen DeMotta.

CHAPTER 9
LINCOLN

It's past midnight by the time I get home, but Pierre is waiting for me like he always is. I find him in my basement, or my *secret lair*. The bank of computer screens illuminates the familiar features of his face in the otherwise dark room.

"You are late," he accuses.

I resist the urge to remind him that I'm a grown man and I never asked him to wait up for me. He's still pissed at me for leaving unexpectedly, and on top of that he always worries when I leave. And now, with Imogen here too, if something were to happen to me, then he would be left with the burden of protecting her. And my oldest friend doesn't deserve to carry the weight of that. He shouldn't have to pay for my mistakes. "I had to stop off and change." I drop the bag at his feet.

"Change your clothes?"

"Yes. They got a little . . . messy."

He makes a soft humming noise. "That is very unlike you."

"This was a special case." I fall into the chair beside him and scan the monitors, glancing over the coding programs as they continue to run in an endless loop and the security cameras and heat sensors that cover the perimeter of my property. After a moment, I satisfy myself that everything is as it should be.

"Did Edgar assist you?" Pierre asks.

"No, there was no time to involve him."

Edgar North is my link with the outside world. A man with infinite connections in the criminal underworld, and one who has reason to hate, and to hunt, the Brotherhood as much as I do. In an alternate universe, one where my sister didn't die, I guess he'd be my brother-in-law, maybe a doting father to my nieces and nephews by now. As it is, he's a man just like me. Living like a ghost and hell-bent on revenge.

"It was someone from the auction you paid a visit to, then?" Pierre asks, perceptive to a fault.

"Yes."

I feel his disapproval radiating from him in waves.

"What, Pierre?"

He holds up his hands in surrender. "I said nothing."

"I can hear you judging me."

"*Merde!* You have spent eighteen years taking every precaution necessary, and now you go and . . ." He mutters some more French curse words.

"Now I what?"

"Now you draw attention by killing someone who is directly linked to the girl, and doing so in a manner which is likely to draw scrutiny. I do not understand it." His accent grows more pronounced the angrier he gets.

"It may draw attention but not to us. He's one of dozens of Pawns involved in those auctions."

"So why this one, Lincoln?"

"Because he touched her, Pierre. And I saw the fear in her eyes when he did. That's why." I don't add that I would hunt down every last one of them and give them the same treatment if I could, because he already knows that. One day, I will.

He remains silent. Deep in thought.

"How has she been?"

He snorts. "She spends her days reading in your library or

the garden and her nights watching television in her room. She does not make a mess. She speaks when spoken to. She eats whatever I cook. A perfect little pet, waiting for her master's return."

An unexpected growl rumbles in my chest. She is not my pet and I'm certainly not her master. "Did you encourage her to talk? To make some decisions for herself? Ask her what she wanted to eat?"

He frowns. "I am not her babysitter, nor her therapist, Lincoln."

I bite my tongue, because he's still annoyed with me for bringing her here, and with good reason. Experience tells me there's no point in arguing with him when he's like this. Instead I stare at the screens, waiting for him to get so uncomfortable with the silence that he can't resist filling it. "Of course I asked her what she wished to eat, and her response was always the same—that whatever I was eating would be fine. Except for breakfast, which as you know for me consists of coffee and more coffee. Meanwhile she would ask for a disgusting blend of oatmeal made with only water." He makes a gagging sound.

"But that's a good thing? She asked for what she wanted."

"*Non.*" He shakes his head. "Because she does not *like* the oatmeal. I can tell from the little sounds she does *not* make while eating. And I . . ." He jabs his finger into his chest. "I am forced to make the foul-smelling sludge when she does not even enjoy it. Did you know she has never been exposed to good music? She did not even know who Bruce Springsteen was!" He appears particularly furious about that and it makes me grin.

"She's twenty-one, not fifty-one, old friend. And not everyone agrees with your questionable taste in music."

He gasps loudly, like I've just insulted his mother and not his favorite music artist. "My questionable taste? This from a man who enjoys the sounds of people screaming and wailing into a microphone?"

I unlace my boots. "It's called heavy metal, and you know

that's not all I listen to." As pleasant as this conversation is, it's not my most pressing concern. "Back to Imogen," I remind him.

He harrumphs, arms folded over his chest, still not forgiving me for my dig at the Boss. "As I said, she has done little but read, listen to music and watch TV. She is meek and obedient."

I rub my temples. I'm tired and my conversation with Pierre is leaving me confused. The whole situation with Imogen has me confused, if I'm honest. I recall clearly the fire in her at the night of the auction. So why the obvious change in her? I understand her being uncertain, given the circumstances of her being here, but she doesn't speak, doesn't ask questions. Is she playing us? Is she one of them? Or did they hide her all this time only to use her to lure me out of hiding?

I intended to bring Imogen here as soon as I saw her name in that damn brochure, but I have no idea what to do with her now that she is. "So she eats oatmeal but doesn't like it?"

"*Oui*. And when I ask why, she tells me that it is *healthy and nutritious*. Like it is a mantra she must repeat to herself in order to ingest such blandness." He snorts with disgust.

"Did you find out anything of interest about her upbringing, aside from her not knowing who some aging rocker is?"

He ignores my barb and rolls his shoulders, like he's shrugging out of his bad mood. "Of course. You asked me to, did you not?"

"I did, and I knew you wouldn't let me down." I considered interrogating her myself, but figured she'd be more likely to open up to the gentle, if often temperamental, blind Frenchman than to the monster who just bought her.

"She was indeed raised by her grandfather, Saul DeMotta, and her upbringing appears to have been very sheltered."

I nod, deep in thought. Imogen's father, Luca, rarely spoke of his father, Saul. They were never close. Saul is a billionaire and mean with it. His grandfather made their money in oil in the early 1900s and the family wealth continues to grow, but he rarely spends a cent he doesn't absolutely have to. A devout Christian and a staunch advocate for *traditional family values*. It's well-documented that he disinherited his only son after he got his girlfriend pregnant when she was just eighteen. The old bigot insisted that they marry or Luca would be cut off. Luca told him to go to hell and just for spite he waited for their child to be born before he married the love of his life.

If only I had known all these years that Imogen was alive and in the care of the meanest man alive. But I was led to believe she perished along with her mother, only a week after her father was killed. A child's body was found, and all of the news reports said it was her. The Brotherhood would never have been merciful enough to let her live.

And then I saw her name in the program.

Every Brotherhood auction has fifty lots. This time there were fifty-one. Each woman has a bio, detailing her age, her "purity level," and whether she has any particular *talents*. There are rarely names attached, mostly numbers. Only the most prized lots are deemed worthy of a name. And alongside Imogen's bio was her name, and the fact that she was the daughter of a traitor. I could practically hear the mob baying for her blood.

"She also spoke of a woman—Larissa." Pierre's voice drags me back to the present. "I got the impression she was almost like a governess. Strict, but nurturing. The girl credits this Larissa with teaching her all she knows. She *claims* to have had a pleasant childhood."

"You think she is lying about that?"

"Don't you?" he scoffs.

"Perhaps she was loved still." From what we know so far, Imogen was taken in by her grandfather with the promise that he would hand her over once she turned twenty-one, to be returned to the Brotherhood to do with as they pleased. Perhaps I simply want to believe that she spent the last eighteen years of her life being loved and cared for by someone. If not by her grandfather, who I would wager is incapable of such emotions, then perhaps by this Larissa woman she told Pierre of. Maybe I just need to believe that because the alternative makes me feel like I can't breathe. It also makes me want to hunt down Saul DeMotta and carve out his still-beating heart. One day . . .

"Would you give up a child that you had loved and raised to the Brotherhood, Lincoln?"

"No," I admit. Her grandfather should be sold at a fucking auction for what he did, no matter what kind of deal he made. "But Larissa? Maybe it was her who showed Imogen kindness? Love?"

"Per'aps." Then he stands and grabs my bag from the floor. "I'll take care of these tomorrow."

"I can do that."

"Agh! I have always been better at getting blood out of clothes than you are. And what else do I have to do?"

I roll my eyes as he walks toward the door. He pauses, his hand resting on the doorframe and his head bent low. "Did you make him suffer, *mon ami*?"

"Of course, Pierre."

"*Bien.*"

He disappears from sight, leaving me alone with my thoughts.

So Imogen is being the perfectly behaved houseguest. Now that I have time to think, I tell myself that's to be expected, given that she's been here for less than a week. And even more so, given that she was quite clearly prepared for an auction. The way she stood on that stage, stoic and defiant proved to me that she had been well primed for what was to come, and if that was the case, she'd have been prepared for the aftermath too. So her obedience actually makes perfect sense.

I can imagine what that kind of training must have been like. Do what you're told when you're told. Be obedient. Don't cause trouble. Look for any opportunity to escape and then take it—the lot's handbook for survival. I can't imagine the horrors she was coached to endure though. She's probably terrified out of her mind, wondering when something awful is going to happen to her.

I should do something about that, but I imagine that no amount of reassurance from me will make her feel at ease, and I suspect only time will do that. Still, I'll try anyway.

CHAPTER 10
IMOGEN

Lincoln must have returned in the middle of the night. I knew he was here before I saw him or even heard his voice. The house smelled of him—of rain and leather and freshly turned earth. I don't know how I feel about him being back here. Pierre and I seem to have settled into something of a routine, and I've found a reassurance in knowing how the day would play out. Now that Lincoln is back, that comfort is gone, and he left so soon after my arrival that I have no idea what the atmosphere in the house will be like with him here.

"What would you like for breakfast, mademoiselle?" Pierre asks me, as he does every morning when I walk into the kitchen. I consider trying something else. Perhaps the waffles I saw in the freezer. Or the bacon I saw in the fridge. One day, I definitely will, but maybe it's Lincoln's return which is making me feel uneasy and out of my comfort zone again, so I choose familiarity and order—oatmeal.

Like he's done the past six mornings, he wrinkles his nose in disgust and then he mutters something in French.

"Why oatmeal?" Lincoln's voice comes up behind me, washing over me and sending a shiver down my spine. I wish I didn't have this kind of response to just his voice, but it's so deep and gruff—always laced with a hint of danger. There were always men at my grandfather's house, and I spent a lot of time in their company, albeit being seen and not heard, but none of them ever affected me in the same way that Lincoln Knight does. I'm not sure why I seem to find some kind of thrill in the way his presence sets me on edge, but what I do know is that it's confusing.

He goes to the counter and pours himself a coffee. He's wearing his mask like usual and all that's visible are those intensely dark eyes beneath his thick crop of black hair.

"It's healthy and nutritious," I reply to his odd question. *Why not oatmeal?*

"Interesting," he mutters. Then he turns to Pierre. "I'll take some eggs and toast in my study."

"Of course, sir."

My stomach growls. Eggs and toast sounds good. Better than oatmeal, but I keep my lips clamped shut. I've asked for oatmeal and that's what I'll eat. If I ask to change now, I could look spoiled. Or weak, which would be even worse.

Without another word, Lincoln leaves and heads to his study. As soon as he's gone, Pierre says, "I'm aware you've enjoyed exploring many of the rooms of the house this past week, mademoiselle."

I freeze. My heart stops beating. I have indeed tried every door in this house, with the exception of Pierre's quarters, which are out of bounds, and discovered all of them but the door to the basement to be unlocked. I found nothing but empty rooms or ones filled with old dusty furniture. But I had no idea Pierre knew I'd been doing that, assuming I'd been quiet enough to avoid detection. How the hell did he know, and what is he planning on doing about it?

Panic surges through my core and I brace myself for whatever punishment is surely headed my way. But Pierre continues busying himself with preparing breakfast. "You will have no doubt noted the absence of a designated study, and that is because Mr. Knight's study is the library, where you enjoy spending most of your days." His voice retains its usual calm and pleasant tone.

So he's not going to reprimand me for snooping? Relief floods my chest and I breathe again. Of course he's not. I was specifically told that I could enter any room of the house that wasn't locked, but I still felt like I was doing something wrong when I was poking through old writing desks and antique dressers. My relief is followed swiftly by disappointment. "Does that means I should stay out of the library now?"

Pierre shakes his head. "*Non*. Not unless he has prohibited you from going in there?"

I recall the conversation I had with Lincoln before he left. "No, he said I could use it as I please."

Is it odd that he gave me permission to share his study with him—his personal space? The library is big but we'd still be in the same room, sharing the same oxygen. Why on earth does the thought of that intrigue me so much? Because he holds the key to me getting out of here, that's why. Nothing to do with how mysterious and brooding he is. Nothing at all.

"Then it's not off-limits, mademoiselle. However I would avoid the room when Mr. Knight is dining, as he will have to remove his mask to eat. But I simply told you so you would not be alarmed to find him there when you are reading."

It's strange that he wears a mask even in his own home. "Does he always wear a mask?"

"When he is around other people, yes."

"But not you?" The words leave my mouth before my brain is engaged.

He turns to me, a half smile on his face. "Really, mademoiselle? What need would he have for a mask in front of a man who cannot see his own hand in front of his face?"

I cover my eyes and feel a blush warming my cheeks. It's easy to forget he's blind when I spend so much time with him. "Of course not. I didn't think about what I was saying. Sorry, Pierre."

He chuckles softly and then goes back to making breakfast. I want to ask why Lincoln wears the mask, but think better of it. I've heard the rumors about him being horribly disfigured and I expect it has something to do with that. Perhaps he has no skin on the lower half of his face—only teeth and bone where lips and flesh should be? Perhaps fangs in place of teeth. Maybe Lincoln Knight truly is a devil.

Whatever lies beneath that mask, I'd like to tell him he has no need of it around me. The kind of devils I fear are not terrifying because of how they look, but because of the kinds of sick and perverted things they like to do to women like me. And by those measures, Lincoln hasn't proven himself to be a devil at all.

At least not yet.

I TOOK MY BOOK INTO THE GARDEN TODAY INstead, purposely avoiding the library and allowing Lincoln his space. Despite him offering me free use of the room, I'm not sure how he'd actually respond to me being in there. Lost in the tribulations of a new novel that's quickly becoming another favorite, *Jane Eyre*, and the English countryside, I read all day, until the sun was low in the sky. I definitely didn't imagine myself as Jane, nor Lincoln as Mr. Rochester. No. Absolutely not.

Pierre brought me a lunch of sandwiches and fruit and he sat with me for a few moments, but other than that my only company have been Jane and Mr. Rochester.

There's a chill in the air now, and the cool breeze dancing over my skin makes me shiver. I wonder if Lincoln is still in the library, or whether he's disappeared to the basement. That was the only door I found locked—protected by one of his high-tech fingerprint systems. What could he possibly be hiding down there? Perhaps he is just like Mr. Rochester, only he's hiding a dirty secret in his basement rather than his attic.

Another shiver whispers over the back of my neck, and this time not from the cold.

What does he have down there?

Lincoln Knight is a man I should stay far away from, but something about him seems to draw me to him. Perhaps an innate curiosity to know more about the mysterious man who bought me, yet doesn't seem to want me near him. The man who loves apple pie and who has earned the loyalty and apparent devotion of such a kind man as Pierre. The Lincoln whose voice makes my legs feel strangely rubbery.

Lincoln is on his way out of his study as I'm entering, and I almost bump into him. Instinctively, I stumble back a few steps in order to avoid the contact, my heart racing wildly. My feet slip, and I almost trip over myself, but he reaches out and catches me before I do, his large hands easily circling my wrists.

As quickly as he grabbed me, he lets me go, leaving only the heat of his touch seared on my skin. "Are you okay?" His voice is a deep throaty growl.

I find myself looking up into his face, staring at the thick black mask and those intensely dark eyes, the ones that are scrutinizing me so intently now.

Oh, no! I messed up. I showed fear.

But was it fear that made me stagger back from his touch? It felt the same—sent my pulse racing and adrenaline coursing around my body. But it felt different too. Dangerous. The same fluttering feeling deep in my belly from when I used to ride my bike down the steepest hill on my grandfather's estate. I'd close my eyes and freewheel all the way to the bottom, picking up speed. Never knowing if I'd fall, or veer off course and crash into one of the nearby trees.

I fell off many times, but it didn't stop me doing it over and over again. Amid all of the monotony of the rules I had to follow, and the unending task of proving myself worthy of the sacrifice my grandfather made when he saved my life, it was how I reminded myself I was still breathing—that I still had something left to breathe for. This feels like that kind of fear, the kind you seek out because it makes you feel alive. Only here, with Lincoln, it's a million times more intense.

"I'm okay, sir. I was distracted."

His eyes narrow. "You didn't come into the library today."

Have I made a mistake? Did he expect me to join him? "I was enjoying the garden, sir. The weather was beautiful today."

I let my eyes wander a little, over his neck and the thick vein pulsing in the underside of his jaw. Scars peek out from beneath the collar of his T-shirt on his right side, gnarled and twisted like the knotted brambles that cover this estate, all of them covered by the shadowy ink that winds around the base of his throat. He breathes heavily, making his muscles strain against the black fabric of his T-shirt. Despite knowing that it would be wrong to touch him, I yearn to trace my fingertips over his chest and see if it's made of iron or flesh. To trail them up his neck, feel his scars, remove his mask and see the man who lies beneath. I have never touched anyone the way I'd like to touch Lincoln, and it makes me feel equally excited and anxious.

"Beautiful indeed," he says, his voice still deep but tinged with something that wasn't there before. If I knew what desire sounded like, I would be sure that's what it was. The longing in his tone gives me that feeling again, the fluttering tightening deep in my core. Like I'm freewheeling headfirst into something inherently dangerous, yet thrilling all the same.

He lifts his hand to my face, and his fingertips almost brush my cheek—so close that I feel the ghost of them on my skin. For just a heartbeat they hover there while I stare into his eyes and brace myself for the inevitable, where he shows his true colors and takes whatever it is he wants from me.

THE AUCTION

But then the lingering warmth from his almost-touch is gone, and his hand drops to his side.

"Good night, Imogen." Any tenderness in him is gone now too. He's cold and detached again as he walks past me and down the hallway. My gaze follows his retreating back, wondering what might have happened if I had said something more. What if I had done as I had when I was a child, embraced the thrill of excitement, closed my eyes and raced down that hill? Leaned into his touch instead of standing frozen to the spot. Would I have veered off course, crashed completely, or would it have been the most exciting ride of my life?

What if that's what he expected me to do? Is that the kind of woman he paid ten million dollars for?

I wish I knew the answer, because it would make my life a whole lot easier, wouldn't it?

Or perhaps *easy* isn't the word. My life could never have been described as easy. But it was safe. Regimented. I always knew what was expected of me and when. My life had purpose. I had goals. Keep myself pure. Learn how to survive life after the auction. Take happiness in the smallest of pleasures. And I always knew exactly what I had to do to achieve those goals. I learned to take a life that could so easily have been unfulfilling, and color it with meaning and purpose.

Yet here, I find myself with no such meaningful purpose. No daily tasks to check off my list. No need to *survive* the daily horrors of abuse and degradation that I was taught to expect. Those same horrors that I imagine all fifty of the women who were sold before me are currently enduring. Why was I the lucky one? And how strange to consider myself lucky, given the circumstances I'm faced with. But compared to my counterparts, I'm extremely fortunate and I know that. Instead of facing torture and horror, I'm finding pockets of happiness in almost every moment, so many that it's becoming increasingly difficult to focus on my ultimate goal—my freedom.

Because, ironically, within the walls of Lincoln's fortress, I find myself with a kind of autonomy I've never had before. Since I've been here, I've been expected to be nothing but me. And that's the kind of freedom I've secretly yearned for, but never even dared to consider. Trouble is I've been who *they* wanted me to be for so long I'm not sure who I actually am. I feel bolder here, but I've also never felt so confused and conflicted as I do in this house.

And I've also never felt more alive.

CHAPTER 11
LINCOLN

It's been three days since I got back. Three days of her scent lingering wherever she's been—citrus fruits and the subtle hint of wildflowers—and three days of me trying not to be alone with her, at least not in close proximity. I almost crossed a line with her that night in the library. I almost touched her skin, and it would have been so easy to let myself feel the soft silk of her cheek, especially when it seemed like she wanted me to. But then where would that have led? For surely one touch would never be enough where she's concerned. And doing *anything* with her is monstrous and unthinkable. I'm heinous for even considering it.

I drop into the chair in front of the bank of screens in my basement *lair*. Eight of them attached to different computers which run endlessly. Two monitor security and heat detection cameras. Two monitoring my investments and programmed with a code that buys and sells stock based on the market fluctuation. It's a program I should probably have patented, except it would get me into a whole heap of trouble with Wall Street if I did. No need for brokers when a simple program can do the work of one hundred of them—not to mention it's faster, smarter and free from human error.

And while it would please me to no end to piss off all those rich entitled men in suits, I'm not in the habit of drawing unnecessary attention to myself. I exist in a state of nonexistence. The reclusive billionaire. Disfigured. Psychotic. Driven mad by the loss of his good looks and locked away in his secret hideaway, far from the prying eyes of the world. There are plenty of rumors out there about me, some so ridiculous they could have come straight from the mind of a horror fiction writer. And I've heard them all—from slaughtering my entire family in the house fire that scarred me, to being a devil worshipper. I do nothing to quash any of them, because for the most part they serve me well.

The other four screens run different kinds of programs. One is still tracing the money I paid to the Brotherhood, but every time the trail stops, it bounces and picks up somewhere else. The others are primarily focused on finding people—specifically members of the Brotherhood and the women sold at their auctions. The only way to ease my conscience is to try and rescue as many of the women as I can find, while also trying to take down as many of the sick fucks who ply this trade as possible. The Brotherhood are an elite organization made up of only the finest and cruelest minds in the world. Insidious and ruthless. They are masters of disguise, who have infiltrated every major institution and influential government in some way. They are ghosts, like me. Their ranks are organized like a game of chess. They have many Pawns. Soldiers who are dispensable and never provided with information other than that which is absolutely necessary to the task. I expect some of them don't fully understand the organization they're working for. They mostly do it for the kudos, the hope that one day they may rise through the ranks and become untouchable too. And some of them simply do it for the thrill, because the words *the Brotherhood*, spoken only ever in the ghost of a whisper, give them a boner.

Then there are the Bishops. The *respectable* faces of the organization—politicians and businessmen who further the Brotherhood's agendas through any means at their disposal. Ruthless and cruel, but with the charisma of a beloved dictator. And of course there are the Knights—the protectors. The generals who are the link between the Pawns and the power. The Knights report to the Rooks, and the Rooks to the Queen, the highest rank before the King himself.

Each level is closely guarded with minimal interaction. Every single member has a single handler who they communicate with. I've met many Knights, killed plenty too. I've only ever met two Bishops. The first was on the day my sister died, and I beat him to death with my bare hands. The second one was fifteen years ago. I killed him too. Slipped digitalis into his martini and watched him slump face forward into his date's ample breasts. I was blinkered back then. Focused only on wiping out as many of them as I could, until I realized my strategy was all wrong. Kill a Bishop and there are dozens waiting to take his place. Like a snake, the only way to take out the Brotherhood is to sever its head. Take its King. Bloody vengeance used to be the only balm to soothe the constant rage, fueled by my crushing guilt, yet now I find myself with another, altogether more effective and more pleasant, form of solace—and that is simply her presence.

I glance at the screen on the top right and frown. This one is focused on tracing the other women from the auction last week. But there is far too little progress and it's happening far too slowly. I roll my neck, trying to keep a lid on my frustration.

Pierre's footsteps alert me to his presence and I'm thankful for his company. This basement has always been cold and clinical, and that's how I like it. Or how I used to like it. But the blandness of this space feels a stark contrast to the color and texture of life above me in the main house. There's a brightness and a warmth there now that has nothing to do with the fire Pierre has started lighting in the library every evening, and everything to do with the person he's lighting it for.

"Have you found anything yet?" Pierre asks, wheeling over the spare chair and then sitting beside me.

"No. Everything is frustratingly slow," I grumble.

"It is always slow, *mon ami*. The Brotherhood are not fool enough to allow the girls to be traced so easily, for it would undermine the integrity of their entire structure, *non*?"

I grunt in response. He speaks the truth. As far as money goes, the auctions are pocket change for the revenue they bring in. Held every two years, they're not run for profit. No, their existence serves a much more sinister and important purpose. An auction is a breeding ground for future marks, already corrupt or primed to be corrupted. Full of arrogant, powerful men, who are so morally bankrupt that they would buy a woman from a fucking brochure where her primary selling point is how *used* she is. And as such, the Brotherhood go to great lengths to protect the identities of their customers, and what they do with the *goods* they buy. They also have a bunch of men who are as smart as me, running programs just like mine, who work just as hard to keep me out as I work to get in.

"I need a lead, Pierre." I run my hands through my hair. "Eighteen years and I've never come close to finding a Rook." The Rooks are the key. The keepers of the secrets who are trusted above all others.

"Your day will come, Lincoln. I feel you getting closer."

I close my eyes and sigh, wishing I could believe him.

Eighteen years of taking souls and exacting vengeance and I never make a dent in their organization. Because every time I take out one of them, it seems two more take their place. They continue growing stronger and richer and more powerful. But if I could find one of them. If I could spend an hour alone with a Rook, I'm sure I could get the information I need to find the

King. The man responsible for taking the only people who ever meant anything to me.

My mind wanders as it often does to the only Rook I ever met. I knew him very well. His name was Luca DeMotta. He was Imogen's father, and I was one of the many Knights who served him. He was calculated and shrewd, and brilliant and loyal. The Brotherhood say I killed him—identified him as a traitor and exacted my just revenge. And every single day I feel the weight of his death on my conscience.

CHAPTER 12
LINCOLN

Imogen wanders into the kitchen at 8:00 a.m., the same time every morning. It's been two weeks since her arrival, and I've started getting here by seven thirty so I can eat my breakfast before she arrives. I don't look up, keeping my head bent low over my laptop, which I've taken to carrying everywhere with me lately. It's an easier way to keep track of the security footage now that I appear to be spending more time in the upper parts of the house rather than my basement. It's also a convenient screen to hide behind while I observe her surreptitiously.

I watch her and Pierre go through their usual morning routine where he asks her what she'd like for breakfast, and every day I see the almost imperceptible flash of disappointment on his face when she replies with her request for oatmeal. Today, it seems he has a plan to change this, and I am anxious to see how she'll respond. She's a woman who seems so content with the smallest of pleasures, yet she refuses to permit herself the simplest joy of eating what she wants for breakfast. It makes me wonder at her upbringing. Was it merely sheltered as she suggests, or was it thoroughly miserable? I suspect the latter, despite her claiming it was *pleasant*.

If circumstances were different, I would take her to the finest eateries in the world. I'd let her sample the richest, most buttery croissants in Paris, and the softest sweetest gelato in Italy, and I would bask in the look on her face as she ate things that truly brought her happiness.

"Ah, we have no oatmeal, mademoiselle. You have eaten all of it. We can purchase more at the next grocery collection, but until then you must choose something different. What else can I fix for you?"

"Um?" She presses her lips together like she's deep in thought. "Do you have grits?"

I suppress a smirk at the disgust on Pierre's face. "No, we do not have grits."

She swallows, appearing anxious for a few seconds before she quickly regains her composure. She's definitely less guarded around Pierre than she is with me, and I can't ignore how much that stings, even if I understand the reason. Pierre is not the sick, twisted fuck who bought her at an auction where other sick, twisted fucks go to play. Sometimes, I catch her looking at me, like she can't quite understand how I could do what I did, and it's almost enough to make me tell her the true reason I was there. But if she knew, then she might hate me more than she already does.

While she's obviously aware I'm in the room, Imogen seems to buy my pretense that I'm focused only on my work. I would dearly like to understand why she's so anxious about choosing breakfast, and what the hell that says about how she's spent the last eighteen years of her life—eighteen years during which I should have been protecting her.

"Wh-what would you suggest, Pierre?" she eventually asks.

His face lights up in a way I haven't seen for a long time, and he claps his hands together. "I would suggest pancakes with bacon and a healthy soupçon of maple syrup." He makes a chef's kiss gesture.

Imogen's eyes go wide. "For breakfast?"

He scowls. "When else would one eat such a delicacy?"

Without waiting for her reply, he starts mumbling happily to himself while he begins to prepare the meal. Then his mumbling turns to singing, a French ditty I haven't heard from him in as long as I can remember.

From the corner of my eye, I can see her observing him working, a soft smile playing on her lips. Every so often I feel her looking at me instead, even though I can't be sure. But when I risk stealing a glance at her, I catch her studying me and our eyes lock. She bites down on her lip, like she was just caught doing something she shouldn't be, but neither of us look away. We stare at each other across the kitchen, neither of us speaking while something unexpected and overly familiar plays out between us. Perhaps she doesn't hate me at all. No, there is something much more nuanced than that between us. This is something more than the obedience she was taught to show. More than the captive trying to please her captor. It's raw and primal and hopeless to ignore. Her green eyes sparkle and I find it impossible to look away and break the connection. Her breathing grows heavier and a flush creeps over her cheeks as the few seconds seem to stretch out for eternity.

"Bon appétit!" Pierre walks between us, severing the connection as he places her plate down in front of her.

I'm pretending to look at my screen again when he moves, but I can feel her eyes on me still, her gaze like a caress on my skin. Pierre breaks the silence once more, encouraging her to *mange* before demanding to know whether his pancakes are better than her oatmeal. She tells him that yes, they are. Then she proceeds to clear her plate and I try to tune out the soft satisfied little sounds she makes when she does.

THE NIGHTS GET COLD INSIDE THE HOUSE DESPITE the spring weather and Pierre has lit the fire in the library. She sits beside it on the worn oxblood leather armchair, her feet tucked beneath her and her eyes glued to the book in her hands as she reads by the pale lamplight. The glow from the flames flickers over her face, highlighting the plump bow of her lips. I pause in the doorway, my mask tucked away in my pocket. Even if she were to look up, she wouldn't see my face in the shadows.

I recall her with Pierre earlier today, how her smile reached her eyes when she tasted her pancakes with bacon. The soft humming sounds she made when she licked syrup from her lips and how much I wanted to do the same. I long to kiss her. To part her lips with my tongue and taste her sweetness. To trail my mouth over her skin, until I reach all the places where I absolutely shouldn't touch. And despite how utterly wrong those thoughts are, I cannot stop them. I no longer even try. As long as I simply think, and don't act upon them, then she will come to no harm. I may die from a severe case of blue balls, but she'll be just fine.

"You'll strain your eyes reading in the darkness," I say, my voice rough from lack of use—the mask will do that, creating more than just a physical barrier. Some days I walk through this house barely speaking more than a few words. Today I've spent most of my day in the basement, chasing leads. When I realized it was almost nine, the time she usually drifts off to bed, I couldn't stop myself from coming to see her. Hearing her voice. Inhaling her scent. From filling my senses with everything that's her, like an addict in need of his next fix.

She lifts her head, a fleeting look of surprise alighting her delicate features, and like the flames it quickly shifts into something different. Something dangerous. She places her book on the table beside her and stands before slowly crossing the room, like a cautious cub unsure if a strange lion is an ally or a threat. The only sounds in the room are the crackling fire and the soft padding of her bare feet on the wooden floor.

I should walk out now and let her remain in the light instead of allowing her into the shadows with me. All kinds of bad things can happen in the shadows.

I don't leave and she doesn't stop walking toward me, not until she's so close that I feel the heat from her skin through our clothes. She tilts her head, studying me too intently, her green eyes narrowed as she tries to see what cannot be seen. I remain in the shadow, my face obscured by the darkness, but she still sees me. Not my face, but my blackened soul, in a way that no one ever has before. And my fierce little angel doesn't run when confronted with the monster. I feel exposed in a way I'm unused to, but I can't move. In fact, I don't want to, unable to back away from her scrutinous gaze.

"I'm used to reading in the dark, sir. My eyes are accustomed to it. I see more than most."

Yes, she most assuredly does. "And what do you see now, Imogen?"

"I'm not sure yet, sir." Her voice is a breathy whisper, and the way she's gazing up at me now, eyes wide and pleading, makes me want to reach out and touch her. Kiss her. Claim her.

I allow myself the sin of reaching out and letting the pad of my thumb sweep over her cheek, just enough to feel the soft silk of her skin and commit it to memory. Instead of flinching, she turns her cheek into my touch, showing no reluctance or fear. And I could let her in so easily. Drop the mask and let her see the man she thinks I am. But I'm not the Lincoln Knight she thinks she knows, and she should fear me.

"I'm the monster they say I am, Imogen. Don't ever forget that."

Her lips part but she doesn't make a sound. Instead she lets unspoken words hang in the air between us. One wrong move and I will take her. Devour her whole. I want her so badly it terrifies me, more than anything ever has before. I yearn to run my hands over every single curve and commit every one to memory. To take her mouth in a bruising kiss—the kind that musicians will write songs about for centuries. She is beauty personified, but my attraction to her is so much more than that. It's not just the way her green eyes see into my soul, but the way she sees the whole world. She's been through the fires of hell yet she's like molded glass, only strengthened by the flames.

But this is wrong.

I drop my hand, feeling the loss of her warmth so acutely that it sends a shiver down my spine. She blinks. Once. Twice. Confused.

"Good night, Imogen."

I sink back into the hallway and leave her to the sanctuary of her books. They will never betray her. My foot is on the bottom stair when I hear her soft voice say, "Good night, Lincoln."

It almost makes me falter. It would take mere seconds for me to go back for her, scoop her into my arms and carry her to my bed, where I would spend the rest of this night tasting and touching and fucking her.

But it's the memory of the promise I made to her father that stops me. Imogen DeMotta might be mine, but I can't fucking have her.

CHAPTER 13
LINCOLN

Living in this house with her is torture—the most exquisite kind of torture that exists. Imogen DeMotta is sweet and vulnerable, yet she is equally dangerous and addictive. I made the costly mistake of touching her skin a few nights ago in the library, and now the desire to do so again grows stronger with each passing moment. And no matter how much I tell myself I should avoid her, I cannot.

I feel her presence whenever she's anywhere near me, like a strange crackling of electricity directly beneath the epidermis of my skin. I slip on my mask, the one I always keep in my pocket when I'm in the upper parts of the house now. By the time she's reached Pierre and I, as we sit on either side of my desk in the library, my face is concealed once more.

She glances at the chess set on the desk, and then at the two of us. Her tongue darts out to wet her lips and a tiny flicker of emotion crosses her face before she's back to neutral. Unreadable. I'm not sure what I saw there. It looked like fear, but from what I know of her, she is not easily scared. So, perhaps she's nervous. "I need some things. I'm sorry I should have asked for them sooner, but I haven't been able to keep track of the dates since I got here."

What dates?

Realization dawns on me. Of course, she's been here for over three weeks already and I can think of one obvious reason she'd need to keep track of the specific days. "Did you get your period?" I ask, saving her the trouble of saying it aloud.

"Yes."

Pierre takes one of my pawns. "There are some things in your bathroom, mademoiselle."

"I know. I saw them, but I can't use tampons. I prefer pads."

Pierre winces. "I did not think, sir," he whispers. "I assumed all ladies used tampons, *non*?"

Imogen's cheeks are flushing a light shade of pink now, and as adorable and intriguing as it is, I would prefer to spare her any further embarrassment, in front of Pierre at least. "I'll go into town and get some pads. Is there any particular brand you prefer?"

She shakes her head. "As long as they're the unscented kind, please."

I push back my chair. The nearest town is at least a two-hour drive from here. "It will take me some time, but I'll be back as soon as I can."

"Thank you, sir." She gives me a polite nod and then slips away. Only when she's out of the room and probably thinks she's far from my line of sight, do her steps falter and she lets her hand go to her stomach before sucking in a deep breath. If I didn't pay such close attention to her, I wouldn't have noticed. I make a mental note to get her some Advil too.

THE STORE CLERK EYES ME SUSPICIOUSLY, WHICH I suppose I can't blame her for. I look oddly out of place in this small-town drugstore, dressed all in black and wearing a mask. Although since the whole COVID shit show, the world in general has grown more accepting of face coverings.

"I have emphysema," I tell her, noting her name badge. "Can't risk getting sick, Alma."

Her eyes narrow for an instant, but then she notices the giant pack of pads in my hand and something about that, or perhaps it was me using her name, seems to warm her to me. "You shopping for your lady?" she asks, cracking her gum before flashing me a smile.

"Yeah. These are the good kind, right?" I hold up the packet. I opted for the most expensive ones in the hopes that equates to quality. While I have zero qualms about purchasing sanitary products, this is the first time I've ever actually done so and I have no idea what I'm doing. There are also a confusing amount of products on offer.

She nods.

"And they're not scented?"

She wrinkles her nose. "Don't sell those fancy scented ones around here. I mean who wants their hoo-ha smelling like a cheap can of air freshener."

I place the packets on the counter. "Can I get some Advil too?"

The cashier makes a sad face now. "Oh, does she have cramps? Poor honey. They're the worst." She grabs a pack of Advil from behind the counter. "That's the best thing about reaching a certain age, you know?" She winks at me like she's letting me in on a secret. "I hope she has lots of chocolate on hand too." After that moment of unexpected kindness, she starts ringing up the items on the old-fashioned register.

Chocolate, why the fuck would she need chocolate? My experience of women is generally limited to one night, and since I'm not averse to period sex, I've found an orgasm is usually a decent cure for cramps, at least that's what I've been reliably informed.

And now I'm getting a very inappropriate hard-on thinking about how orgasms would be a much more fun way of helping Imogen with hers. What the fuck is wrong with me?

I grab a pack of Milky Ways and some Reese's Peanut Butter Cups from the stand near the counter and add them to my order.

"Mine used to be every four weeks like clockwork until I had my first baby, and then . . ." Alma goes on to tell me about her first pregnancy and the incredibly traumatic birth, and I half listen while I grab another two packs of pads. Might as well stock up a little. I grab another few packs of chocolate too. "Do you have any diaries? Or calendars?"

"Not much call for them in May honey," she says. "But you know we might have a calendar or two left over from January. Let me go check."

Alma disappears into the back room and a few minutes later emerges triumphantly, clutching two calendars. "I found these. Take your pick."

One is a charity calendar featuring the firefighters of Hillcrest, wherever the fuck that is, and the other has tulips on the front. I opt for the latter, and tell myself it's got nothing to do with Imogen staring at images of half-naked men who aren't me.

IT'S LATE BY THE TIME I GET BACK TO THE HOUSE and Imogen is in her room. Her door is half open but I knock and wait for her to invite me in. She's sitting up in bed, watching TV and the small smile on her face when she sees the brown paper grocery bag in my arms makes listening to Alma's incredibly vivid description of her *hoo-ha blowing out* worth every second.

"I got the things you needed."

"Pads?" She holds out her hands and I take a pack out and toss them to her. Immediately she sprints to the bathroom and closes the door. I stand awkwardly, still hovering by the doorway and then realize what a creep I'm being waiting for her to put a pad on. I place the paper bag on her bed, ready to leave when she calls out. "I'll be right out. Just one minute."

And now I feel like I have to stay. No, I want to stay. Because that sounded like she wanted me to and how could I possibly deny myself a chance to be in her company? A minute later she walks out of the bathroom. "Fixed now. Thank you, sir." Her eyes dart to the bag on the bed, and no doubt she sees the candy peeking out of the top. "Is that . . ." She stops speaking immediately, as though she remembers where she is and the grin that was about to light up her face disappears.

I hate that she won't let herself be human around me. I might look like a monster, but I'm not. At least not for her. Never for her.

On the other hand, I'm definitely a sick fuck for noticing her nipples beneath that T-shirt and wondering what it would be like to kiss them, but I would never act on that impulse. She never has to worry about being touched when she doesn't want to be ever again. The decisions about her body will only ever be hers. She has nothing to be afraid of in this house and I have no idea how to assure her of that.

I tip out the contents of the bag onto her bed. "There's Advil in case you have cramps and the store lady told me that chocolate is a thing. I don't know much about that, but I got you a few different kinds."

"And this?" She picks up the calendar and stares at it like it's the most incredible thing in the world.

"A calendar. So you can track your cycle. For next time."

Her slender throat works as she swallows, like she's trying to choke down whatever emotion it is she's feeling. But at least she's feeling something and I so desperately want that for her. I want her to feel a whole kaleidoscope of feelings and emotions. To feel loved and have all of those things she never had before now right here. Even if that means I'll have to endure the torture of being close without touching her. "Thank you, sir."

Fuck, I want to touch her though. Wrap her in my arms and tell her that she's safe here, that I'll never let anyone hurt her. But if I hug her, then I might smell her hair or her skin. She might melt into me, because she's been trained to be obedient, and I might let her. I might kiss her forehead and then her lips, then allow my hands to wander beneath her T-shirt. I might do any one of the things I'd like to do to her whenever she's near me. and how can I be sure that's what she wants and not simply what she thinks I expect from her. So instead, I leave.

CHAPTER 14
LINCOLN

The light from her TV is on when I walk past her room again. It's after 1:00 a.m. and I assume she must have fallen asleep. For that reason, I allow myself to stick my head inside and check on her. But instead of finding her sleeping, she's doubled over, bathed in the blue light from the screen, her arms clutched over her stomach like she's in pain.

"Imogen, are you okay?"

She looks up, startled. "Just cramps, sir."

I cross the room to her. "Did you take the Advil?"

She winces, unable to hide the pain on her face. "They worked a little. The cramps just come and go is all. Like bursts of pain every so often." She sucks in a deep breath. "I'll be fine."

Given who she was raised by and the little I've gleaned about her childhood, I suspect all her life she's been conditioned to ignore pain. To brush it off and never allow anyone to care for her. Or more likely never had anyone willing to and that thought makes the guilt I feel at not protecting her from that life even more crushing. "I'll be right back."

A few minutes and a visit to the kitchen later, I return with a hot water bottle.

"What's that for?" She blinks at me.

"No one ever taught you that heat is good for stomach pain?"

She shakes her head.

Without thinking, I sit on the bed beside her. "May I?"

"Yes, sir," she whispers.

I shake off the anger those words provoke in me right now. They make me feel like her fucking owner. And I'm well aware that's all on me, that she has no idea why I had to participate in that evil auction, but it still fucking stings.

I pull down the covers a little and rest the hot water bottle on her lower abdomen, over her T-shirt. "There?"

She nods, closing her eyes and lying back against the pillow. "Yes," she says on a relieved sigh. "That feels so nice."

"You can refill it with boiling water when it cools."

"Thank you, sir." Now that word doesn't make me feel any anger at all. In fact, it travels straight to my dick. Maybe it's the soft moan to her voice. Or that they sound like words spoken because of actual sincerity rather than obedience. Glancing around the room, I notice three empty Milky Way wrappers on her nightstand and she immediately blushes when she sees me looking.

"I've never tasted them before. They were really good." She's apologetic, a tone she often adopts around me, and it's a quirk I despise. She has no reason to apologize to me, for anything. Ever. She could raze this house to the ground and my pressing concern would be whether she'd burned herself in the process.

I want to kiss her forehead and tell her she deserves all the candy in the world. "I would have eaten all six of them, and the peanut butter cups."

Her lips curve in a radiant fucking smile, a smile that makes me want to protect her and defile her at the same time. I feel so many conflicting emotions around her. Every second I spend alone with her tests my resolve to its limits, and feels like it brings us closer to an inevitable outcome. Me. Her. Naked.

I screw my eyes closed and chase such thoughts away. It's not good for either of us, for me, to be sitting on her bed like this, and besides how wrong it is to do the things I want to do to her, she's far too distracting. I have a mission to focus on. Goals to accomplish. "Good night, Imogen."

The storm that's been threatening all evening finally breaks, and thunder cracks in the sky. Her eyes snap open as she steals a quick glance at the window. "Would you sit with me?"

"You want me to sit with you?"

She shivers. "Sorry. Thunder always makes me a little on edge."

Of course it does, and I should have anticipated it. If thunder still makes me think of that night, then it's unsurprising that it's left such a profound imprint on her young memory.

There was a storm the night her father was killed—the same night I found her and her mother cowering in the woods behind their safe house. I'd never heard thunder so deafening before, nor since. She was just three years old then, but how much of that fateful night does she recall? Hopefully none of it at all. Nothing except for the thunder anyhow.

She schools her face into a neutral stance once more, but the ghost of her fear is still here with us. "I'm okay. It was a silly thing to ask."

Both of us wear masks, and now hers is back in place. But I long to see it slip again, and I'm aware of the irony of the masked man longing to see behind hers. But I would let her see beneath mine, if she truly wanted to. Actually, I think there's not a lot in this world I wouldn't do for her. "Would you like me to sit with you, Imogen?"

Her eyes shine with surprise. "Yes please, sir."

I kick off my shoes and then grab a pillow, propping it up against the headboard beside her. I'm hyperaware of the proximity of her and the slight increase in her breathing. It mirrors the spike in my heart rate. And I notice more acutely how small her body is in comparison to mine. How easy it would be to roll on top of her and let my hands wander to all the places I dream of touching.

"What are you watching?" I hope to God it's nothing remotely sexy, because I'm not sure that will help the situation in my pants right now.

"A movie about a zombie apocalypse but I think actually the zombies are the good guys."

Not what I was expecting, but definitely feels like safe territory. "Is this the kind of thing you usually watch?"

"I don't have a usual. I'm still trying to figure out what I like, so I'm working my way through the different top tens."

So she wasn't exposed to much of the outside world? Interesting but not unsurprising. "You didn't watch a lot of TV before you came here?"

She shakes her head. "Not much. I wasn't allowed to. But very occasionally, when my grandfather was away, and if I'd done all my lessons and stayed out from under Larissa's feet or hadn't caused any trouble, I was allowed to watch an hour of TV. I used to watch Nickelodeon."

I can't imagine her ever causing any trouble as a child. And I'm keen to know more about what happened to her if she ever did cause any. I'm especially keen to know more about Larissa. Did she truly show Imogen the care and understanding that she seems to indicate, or was it simply that Larissa wasn't as cruel as her grandfather? And was she another Pawn in the Brotherhood's game? When I eventually confront Saul DeMotta, which I will surely do one day, will Larissa be an ally or an enemy? As much as I'd love to ask her more questions and tease out the information I seek, I'm also cautious about pushing Imogen too far too soon.

So I remain quiet, allowing her to fill the silence. "I always preferred reading anyway. I didn't have a lot of books, but I used to read my favorite over and over again. So, your library is like heaven to me." She smiles and it's a beautiful thing.

"And what was your favorite book?"

Her face tilts toward me, her green eyes sparkling. "*The Secret Garden.*"

I've heard of it of course, but never read it for myself.

"I used to imagine I was Mary, and I'd find a garden in my grandfather's estate and maybe my own Colin and Dickon," she says with a dreamy sigh. "I think I just admired the characters, and wished I could be as brave and courageous and strong as they were, you know?"

She goes back to watching the movie, no doubt worrying that she's shown too much of herself. And as much as that hurts, I understand her motives for keeping her guard up around me. Given the circumstances of her being here, and the kind of man she must believe me to be, it would be foolish to show her emotions so readily. And Imogen DeMotta is no fool. But I've no idea why she wished she were braver and stronger and more courageous, because she is all of those things and so much more. And I wish I were brave enough to tell her so.

Instead I sit quietly beside her, with my arms folded over my chest, and we watch her awful movie. I try not to think about the scent of her skin, or the soft steady cadence of her breathing. Try not to steal glances at the curve of her neck or the way her nipples continue to peek through the fabric of her T-shirt. I even pretend not to notice when her foot grazes mine. And when I shift position and her breath catches in her throat, I convince myself that it's because she was engrossed in the movie and forgot I was there, and not because she thought I was going to touch her.

I don't allow myself too much time to ponder whether my touch would be welcome or not. Nor which would be worse, her rejection or her submission.

When the hero gets the girl at the end, and he kisses her like he'll never get the chance to again, I try not to imagine what it would be like to kiss Imogen like that. To feel her supple skin under my hands. To have her under me. To mold her tight cunt to the shape of my cock. Because sometimes, the way she looks at me makes me think she'd like that as much as I would.

I think she'd like me to be her hero. But I'm not the hero here—I'm the villain.

CHAPTER 15
IMOGEN

The credits roll over the screen and an acute pang of sadness washes over me. If the movie is over, will Lincoln leave? It's been unexpectedly lovely having him sitting here with me. His presence is solid and reassuring.

I didn't mean to ask him to stay, but the thunderstorm threw me. On the nights when Larissa stayed at my grandfather's house, if there was a storm I would crawl into bed with her and she would gently scold me, before letting me curl up beneath the covers. And on the nights she wasn't there, I would hide under the covers with my copy of *The Secret Garden* and lose myself in the English countryside.

I have no idea why thunder scares me so much, but it has for as long as I can recall. I have a vague memory of being trapped somewhere in a storm once, but it's nothing more than the avalanche of thunder and the sensation of soaking wet clothes clinging to me. I think I remember my mother's voice too, but it's all too foggy and muddled to make sense of.

"Have your cramps gone?" Lincoln's deep soothing voice pulls me from that old memory.

"Yes, thank you. The hot water bottle did the trick." Or perhaps it was the distraction of the movie, and of him.

I've been acutely aware of him the entire time, but not in any uncomfortable way. More like in a fascinating way. Surreptitiously studying the tattoos on his forearms and marveling at the thick vines that wind along his veins. Stealing glances at the way his thighs stretch his pants so taut. I don't think I've ever seen a man with thighs as big as his. Some of my grandfather's drivers were big men, and usually they were mean with it, but Lincoln is the largest man I've ever seen.

Yet for all his size and obvious strength, he's never mean. Cold and detached. Grumpy. But not mean. There's a difference, and I would know. I could never imagine him squashing a snail under the heel of his boot just because a small child took some delight in it, or pulling the wings off a butterfly when it made that same child smile.

"That's good." Once again, his voice anchors me back to the much more pleasant present. "I should let you get some sleep." He climbs off the bed.

"Thank you for sitting with me, sir."

He nods once, rubbing a hand over the mask covering his jaw. "Good night, Imogen."

"Good night, sir."

He slips out of the room and I watch him with a strange and heavy ache in my chest. I have no idea what this feeling is. It's a little like when Larissa would go away for weeks at a time in order to visit her family in Greece. A longing to be near someone.

Except it's different. I don't just feel it in my chest, but low in my belly too. I felt it grow stronger when the hero kissed his girl at the end of the film, and when he laid her down on the bed—a pulling feeling, or perhaps a deep ache. The scene faded to black and I imagined what might have happened next. Would Max have been rough with Sammi, or gentle? I suspect the latter, given how tenderly he kissed her. None of the depictions of sex Larissa showed me involved the kind of sex I imagine movie characters having. They were only ever focused on the man's experience, and in some videos, multiple men at once. They invoked mostly feelings of revulsion and horror, and they were nothing like the scenes I imagine in my head.

After the scene in tonight's movie, I stole a glance at Lincoln. That deep ache grew more insistent and had nothing to do with my period cramps. And then I found myself imagining that it was me and him and not the characters on the screen. I pictured him lying on top of me and kissing me the same way Max kissed Sammi. Until that deep achy feeling in my core grew stronger and more insistent.

It's still there now, dulled but persistent. I wish a hot water bottle could fix this kind of pain, but I know instinctively that it won't. Despite my limited experience of sex, I suspect that's the only remedy for this kind of longing feeling.

I consider sliding my hand into my panties and touching myself there. If it weren't for the blood, or the fact that since the moment I learned about sex I've been taught that to do so would be a violation of my body, I would.

One of my many conversations with Larissa plays in my mind. I was fifteen and struggling with some of the changes in my body and the intense feelings I was having. We discussed female orgasms and why self-pleasure was forbidden. *A woman's pleasure is an unnecessary distraction, Imogen. Do not be weak. The ability to bring a man to climax is a powerful tool in your arsenal, sometimes one of the only tools at our disposal. Because men are weak, and they think with their dicks.* Then she took my face in her hands. *Do not allow yourself to be controlled by your hormones, my sweet child. Do not give in to your base desires.*

Instead of giving in to the urge, I turn off the TV and roll onto my side. And I find myself snuggling into the pillow Lincoln was using. Burying my face into the soft cotton until the scent of him fills my senses—fresh and clean and comforting.

I fall asleep with images of him in my head, and then I dream of a faceless hero whose kisses feel like fire.

CHAPTER 16
LINCOLN

Uncharacteristically of me, I place a call to a rare antiques dealer I met in New York many years ago, when I was still furnishing this house. Ordinarily, Edgar would be my go-between with the outside world, but this feels . . . personal. Or maybe I just don't want him to ask questions about what I'm doing. Because I don't even know what the hell I'm doing.

I searched for the shop online and confirmed it's still trading, and Harriet, the woman I met, is still listed as the owner.

She answers after a few rings. "Hardman Antiques. This is Harriet Hardman speaking."

I smile to myself. Her landline telephone number and professional telephone manner are almost an antique in today's fast-paced technological world. It makes me feel nostalgic for a forgotten time in my life, a time before I was who I am today.

"Harriet. My name is Lincoln Knight. We met some years ago."

"Of course we did. I remember you well, Mr. Knight. I believe you put two of my children through college." She laughs softly. "Are you looking for some new furniture?"

"Not exactly. I'm looking for a book."

"A book?" She sounds surprised.

"A first edition if possible."

"Books aren't really my specialty, but I have a friend who could help."

I bristle at the thought. I abhor dealing with new people and avoid it as much as possible, especially when involving anything remotely personal. "I'd rather deal with you."

She pauses for a few beats. "Of course. I can arrange the transaction if you'd prefer. Which book is it you're looking for?"

"The Secret Garden."

"Oh, that is a beautiful book, and we should be able to get you a copy of that quite quickly. Do you have a price range in mind?"

"Whatever it costs. I want one in the best condition you can find."

"Oh, delightful," she squeals. "Is it for your collection, Mr. Knight, or a gift?"

Even more uncharacteristically, I find myself replying with the truth. "It's a gift." A long overdue one, although I don't reveal that. "I'll email you details of the PO box to send it to, and I'll wire the money as soon as you confirm you have the item in your possession."

"Perfect, Mr. Knight. I imagine we can obtain a copy by tomorrow."

"Thank you, Harriet."

"My pleasure. It was wonderful to hear from you."

I end the call and lean back in my chair, and can't help picturing the happiness on Imogen's face when she sees the book. At least I hope it will make her happy.

There's no denying the fact that I've trapped her here against her will, yet she seems to have an ability to find happiness in the smallest of things. I recall her squeal of delight in discovering a rose growing out of the brambles in the garden, the way she savors a slice of apple pie, how excited she was over a simple calendar. She's an incredible young woman who deserves the world, and if I cannot give her the world, I will bring whatever she wants of the world to her.

CHAPTER 17
IMOGEN

I have wandered around this house for the past five days in something of a daydream, and I have no idea what's wrong with me. Because the daydreams are all about Lincoln Knight, and all of the things I'd like him to do to me. Something like the things men did to women in the videos Larissa used to prepare me for life after the auction, and the very same things I could never imagine myself wanting.

But my fantasies about Lincoln are different. In them, he's tender and kind and not brutal or forceful. Surely that kind of sex happens too?

It does in my head anyway, and now it's all I can think about. And every time I do, it makes me wet between my thighs and causes that deep ache in my abdomen to bloom. He was so sweet and caring a few nights ago, and it was in a way I don't recall ever experiencing before.

Larissa was my primary caregiver when I was a child, but even on her best days, I cannot recall her being quite so tender as Lincoln was. The way he thought to get me a hot water bottle for my cramps, and how effective it was. Larissa was very much of the suck-it-up-and-get-on-with-it school of pain relief. Not because she was unkind; it was simply her nature.

Yet Lincoln, a man I expect to be cruel and unfeeling, has shown me more tenderness and compassion in a few weeks than I have experienced in my whole life. And it's making me confused, and more importantly, it's distracting me from my primary goal—to get out of here.

Even now, when I know I should be exploring the house and looking for an escape, the memory of that night on my bed is so clear and vivid, and I replay it frequently. Every subtle movement he made. The reassuring steady cadence of his breathing. The heat from his body as it warmed my skin even without him touching me. Although for almost the entire time he was there, I imagined what it would feel like to have him touch me.

By the time the movie was over, I found myself wondering what it would be like if he lost control and rolled on top of me, taking what he paid for. I have no idea why he won't, unless perhaps I'm not what he expected. Not what he wants. But if that were the case, he'd discard me, wouldn't he? I'm certain he wouldn't be so nice to me if it were that simple. Most men who participate in auctions from the Brotherhood would do much worse.

I wander into the library, hoping to find a book that will distract me. Or maybe an epic love story that will be enough to sate my appetite for sex and romance, so that I can stop having inappropriate thoughts about the man who bought me at an auction!

I definitely need to be referred to a psychiatrist, don't I? And if not for that, then for talking to myself and expecting an answer.

The spot beside the fireplace, the comfy leather armchair and the reading table beside it, has become *my* space in this house. A place so comfortable and familiar to me that it makes me feel warm inside even by thinking about it. That I've been allowed to carve such a place for myself in this fortress where I'm held prisoner is very special to me. I'm grateful and happy for every minute I get to spend there, and I'm also highly sensitive to any changes to my little corner of the world.

So I immediately spot the extra book on the reading table, and I'm certain that I didn't leave it there. Has Lincoln been enjoying my little spot by the fireplace too? Eager to discover what book he's been reading and gather a little insight about his taste in literature, I hurry over to it.

I see the title first and my steps falter until I almost stumble over my own feet. How did that get here? I have scoured this library and I know a copy of that book wasn't in here before today.

I trace my fingers over the gilded gold lettering and a sob bubbles up from my chest. I scold myself. *Emotion is weakness.* Still, my lip wobbles and I bite down on it to stop myself from crying, but a rogue tear spills down my cheek anyway. My hand trembles when I pick up the book, running my palm over the soft green leather cover before holding it briefly to my chest, close to my heart where this story has lived since I was a child.

Then I bring it to my nose, inhaling the familiar scent of old paper, and a hundred memories come flooding back to me. Some horrible but mostly good. Reading beneath a chestnut tree while butterflies danced in the tall grass. Hiding beneath the covers in a thunderstorm with a flashlight while I pretended to be Mary on her adventures with Colin and Dickon. No matter how dark or desperate I would feel sometimes about my life and the fate that awaited me, this book would take me away from it all. It was my life raft in any storm. I open the cover to the first page and find it inscribed with black cursive writing. The words cause a physical ache deep in my chest.

For Imogen. Who is braver, stronger and more courageous than any character from any story ever written.

More tears burn behind my eyes. Lincoln did this? He remembered our conversation about my love for this book. He thought enough about me to obtain a copy and write this message inside. While he was incredibly caring toward me the other night, this might be the kindest and most wonderful thing anyone has ever done for me. Ever.

His footsteps alert me to his presence as he walks into the room. They're unmistakable to me now, much heavier and slightly faster than Pierre's. I pivot to face him, clutching the book in my hands.

"Did you do this for me, sir?"

He's at his desk already, opening up his laptop. "Do what?" he asks, not gracing me with any eye contact. So I drift closer, until I'm standing in front of his desk.

Eventually he looks up.

"The book?" I ask.

His right eye twitches. "Yes."

"It's the nicest thing anyone has ever done for me. Thank you."

He shrugs. "My antiques dealer came across a copy and I recalled you telling me it was your favorite."

"It is." I'm still overwhelmed with emotion. Gratitude. Happiness. Not to mention the lingering fantasies of him on top of me leaving me confused and excited at the same time.

My eyes wander over his torso, from the hard muscles straining against the fabric of his shirt to his forearms covered with dark ink and thick veins that stretch all the way to his knuckles, leading to his powerful hands. I recall how tenderly he pressed the hot water bottle onto my stomach and wonder how gentle he'd be with the rest of my body. How skilled those hands would be at touching me in the places I'm aching to be touched.

He's pretending like this isn't a big deal, but we both know that it is, and I wish I could understand why he hides his true self from me. Not the man behind the literal mask, but the one behind the other mask he wears—the one not made of fabric or ceramic, but of pain and guilt. I wonder if he knows that he doesn't need to wear either of his masks around me, not his literal or his metaphorical one. I see him anyway, even if he doesn't realize that yet. But the words he wrote inside the book don't fit with the cold and detached man sitting in front of me right now. I suspect that is the man the whole world gets to see. But this is not the one who wrote those beautiful words, or the same man who sat with me because I was scared of a little thunder. I expect that version of him is reserved for a few select people. Perhaps only for me? I hope so. It makes me feel special to know that I get a glimpse of that different part of him. "The inscription is beautiful, sir. Did you write it?"

The muscles of his jaw twitch visibly beneath his mask. "Yes."

My heart is racing. Stomach fluttering. "Did you mean it?"

"I'm not in the habit of writing things I don't mean, Imogen."

He thinks I'm all those things! Now it's not only my heart racing, but it feel like there's actual lightning zapping through my veins. I want to thank him again, but I'm afraid if I speak, I might let all these feelings that are swirling around inside me out. Emotion is weakness. But when Lincoln Knight does things like this, it makes me wonder if that weakness is a price worth paying.

His dark eyes are burning into mine, making heat sear through my core. That wet sticky feeling is happening between my legs again and I'm sure my pussy is pulsing with its own heartbeat. I squeeze my thighs together to try and stop the feeling, but it has no effect at all. Surely this is it and he's going to leap across his desk and kiss me—the girl he thinks is strong and brave and courageous. After what feels like forever, he speaks. "Is there anything else, Imogen?"

And just like that he crushes the flicker of hope burning inside me. "No, sir."

He drops his head and goes back to his laptop. With my book clutched in my hand, I go to my second favorite place in this house, my very own secret garden.

Pierre is sitting outside at the small table and chairs when I get there, his face tilted toward the sunshine and his eyes closed.

"Good afternoon, mademoiselle."

I sit with him. "Good afternoon, Pierre."

"It is a beautiful day, is it not?"

"It certainly is." I glance around the garden and wonder if he has any idea how overgrown it is. So many colors and scents all fighting for their own space. The yellow chocolate daisies struggling to flower through the tangles of bright green ivy, and the clematis being strangled by the fleabane. I imagine it was truly beautiful once and it seems a shame to not at least try and bring a little order to it, while maintaining it's beautiful wildness. "Does Mr. Knight have a gardener?"

Pierre scoffs. "*Non.* Never."

"Do you think he would mind if I did a little gardening? I could clear some space to grow vegetables and maybe some fruit."

"I already grow vegetables." He jerks his head to a few raised beds which also appear to be overgrown.

"I could make a little more room? Now that I'm here and there's an extra mouth to feed?"

"There is no need, mademoiselle. You do not need to work to earn your keep."

"It wouldn't be work. I'd enjoy it."

He hums, seeming distracted today. It seems there's something on his mind and I'm worried it's something to do with me. Have I been too overt in my mooning over his boss? Maybe it's the inscription written in the book in my hands that makes me feel bold enough to ask. "Do you wish I weren't here, Pierre?"

He smacks his lips together and makes a sighing noise. "Ah, I will admit, I would rather you were not here, mademoiselle."

That hurts more than I thought it would, or at least more than I should have ever allowed it to. But I thought Pierre genuinely cared for me, and to find out he would rather I weren't here makes my heart break a little. Or perhaps I'm still reeling from being so easily dismissed by Lincoln. Either way, I'm hurt and I blink back tears and scrub at the few that I allow to fall with the sleeve of my sweater.

"That does not mean I do not enjoy your company," he adds.

I don't need sympathy though, not from him or Lincoln. I tip my chin and roll back my shoulders. "You don't have to say that, Pierre. I'm used to being places I'm not wanted."

He snorts a laugh. "Oh! Not wanted? If you were not wanted, then you would not be here. *Non?*"

Perhaps there's a ring of truth to that. "But *you* don't want me here?"

"That I would rather you were not here does not mean the same thing as not wanting you here, *mon chou*. Per'aps, I simply believe you would be better off elsewhere."

I disagree. Especially when I think about the places I could have ended up instead. I remember all too well the vile catcalls and disgusting comments made by the other men at the auction, and the reason all fifty women before me were paraded around like objects, to be used and abused. And so I feel incredibly lucky to be here in this house with Pierre, and even Lincoln, who despite his mask, his reputation, and his apparent apathy toward me at times, has shown me nothing but kindness.

Why does a man like that even go to an auction? It doesn't fit the Lincoln I've come to know at all. And as guarded as he is, I've seen enough between the cracks of his facade to recognize his true nature, and that's not a man who buys women for sport. So why does a man like him pay ten million dollars for a girl like me?

"Why does Mr. Knight want me here?"

Pierre shakes his head. "You will have to ask him that, *mon chou*."

Perhaps I would if he weren't so closed off. Or if he didn't walk away or dismiss me every single time I get close to him, physically or otherwise. "What does *mon chou* mean?"

His lips twitch in a smile. "Little cabbage."

I let out an unexpected burst of laughter and it feels so good. I can't remember the last time I laughed out loud. "Cabbage? It sounded so sweet but you actually just called me a cabbage?"

His smirk grows wider. "It is sweet. Where I am from, it is a term of affection." He reaches out and pats my forearm. "You are very much welcome here, *mon chou*. But I wish for you that you were somewhere living a life full of love and happiness."

A life full of love and happiness hasn't ever been a goal for a girl like me. Survival has always been my primary objective. And freedom my ultimate prize, for then I may have a chance at some peace at least. And freedom means leaving this place.

Pierre pats my hand and I feel an overwhelming rush of affection for him.

Love and happiness? I might not have much experience in those things, but I'm sure I've never experienced them in as much abundance as I do right here in this house. Do I give up my dream of freedom for the promise of the former? It's not the most terrifying prospect in the world to me, especially not given what I imagined my future would be just a few short months ago. "Perhaps I could live that kind of life here?"

He simply smiles and says, "Per'aps."

CHAPTER 18
LINCOLN

I watched her with Pierre yesterday, and saw for myself how much more at ease she appears to be with him than me. Then I witnessed my old friend smile like I haven't seen him do for many years. But it was her laughter that almost broke me. It was the most beautiful thing I think I've ever heard.

She was grateful for the book, of course, and she clutched it to her chest like it was the only thing tethering her to this earth. And for a moment, I thought she might see me differently . . . and then she called me sir. She's still behaving as she believes I expect her to—as she was programmed to.

Will she ever laugh so freely around me as she does with Pierre? I'm not sure she'll ever be able to look at me as anything other than the monster who bought her, and that shouldn't matter to me. I paid those sick fucks ten million dollars simply to keep her safe. That was my only motive. Not to build some kind of relationship with her.

Whatever my intentions were, or are, it's clear she feels able to let her guard down around Pierre in a way she can't around me. And I want her to be her true self. I want her to find out who she is and become the incredible woman she was born to be, not the obedient pet she was trained to be. And if she can't do that around me, then maybe the best thing I can do for her is to stay away as much as possible.

Pierre will forgive me for slipping away in the middle of the night without saying a word, and I expect Imogen will too. Maybe it will be a relief to her that I'm not there, given how on edge she seems to be around me lately. Like she's constantly waiting for me to do something dangerous. To act upon the base desires I have for her. Maybe she's even convinced herself that she'd want that too. But if she has, then it's only because she doesn't know any better. Because if she knew who I truly was, and all the blood I've spilled in my need for vengeance, then she would never look at me that way again. And it would be no less than I deserve.

After I land the plane on the disused airstrip, I wait for the headlights to approach and climb out. A few moments later, I'm standing face-to-face with Edgar. He nods in greeting and then hands me the keys to the black sedan he just climbed out of.

I trade him the keys to the plane. "Refuel her for me, and I'll meet you here same time tomorrow." I speak slowly, enabling him to read my lips with ease.

"Sure, boss. Everything you asked for is in the car."

I sign my thanks to him before we part ways. As promised, Edgar has left me a map on the front seat and I study it quickly. Usually I'd thoroughly analyze the area beforehand and commit it to memory, but this tip off came in late last night and rumor has it the occupants of the house I'm headed to are about to pack up and leave soon. That means the girl is either going with them, or she'll be left behind in the ground. It's been four weeks since the auction and my stomach rolls at the state I might find her in.

It takes me forty minutes to drive to the compound, an old farmhouse deep in the forests of Appalachia. The house is made even more insidious for its subtlety, appearing more like a run-down homestead than the headquarters of Henry Finch, responsible for most of the meth circulating in the entire state of Kentucky. Generally, I don't give a fuck about meth dealers and their ilk because they rarely find themselves in the unfortunate position of being on my radar.

But when Henry bought a girl at the auction four weeks ago, he landed himself firmly on my shit list.

I'm sure he and his men could, and do, have their use of any number of girls. Those enticed by the money and those who are simply desperate for their next fix. But there's something about buying a woman at a Brotherhood auction that becomes more than a fucked-up erotic power play. Instead it becomes like some sick, twisted status symbol. Living, breathing proof that he's playing with the big dogs now. Stupid fuck.

I park the car half a mile from the compound, grab the bag Edgar left in the trunk for me and go the rest of the way by foot, finding my way through the trees and the rusted old farm equipment being eaten up by the tall grass. It doesn't take me long to find a prime spot for surveillance and to set up my infrared alert system. For the next few hours, all I do is watch them. When dusk falls, I switch to night-vision binoculars and decide I'll wait for full nightfall to make my move.

One of the quickest things I learn about Henry Finch is his sheer fucking arrogance. He has little in the way of security around the main house—just a few men patrolling the perimeter. The bulk of his security is situated at the exterior of the second barn behind the main house along with only two cameras that I can detect. The barn is reinforced with huge steel doors and has at least six guards patrolling the perimeter. I figure that must be where he keeps his most valuable assets, that being his drugs and his cash. Experience with men like him tells me that Lot 17, the girl I'm looking for, won't be in there. She'll be somewhere in the main house. Close enough for her to serve him in whatever way he chooses.

Henry Finch seems to believe himself untouchable, and I suspect because most of the people from the local town don't give a fuck about his operation here so long as he doesn't bother them—and he doesn't. I'm also sure that his cousin being the local sheriff is a big help too.

As soon as it's pitch-dark, I make use of my night-vision goggles and inch my way to the main house. I encounter the first of Finch's soldiers when I reach the smaller barn at the side of the house. His eyes bug out when he almost bumps into me, but before he can raise the alarm, I slip my knife into his carotid artery and he drops to the floor, clutching his throat and sputtering. I take his semiautomatic and drape it across my body before moving on, my boots barely making a sound on the grass. When I pass by the barn's rusting doors, I take a quick look inside and get my first glimpse of the truth behind the run-down facade. A black armored SUV and some false plates sit idly on the floor, waiting to be used.

I dip out of the barn again and head toward the farmhouse, encountering another of Finch's guards and disposing of him the same way as his colleague. I take his gun too, and hang it across my other shoulder. The door is unlocked—another sign of Henry's arrogance.

The hallway is decorated in a way befitting the derelict exterior. Floral wallpaper, faded and peeling. A worn carpet, threadbare in places and faded from the sunlight that must stream through the tall windows during the daytime. I suspect it's a lot like my own house: a mask disguising the true veneer beneath.

A floorboard creaks beneath my feet and I freeze, waiting for someone to hear me. When the house stays still and silent, I head upstairs. There's life up here. Sounds. Muffled voices. The low hum of a TV. The shuffling of feet. And scents. Gun oil, disinfectant, and a hint of copper. A door opens ahead and a man walks out, locking it behind him before he zips up his fly. He has a smug smirk on his face that immediately makes me want to ram the butt of my knife through his teeth, but I stick to the shadows while he walks into the room next door. Light from the room spills out into the hallway as he leaves it open.

"She's all yours, buddy."

Laughter. "Did you leave her conscious this time?" More laughter. It makes my blood boil to hear them laughing while they talk about another human being this way. If I had time, I'd skin every one of them alive. "I like to hear her scream when I fuck her."

I squeeze the handle of my knife tightly, until the skin stretches taut over my knuckles. Just a few more minutes and I'll make him pay.

"You sure you don't want a turn, boss?"

Boss? Is he talking to Finch?

"Nah. She's got a bit baggy for me now, you know what I mean?" More raucous laughter.

My grip tightens further and I force myself not to go in there and slit every one of their throats. But rescuing Lot 17 is my primary goal. Once she's safe, then I'll come back and kill every last one of them.

Another man walks out of the room and pulls the door closed, leaving the hallway in darkness once more. He drags on a cigarette, the amber glow from the lit end highlighting his features for an instant—a jagged scar runs the length of his jaw. He scratches his head, ruffling a thick mop of greasy hair and then flicks the butt onto the floor before stubbing it out with the toe of his boot.

He unlocks the door. "You awake, bitch? Billy has come to play." He cackles, the sound cut off as the door swings closed behind him.

You're about to laugh for the very last fucking time, Billy.

I creep along the hallway and gently turn the handle, relieved to feel it move beneath my hand before I push the door open a crack. Billy, the sick piece of shit, is already taking off his pants, and there's a girl lying on a bed, on top of filthy bloodied sheets. Even with my mask on, I can smell the foul odor of unwashed bodies, blood and cum. The girl is unmoving, but that doesn't deter Billy.

THE AUCTION

I slip inside the room and close the door behind me. The soft click has him spinning around, dick in his hand and a smirk on his face. I guess he was expecting one of his buddies. His mouth drops open, and before he can speak or alert anyone to my presence, I shove two fingers into his mouth, pressing his tongue down hard and gripping the underside of his jaw with my thumb. I hold my knife in front of his face. "Speak and I'll slice you from balls to nose, you understand me?"

He nods jerkily.

"How many men are in the next room? Blink once for each of them."

He blinks four times.

"Is your boss, Mr. Finch, in there?"

He stares at me, eyes filled with fear and saliva running down his chin.

"I'm only interested in your boss, Billy. Answer me and I'll let you go. Blink once for no and twice for yes."

He blinks twice.

"Good. Now I'm going to let you in on a little secret, Billy." I squeeze harder, until he gags and tears leak from the corners of his eyes. "I'm a liar."

I slice his throat and keep hold of his jaw while the blood and the life drains out of him, and then I gently lower him to the floor. When I'm sure he's dead, I turn my attention to the girl on the bed. She's conscious but staring into space. Almost like she's catatonic. Her dark hair is matted with bodily fluids, her naked body covered in sores and burns and welts. I'd say she was around the same age as Imogen.

Suddenly, indescribable rage is burning through every sinew of my body. Not just for what this poor girl has endured, but because it makes me think of the fate that could have been my girl's too. I wish I could revive Billy and kill him again, slowly and painfully, but my priority is getting this girl out of here.

I drop my backpack onto the floor and pull out the T-shirt

and leggings Edgar provided. Then I gently perch myself on the very edge of the bed, so I'm nowhere close to touching her. "Hey," I say gently. "I'm going to get you out of here. You want to get out of here?"

To my relief, she turns and blinks at me. At first sight, I'm scary to most people with my mask and tattoos, but I suspect she's seen and been subjected to horrors much worse than me. It breaks my fucking heart that I didn't get to her sooner. I should have shut down that fucking auction and got every single one of those girls out of there. I have no idea how I'd have done that, but I should have at least fucking tried. Yet always I'm driven by my need for revenge against the Brotherhood. Shutting down one auction wouldn't solve the long-term problem of eradicating their evil from the world, and it would also likely get me killed.

"They won't let me leave," she says, her voice cracked and raw.

"I know. But that's why I'm here."

"A-are you real?" she whispers, her fingers gently reaching out to me, like she's grasping at a mirage.

I allow her fingertips to brush over my mask. "Yeah, I'm real." I leave the clothes next to her. "Put these on and I'll be right back, okay?"

"No," she croaks. "If you're really here to get me out, you can't leave me."

"I'll just be—"

"No!" She grabs hold of my forearm. "Please don't leave me. I'd rather die than stay here."

I know she means that, and so I reluctantly agree, turning my back while she dresses. She does so more quickly than I expected, no doubt thanks to the adrenaline coursing through her and giving her a much-needed burst of energy.

She kicks Billy in the face as she passes him and I smirk behind my mask. "What's your name?" I ask her.

"Leah. Yours?"

I ignore her question. "Let's go, Leah. Do whatever I tell you to, okay?"

She nods to the guns draped over my chest. "Can I have one of those?"

"Have you ever used one?"

"Used my daddy's shotgun once. Can't be all that different."

I scrutinize her face, trying to get a read on her. Is she going to fucking shoot me? Does she believe I'm like one of the monsters outside?

"What if something happens to you? I really need to get out of here, mister. Please?" I can't ignore the desperate plea to her voice or the haunted look in her eyes.

"Fine. Don't shoot it unless you absolutely have to, okay?"

She nods, licking some dried blood from her lip.

I pass her a gun and she holds it like she's used one before. That puts me on edge, but I don't have time to change my mind now. If she didn't remind me so much of Imogen, I'd have told her she'd have to trust me instead of handing her a fucking gun. "I'm going to go next door and deal with the four sick fucks in there. You wait outside for me, okay?"

She nods.

I open the door a crack and find the hallway clear, so I signal her to follow. The floorboards creak and I wince. Her breathing gets heavy real fast. She stumbles into me and then gasps loudly. The door opens and one of the men steps out. I grab him quickly, slicing my blade through his neck. Leah screams. The other three come rushing out of the room and she opens fire, bullets zipping through the open doorway. She takes two of them out but the third ducks to the floor and aims a gun at her. I crush his skull with my boot before he can fire off a round.

She stares at me, eyes wide with shock and horror and then she starts babbling. "I shot them . . . I know you said . . . but I . . . I . . ." She takes deep ragged breaths, her wide brown eyes staring at me. "They did things to me." Then she sinks to the floor, letting the gun fall from her hands.

Giving her a gun was a mistake, but we're in this now.

Footsteps thunder through the downstairs hallway, more of Finch's men alerted by the gunfire. Leaving Leah on the floor, I crouch at the top of the stairs and pick off three of them as they charge up the stairway. The rest take cover, firing off shots that get nowhere close to me.

I run back to Leah and duck down on the floor beside her. "You're going to be okay."

She's trembling violently, babbling to herself. I grip her jaw firmly enough to get her attention. "We have to get out of here and we can't go down the stairs. Do you know any other ways out of this place?"

She nods. "The b-basement. They brought me through the basement."

Fuck this! "That means going downstairs."

"No, there's a staircase at the other end of the house."

If she knows that, Finch's men will know about it too, but it's a better option than the main staircase right now. "Then we have to move." I pull her up and shove the gun back into her hands, and then she leads me to the stairs.

Slipping on the night-vision goggles from my utility belt, I cautiously take a step down and find nobody. Seems like they all headed for the house to protect the boss when they heard the gunshots. I hope to fuck there is an exit down here. I make it to the bottom with Leah close behind me, and the sound of thundering footsteps in the upstairs hallway, coming straight after us.

"Through there." She indicates a doorway ahead of us. I take a deep breath and yank it open it to reveal a dimly lit hallway. "It leads to a garage."

The barn? There must be keys to the vehicles in there somewhere.

Blood thunders through my veins as I take her hand and run

THE AUCTION

through the hallway to another set of stairs. Footsteps follow after us. Leah is still shaking, but I don't have time to reassure her, so I keep us moving until we get to the barn. I see the armored SUV and a couple of motorcycles. My eyes dart around the room, looking for a place where they might leave the keys. And then I spy the small metal box on the wall with a key-code system.

There are voices outside now too. Growing closer. "What are we going to do?" Leah asks, gazing at me with wide innocent eyes. Here in the harsh light of the barn I can see the deep bruises on her face more clearly. The dried blood around her mouth, nose and ears. The ligature marks on her neck and the fingerprint bruises that cover her arms.

Sick fucks.

"We'll shoot our way out of here if we have to. Okay?"

She nods, cradling the gun to her like it's her lifeline.

I shoot open the lock and work through the keys until I find the one with a fob that will open the SUV. I press it and the car beeps to life. More thundering footsteps. Leah shrieks and I spin around and see the two guys come charging into the barn. I duck and sniper them both as their bullets whizz past me. Then I feel the cold barrel at my neck.

"Take off the fucking mask," the voice commands. I already know this is Henry Finch from a voice clip I heard of a police interview I uncovered when I was researching him. So, Billy was a lying piece of shit . . . I grind my jaw. Thoughts of Imogen fill my head. I have a knife strapped to my thigh. I can take Finch out before he even blinks. But if the worst happens, my girl will be safe with Pierre. Nobody will find them at RooksBlood.

A shot rings out. The back of my neck is splattered with something warm and sticky.

"Let's go," Leah yells.

I spin around and find Henry Finch face down, the back of his head blown wide open. Leah is holding the gun, standing beside the SUV with the door pulled wide open. She climbs inside and I run after her, shooting out the tires on the four motorcycles before I jump into the car beside her.

I CHECK THE REARVIEW MIRROR AS SOON AS we've cleared the grounds of the compound and sigh with relief when I find nobody following us. I'll have Edgar and some of his men torch the entire place and get our car back as soon as the heat dies down. Beside me, Leah is quiet, but she continues trembling now the immediate danger is gone. We've been driving for over ten minutes before she finally speaks.

"I killed them," she whispers.

"You also saved my life," I tell her.

She stares out the window, taking in a deep breath. "I ruined your plan to get out quietly."

True. She fucked it all to hell. But Edgar and I can work with the carnage we just left behind. "Well, with all those dead bodies back there, it will look like a drugs war. You probably did me a favor," I assure her.

She turns to face me now, her face drawn and pale. "Who are you?"

I keep my eyes on the road. "Nobody important."

"Are you like a secret vigilante superhero? Is that why you wear a mask?"

The absurdity of that idea almost makes me bark out a laugh. "Not either of those things."

She sighs and leans back in the seat. "So what happens now, Mr. Nobody?"

"I'm going to take you to a safe house and you can stay there for as long as you need to. You'll be given a prepaid credit card with enough money to start over. It's up to you what you do next, Leah."

"And that's it. You're just going to leave me?"

A pang of guilt lances through me, but I'm not her fucking savior. Definitely not anybody's hero. I already did my part, so why do I suddenly feel like shit for just dropping her at a safe house? "The house is in a nice little town. The neighbors are good people and we work with a charity from Chicago who can help you get back on your feet. You won't be entirely alone."

"I will be though, won't I?" she sniffs.

"Do you have family somewhere?"

"No."

"Friends?"

She shakes her head. "No."

"How did you end up at the auction?"

"I met this guy who offered me some work in a club. Next thing I knew I was in some house with a whole load of other girls and . . ." She swallows. "So how do I just go back to normal life after everything that just happened? After I killed three guys."

"There's not a single person with any kind of moral compass who would judge you for what you did, Leah. And as for what you do next, that's really up to you. Get some therapy. Go to the cops if that will make you feel better. I know it won't be easy, but those sick fucks have taken enough, haven't they? Are you going to let them beat you, or are you going to live the best fucking life you can?"

I give a lot of them this same speech, and I mean every word of it, even if I'm always aware of the irony. Am I living the best life I can? Not even close, but I am doing what I can to pay for my sins, and maybe that's the best life there can ever be for a man like me.

"Who are you?" she asks again. "How will I ever be able to pay you back if I don't know who you are."

"You want to pay me back? Promise me you'll do everything you can to have a good life. Get some help and make some friends and go live, Leah. That's all I want from you."

She picks at the edge of her T-shirt. "I'll try, Mr. Nobody."

CHAPTER 19
IMOGEN

Pierre sits beside me on the wrought iron bench we uncovered together earlier this morning. I pull off my headphones and let them dangle around my neck. They're the ones he kindly loaned me after lunch when he complained that my choice of music was *an abomination*.

He rests his hands on his thighs and lets out a contented sigh, his face tilted up toward the sun. "I see now why this bench is here. It faces south and gets the best of the sun's rays for the day."

"It's beautiful," I agree.

"Were you listening to your awful music, mademoiselle?"

"Actually, I thought I'd give the Boss a try. I was listening to 'Thunder Road.'"

His entire face fills with delight. "Ah, a classic. And what, pray, did you think of it?"

"I like it. Some of the lyrics are beautiful—poetic. It's pretty sad though."

"Sad?" he scoffs. "How so?"

"When he sings about the ghosts of all the lovers she's lost and how they're gone when she gets to her porch. It's a song about regret and missed opportunities."

He searches for my hand, giving it a gentle squeeze when

he finds it, his touch gentle and reassuring. It makes me feel strange—good strange. Like I've known him a lot longer than a month. "Or per'aps, mademoiselle, it is a song of hope and new opportunity?"

Maybe. Did I focus on Mary's past rather than the future she could have if she just took the guy's hand and climbed into his car? "Then I'll listen to it again."

He gives my hand another gentle squeeze. "That is the beauty of songs, they mean different things to each of us. But it is per'aps fate that you chose that particular song of his to listen to, as it happens to be my favorite one."

"Really? That sounds like fate."

He nods. "And you, mademoiselle. What is your favorite song?"

"I don't have one yet. But I did enjoy 'Style' by Taylor Swift."

He snorts. "Then let us not discuss music any further. Tell me something else you like. What is your favorite color?"

"Purple," I reply without hesitation.

Pierre huffs a gentle laugh. "That was an emphatic response."

I shrug. "It's always been my favorite color. It's just so vibrant and unapologetic. There should me more purple in the world. What's your favorite col—" I wince at my insensitivity.

He must sense my embarrassment. "It is okay, mademoiselle. I was not always blind, and I remember colors."

"I'm sorry, Pierre. Sometimes I forget that you cannot see."

He smiles warmly. "And that is exactly how I like it, *mon chou*."

I smile, adoring his pet name for me. But it makes me feel both happy and sad that I was too young to recall my parents having any such names for me. I'm sure they would have though, and I'm certain my father would have been wise and kind like Pierre.

"Green," he says, reminding me of the question I almost asked.

"Green is a beautiful color. There are so many shades of green in this garden, Pierre. Deep rich emeralds, vibrant sage, and pale fern."

He takes a deep inhale. "I know. I can smell them all."

I gasp my amazement. "You can smell color? Is that a thing?"

He laughs and gently pats my hand. "No, *mon chou*. But I can smell the wildflowers, the greenery, apples, mint, sage. All the scents of the earth."

"Oh." I feel my cheeks heat with embarrassment at my foolishness.

"I suppose in a way it is the same as smelling colors," he muses.

I regard him with curiosity. There is so much more I'd love to know about him, but my politeness and breeding stops me from prying as much as I'd like to. "Is it true that when you lose one sense the others are heightened?"

He considers my question before answering. "I do not know. But I suppose when one sense is no longer available, then we pay more attention to the others, and in that way, then yes, they would be heightened."

His kindness and patience embolden me to risk a more personal question. "How old were you when you lost your sight, Pierre?"

"Thirty-six, mademoiselle. Eighteen long years ago."

That makes him fifty-four. "What happened? Was it an accident?"

He bristles, subtly shifting his body away from me, and I already regret asking the question because it seems to have upset him. Understandably so, I suppose. "*Non*. Definitely not an accident, *mon chou*. It was a very deliberate event."

I risk touching him, resting my hand gently over his, the way he did with mine a moment ago, and I'm filled with gratitude when he doesn't pull away. "I'm sorry, Pierre."

He clears his throat and rolls back his shoulders. "All of us in this house know pain, *non*?"

We do. I'd like to understand more about his, and more about Lincoln's too. I want to know the stories behind his scars, and not just the visible ones on his face that he covers, but the ones he seems to carry deep inside him. Why he hides himself in this fortress, and where he goes when he leaves for days at a time.

"Now tell me more about your plans for the garden," Pierre insists, and I recognize it as an attempt to change the subject.

Before I do that, I feel the need to explain why I pry. "I'm sorry I ask so many questions, Pierre. But I . . ." I suck in a breath because I'm about to admit a vulnerability, and that goes against everything I've ever been taught. "I feel like I know so little about the world, and it seems so different from the one I grew up in. I was taught a lot of things most kids aren't, I suppose. I probably witnessed things others wouldn't have too. I was taught how to survive, but in a lot of ways, I feel . . . well, almost like a child."

"Oh, *mon chou*." The tenderness in his tone chases away any lingering doubt I had at allowing myself to be vulnerable with him. "You are smart and quick-witted, yet you possess the most wonderful naivete and sense of curiosity that, yes per'aps is a childlike wonder, but it is also a beautiful part of you." He pats my hand again. "Do not ever lose that."

What a beautiful thing to say. My eyes fill with tears. Curious? I suppose I always have been, but that I am allowed to be so openly here is a revelation. "I was never permitted to ask too many questions growing up. My grandfather was very much of the opinion that children should be seen and not heard."

He tuts. "You make ask all the questions you wish, mademoiselle. But that does not always mean you will be granted an answer. Now, tell me about your plans for the garden."

I have so many I don't know where to start. I've never been a gardener, but I do have a keen interest and good knowledge of flowers and plants. And something about being here amongst the overgrown rosebushes and tangled vines strangling the wildflowers, holding their delicately colored petals captive, makes me want to strip back the layers of neglect and reveal the beauty beneath. Not so much that it would lose its wild charm, but enough that we could walk along the small stone paths without brambles and thorns scratching my calves. "I thought maybe the wild roses could be trimmed back first. They're so overgrown with thorns it's difficult to see their delicate blooms."

He nods. "A fine place to start, mademoiselle. I am sure there are some pruning shears out here somewhere."

"Yes, there are." I found some this morning hidden inside a small stone bunker. "They're a little rusty but I'm sure with a little oil and sharpening they'll work just fine."

Pierre stands and offers me the crook of his elbow, like an old-fashioned gentleman in the movies I've been watching. "Come show me the changes you wish to make."

I link my arm through his, a huge smile on my face as we walk through the garden together and I chatter excitedly about the subtle changes I'd like to make. And he listens intently while I describe the purple fireweed and lupines, the vibrant pink of the bitterroot and the bright yellow coneflowers, nestled amongst the Indian basket grass.

"How do you know the names of all these wildflowers, *mon chou*?"

"I had a book about wildflowers when I was growing up. I'm sure I could identify every one that grows in North America." I smile, recalling the worn brown edges of that book. I read it from cover to cover at least one hundred times. I would use it to identify the blooms when I'd go exploring on my grandfather's estate. There weren't nearly as many as there are here though. The groundskeepers used to cut back all the flowers as soon as they bloomed, something that always made me inexplicably sad.

He pats my hand. "As I said, very smart. Now, I am detecting a chill in the air, which tells me it's time for me to start preparing dinner."

"Do you need me to help?"

"*Non, mon chou*. You stay here and continue making plans for your garden."

He goes back into the house and I do just as he suggested, my head filled with ideas and my entire body buzzing with excitement. My very own secret garden.

CHAPTER 20
IMOGEN

Despite savoring every single word of it, I still managed to read through *The Secret Garden* in less than a day, and now the book sits in pride of place on the antique walnut dresser in my room. Always there whenever I need to escape into its pages.

Now I find myself in the library searching for a new read, once again entertaining the notion of the epic romance novel that might allow me to live vicariously through its pages. At this point, I'm willing to do anything to stop the highly improper and ridiculous thoughts I keep having about Lincoln. He left the day after he gave me the book—slipped out in the middle of the night without so much as a goodbye. From Pierre's grumblings I assume his leaving was a surprise to him too.

I scan the rows upon rows of shelves, examining the titles and not knowing which ones might be the kind of story I'm looking for. Until I spot one that has a title that must be about romance—*Lady Chatterley's Lover*. Larissa had a copy of this book. I saw her reading it once, and when I, being a curious child at that age, inquired about it, she scolded me. Then she told me it was a book for adults, full of sin and wickedness, and that if I ever looked between its pages, I would go to hell. I think I was about seven years old at the time, and I never questioned her logic, nor why she was reading it if it led directly to hell, but it's a memory I'd forgotten until now.

I slip the book from its snug spot on the shelf and head to my armchair. Tenderly, I open the first page, my fingers trembling slightly as I dislodge the scent of old paper and ink. I glance around nervously, ensuring I'm alone before I continue reading. The harsh memory of Larissa's words makes me feel like I'm doing something wrong, even though I'm most definitely an adult now. And if it did indeed lead directly to hell, then Larissa would be there.

The text is small and the language unusual, but I soon find myself lost in the pages, rooting for Constance to find her chance at true happiness and escape her loneliness. Quickly, the pages become shorter, or my reading grows much faster. From the first kiss on Connie's cheek every page becomes more thrilling and exciting, until . . .

My eyes linger on the words. A flush heats my cheeks. Not because of the content, or the detail, but because of the tenderness—the quiet reverence with which Oliver touches Connie. Yet the passion between them is so fierce that it ignites the pages. A far cry from the *preparation* I had for the act of sex. The vulgar, crude videos that were only ever about female submission and male pleasure. Base animalistic acts devoid of desire and connection, nothing like the depiction in the book. I wonder which of them is the true reflection of what happens between a man and woman? My rational mind tells me it can be both—perhaps even the most vulgar of acts can be tender with the right person.

I close the book and clutch it to my chest, too breathless with want and too unsure of what to do with all these feelings flooding my body to read any more. Closing my eyes, I tuck my feet beneath me and lean back into the chair, the scent of leather reminding me of Lincoln, and suddenly my thoughts are no longer of characters from a book, but of him. I long to be touched the way Connie is. I want to feel his lips on my cheek and his powerful hands gently caressing my skin, stroking me between my thighs, in that place that has started to ache only for him. And the though the thoughts are sinful and might send me straight to hell, maybe that's not the worst that could happen. Not if I get to be loved the way Oliver loves Connie. And if I got to be loved that way by Lincoln . . .

My heart is beating so wildly it might just pound straight out of my chest and fly away. But, *if* that were to happen . . . If Lincoln were to touch me the way I'd like him to, well then I think I'd walk straight into hell of my own free will.

CHAPTER 21
IMOGEN

According to the colossal grandfather clock in the hallway, it's a little after eight, and traditionally the time when Pierre retreats to his own room on the ground floor of the house. I'm curious to see inside, but too respectful of his privacy to ever venture in.

However, I'm feeling . . . not exactly lonely, but like I want some company. It's an unfamiliar feeling when I've always been so used to being on my own, and more than content with the company of books. And as well as that, I've been dreaming of a drink that some characters had in a TV show I watched last night.

I pause outside Pierre's room. A faint amber light peeks out beneath the door and the muffled sound of the TV carries through the solid oak door.

I take a deep breath, steeling myself for his potential rejection, and knock.

The TV is silenced and the sound of Pierre's footsteps signals his approach. A few seconds later, he opens the door, wearing the most adorable silk pajamas with a peacock pattern. For some reason they endear me to him even more. "Are you okay, mademoiselle?"

I swallow down my nerves, masking them with practiced ease. "I wondered if you'd like some hot chocolate? I believe I saw some in the pantry."

He frowns. "You want me to make you some hot chocolate?"

"No. I can make the chocolate. What I wondered is would you like to join me for some?"

"Hot chocolate?" he says, seemingly mystified.

"I've heard it's nice, and I've never tried it. I didn't want to make some just for myself, so . . ." I leave the rest of the question unspoken. "I could make it and bring it to you?"

He clears his throat and there's a few awkward seconds that sow the first seeds of regret at interrupting him. But then he offers me a faint smile. "I would be delighted to try some of your chocolate, mademoiselle. The instructions on how to make it are on the tin, I believe."

I smile, relieved and full of joy that he's agreed to my suggestion. With a little luck, he'll let me drink it in his sitting room with him, but even if he doesn't, it will be nice to do something nice for him, given how well he takes care of me, even if it is a small thing.

AS PIERRE SAID THERE WOULD BE, THERE WERE instructions on how to prepare the chocolate on the tin. I followed them to the letter and then added a sprinkling of tiny marshmallows that I found high up on a shelf, just like I saw them do in the TV show. And fifteen minutes later, I return to Pierre's sitting room carrying two mugs of steaming delicious-smelling hot chocolate. He's left the door ajar and I poke my head inside the room, but Pierre has already heard my approach and he beckons me inside, pausing the TV.

I pass him the mug and he lifts it to his nose and inhales

deeply. "Smells delicious, *mon chou*. How did you know that this was my guilty pleasure?"

"I didn't," I giggle. "But I'm very glad that it is."

He pats the seat beside him on the sofa. "You may sit and drink it in here, so long as you are quiet and don't interrupt my movie."

"Deal!" I agree without hesitation.

He switches the TV on and we both settle back against the sofa. A giant green monster of a man appears on the screen, grunting and slamming his fist.

"Why is he so angry?" I whisper.

Pierre sighs. "Because he is the Incredible Hulk. He is always angry."

"The Hulk? Is he an alien?"

"No. He's a man who was exposed to gamma radiation."

I stare at the screen and now a beautiful red-haired woman in a skintight leather suit is on the screen with the Hulk character. "Wow! Who is she?"

Pierre pauses the TV again. "Did we not just agree on your silence, *mon chou*?"

"Sorry. It would just be easier for me to follow if I knew who main the characters were."

"There are many main characters. They are the Avengers."

"The Avengers?"

He sighs and pinches the bridge of his nose. "You have never heard of the Avengers, I assume?"

"No, but they sound cool. Are they like vigilantes?"

"No, they are superheroes. Captain America. Thor—"

"Thor is the god of thunder," I tell him proudly.

He mutters a French curse under his breath and then he puts his chocolate on the table and turns off the movie. My heart sinks. He did ask me to let him watch his movie in silence, and I did agree.

Before I can apologize, Pierre speaks. "I can see I am going to have to give you an education, *mon chou*. One cannot have their first introduction to the Marvel universe midway through *The Avengers*." He holds a button on the TV remote and for some reason I can't fathom, he speaks into it. "*Iron Man*."

I stare at him, transfixed and confused, feeling like I've stepped into an alternate universe. And I'm even more stupefied when a few seconds later, a movie called *Iron Man* appears on the screen.

"How did you do that?"

"It's called voice recognition software, mademoiselle."

"It's incredible. You spoke into the remote and the TV heard you."

He laughs softly. "It's very common technology, mademoiselle." He picks up his chocolate and settles back against the sofa again. "Any introduction to the Marvel universe has to start with *Iron Man*," he declares with confidence.

I'm still perplexed, but I wrap my hands around my mug and settle in to watch the movie.

Two hours later when the credits roll, I am obsessed with Tony Stark and Pepper Potts and I'm eager to watch the second Iron Man. Then I'm reliably informed by Pierre that I need to watch *Captain America* after that, followed by *Thor*.

"When can I get to the movie with the kickass sexy woman in the leather suit?"

"Ah, Natasha Romanoff," he says with a knowing smile. "Black Widow."

"Like the spider! When does she get a movie?"

"Patience, mademoiselle. *Iron Man 2* is next. We can watch it tomorrow after dinner if you would like."

I'm filled with so much affection for him that I almost throw my arms around his shoulders and hug him fiercely, but as always my years of conditioning and the realization that I've shown too much emotion already stops me. Instead, I offer Pierre a polite yet heartfelt thank-you.

"It has been my pleasure, mademoiselle."

Mine too. "I appreciate you letting me into your personal space, Pierre. I know you enjoy your time alone."

He smiles. "I do, mademoiselle. And while this cannot be an everyday occurrence, it would be nice to watch a movie with you from time to time."

"I would love that, Pierre."

I know he usually watches TV until the early hours of the morning and I don't want to encroach on any more of his time, so I wish him good-night. And then I head to bed and wonder what this warm fuzzy feeling is I'm experiencing. It's completely different from how I feel whenever I spend time with Lincoln. Being with him is thrilling, and it usually leaves me breathless—filled with excitement and adrenaline. While time with Pierre leaves me peaceful and content. I think for the very first time in my life . . . maybe I've found myself a true friend.

CHAPTER 22
LINCOLN

After I leave Leah at the safe house, I find a hotel, shower and sleep for twelve hours. I decide to drive back from Kentucky the next day, and the closer I get to home, the more anxious I get to see Imogen.

Pierre's name flashes on the screen in my car and that simmering anxiety tangles itself into a knot in my chest. He rarely contacts me when I'm away and instinctively I know something must be wrong. I answer his call and immediately his voice fills the car.

"Imogen has hurt herself, sir."

That knot of anxiety splinters out, wrapping itself around my heart.

"Hurt herself how?"

"She broke a glass and one of the shards must have cut her. But she's bleeding profusely. I believe the wound needs stitches. I would try, but I'm not as steady handed as I once was."

"It's okay, Pierre," I assure him. It's not his lack of sight which makes him so ill-equipped for the job. He's stitched me up many times since being blinded, but that was before his hands were destroyed by arthritis.

Panic grips me. He has no way of knowing how badly

injured she is. Perhaps she's downplaying it. Hoping to lose so much blood that I have no option but to take her to hospital—it's a risky strategy for her to employ, but one I would no doubt try myself if I suspected it might work. It won't. I have a skilled surgeon I could call upon if necessary. I contemplate calling him anyway, just in case he's needed, but decide against it. Money buys a lot of silence, but I'd prefer as few people as possible to know of her existence. "I'm already on my way back. I'll be there within the hour. Keep pressure on the wound and try to minimize the bleeding as much as you can."

"Of course, sir."

I RUN THROUGH THE HOUSE SO FAST THAT MY shoes slip on the polished tile floors. When I reach my study, I falter. Seeing her sitting on the chair, her hand wrapped in a blood-soaked washcloth, looking so pale and vulnerable . . . I am almost knocked off my feet by the wave of guilt I feel.

She's staring at me, mouth gaping in shock, and that's when I realize that I'm not wearing my mask. This is the first time she's ever seen my face. I push down the rush of emotions that floods my chest, ignore the voice inside my head that tells me how repulsed she must be to have to look at my scars, and I drop to my knees in front of her.

"I have everything you need, already prepared, sir," Pierre says.

She holds out her injured hand, her gaze finally dropping from my face. "I'm sorry, I didn't mean to be so clumsy, I just . . ."

"It's okay. I'm here. We'll get you fixed up. Okay?" I keep my voice calm and reassuring while internally I'm building myself up to confront how bad a state her hand may be in when I unwrap this cloth. She told Pierre it was just a cut, but she's tougher than most and has likely been conditioned to downplay her pain all her life.

I unwrap the washcloth slowly, and it's a relief when I see only one finger has been cut. It's a deep gash though. Fresh blood is still oozing from the wound.

"This is going to need a couple of stitches. Okay?"

She nods, her eyes back on my face now. Wide and unblinking. Staring at my scars. I choke down the discomfort and focus on her. "I have nothing for the pain other than a little Scotch. Would you like Pierre to bring some?"

"No. I can take it. I've had stitches before. In my knee." She lifts her knee as though to show me, but I'm too focused on her bleeding finger. "I had no anesthesia then either."

I want to ask why that was, but I suspect I already know. Her grandfather and the Brotherhood kept her a secret. Taking her to a hospital would have alerted the outside world to the fact she was still alive. And now here she is, bleeding all over my study floor and I find myself spiraling into a panic. I can disembowel a man without breaking a sweat, but seeing her bleeding and injured is terrifying.

I grab some alcohol from the tray Pierre has laid out on my desk and carefully take hold of the tip of her injured finger. "This will sting," I warn her.

"I know." She swallows and then visibly braces herself for what's to come. Although she winces when I pour the alcohol over the wound, she doesn't pull away or flinch. I push away any thoughts of why she might be so accustomed to pain and focus on patching her up, working as gently as possible when I pierce her delicate skin with the needle.

It takes five stitches to close the wound and at least they're neat enough that the scar won't be overly visible. She keeps her eyes on the floor the entire time, refusing to look at my face. A choice I can hardly blame her for, given that I can barely stand to look at it myself.

I cut the thread and place the instruments on the tray for Pierre, who quickly takes them from the room, leaving Imogen and me alone.

She remains seated on the chair, looking so small and vulnerable that I want to wrap her in my arms and promise her the world.

"I think I'll take a little of that Scotch now," she says, still refusing to look at me.

I grab the bottle along with two heavy tumblers, pouring each of us a measure. She takes hers from me, the fingertips of her good hand brushing over mine and sending shock waves along my hand and forearm. She sniffs the liquor first, then wrinkles her nose in disgust.

I wonder if she's ever tasted Scotch before. It wouldn't surprise me that her puritan grandfather never allowed liquor in the house. Before I can ask her, she downs the entire contents of her glass in one gulp. She screws her eyes closed and sticks out her tongue, making a gagging noise. "Oh, dear god that's disgusting." She rubs her throat. "And why is it burning?"

I feel my lips curving in a smirk. "Have you ever drank Scotch before?"

She shakes her head, eyes streaming.

"Any kind of whisky?"

"No. No hard liquor ever."

"Never?"

"I wasn't allowed alcohol. I did have one glass of champagne the day I turned twenty-one, but I didn't really care for it."

Her upbringing intrigues me greatly, but I'm hesitant to pry for fear of what I might accidentally reveal, or what memories I might make her relive. From what I've gleaned so far, her upbringing was very strict and regimented. Her father's was too as I recall. It was one of the reasons he was so eager to join the Brotherhood. Still, I'm too intrigued not to ask. "What other things have you never tried, Imogen?"

The question was intended entirely innocently, but from the way she looks up at me through her darkened lashes, I'm not sure it landed that way. And now I have no doubt we are both thinking about the one very obvious thing she's never done.

I put an end to that avenue of conversation by adding, "Did you go to regular school?" The answer is one I can already guess, and she confirms my suspicion by shaking her head.

"Never had friends. Went to parties. Or the mall. Or . . ." her slender throat works as she swallows. "Anything really. You could say I was very . . ." she considers her next word very carefully " . . . protected."

I would say she was hidden away and kept as a prisoner, and I'm also aware of the irony that I feel any anger about that fact, given that I'm currently doing the same. While I might tell myself it's for her protection too, I wonder if she would believe me so readily. I'm desperate to know more, but I'm cautious about unpicking the layers of her psyche when she doesn't yet trust me.

Instead I brush my fingertips over the bandage on her hand. "How is this feeling now?"

"It's okay." Her eyes linger on my face. On my scars.

Instinctively I hide them, dropping my head and staring at the droplets of her blood on the parquet floor. I usually reserve the privilege of seeing my scars for the people I'm about to kill. What if she heard the urban legends of the monster who betrayed the Brotherhood, and the scars he bears for his sins? And what if that's enough for her to recognize who I really am? Or what if she doesn't know any of that, but she's repulsed by me anyway?

She jumps up from the chair. "Lincoln." Her voice is soft and warm, like molasses in the summertime. "I'm sorry if I made you feel uncomfortable." I refuse to look at her, so she takes a step closer. "I've just never seen your face before."

"I'll ensure it doesn't happen again," I snarl, allowing some of my anger to bleed out into my tone.

"What? No!" Her cry is pained. "Why would you do that?"

THE AUCTION

I lift my head and let her see the face she's so desperate to stare at. My hands ball into fists, trying to keep any more of the guilt and shame inside me from spilling out. "Why wouldn't I, Imogen?"

Tears fill her bright green eyes. "Because I like seeing your face. It makes you look more . . . human." She whispers the last word.

Is she fucking with me? "Some would say it makes me look more monster than human."

"No." She shakes her head vehemently. "So, you have some scars. We all do. Some of them are just on the inside and easier to hide. I'm sure they all make us feel like monsters sometimes." The pain in her voice is so acute I can almost feel it. Her sadness and despair wash over me. This is the most she's ever willingly revealed of herself. What scars does my little angel hide inside?

"Except that I am actually a monster."

She takes a half step toward me. Now we're so close I can smell the sweet scent of her skin. Feel warmth radiating from her body, like the heat from an open flame. I suppress a growl, filled with need and desire. It's wrong to want her the way I do. Sinful to think about taking her innocence and defiling her body. She doesn't know who I really am, and if she did . . .

"You're not a monster to me, Lincoln."

Tentatively, she reaches up and brushes the fingertips of her good hand over my scars. I flinch at her touch, an electric current passing through my entire body.

She bites on her lip and pulls her hand back like she's been burned, but not far enough from me that I don't still feel the lingering warmth of her touch. "I'm sorry, I should have asked your permission."

I remain rooted in place, hypnotized by her bright green eyes, until once again her fingertips skate delicately over my scarred flesh. Tracing the thick twisted knots and ugly reddened welts as if they're the key to discovering something in me. Nobody has touched my scars since the surgeon who patched me up and this feels like it's too much, but not enough. Her touch is a balm to my tortured soul and I never ever want her to stop.

She inches closer. "I think your scars are perfect," she says, no hint of revulsion or sarcasm.

My throat constricts. "Perfect how?"

"Perfect because they're a part of who you are. And despite what people say, and what you might believe, you are not a monster, Lincoln Knight. Trust me, I would know."

I hate that she knows men who are worse than I am, but that doesn't make me any better. "Don't be fooled by my name, Imogen. There is nothing honorable about me." And there is definitely nothing honorable about the way my dick is growing harder with each second she has her hands on me. Nor any of the filthy things I'm thinking about doing to her right now. I could show her how much pleasure even a monster like me could make her feel, and how much pleasure can be found in sin. But nothing about her pleasure should ever be sinful; it should be glorious and without shame. And that is why it can't ever be with me.

"I never said you were honorable. Although . . ." She chews on her luscious lower lip, until jealous need spikes inside me. I want to nibble on her lip—on all the parts of her. "You have acted very honorably since my arrival, sir. Nothing but a single touch of your thumb on my skin before you stitched my wound today."

Does she think about that night in the library too, when I was a whisper away from losing control?

"Aside from that, not a single slip in all this time." Her pupils grow darker, as I'm sure mine do too.

It would be futile to deny my attraction to her when it's so evident. She only has to glance down to see the hard evidence of my desire for her. Painfully hard. "It would be wrong," is all I can manage.

THE AUCTION

The spot between her brows pinches into an adorable frown. "Why?"

This has to stop. She has to stop pushing me, believing me to be someone I'm not—a man she should be flirting with. I opt for cruelty in the hopes it will make her run from me, which would be the wise choice. "Because I own you, Imogen."

She doesn't run. Instead she tips her jaw, darting out her tongue to wet the lips I'm so desperate to kiss. "So take me."

Fuck it all to hell. The very last shreds of any kind of morals or restraint crumble to dust.

CHAPTER 23
IMOGEN

Lincoln's eyes blaze with so much heat that my skin burns under his gaze. What have I done? Have I pushed him too far? Am I actually prepared for any of what might happen now?

His lips crash against mine, brutal and tender at the same time. He licks the seam of my lips and I part them willingly, allowing his warm velvety tongue to slip into my mouth. He flicks it against mine, causing a desperate moan to roll out of my throat. Unable to do anything but feel, I melt into his hard body. And there are so many feelings, all of them new and exciting—explosive and overwhelming. I revel in them all. And I want more.

Lincoln's powerful arms snake around my waist, crushing me against him, and now I'm entirely lost to the sensations flooding my body. Without intending to, I find my good hand threading through his dark hair. It's as silky and thick as I've imagined it would be. His tongue continues exploring my mouth and I can only respond on instinct, hoping that what I'm doing is right. It certainly feels right, so very right. And from the sensation of his rock-hard length digging into my stomach, I assume he's enjoying this too.

My head is spinning. My panties are damp and sticky. His

fingers brush against my stomach and my lower abdomen feels like it's being pulled into itself, causing a delicious burning ache. His kisses linger, my lips feeling tender and bruised but in the most delectable way possible. I could spend hours doing nothing but being kissed by him.

Much too soon, he pulls back, and we both pant for breath.

"Fuck!" he grunts.

What does that mean and why does he sound so annoyed? Whatever the reason, I don't want this to end. Instinctively, I grind my hips against his, seeking a little relief from the deep throbbing ache between my thighs, finding it in the thick ridge of his length straining against his pants. Pleasure skitters up my spine.

Lincoln groans, a sound so feral and full of longing that it makes my legs tremble. He stares at me, dark eyes still raging full of fire.

"Please, sir," I whisper.

His lips find mine once more and he kisses me again, less urgently this time, yet still possessive and dominating. I'm not sure anything in the world could ever feel better than this. Seeking that same sweet relief I found a few moments ago, I rock my hips against his.

A growl rumbles deep in his throat, and the sound sends shivers of ecstasy hurtling through me. He slides a hand down over my ass and then the outside of my thigh before slipping it beneath my dress. And now his warm rough hand is gliding over my skin. My heart rate spikes and my breath stutters in my throat.

I rub against him instinctively and his hand moves up my thigh.

I'm sure my heart rate just doubled.

Moaning softly, I flick my tongue against his as I grow more confident. His soft grunt tells me he likes it. He still has his hand beneath my dress, gently caressing my skin, but he's not yet touching me where I yearn to be touched. When my thighs part a little of their own volition, I realize my brain has fully checked out of this situation and is letting my needy lady parts run the show. Lincoln responds by herding me back a few steps until my ass bumps against his desk. I shuffle backward, perching on the edge of it while he slides his hand between my thighs, pushing aside my, now very damp, panties. And I tell myself that this is okay to want this, because giving him pleasure is exactly what I was trained for. And he's definitely enjoying this.

My body pulses with electric energy.

I cling to him, desperate for more of whatever he's offering, wondering how it's possible to feel this much desire and bliss, when he ups the ante, swirling the pad of his index finger over a particular spot that has euphoria spiking hot and fierce through my entire body.

"Oh!" I gasp, wrenching my lips from his as my full body trembles.

He keeps his other arm locked firmly around my waist, holding on to me, and smirks, before repeating the action. Then he runs his nose over my neck and growls. "Do you like that, angel?"

I nod, biting down on my lip so that I don't moan out loud and reveal myself to be too needy and desperate, because men don't like that. But is that my clitoris he's toying with?

"Have you ever made yourself come, Imogen?"

I shake my head. "I don't know how to, sir."

His eyes narrow on my face, trying to assess whether that's true.

"I never tried. They told me it was wrong."

He arches an eyebrow, swirling his fingers over my hypersensitive flesh. "Does this feel wrong?"

"God, no!" I moan aloud now, no longer able to stop myself.

And far from not liking it, me being vocal seems to please him. He gives a soft satisfied growl. "There are so many ways your body can feel pleasure, Imogen. Would you like me to show you?"

I nod, my cheek brushing the fabric of his T-shirt over the hard muscle of his chest. "Yes, sir."

He circles my entrance, and every single nerve ending in my body is screaming for him to relieve this deep bone-aching need he's stoked in me. Even though I have no idea how I could know what it is I need him to do, instinct tells me that if he pushes that finger inside of me, it will make everything better.

"Has anything or anyone ever been inside you, angel?"

He inches the tip in the slightest fraction of an inch and I tremble. "N-no. Nothing. Not even a tampon."

He closes his eyes and mutters a string of curses.

"Please, Lincoln," I beg, ashamed of myself for allowing my body to have this much control over my mind. Although not my entire body, just this single part of me where he has his hands. Nothing in this entire world feels more necessary than what he's about to do.

"Fuck, Imogen," he groans, pained. But I'm sure it's me who's suffering here. He's the one with all the power. He has all the control. It goes against everything I have been taught my whole life to let go this much, but I'm a trembling mess made up of nothing but desperate need and a desire so fierce that it's searing through my flesh.

I grasp his shirt in my fist, pressing my forehead to his chest and clinging to him like he's my only chance of survival. "Linc," I pant out only half his name in a plea.

He rests his lips on the top of my head and tightens his grip around my waist before he sinks his thick finger inside me.

I see stars. Every single particle of energy in my body rushes to the place between my thighs. Nothing exists outside of this room. There's nothing except for me and him. And nothing before in my entire life has ever felt so right.

There's a rush of slick arousal. A deep pulling sensation in my core. The feeling that I'm floating.

"You're doing so well for me." His free hand slides to the

back of my head, palming it possessively, while also grounding me back to reality as he works his finger deeper and grinds the heel of his palm against my clitoris.

I groan. Another rush of wetness.

"Such a tight little pussy," he groans against my skin.

Oh, god! Overwhelming need and the burning requisite for some kind of release of all this pent-up feeling thunders around my body. I have to let it out before I implode.

"Let go for me, angel." His deep growling voice washes over me, soothing and encouraging. He probes deeper. My head is whirling. Vision blurry. I can't hold on. I don't want to. White-hot euphoria detonates in my core. Starlight explodes in my vision. My body goes rigid, both fighting and clinging to this strange and wonderful feeling that's dominating my entire consciousness. I let out a garbled cry, something between a curse and a prayer.

What the hell was that?

Lincoln holds me tighter, his skilled fingers massaging my tender flesh. "That's my good girl," he growls, all dominance and possession and fire.

It takes minutes for my body to stop shaking, for me to uncurl my fingers and toes. I melt against him like a candle left too long in front of an open fire. My entire being hums with relief and contentment as I bask in the aftermath of what I assume must have been an orgasm. And if that's what they feel like, how does a person ever go back to a normal life knowing that that kind of pleasure exists in this world? Why did nobody ever prepare me for this? Not even Lady Chatterley and Oliver could explain just how life-changing a climax would be.

Lincoln's lips are pressed firmly against my forehead. "You did so good for me."

Something about his praise unravels me.

A tear runs down my cheek.

I was never prepared for this because this was never supposed to happen. This kind of experience isn't the norm for girls and women sold at auctions. More tears run down my face and I don't try to stop them. I can't recall the last time I cried so openly, but it feels good. Necessary.

"Imogen?" His voice is tinged with concern. He slides his finger out of me, and the loss feels so great that I sob out loud. He brushes my hair back from my face, and as he does, I notice his palm streaked with blood. It freaks me out less than I thought it would. *That*, I was prepared for. "Are you okay?"

I nod, lip caught between my teeth so that I don't sob again. When I can trust myself to speak, I whisper, "It was intense. I feel like I fell apart."

He dusts his lips over mine, wrapping both his arms around me. "I have never seen anything more beautiful than your undoing, angel."

Bending low, he rests his forehead against mine and our warm breath mingles in the space between us. There's a connection like I've never experienced before in my life. Like my soul has been anchored to his, and I might die if he lets me go. It's warm and safe and everything I have ever wanted.

And then he breaks it.

Without warning, he takes a half step back, creating a physical space between us, and his arms slip from around me. My legs wobble. He glances at his blood-streaked palm, and raw shame and guilt flash in his dark eyes. Surely he knew that would happen?

"You should go to bed, Imogen." His tone is cold now. Detached. He's an entirely different person than the man from a moment ago.

Is he upset about the blood? Or is he upset with me?

"Did I do something wrong?" I hear the tremor in my own voice, and under normal circumstances, I would despise such a weakness and do whatever I needed to correct it. But he has cracked me wide open, and now he's just going to leave me to put myself back together? Pretend like this didn't happen?

He pinches the spot between his brows and paces across to the other side of the library. "No," he grits out the word. "Just go." When I don't move, he yells, "Leave. Now."

And now I get it. It wasn't only me who lost control. He did too and he's hating himself for it. I don't understand any of this. By his own admission, Lincoln Knight is supposed to be a monster. He paid ten million dollars for me at some twisted auction, where my purity and obedience were the selling point. Yet he's consumed with guilt for touching me. Why?

Whatever it is, I should be grateful for his lack of interest in me because it provides me with an opportunity. It allows me to refocus on the only thing I should be focusing on—the one I keep forgetting about. My freedom. If he's not strong enough to get past his guilt, or shame, or whatever the hell it is that's holding him back, then it only helps me push forward.

I slide off his desk and walk out of his office, the dull throbbing between my thighs growing more intense with every step I take—a reminder of what I just gave him, and what he just threw away.

CHAPTER 24
LINCOLN

I am a monster. No, I'm a fucking animal. How the hell did I go from dressing her wound to . . . to finger-fucking her so hard that her blood ran down my fingers and into my palm. I glance at my hand now, see the dried blood, and feel an intense wave of guilt laced with animal desire. Unwelcome images of Leah, broken and bloodied, fill my head and I push them away.

This is entirely different. I would never intentionally hurt Imogen. And I would never take advantage of her. Although maybe I just did. Because what just happened was one hundred kinds of wrong.

I pace up and down my room, cursing my own stupidity and my complete lack of control. It doesn't matter that she wanted it. It doesn't matter how she moaned my fucking name, or that I made her come. It was immoral. She doesn't know who I really am. Doesn't know how fucked-up this truly is.

Where is she now? I wonder. I sent her to bed and she probably obeyed me, taught to do so by the animals who raised her. Animals just like me. Is she feeling any shame about what just happened? I hope not because she has no reason to. She's probably feeling confused though, after I used her like that and then sent her away.

One day she'll understand it was for her own good.

My mind is filled with her. Sparkling green eyes and full pink lips. The taste of her lips. Her soft moans. The way her body convulsed when she came for me. The rippling of her tight cunt around my fingers.

Christ! What if I hadn't sent her away though. What if I'd carried on? Peeled her soft cotton panties down her long slender legs and then spread her wide open for me. Tasted the sweet arousal from her pussy and then sunk myself inside her tight heat.

My cock is aching at the thought, desperate for some relief. I lie on the bed and unzip my pants, hurriedly freeing my length from the confines of my boxers and squeezing the base of my shaft hard. I groan at the sweet relief it brings. It's not sweet enough though. Not as sweet as her.

I squeeze harder, imagining sinking my cock deep inside her tight virgin cunt. Fantasizing about the soft needy little noises she'd make as I filled her up and claimed her for my own. I can almost feel the sting of her nails scratching my back as she'd cling to me, torn between pain and pleasure. And I'd bring her so much pleasure. Playing with her needy little clit while I fucked her. Making her come for me over and over. Tasting her skin. Sucking on the stiff peaks of her nipples. And then I'd let my mouth move farther down her body, eating her own cum out of her sweet cunt before I came inside her.

I stroke my shaft, coating it in the precum already weeping from the crown. I imagine how she'd taste, my tongue buried in her folds and her thighs wrapped around my head. Even the thought of her is all-consuming. I recall the feel of her tight center squeezing around my finger and the intoxicating scent of her cum. The cum still coating my fingers.

This is so fucking wrong, but I'm going to hell anyway. So I place my hand over my mouth and nose and inhale deeply, and I can almost taste her. The sweet smell of her juices, tinged with the coppery tang of her blood. My pure little angel. What

THE AUCTION

I'd give to fuck her. Defile her in all the filthy ways I'm dreaming of. Sink my cock into all her tight pretty holes. Watch as I stretch her wide open for me. Only ever for me.

I tug harder. Squeeze tighter. Jerk faster. Breathe deeper until she's all I can taste and smell and feel.

Pleasure ignites inside me, white-hot searing euphoria burning in my veins. I quicken my pace. Dart out my tongue to taste her on me. And I come with a blinding rush of adrenaline and euphoria, the kind of release that almost steals a soul from a man's body. Ribbons of white-hot cum streak over my hand and onto my T-shirt.

I pant for breath, eyes closed as images of her swirl around my head. Of her naked. On her knees. With my cock inside her. Pliant and submissive. The one woman I shouldn't have any such kind of thoughts for. The reason they say I'm a freak and a monster is because I fucking am one.

CHAPTER 25
LINCOLN

"You're leaving again? Already?" Pierre scolds me, having followed me down to the basement as soon he got out of bed.

I nod, sheathing my hunting knife and stuffing it into my bag. "You should have seen her, Pierre. I can't even imagine what those sick fucks did to her."

He frowns. "The girl you rescued?"

I've rescued hundreds of these girls and women over the years, so why am I still haunted by this last one? Is it because Leah saved my life, or because the carnage we survived created a connection between us—the kind I don't usually establish with the women I rescue—and because of that, she shared a small piece of herself with me. Or maybe I'm haunted by what I did last night to the woman upstairs in my guest room. A line I promised myself I would never cross. But I'm not going to admit that to Pierre. "Her name is Leah, and yes."

He folds his arms across his chest. "The same as they have done to them all, I imagine, *mon ami*. Why does this one have you so rattled? So desperate to leave again? Have you found out where another is being kept?"

"No." I swallow down my anger because he doesn't deserve it. "But I . . . Fuck!" I roar the word and he flinches. "I should have saved every last fucking one of them, Pierre. What about all the women that are still out there, suffering and in pain? I should have shut down that fucking auction instead of . . ."

"Instead of what, sir?"

My anger explodes out of me. "Instead of fucking participating in it."

He shakes his head. "And how exactly would you have done that? You are one man, Lincoln. Two with Edgar, but even together, and even with his contacts, you are not enough to take down a Brotherhood army. You would have only gotten yourself killed, and then what would have happened to Imogen? She would have been sold like cattle and there would be nobody to save her."

Imogen? Her name alone fills me with shame and desire, and the thought of what would have happened to her had I not intervened almost makes my legs buckle. If I hadn't bought her, she'd be somewhere out there now, broken and abused just like Leah. An indescribable rage burns through every fiber of my being.

Pierre rests his hands on either side of my face. "You cannot save them all, *mon ami*."

"But I should, Pierre."

He nods. "I know, and I also know you well enough to know that you do all you can. It is not enough, but it never will be. There can never be enough good done to undo all their wrongs. But that does not mean you stop trying, or that you stop fighting for the ones you can save, does it?"

I drop my head, knowing he's right, but unable to rectify that truth with how inadequate I feel.

"So stay here and continue with the search the best way you can."

I wrench my head from his gentle grip. "No. I have to go." We both have our demons, and he knows better than anyone how I like to exorcise mine.

"So once again, I'm left to babysit the child?" he grumbles.

"It's not enough that I'm your butler, now I'm a glorified baby-sitter too?"

He drops into the chair with a sigh, cursing in French under his breath.

"She's not a child," I snap before walking into my armory room to select some weapons for my trip.

Pierre hurries after me. "You have had sex with her, haven't you?" he scoffs in amusement. "That is why you are running away."

I hate that he knows me so well. "I didn't have sex with her," I growl through gritted teeth.

"Then what? Something happened? Because you only got home last night, and I don't need my sight to be able to see the tension between the two of you, Lincoln."

I ignore him and select a set of titanium knuckle-dusters from a rack.

"Lincoln!"

"Something happened, okay!" I snarl. "I touched her but we didn't have sex."

He frowns. "So?"

"So what? You fucking know, Pierre."

"*Vie de merde!*" He slaps his forehead and storms back out into the control room.

My stupidity makes me follow him. "What does that mean?"

"Fuck my life," he replies deadpan.

I growl. "I know what your French curses mean, Pierre. Why are you saying it?"

"Because you are exhausting, *mon ami*. You constantly beat yourself up over something you have no control over. And you refuse to allow yourself any kind of happiness because you are sure you do not deserve it. If you and the girl like each other, which is blatantly obvious to even a blind man!" He waves his hand in front of his eyes. "Then what is the problem?"

"She's—" I don't even finish the sentence. He knows who she is.

"You have not been a part of her life since she was a small child. She is a woman now, and not the little girl you once knew."

"I fucking *bought* her, Pierre."

"*Oui!*" He nods. "But you did so to save her from a life of pain and degradation. She is more free here than she's likely ever been in her life. And she is falling in love with you."

I grind my jaw. "If that's true, then she's falling in love with an illusion."

He shakes his head. "*Imbécile!*"

"I'm trying to do the right thing," I bark. How can he not fucking see that?

"By running away when things get too uncomfortable for you to handle? But it is okay, *non*? Because Pierre is here to pick up the pieces . . . to babysit . . . to buttle . . ." He sinks back in his chair again and drops his head into his hands.

I've been too blinded to my own misery to see how difficult it might have been for him to have her here, reminding him of all he lost. His daughter, Francesca, would be twenty-eight now. Not that much older than Imogen. He should have watched her graduate college, maybe be preparing to walk her down the aisle, or bouncing some grandbabies on his knee. Instead he's stuck here in this place with me, and now he's guiding Imogen through this whole fucked-up mess in the best way he knows how. While he has always been fully on board with my mission against the Brotherhood, he never agreed to do any of that other stuff.

I perch on the desk beside him and place a comforting hand on his shoulder. "You're not my butler, a babysitter, or my servant, Pierre. I have never asked you to be any of those things."

"How else would I keep myself from going crazy?" he mutters.

"You are my friend though, and I'm sorry if her being here brings up any bad memories for you."

He lifts his head and wipes a tear from his eyes. "The problem is she reminds me of too many good memories." He offers a faint smile. "She is a very smart and sweet girl. Resilient too."

"She is all that." *And so much fucking more.* "I'm sorry that I put this on you. I know you never signed up for this."

"I signed up for all of it. Whatever it takes, remember?" He holds up his gnarled hands. "I only wish I could be more use."

I stare at his hands. Once the instruments of an incredibly skilled surgeon. The Brotherhood took that from him when they crushed every bone in them after he saved someone they thought he shouldn't. Then they made him watch while they raped and murdered his wife and child before they took his eyes, ensuring it would be the last thing he ever saw. I found him shortly after and he swore a lifetime of service to my cause—revenge.

I only wish he could have seen what I did to the sick fucks who hurt his family. He heard though. He listened to their screams for days, begging me to prolong their agony for as long as they could stand. I was happy to oblige. "I would probably starve without your cooking. And besides, you have more than paid your debt to me, Pierre."

He sniffs. "Well, that is debatable. I will forever be in your debt. And I actually like the babysitting part. We've been working our way through the Marvel movies, and she is also becoming a Bruce Springsteen fan."

That makes me smile. I like that they both have each other for company. And watching their bond develop while painful in some ways, because it is richer and deeper than the one I have with her, is still beautiful to witness. I enjoy seeing the two people I care most about in the whole world finding comfort and happiness in each other. "I figured as much, old man. I've never seen you so happy."

THE AUCTION

He scoffs. "I wouldn't say happy exactly. But she gives me a reason to smile."

Yeah, me too. And I took advantage of her in the worst fucking way.

Sensing my emotion the way he so easily can, he sighs. "The guilt will kill you one day." He stands and places a comforting hand on my arm. "It is time to let it go."

He walks out of the room, leaving me to wallow. Although I can acknowledge the truth in his words, I can't let it go. Not any of it. Not until the Brotherhood are wiped from existence. And to do that I need to find their King.

It's a little after 6:00 a.m. when I'm ready to leave, and if she's awake, she's not out of bed yet. I step into the garden, and even out here, all I'm reminded of is her. Especially out here. The place she enjoys spending so much time and the place where she shines with happiness. The scent of wildflowers and jasmine will always remind me of her smile.

Carefully, I place the parcel on the table, tied with a purple ribbon and I imagine the delight and surprise on her face when she opens it. It's almost enough to make me stay.

Almost.

CHAPTER 26
IMOGEN

The house seems eerily quiet when I go downstairs. Every step I take intensifies the ache between my thighs, and every throb intensifies my guilt and shame. How low did I stoop to practically beg for his touch? And how much further would I let myself slide, given that I long for it again?

Pierre is alone in the kitchen when I enter. He greets me pleasantly, like always, but he seems a little annoyed. Does he know what took place last night and is he angry with me about it, just like Lincoln seemed to be. More shame and guilt washes over me.

"What is it to be, mademoiselle?"

"I'm not feeling very hungry actually, Pierre."

"You must eat something, *mon chou*. How about a little toast?" His concerned tone suggests he's not angry with me at all.

"Yes, a little toast would be nice. Thank you. Where is Mr. Knight?"

"Ach!" He takes the bread from its ceramic home. "He left early this morning."

And now I have a generous helping of sadness to accompany my guilt. Nice! Lincoln has obviously gone because of me and that fact is inescapable.

THE AUCTION

"I believe he has left you something on the table in the garden, *mon chou*."

I peer through the window and sure enough there is a small brown paper parcel, tied with a bright purple ribbon. Another gift? And now I'm flooded with elation and hopefulness. It's all making me feel dizzy.

"Well, go and see what it is," Pierre gently scolds me, making a tutting sound.

I rush out of the kitchen and into the garden to fetch my parcel, barely able to contain my curiosity. It's a small parcel, no bigger than a book, but a different shape. Tentatively, I trace my fingertips over the soft purple ribbon, before gliding over the smooth brown paper. It's all packaged so neatly. Did he wrap this himself, or have someone do it for him? I want it to be the former, and I imagine his large powerful hands carefully folding the fragile paper, and then tying the delicate ribbon, his brow furrowed in concentration. The image I conjure of him in my mind's eye makes heat bloom in my core.

Gently, I tug open the purple bow, and then slowly unfurl the paper. I used to get one gift every single Christmas from Larissa, and I would open it like this, savoring the anticipation. I cannot even imagine what might lie beneath this paper, and I haven't held the package and tried to guess, for fear that I might guess correctly and ruin the surprise.

As I peel back the paper, the bright purple fabric is revealed inch by inch. Unable to contain my excitement any longer, I pull the wrapping all the way off, and an unexpected sob catches in my throat. I pick up the purple gardening gloves and hold them to my cheek. They're made of thick purple suede with palms crafted from some kind of flexible rubber—thick and sturdy enough to prevent thorns from piercing through the fabric. And also there in the package, the blades glinting in the sunlight, are a shiny new pair of pruning shears.

Pierre must have told Lincoln about my plans for the garden, and my love of purple. And he must have got these for me during his last trip. Tears, unbidden and unwelcome, well in my eyes. He might explain the book away as a coincidence, even if the inscription was not, but this . . . this was thoughtful and deliberate. It makes my heart ache with happiness and sadness at the same time. If he can do this, if he can be this sweet and kind, how can he be so cold and detached too? How can he push me away when I show him the most vulnerable parts of myself?

"Do you like your gift, *mon chou*?" Pierre snaps me from my thoughts of Lincoln.

"I love it, Pierre."

"It is for the garden, *non*?"

"Yes. Some gloves and pruning shears."

He smiles. "Then you will be able to get to work on your grand plan."

"You told him?"

"*Oui, mon chou*. He likes to know how you are settling in and how you pass the time while he is away."

Another thing that makes sense, but also doesn't. For some unfathomable reason, Lincoln seems to care for me, or at least about my well-being. The way he tended to my wound last night was proof enough of that. Absentmindedly, I brush the pad of my thumb over the plaster on my pointer finger. Yet he ran away the moment there was any kind of actual connection between us.

"Your toast is ready, mademoiselle. Come eat if you are to be toiling in this garden all day."

I follow Pierre back into the house, with my new gifts clutched to my chest. A reminder of the enigma that is Lincoln Knight.

CHAPTER 27
IMOGEN

I wake in a cold sweat, my limbs twisted in the sheets, my heart pounding and a persistent, throbbing ache between my thighs. In my dream, Lincoln was here. He came home and snuck into my room in the night. Whispered in my ear how much he missed me, and how he couldn't stay away—even now the mere memory of the deep timbre of his voice sends a shiver down my spine. Then he pulled the bedclothes off, slowly inching them over my body until I was fully revealed to him. I still feel the weight of him easing himself onto the bed as he crawled over me, his mask in place and wearing black camo gear, growling his intent to do all manner of wicked things to me.

Then his mask had disappeared, and he was trailing his sinfully delicious mouth over my hardened nipples while he peeled off my panties.

"Do you want me inside you?" His voice deep and gruff still resounds in my head.

And then I woke up, hot and needy and aching. I roll onto my back and suck in deep breaths, but nothing seems to calm my racing pulse. The deep pulling in my abdomen grows stronger and all I can see is Lincoln's strong hands delving between my thighs. I can almost feel his finger pushing inside me.

I screw my eyes closed but the images intensify. The ache grows stronger and more insistent.

It's wrong to touch myself. Wrong to bring myself pleasure.

I take a deep calming breath.

It doesn't work. Nothing works. There's no room in my head for anything but this bone-deep longing for release. I slip my hand inside my panties. Perhaps if I touch myself, just briefly, I can stop the infernal throbbing.

I swipe the pad of my index finger over the swollen bud of flesh and realize I was wrong, even the slightest contact sends pleasure rocketing through my entire being. My skin grows hot with shame when I find my flesh already slick with my arousal, but it feels too good to stop.

I recall Lincoln's fingers on me, and try to mimic what he did. My movements aren't as refined as his are, but I move on instinct—increasing the pressure and speed and ramping up the euphoria. I venture closer to my entrance and consider sliding a finger inside myself. My body screams at me to do it, but that would feel like stepping over a line that I shouldn't cross. And what if Lincoln were to somehow know I'd done that? I'm still his property and I'm not sure if *this* is even allowed.

I go back to toying with my clit, which is more than enough pleasure for me to handle. The euphoric sensation builds quickly, cresting and falling as I bring myself close to the edge of something. I wonder if I can even do this myself. It feels good, satisfying, but not as intense as what Lincoln did.

I close my eyes again and recall my dream, and it mingles with my memory of our night in the library. I imagine it's his hands on me. I can hear the filthy words he growls in my ear. Feel the scratch of his beard on my skin.

I get closer as my fingers work faster, slipping and sliding over my soaking flesh.

So close . . .

Blinding white euphoria washes over me. A moan is ripped

from my chest and I slap my hand over my mouth to drown out the sound. My head swims with warm fuzzy feelings and my limbs tingle with pleasure.

I gasp for breath as I slide my slick fingers out of my panties.

I know I should feel ashamed, but mostly I just feel satisfied . . . and a little proud. I just did that. I just made my body do this incredible thing, all on my own. I brought myself intense physical pleasure with just two fingers. Wow!

And I could do it again if I wanted to. Every single day for the rest of my life. For now, I'm sated enough.

I yawn, my eyelids already fluttering closed again before I fall into a dreamless sleep.

CHAPTER 28
LINCOLN

Blood drips down my chin and I scrub it away with the back of my gloved hand, acknowledging the mess of man at my feet, who is no longer recognizable as human. I'm getting sloppy. Too caught up in my own guilt and anger to think clearly.

I left the house a week ago, and I've spent all that time chasing down Pawns. Plentiful and easy to find, but with no information of any value. Ten years of torturing hundreds of the fuckers for days taught me that. That still hasn't stopped me from destroying the piece of shit currently lying in a pool of his own bodily fluids though, or the five others that have come before him this week. It gets me nowhere in respect of my mission to take down the Brotherhood, but it does make me forget about her, at least for a while.

The only time I'm not torturing myself thinking about Imogen is when I'm torturing someone else. I can't escape her. She's consuming me and there's not a single thing I can do to stop it. I'm a smart man, a man of logic and reason, until it comes to her, when I lose all sense of rational thought. Not to mention all sense of what's right and wrong. Because what I did to her, and what I still want to do, is all kinds of fucking fucked-up.

And that I'm twice her age and I bought her at a fucking auction aren't even the worst of it.

But at least she's aware of those facts, and I can use them to push her away. Not that I'm doing a very good job of that so far. I seem to be pulling her to me instead, or perhaps it's me being pulled to her. A draw to what I find inescapable and infuriatingly impossible to resist. That's why I've been on a killing spree across the West Coast of America. Drawing attention to myself after eighteen years of meticulously hiding myself away.

Lincoln Knight is a carefully constructed persona, hidden behind layer upon layer of falsehoods. Dig too deep and you'd start to find some anomalies in his past. Like the fact that he doesn't actually exist, despite his social security number and his birth certificate stating he was born to Bella and Marvin Knight in Gatlinburg, Tennessee. Nobody digs too deep. They want to know about my personal life, how I got my scars, who I'm secretly fucking, but never whether I actually exist at all.

A police siren passing by a few streets away reminds me I need to get out of here. I wipe my clothes and gloves clean of the Pawn's blood and slip out the back door, heading to my car. There's a message from Edgar on my cell phone.

Where to next?

My jaw tics. He's been following behind me, cleaning up some of the mess I've left in my wake. Not literally speaking of course, but his connections with law enforcement as well as the kinds of people who can be persuaded to take the credit for some of my misdemeanors make him indispensable. There are a surprising number of local crooks who are willing to take the credit for the kind of torture I'm capable of. Not to the cops, obviously, but to their peers, for sure.

Where to next? I've been away for a week and achieved what?

Do I feel better about losing control with Imogen? No, not even close. Have I atoned for any of my sins? Also no. So what the fuck am I doing other than keeping Edgar busy and potentially drawing attention to myself, and thereby fucking up the main goal? And also, I miss her. I really fucking miss her. I'm soaked in someone else's blood, bathing in the consequences of my sins, but I'm certain that just seeing her smile could make me feel clean again.

I type out my reply.

I think it might be time to go home.

A few seconds later, his reply lands. **Good idea.**

Thanks for everything.

Anytime.

I toss the phone onto the passenger seat and start up the engine, ready to head for home, while thinking about the mess I just left for Edgar. I wonder sometimes why he continues to do it. It's been eighteen years since my sister, Olivia, died, and as far as I know, he's never found anyone else. I'm sure there have been women, but none that have lasted.

We met the day after she died, the same day he got out of prison for aggravated assault against his stepfather. Like me, Edgar had a difficult upbringing, one that led him to some places he shouldn't have gone. He insisted on seeing her body, and I took him back to that house and showed him the place where I'd buried her. He dug up her corpse with his own bare hands. Then he held on to her for hours. I've never seen a man cry like that before. Never seen him shed a single tear ever since, but I often wondered what a love like that must feel like. She was the other half of him, he told me. His missing piece, and without her, he would never be whole.

He joined my cause that same day and has been by my side ever since. He was by my side the day of the explosion that *killed* me, or at least it killed who I was. The charred body left behind was actually a guy named Parker, but he was identified as me due to the skull tattoo on the inside of his left wrist—matching ones we both got when we were stupid fourteen-year-old kids.

We were recruited by the Brotherhood a few days apart, and in a lot of ways we were alike, at least on the surface—young, too smart for our own good, and full of ideas about ruling the world. We ended up in the same foster home together, and we gave each other the tattoos after our first successful assignment. At the time we were given little information and a set of instructions—to steal some papers from a guy's briefcase while he was having dinner with a redhead. I was never content with limited information though; I always wanted to know more, while Parker was never curious. Later, I pieced together that those papers brought down a prominent senator, who had been stupid enough to piss off the Brotherhood.

Parker was a mere Pawn though—one who'd been a guard at the auction where Olivia was sold—so despite our shared history, the Brotherhood never suspected me. I should have known he was a sick fuck. Even when we were fifteen, all the signs were there, but I suppose I chose to ignore them.

As I had no dental records, and the burned corpse had no fingerprints left—at least not after Edgar and I seared them off with a hot poker—the Brotherhood assumed they'd completed their mission. The explosion left Parker dead and Edgar deaf for life, but it gave me the freedom to become Lincoln Knight.

For Olivia, for Imogen and the other family I lost, Lincoln needs to stop making reckless decisions and get back to focusing on the primary goal: erasing the Brotherhood from existence.

CHAPTER 29
IMOGEN

For someone who has spent the majority of her life either alone, or wishing she were, you would think I'd be pretty thrilled with Lincoln's latest expedition. He's been gone for eight days, longer than he's ever left the mansion before, and now I'm certain that his absence has something to do with what happened the night before he left.

What if he's gone to another auction? Is he out there looking for a replacement for me? Am I not what he expected? Too naive? Too passive? Not passive enough? Undesirable?

I'm driving myself crazy with questions. Questions with answers that shouldn't even matter to me.

So what if he's with other women. He's not mine. And no matter how much money he paid for me, I'm not his either. The simple fact that he made my body do something incredible doesn't mean anything. Clearly, whatever I felt about that night in his study is not reciprocated.

Pierre has cleared the dinner dishes and retreated to his quarters. It rained all day today, so we indulged in our daily Marvel movie this afternoon with *The Avengers*, and I got to see Black Widow in action. She's definitely my favorite. I adore how she doesn't even need any magical powers or special suit, yet she

THE AUCTION

holds her own with the rest of them. Not just holds her own, she kicks ass.

Judging by the way Pierre always starts to fidget and cough afterward, I've realized that a few hours is his tolerance level for allowing anyone to be in his personal space. So, I didn't ask to join him this evening, and he didn't invite me to. And now I'm alone in the kitchen . . . Well, not entirely, I suppose. Who is ever truly alone when there are books to escape into. I open mine, determined to lose myself in a world that's anywhere but here. After my foray into romance with *Lady Chatterley's Lover*, I'm working my way through the entire romantic fiction section of the library, which isn't all that big. Yet, once again when I read about the passion between the characters, I can't help but imagine they're Lincoln and me.

What on earth is wrong with me? The me who walked into this house six weeks ago would be so disappointed in the me right now. Larissa would be disappointed. My grandfather too. All those years of training and discipline, unraveled in a few moments.

The main doors slam closed. Pierre obviously hasn't left, so that must mean Lincoln is home.

Despite the pep talk I just gave myself, butterflies take flight in the pit of my stomach and a bolt of excitement races up my spine. I don't want to care about his return, but I do. I shouldn't have allowed myself to miss him, but I have anyway. Still, I resist the urge to run out into the hallway and see him, remaining in my seat with my eyes glued to the pages of my book like it's the most fascinating thing in the world. Before Lincoln Knight, it probably was. But we shared a connection last week. Even if it wasn't enough of one for him, it changed everything for me. And now my world feels less colorful without his presence.

I listen to his footsteps approaching. He has to pass the kitchen to get to either his study in the library or his bedroom, and I brace myself for the rejection of him simply walking by as though I don't exist. He'll know I'm here because the light is on. I'm aware of my own desperate need for his acknowledgment, and while it makes me feel childish and naive, I cannot seem to stop myself. I pray he'll stop and come inside. The footsteps stop outside the room, and I hold my breath. Waiting.

Then he proceeds down the hallway. I swallow down a sob when I hear the door to the library opening. Eight whole days and he couldn't even come in here and say hello. Couldn't even be bothered to ask if I'm okay or see if I'm still breathing. I bet he's found my replacement already. Maybe he's going to discard me like a used tissue. Whatever happened last week, for some reason I displeased him. I obviously did something wrong. And I absolutely shouldn't care about that, because I was raised better than this. Larissa always taught me never to have this kind of attachment to a man, because it gives them too much control. She was right. I fear he could break and build me with a single word. But if I'm no use to him, then I'm dispensable, and being dispensable is dangerous for a girl like me.

Setting down my book, I remind myself who I am and what I'm capable of. I was raised for this life, to survive it at all costs.

Determined to prove that I can be whatever he needs, I make my way to the library. There has to be a reason he bought me from that god-awful auction, and whatever that reason is, I can handle it.

I find the door half open, so I step inside without knocking to witness him staring out the window. Upon hearing my footsteps, he turns around, glaring at me and my intrusion. He's not wearing his mask and that makes me happy, because he looks so much better without it. I'm reminded of that very first time I saw his face, and how despite the pain of him stitching my now-healed finger, I was transfixed by him. He has always called himself a monster, but all I saw was how strikingly handsome he is, and the sincerity of his smile. But there's something about the disdain on his face now that ignites the anger which has been brewing inside me for over a week. And despite all my best intentions to be the perfect little whatever-the-hell-it-is he wants, I let my emotion spill out.

"So, did you find a replacement?" I want to reel those words back in as soon as they've left my mouth.

He scowls, his dark brow furrowed like he's annoyed, or worried. "A replacement for what?"

Panic overwhelms me now. I spoke out of turn and ignored all of my conditioning, and now I've probably made the whole situation worse.

I take a deep breath.

One, two, buckle my shoe.

It's been a long time since I've recited that nursery rhyme, and I was beginning to think I might not need it any longer, but moments like these remind me that I cannot undo . . . no, I cannot throw away all my years of conditioning in a couple months. The mantra soothes me like always. When I find my calm, I answer his question. "For me."

He walks around his desk. Every step he takes seems so careful and considered, but I can feel the tension radiating from him, like he's a volcano quietly simmering before he eventually erupts. "Imogen, what are you talking about?"

I remain still, resisting the urge to fold my arms across my chest and create a barrier between me and the wall of muscle and anger bearing down on me. I soften my tone. "Was it the blood? Did it upset you? I don't believe it will happen again. That's supposed to happen the first time from what I've been told."

He blinks, his hard expression softening with confusion. "You think I was upset about a little blood?"

"I don't know. Something seemed to upset you. If it wasn't the blood . . . is it just me? Am I not what you expected? If I'm not what you want, then I can do better, sir?"

"Imogen!" He growls my name, taking another step until he's closed the distance between us.

I tremble at his closeness. "I can be what you want if you just let me try."

He screws his eyes shut like he's in physical pain. What is it about me that makes him so conflicted? "Lincoln, please tell me what I did wrong?"

His eyes snap open, and they're different. Blazing with heat. "What do you want from me, Imogen? Would it make you feel better if I told you that after I sent you away, I jerked off just to the memory of my finger inside you? That I didn't wash my hands after I touched you and it was the scent of your cum and your virgin blood that tipped me over the edge." He fists a hand in my hair, angling my head until I'm staring up into his face. My legs tremble at the contact. "Or that it took every ounce of willpower I possess not to come to your room and fuck every single part of you? Not just once, but over and over again until you screamed for mercy?" He runs his nose over my jawline and my knees completely buckle, but he holds me up. "Would it?"

Oh, dear god. A breath shudders out of me. "Y-yes, sir," I whisper, staring into his eyes and sure I must be dreaming, because it's only in my dreams when he wants me just as much as I want him. But this is so much more vivid, his words so much more possessive and erotic than in any fantasy I could conjure. "It would. It does." He stares at me intently, doing that thing where it's like he's trying to read my mind. "So why didn't you come to my room? Why did you leave instead?"

He inhales deeply, like he's drinking me in, like he can absorb my essence straight into his bloodstream, and it makes goose bumps prickle out all over my flesh. "Because it's wrong to want to do those things to you, Imogen. So very fucking wrong."

I'm scared and excited and confused. Is this wrong? Perhaps it's entirely messed up for me to so desperately want him to do those filthy things he just spoke about. But is it wrong for me to want to freely give myself to him? I can't help but wonder if I'd be feeling like this if I wasn't his prisoner and we were just two people who met in a bar, like in a movie. But I am sure of one thing. Tentatively, I place my hands on his chest. "This doesn't feel wrong to me."

"But it is," he groans, sounding torn.

"If it is, then I don't care, Lincoln. All I know is that I've been miserable here this last week, thinking I'd done something wrong and—"

"You haven't done anything wrong, angel. You are perfect." He takes hold of my hands and kisses my fingertips.

Perfect? Me? Never in my life have I felt like anything close to that, but with him . . . for him, and in this moment, I believe I am. "Then please touch me again, sir. Please?" I sound desperate and needy, but I don't care. The only thing that matters is his touch. I want him to sate the constant ache between my thighs, the place where wetness is already seeping into my panties.

"Imogen, you could tempt even a saint into hell with those pretty lips, not to mention . . ." He sinks his teeth into his bottom lip, tips his head to the ceiling and groans.

"Not to mention what, sir?" I purr the last word, feeling strangely empowered.

He slides his hand between my thighs, hitching up my dress and quickly finding my panties. "This sweet virgin pussy," he growls. "I have spent every moment of the past eight days thinking about how good it would feel to sink my cock inside you, angel. But I won't be gentle. So don't ask for this again unless you're sure you want it."

My entire body shivers with anticipation. Last week in the library was incredible. I experienced life-altering pleasure, and we didn't even have sex. It's unfathomable to me that anything can feel better than what he did to me that night, but instinctively I know that there is so much more. And even though there are slivers of anxiety splintering through my excitement, they're overwhelmed by the desire to have more. More of that same feeling. More of him. "I want it."

He lifts me as though I'm weightless, wrapping my legs around his waist and carrying me to the antique leather sofa. He sits so I'm straddling him, and then he pulls aside my panties, sweeping two fingers through my already-slick center. "So wet already, angel. Have you made yourself come again while I've been away?"

My cheeks flush with heat. "Yes, sir."

He groans, pulling me closer while his fingers go on teasing me. That now-familiar pleasure is already building deep in my core. "How, Imogen? What did you do?"

"I tried to copy what you did, sir. I touched myself where you're touching me now."

A growl rumbles in his throat. "Did you play with this needy little clit?" He pinches it gently, and I cry out as wet heat slicks between my thighs.

"Y-yes!"

"And did you do this too?" He pushes a finger inside me and my vision blurs.

"No."

He arches an eyebrow. "You didn't?"

"No, sir."

"That surprises me when you were so needy for me to be inside you. Why didn't you try it for yourself, angel?" He twists his finger, rubbing at a sweet sensitive spot deep inside that almost has me mewling like a kitten.

"I wasn't sure if I was allowed to."

He hums, running his teeth over the skin of my throat. "You thought I might be able to tell if you'd touched yourself like that? And that I'd be angry if I discovered you'd slipped your fingers into *my* cunt?"

Even the crude way he talks about me and my body makes me wet and needy. I have no idea who I'm becoming. I nod, biting down on my lip because he's still toying with me, still driving his finger in and out of me while we talk, and I'm close to that feeling of blissful oblivion already.

"This is *mine*, Imogen." He pushes deeper, like he's claiming the territory. "But it's your body. You can touch yourself however and whenever you want to, and I will never be angry. Okay?"

I nod again.

"Good girl." He rubs the pad of his thumb over my clit and fireworks explode in my core. It's sudden and euphoric, and I cling to the back of his neck while I ride the waves of ecstasy. I'm still trembling when he presses his mouth against my ear. "I'll teach you how to make yourself come like this. How to find your G-spot . . ." He does something with his fingers that has another orgasm washing over me. It's so much more intense than the one I gave myself. I cry out his name, bucking my hips against his hand while my cum drips out of me. "That's my girl," he soothes. "But we're not done yet."

He cups the back of my head possessively, pressing my face into the crook of his neck. And then he adds a second finger and the burning stretch makes me gasp, even as another wave of wet heat slicks between my thighs.

"Relax, angel," he murmurs into my ear. "I need to make you nice and relaxed and wet before I sink my cock into you. Because I already told you I'm not going to be gentle. And you want my cock to fill you up, don't you?"

I whimper, shameless with need. The sensations surging through my body are like nothing I've ever felt before in my life. I had no idea the human body was capable of feeling this much pleasure . . . this much anything.

"Words, Imogen." His tone is deep and commanding. The timbre of his voice seeps into my bones, warming me from the inside.

I cling to his neck, my fingernails scraping over his skin and my body molded to his. "Y-yes."

"That's my girl." He works his fingers skillfully, causing a deep aching pleasure to throb in my core. Resting his lips against my ear, he allows his warm breath to dance over my skin. "I'm going to sink my cock so deep inside you that you'll still feel me there every time you move for the rest of the week. Your tight little cunt will be forever molded to me, Imogen. You belong to me. Always."

His words are enough to send me over the edge once more, and this time it's even more intense, more mind-blowing. While my body continues spasming, he holds his fingers still, gently sweeping the pad of his thumb over my sensitive clit.

"Lincoln," I whimper his name.

He presses a gentle kiss on my temple and it's *everything*. Despite the ministrations of his skilled fingers, it's the tenderness, and the reverent way he touches me that's my undoing. "I know, angel." Slowly, he begins moving his fingers inside me again, reigniting the dying embers of my last orgasm.

Oh, god! I try to squeeze my thighs together but his huge bear paw–like hand between my legs prevents me from doing so. "I c-can't," I stammer, fearful of the new and intense sensations flooding my entire being.

"What can't you do, Imogen?" he asks, lips still pressed against my skin. "What are you afraid of?"

"What if I . . . I feel like I'm going to . . ." I gasp in a breath. "It's like I'm not in control of my own body." All my life I've thrived on control. Losing it is weak and it leaves me vulnerable. It makes me unsafe.

He growls. "That's because you're not. I am. But you don't have to be afraid of that, you can lose control when you're with me."

Can I? Do I trust him enough to give this willingly? I let out a shaky breath and give a single nod of my head.

"Good girl," he soothes, sweeping the pads of his fingers over a spot deep inside me that makes electric pleasure coil deep in my core. "You're going to come as many times as I need you to, until you're wet enough for me to fuck you."

Given that the filthy sound of my arousal as he moves his fingers in and out of me is unmistakable, surely I must be wet enough already.

He rubs his nose along the column of my throat. "I know you're soaked, angel, but I need you dripping down your fucking thighs for me. I'm not going to stop until you're drenched in your own cum."

CHAPTER 30
IMOGEN

My head is spinning. Legs shaking. Endorphins charging around my body at lightning speed. I cling to Lincoln's neck, inhaling his unique fresh scent, as he carries me upstairs—to bed I hope, to finish what he started. To deliver on his promise to fuck me. He's made my body do things I had no idea it was capable of. He took off my panties at some point, and the sticky residue of what he just did to me in the library clings to the top of my thighs, still seeping out of me now.

He walks into my room rather than his and lays me down gently on the bed. I gaze up at him through hooded eyes. I've felt the length of him through his pants and he seems so big I'm not sure how he'll fit inside me. But I'm desperate for him to try anyway.

I lick my dry lips. "Can I see you, sir? All of you."

"You want to see all my scars, angel?"

I nod. "Yes, sir." It's intoxicating, knowing that this powerful man will do as I ask, simply because I ask him to. I could get drunk on this feeling alone.

Slowly he peels his T-shirt off over his head, and when he lifts his arms I can fully see the extent of scarring on his right side. It's covered in thick white knots and patches of skin that look like they've been through a meat grinder yet somehow stayed intact.

From the top of the underside of his biceps wrapping almost halfway across his chest and disappearing beneath his waistband. All of it is covered in thick black tattoos, roses and vines and chess pieces, stark against his mottled skin. He tosses the T-shirt onto the floor and his eyes lock on mine before his hands drop to his belt. Tantalizingly slow, he unbuckles it and then pulls it through the loops. The sound makes me shiver with pleasure.

"Spread your legs for me. Let me see the mess we made of your sweet pussy while I strip for you."

I bite my lip, spreading my thighs wide. The metallic sound of his zipper makes me tremble. Then he reaches into his pants and pulls out his dick. Oh, dear lord, it's huge. He wraps his hand around the base of his shaft, lined with thick veins, until a bead of pearly cum forms on the purple head of him.

My pulse spikes and I suck in a breath that makes him smirk. "I'll make it fit, baby."

I have no idea how, but I believe him. And more importantly, I trust him not to hurt me. Which is ironic, isn't it? Given how I came to be here. I should be afraid of him, of this giant bear of a man and his huge muscles, a man who could so easily overpower me at any moment he chooses. I should be terrified of his promise to *not be gentle*, and whether that means he'll be rough with me and it will hurt. But I'm not.

He tugs on his shaft and grunts with pleasure. A pang of jealousy lances through me. I want his grunts and groans for my own. I want to be responsible for his pleasure. Does he feel the same way about mine? "Please, sir?" I whimper.

He tuts. "So impatient." Then he pulls off his pants, yanking his boots and socks off along with them. He crawls over me, running his nose over my ankle, my calf, the inside of my thigh, his thick dark hair brushes over my wet center and I gasp aloud at the unfamiliar but incredibly erotic sensation. "Needy little angel."

Needy? I'm practically vibrating with desire. Lincoln's mask and clothes might be gone, but his control isn't. He has the patience of a man who wants to memorize every inch of my skin. He nudges the tip of his nose at the apex of my thighs and I squeal, but he quickly moves on, tongue swirling over my stomach and then the tiny scars from the keyhole surgery the Brotherhood forced upon me. I hate those scars and what they represent, but his attention makes even them feel like a beautiful part of me. Then he finds my nipples, which weren't aching until he touched them . . . and now, now they feel like they have a heartbeat all their own. I didn't know nipples could do that.

He settles between my thighs, notching the head of his giant dick at my entrance. I buck my hips a little, chasing the relief I know he can so easily give me. "I can't get pregnant, sir," I assure him. The Brotherhood made sure of that.

"I know, angel." He drags his teeth over my collarbone before staring into my eyes. "Are you sure you want this?"

"Yes. Absolutely sure."

He sinks the tip of his cock inside me, and as much as he prepared me with his fingers, this is a whole new level of ecstasy, laced with a burning pain that makes me feel alive. "Christ, you're so fucking tight," he growls, the words sounding like they're being torn from his throat.

"I'm sorry, sir. I can't help it."

He presses his forehead against mine. "It's not a complaint, baby. You feel so good I might come as soon as I get all the way inside you."

I wrap my arms around his wide shoulders, desperate for him to finally lose the control he's been so tightly clinging to, and even more importantly, to lose it for me. "I want all of you," I whine.

"Yeah?" he growls.

"Yes, sir."

He sinks deeper. "Then take me. Take every fucking inch of me."

"Linc!" I cry his name into the darkness as he fills me completely and my entire body is burning with hot desperate need.

My nails dig into his shoulder blades while he stretches me wider than I imagined possible.

"Good girl," he soothes. "See how well you're taking my cock. It's like you were made for me."

I melt under his praise, so overwhelmed with feeling that tears squeeze from my eyes. He kisses them away. "Are you okay? Do you need me to stop?"

I shake my head vehemently. "No, sir. Please don't. It feels . . . so good. So much."

He buries his head in the crook of my neck. "My good girl," he soothes. "Just hold on to me and I'll take care of you."

I cling to him and he fucks me hard, driving his huge dick in and out of me. And I have never felt anything so all-consuming, such a mind-altering euphoria in my whole life. And if enjoying this means I go to hell, then I'd gladly spend an eternity with the devil for the promise of a life filled with this.

He kisses my neck and rolls his hips and I see stars. Another orgasm crashes over me, unexpected and glorious.

"There she is," he grunts. "My needy girl."

Then he pushes himself up and throws my legs over his shoulders. His hair falls, covering his eyes as he looks down at me, wild with untamed desire.

Wow, he is truly beautiful.

He sinks into me, getting deeper in this position and rubs my sensitive swollen clit with his thumb.

"Linc," I whine. No, I can't come again. My body won't survive it. But I do. Overstimulated and insanely sensitive, another climax shakes the breath from my body.

"It's okay," he soothes. Then he rocks his hips once, twice more before he throws his head back and roars his release, like he's just given me everything he's spent years holding back. Like I just unraveled him.

Me. The girl who was always overlooked and forgotten. Now she's seen.

CHAPTER 31
LINCOLN

I can't remember the last time I fucked a virgin, but I'm sure they weren't as tight as this. Imogen's snug cunt milks my cock as I make her come again, her wet heat slicking my entire shaft, covering the tops of her thighs.

I stay inside her, my dick pulsing in her throbbing pussy. Her eyelashes flutter against her cheeks as she pants for breath. Her hands are on my shoulders, fingernails digging into the muscle. I hope when I look at them in the mirror later, she's left her mark on my skin, just like she's left one on my heart and soul. I knew as soon as she came to this house she'd be the ruin of me, and despite all the promises I made to myself about the lines I wouldn't cross, here I am filling her with my cock. It's still wrong. I'm still going to be eaten alive by guilt, but fuck it, she's worth it. I could spend an eternity in the deepest darkest pits of hell and it would be worth it just for this moment.

I suppose she's not my ruin at all. She is the salvation I don't deserve.

I already want her again. Want to flip her over with her perfect ass in the air while I fuck her from behind. Instead, I gently lower her legs to the mattress and slide out of her. She winces and I feel like an insensitive jerk for being so rough with her. The fact that I prewarned her is no consolation to me right now.

I brush the strands of hair from her damp forehead. "How are you doing, angel?"

"Will it always be like that?" she asks, all wide-eyed and innocent while looking thoroughly fucked at the same time.

"You mean will it hurt?"

She shakes her head. "Will it always feel that . . . incredible?"

I suppress a satisfied smile and I drop a kiss on her forehead. "Angel, it's only going to get better."

"Better?" She beams, her face flushed pink and her green eyes sparkling. The real Imogen beneath the veneer of obedience and expectations. I want this side of her. All the damn time.

"Better." And much fucking filthier. I keep that last thought to myself. "If it weren't your first time, I would fuck you again right now."

She snakes her arms around my neck. "I can take more. I want more, Linc."

I love that she's calling me Linc. Nobody has ever called me that, and nobody else ever will. I nip at her neck. "My greedy little angel."

"I've never felt anything that made me feel so good before. Is that normal?"

Nothing about me and her together could be described as normal. Nothing about what we just did either. It was explosive and addictive. I've had plenty of sex before her, but she's the first human being I've ever wanted to be so close to. Sex has always been transactional. It was a necessary arrangement, given the life I lead, but also it was all I ever wanted. No feelings. No attachment. With her though, there could never be enough of either. I could crawl inside her skin and it wouldn't be enough. "I'm not sure what you would consider normal, Imogen."

"Well, I suppose I have no idea. But I was warned that it would hurt . . . a lot. I was never told about the other stuff."

I roll onto my side and she does the same. The way she's studying my face feels too intimate, too intense. But I'm unable to resist the plea in her bright green eyes, or the gravitational pull of her. And this is an opportunity to discover more about her childhood without appearing like I'm searching for information. Because any information about the Brotherhood is always welcome, but I'm more interested in knowing all about her. "Who warned you it would hurt?"

"Larissa. My grandfather's housekeeper."

Ah yes, the governess figure Pierre told me of, who was definitely much more than that. "You two discussed sex?"

She nods. "We talked about a lot of stuff. She . . ." Her slender throat works, as though something is stuck inside her. "She was the only person I had really. So anything I learned about life experiences, I learned from her. She tried to prepare me for what would happen after the auction as best she could."

White-hot rage sears through my veins. The mere thought of what my innocent angel was prepared for. What kind of violence and abuse was she expecting, and what the hell did Larissa have to show or tell her to do that? Or was there more? Was she taught to defend herself? Forced to fight? Shown how to please a man to seduce or subdue him? It all stokes my ever-present need for vengeance to dangerous levels. And there were fifty women sold before her. Forty-eight of whom I haven't yet managed to free from their torment.

I swallow all of the anger, pushing it down deep where it won't reach my girl and taint her with its darkness. I tuck a curl behind her ear and soften my voice. "What did she prepare you for?"

A faint smile tugs the corner of her lips. "Not for this. *You are nothing like what I was told to expect.*"

Her choice of words makes the hair on the back of my neck stand on end. "You were told about me specifically?"

She shakes her head. "No. I had no idea who would be there or who would buy me." Those words fill me with shame. Yes, I bought her, like a prize heifer at a fucking cattle auction. But I did it for the right reasons. I did it to save her. At least that's what I need to believe, otherwise my soul is even more damned than it was before.

"I was taught to expect pain and cruelty," she says flatly, and that fuels my rage further. "I was never taught about what an orgasm might feel like or given any indication that I would feel any kind of pleasure from sex."

I suppress a snarl, in case she worries it's aimed at her. "And you were never allowed to touch yourself to give yourself any pleasure?"

"No."

"And you didn't ever try anyway?"

Her jaw clenches and her eyes narrow a fraction. Her guard is up again and I could kick myself for pressing too hard too soon. "I was an obedient child, Mr. Knight."

Mr. Knight? I cup her chin, squeezing hard enough that she knows I'm not playing. "Don't call me Mr. Knight, Imogen. I've just been inside you and I'd say we're past that, aren't we? I am simply asking a question."

"I'm sorry." Her eyelashes flutter against her cheeks. "But you sounded like you didn't believe me."

I file away her reaction to being taken as a liar for future exploration. "You weren't allowed to touch yourself and I assumed it was because you were taught it was wrong, or something to be ashamed of. But you talk so openly and unashamedly about sex, so that makes me think perhaps there was another reason. I'm merely curious. Exploring one's own body and pleasure is a natural part of human development. I'm not sure I could have abstained, no matter how many people told me I should."

"Perhaps I am more disciplined than you, sir."

I let the *sir* go, because I can't be sure whether it's sass or her submissive conditioning kicking in. Although I would much prefer it was the former. "I'm sure you are, angel. But you still haven't answered my question. Why were you not permitted to touch yourself? Or even use a tampon?"

She holds my gaze, but she's cold and detached. All her walls are up now. "So that I didn't sully the property of the Brotherhood. I was told they would know if I had ever touched myself inappropriately, and I was never brave enough to risk taking that chance."

She's wrong. She's the bravest creature I've ever known. I soften my grip, rubbing the underside of her jaw with my thumb. "You are free to touch yourself, and be yourself, in this house, Imogen. Do you understand that?"

"Yes, sir."

She's still closed off to me. Years of brainwashing will take a long time to change, even for someone as strong as her.

I press a kiss on her lips and run my tongue along the seam. She allows me entry into her sweet mouth and I kiss her softly, hoping to reignite the spark of connection we just shared. But she's gone, retreated into herself, and I can't blame her. I'm loath to even imagine the horrors she was prepared for and almost subjected to, so I cannot fathom the armor she had to develop in order to deal with all of that. To be the fearless girl who walked onto that stage in front of a room full of monsters and didn't break.

I go to the restroom and bring back a warm washcloth, and I gently clean the cum from between her thighs. She lies back obediently and lets me tend to her, then politely thanks me afterward. I hate it. I hate the well-trained obedient little pet she's turned into within the space of a few minutes. I hate what they made her—a perfect little fuck doll to be used and abused at will. And given what we just did, it hurts like fuck that she's closed herself off to me so quickly.

I know that she wanted what happened between us tonight.

She was different when she came into my study. Filled with fire and defiance because I'd neglected her. That was the real Imogen, the only one I have any interest in kissing, fucking, or doing anything else with. And if I have to push her boundaries to bring out that side of her, then that's exactly what I'll do, no matter how cruel she might think me for it.

I press a soft peck on her forehead and wish her good-night. That's when I see it, the tiniest flicker of anguish that flashes in her eyes. Despite her walls, she wants me to stay in here with her. And I probably should, given how I just took her virginity the way I did. But if I stay, I'll likely wake her in the night to fuck her again, and I'm not sure I'll be able to tap back into the real her, or whether she'll let me climb on top of her because that's what she's been conditioned to do. And taking her like that would fucking crush me.

So, I leave her alone in the dark, even though I know it will probably hurt her. It guts me to my core to cause her any kind of pain, but the reality is her guard comes down quickest when she's feeling new overwhelming things. Imogen needs to break free of whoever it was she was always taught or expected to be, and unfortunately for my girl, pain is usually the quickest route to any kind of meaningful change.

CHAPTER 32
IMOGEN

I'm so sore that every step I take this morning is a reminder of last night. An evening that started out so perfectly and then ended so horribly—with Lincoln leaving me alone in the dark. And I hate the dark, not that he'd know that because I'd never tell him. After he dug up all those old wounds from my childhood and my past, he left me wide open and bleeding.

He tended to my body so gently, carefully washing me. But my body will heal much quicker than my heart. I let him inside me, not just literally, and he still left. I know I got upset and defensive when I thought he accused me of lying. But I realized my mistake and immediately afterward I went back to being his perfect little angel. Passive and submissive and never emotional or needy. And he left me anyway. Used me and walked away.

Perhaps it was me closing off like that made him turn away. I don't know what to do anymore. Being closed off and unemotional is how I survive. That's how I was taught to survive. And Larissa wouldn't lie to me. She prepared me the best way she knew how. But Lincoln isn't like any of those men she warned me about. He's different, and so maybe all of that preparation is meaningless where he's concerned.

I shower and dress and head downstairs, hoping to see him

while also praying that I don't. What if my body remembers how good he made me feel and I melt into a puddle at his feet? What if I'm too needy? Too clingy? What if he's tired of me already and tosses me aside to find his next virgin? One who doesn't run her mouth too much or react emotionally to being made to feel like a liar.

I see now that that's when it all started to go wrong. But I despise being accused of lying. Unconsciously I scratch at the healed scar on the inside of my wrist—the burn from a poker, and my constant reminder that lying is bad. My grandfather caught me sneaking one of his books from his library, and when I told him it was the first time it happened, he showed me a video of me doing it the week before. I can still smell the burning flesh, still feel the cruel sting of his words when he called me a lying little bitch.

I never lied to him again.

"Would you like some breakfast, mademoiselle?" Pierre's voice jolts me from the memory of searing pain and burned skin and I realize I've wandered into the kitchen in a daze. And I am dazed. Overwhelmed with all the new and confusing sensations and the way they're making me question everything I've ever known—rocking the very bedrock of who I am.

I take a breath. *One, two, buckle my shoe.* I need to remember who I am. Need familiarity so that I can think clearly and remember my goals. Lincoln is a distraction. Larissa warned me of this very thing.

"Yes please, Pierre. Oatmeal would be nice."

He simply smiles and opens a cupboard.

"No pancakes and bacon this morning?" Lincoln's deep voice almost knocks me off my feet. He steps up behind me, the heat from his body at my back. Yes, definitely a distraction.

I twist around, my heart fluttering and my throat closing over as I stare up into his deep brown eyes. He's still not wearing his mask and I'm glad about that, at least. Happy that he clearly doesn't feel the need to, now that I've seen every part of him. "N-no, sir."

His right eye twitches, but other than that his face remains passive. Then he brushes past me and takes a seat at the breakfast table. When Pierre serves our food, he leaves us, quietly muttering about some carrots and potatoes. Suddenly it's just Lincoln and me, and the room is thick with unspoken words.

I desperately want to break the silence. I want to talk about last night and the expectations of this new dynamic of our relationship, but I'm too scared. Not of Lincoln per se, but of doing or saying the wrong thing. What if I make this already-tense situation worse? And what if I already messed up and he's considering whether I'm worth the effort of keeping around? What if I'm useless to him now? And just like that, I realize I'm already in too deep. Because more than any of that, I'm worried about his rejection. I think it would break me.

"Why are you eating oatmeal?" he eventually says, and I don't miss the hint of annoyance in his tone.

I glance at the bowl, full of perfectly nutritious food that I decided to eat, and wonder what about it has made him so grumpy. Unless it's just me he's grumpy with in general. "I—I . . . It's healthy and nutritious," I blurt out my well-practiced mantra. Fuck him and his condescending attitude. Not everyone grew up with the kind of luxury he can afford.

He grinds his jaw, eyes raking over my face and torso. I'm wearing a cute little white sundress today, the one I was wearing that day in the library when I caught him watching me. "You will no longer wear panties without my permission when I am in the house, Imogen."

He goes back to his scrambled eggs and wheat toast like he didn't just say the most bizarre and random thing ever. What the hell does that have to do with oatmeal? I know I should bow my head and eat my breakfast. I'm his property and he can do whatever the hell he likes with me. I hear Larissa's voice in my head. *Emotions are weakness. Never let them see your weakness.* Do I heed her advice, which I seem to rely on less and less lately? It served me well on my grandfather's estate, but I've already figured out the same rules don't apply here. And something about the way Lincoln is sitting there, smug and arrogant and distant, snaps something inside me. "Excuse me?"

He looks up, arching an eyebrow. "Did you not hear what I said?"

"I heard you, but I don't understand you. We were talking about oatmeal and then . . . then you said . . ." I stop talking, aware of my tone going up an octave, my words coming out fast and reckless.

"For the purposes of clarity, I said that you are not to wear panties when I am in the house. Is there something about that particular request that you don't understand?"

Yes! Why the hell you're making it! I want to shout, but instead I tighten my grip on my spoon and channel all my confusion and anger into the poor defenseless piece of silverware. "May I ask for what purpose, sir?" I ask, the hint of snark still there in my tone, unable to stop this new defiant side I'm discovering from spilling free. I don't hate it. And I don't miss his reaction to it either. His lips most definitely twitched, like he was trying to suppress a smirk.

"I would have thought that fairly obvious. No?"

Jackass! "Not entirely."

He wipes his mouth with his napkin and pushes back his chair. "When I slip my hand beneath your dress, or into your leggings, I want nothing between my fingers and your cunt." He walks around the table until he's standing directly in front of me, and I'm looking right at his groin area, where I can already see the outline of his semihard dick through his pants. "If I wish to bend you over this table and fuck you, I don't want panties getting in my way. Does that answer your question?"

My brain misfires. I'm equal parts indignant and turned on.

I have so many questions about the practicalities of such an insane request, but I clamp my lips together, the only way to stop myself from asking them. Is this my life now? Do I become his little pet to play with and use when he pleases? Was I completely wrong thinking he was any different to all the men I was warned about? Tears burn behind my eyes and my throat constricts tightly with the effort of keeping them in.

He holds out his hand. "With that in mind, do you have something for me?"

I look up into his face and he's staring at me, eyes sparkling with hunger. He's waiting for my panties, isn't he? Right now at the breakfast table. I take a breath and recite the nursery rhyme again until it calms me.

Then, obediently, I stand and slip my underwear off before pressing them into his hand. He closes his palm over the soft white material and then walks out of the room without another word.

I sit back down at the table and allow myself the luxury of one single solitary tear. I hate Lincoln Knight.

CHAPTER 33
IMOGEN

So, maybe I don't hate Lincoln Knight.

Or maybe I do, but I still want him to touch me.

But he hasn't, for four whole days, nothing more than a fleeting brush of his skin on mine, which is not the kind of contact I'm aching for.

I pick at the petals of a daisy and let them drop to the ground. The gentle breeze carries the sweet scent of lavender through the air, and I try to enjoy my favorite spot in the garden, but my thoughts are too jumbled. Too consumed with Lincoln. I want him to touch me so badly that my skin burns with longing. Every time he's near me, my entire being hums with desire. Yet he remains infuriatingly distant.

He hasn't come to my room, or invited me into his. He's still sweet to me. He's still not wearing his mask. And when I smile at him, he smiles back, but the time has gone for smiling to be enough. How can he not want more of what happened just a few nights ago? It doesn't seem like he's annoyed with me, and I suppose I assumed that even if he were, he'd still want to touch me, if even for his own pleasure and not mine. Or else what was his stupid no-panty rule for in the first place? And all his big talk about wanting to bend me over the kitchen table, which, as degrading as he may have intended that to be, actually sounded like it would be a lot of fun, was obviously only talk.

Of course there's every possibility that what happened between us just wasn't all that special to him. Given how skilled he is, he must have had plenty of sexual partners. Perhaps sex is always like that for him. That thought in particular makes me feel something new . . . I'm jealous! What on earth have I become? I'm ashamed of myself, honestly.

I stare out across the knotted brambles and the beautiful pink and orange colors of the sunset. The sound of his footsteps makes every nerve in my body come alive with electricity. Maybe this will be where he lifts me into his arms and carries me to bed. Or maybe he'll just lie me down right here in the garden and have his way with me. The thought of him taking me here on the ground, rough and dirty and urgent, does nothing to calm my raging libido. Nothing at all.

He sits down on the chair beside mine and I pretend to be engrossed in the sunset while trying to ignore the heartbeat between my thighs. "What have you been reading today, angel?"

"*Flowers in the Attic*," I tell him. "I finished it already."

"And what did you think of it?"

"It was . . ." I search for the right word " . . . different."

"Would you tell me about it?"

I turn to him and find him staring at me intently. There's something in his eyes that makes me feel like there's an ice cube running down the length of my spine. It's a need. A hunger. As if he'd like to pin me to the ground and devour me whole. So, why doesn't he? "About the book?"

He nods. "I've never read it, although I've heard it's a classic."

I'm suspicious of his motives. Is he teasing me because he does actually know the plot of this story? Is he aware I'm a trembling mess of desire aching for his touch. I try not to let any of that show on my face. "I don't want to spoil it, sir. It's a very good story."

He runs the tip of his pointer finger along my forearm and a shiver runs from the top of my head all the way to the tips of my toes. "I'd rather hear what you think of it."

Angel? Is he calling me that to drive me crazy? Is this some kind of test to see when I'll break? I squeeze my thighs together as his touch on my skin ignites a burning in my center. I try not to think of other things he's done with that particular finger. Per his instructions, I'm not wearing panties and I definitely don't want to leave a wet patch on the back of my dress.

"Well, it's a little complicated."

"I'm sure you can explain it in a way I'll understand." His dark eyes twinkle.

I run my tongue across my lips and eye him, yet he simply waits for me to talk. So I explain the plot, and he listens intently.

"So he raped his sister?" he asks, appearing genuinely curious.

"I don't think either of them considered it to be rape," I say. "At least not as far as I understand what rape is anyway." My ideas around consent are probably very skewed though, given that I was taught from an early that my consent is not actually mine to give.

His eyes narrow. "And what is your understanding, Imogen?"

I feel the heat flush across my cheeks. "I don't know what you mean, sir."

He frowns. "I'm simply asking you a question. What is your understanding of the term? And why does me asking make you feel uncomfortable?"

"I feel like you're making fun of me, sir. You know I don't have much experience beyond . . ." I tip my chin and hold his gaze. "Beyond what happened between you and I."

His frown deepens and he leans back in his chair, his scrutinous gaze making me want to fidget in my seat. "I assure you I would never make fun of you, angel. And as for what you know of sex, our encounters might be your only lived experience, but you were taught about sex before you arrived here."

I nod. I already told him that I was, but I don't understand why he's questioning me. "Yes."

He takes my hand in his and brings it to his lips, dusting them over my knuckles. The space between my thighs grows wetter. "I'm not trying to make you feel uncomfortable, Imogen. I just want to understand you a little better."

As much as I crave his affection, I'm not sure I want him to delve into the deepest parts of my psyche and discover all the parts of me. They're the only parts nobody else can ever touch or take. "But why?"

He grinds his jaw. "Did you like me touching you?"

My cheeks burn hotter. "Yes."

"Did you enjoy having sex?"

I nod.

"Would you like to do that again?"

"Y-yes, sir." *Right now would be ideal.*

"If we're going to have sex, Imogen, then surely we can discuss it too?"

How about we discuss the reason you made your stupid no-panty rule but won't touch me! I bite my tongue and don't say that, because then he'll know how much I want him. And that gives him all the power, and he already has enough. "Yes. And I've never had an issue discussing sex. But that was before I experienced it. And now, I . . ." I swallow.

"Now you can't discuss it without thinking about me fucking you?"

Heat sears between my thighs and I almost choke on my breath before I answer, "Yes."

"And is that an unpleasant thought?"

I look down at my hands and he cups my chin, gently tipping my head up so I can't avoid him again. "No, sir. But it does makes me blush, although not because I'm embarrassed." *Because I want it to happen over and over again.*

"Tell me what you learned before you got here."

THE AUCTION

I roll back my shoulders and remember that I'm not controlled by my raging libido. I'm Imogen DeMotta, daughter of Luca and Carmen DeMotta. I am strong and capable and I am not defined by the man that owns me. He can push and I will bend, but I will never break. "I learned the physicality of it. The mechanics. What parts are supposed to go where. Larissa allowed me to watch some videos too, so I could see for myself what would happen."

He raises one eyebrow. "Videos?"

"I believe it's called porn."

"You learned about sex from porn?" He pinches the bridge of his nose.

I don't understand his reaction. I was told lots of men watch porn and that's why it was used to teach me what to do. "Is that bad?"

"Not necessarily, angel. Depending on the porn, I suppose."

I swallow down my discomfort. "What I didn't learn about was the emotional aspect of it. Nothing about how it would make me feel, and certainly nothing about female orgasms."

He opens his mouth, like he's about to ask me something else, but Pierre interrupts us. "Sir, that information you've been waiting for has come through."

Lincoln stands, presses a tender kiss on my forehead and then goes into the house with Pierre. Like always, it's the tenderness that unravels me. He cares for me, I know he does. So why won't he touch me the way I want him to?

LINCOLN DIDN'T COME BACK TO THE GARDEN AFter abruptly ending our confusing, and somewhat frustrating conversation. So I was left alone, once more, feeling wet and achy and needing some kind of relief. What was the point of him ordering me not to wear any panties if he wasn't planning on touching me? He spoke about wanting unrestricted access, which was infuriating at the time, but I've done as he asked. I've sat beside him in the shortest of sundresses, like this white one I'm wearing today, and he still hasn't touched me.

A flicker of something unfamiliar sparks inside me. What if I simply disobeyed him and wore some panties anyway? I'm sure he wouldn't even notice, but oh, my, what if he does? Suppressing a smile, I head upstairs to my room to change for bed. A thrill of excitement skitters through me.

Is this what rebellion feels like? If it is, I think I like it.

CHAPTER 34
LINCOLN

It has been four long and torturous days since I last touched her, at least touched her in the way I want to. And I'm on the brink of losing either my sanity or having a heart attack from the constant erections. Like an obedient little pet, she has followed my rule about no panties, and every day she grows a little more frustrated by my lack of interest in her. At least my apparent lack of interest. In truth, I'm feral to slide my hand beneath her clothes and feel her. To get my mouth on her. Sink my cock into her heavenly wet cunt.

One of us will surely break soon, and I hope it's her or this will have been for nothing.

Today, she wore that white sundress that drives me crazy, and the amount of times she's dropped something and bent over to pick it up is bordering on ridiculous. I jerked off in the downstairs restroom as soon as she was out of sight after the last one, and still it did nothing to curb my desire for her. Then I found her in the garden and she told me all about the book she was reading. The parallels between fiction and reality became a little too blurred for comfort. Not that our relationship is incestuous, but still . . . fuck me. And when the conversation turned to sex, it was a Herculean feat of willpower not to take her right there beneath the rosebushes.

I sit at the desk in the library, waiting for her to come in and pick up a new book to read before bed. When she enters the room, I keep my head bent low, pretending I'm focused on my work, but from the corner of my eye I catch the distinct outline of her panties against the thin material of her oversized T-shirt. It takes every single ounce of restraint I possess not to smile with triumph. Hell, I'm filled with so much relief I'm close to breaking into fucking song.

"Imogen?" I call her name as she passes straight by my desk.

"Yes, sir?" She bats her eyelashes, feigning her innocence. There she is, the sassy little brat I've been desperate to meet again.

"Come here."

She walks over to stand beside my desk. My palm twitches with anticipation as I reach out and slide my hand up the outside of her thigh, until I reach the soft cotton underwear.

Her breath hitches.

"Did you ask my permission to wear these?"

She presses her lips together and shakes her head.

"Then why are you wearing them, angel?"

Her mouth remains firmly closed. I'm guessing she didn't think her plan through to its entirety and is currently questioning the wisdom of her decision. If only she knew this was the choice she was always supposed to make. Currently, my cock is hard as iron and I'm almost drooling with the prospect of how I'm going to punish her.

"Give me the truth, Imogen," I command.

She tips her jaw a little, some of that defiance I crave spilling out. "I wore no panties for four days and you didn't seem to notice."

I roll my chair a little closer, guiding her between my spread thighs. "I noticed."

"You didn't even touch me once, so I thought maybe you wouldn't care if I wore panties or not."

I run my hands up the back of her legs and cup her ass, pulling her toward me. "If I didn't care, then I would have told you the rule was no longer in place, would I not have?"

"I don't know, sir."

"For future reference, Imogen, if I make a rule, I expect it to be adhered to. I will advise you if the rules change."

She shuffles her feet, awkwardly. "I'm sorry, sir."

"Are you?"

Her eyes narrow a little. "Yes."

"So you didn't pull this little stunt to get a reaction from me? To get my attention?"

I study her face intently. I know she hates to be accused of lying, but is she capable of lying to my face? I suspect she could if she needed to, no matter how uncomfortable it might make her. And I don't hold that against her, it's simply a tool in her arsenal, one she would have needed had she not ended up here with me. "Maybe I did," she whispers.

The truth then. I stand and yank her closer until her body is flush with mine. Her pupils blow wider. "If you want my attention, angel, all you need do is ask for it. With your words, and not by flashing me your bare ass when you bend over."

Her cheeks tinge a light pink.

"And now you'll need to be punished for breaking my rules."

A shudder runs through her body, and whether it's from excitement or fear I cannot entirely tell. While she should fear me, it's not for the reasons she thinks. I glide a hand over her ass and rest it on the small of her back. "I would never harm you, Imogen. You have no need to ever be afraid of any punishment from me. Understand?"

She nods. "Yes, sir."

I scoop her into my arms and carry her up to her bedroom.

All the while, she clings to me, the pulse fluttering in her neck, her breathing shallow and fast. And when I toss her into the middle of her bed, she lets out a tiny squeal that sings to my soul. *That* was pure and unguarded. All her. Everything I want her to be, slipping out in a moment of connection.

"Take off your clothes," I order.

She bites her lip while she obeys my order, giving me a striptease. My mind can't help but wander to dark places. Is that something else she *learned* from Larissa? Something to please her buyer? So I don't enjoy it as much as I should. Still, my cock is aching to be set free by the time she's done. That's all because of her naked body and the thought of what I'm about to do to her rather than her little show though.

She stares up at me expectantly, waiting for further instructions, her breath coming in uneven pants. "Turn over. I want you on all fours with your pretty ass in the air and your legs wide. Show me what I own, angel."

She hesitates for a few seconds, and I like it. That's my girl, right there in the pauses. In the uncertainty and confusion. That's the Imogen I want to tease out, to tempt and frustrate and push to the edge, until the passive little pet who I refuse to trust is all gone.

Slowly she slithers onto her belly and then pushes herself up onto all fours, sticking her perfect peach of an ass in the air for me and spreading wide, until her pink pussy, already glistening with her arousal, is on full display. I clamp down on my lip to stop myself from groaning with appreciation.

Slowly, I take off my clothes, prolonging her torment. The sound of my belt buckle makes her visibly tremble, and my zipper sliding down has her whimpering. Holy fuck this is torturous holding myself back from her, but it's exquisite torture. By the time I crawl onto the bed and kneel between her spread legs she's practically vibrating with anticipation. I deliver a sharp smack to her ass that makes her squeak. It wasn't enough to hurt, but enough to leave my red handprint on her creamy skin. I store the mental image for later.

Before she can ask for more, I slide a finger through her slick folds. "Already wet for me, angel?"

"Yes, sir," she whines.

"You want my hands on you? You want my cock in your tight little cunt?" I push a finger inside her snug heat and her back bows.

"Y-yes!"

I lean over her, lips brushing against her ear. "You're going to get it, baby. Over and over again."

She smiles and I rest my lips on her temple while I play with her pussy, curling my finger inside her the way she likes while I tease her needy clit. I bring her to the edge.

And then I leave her there.

She whines with frustration until I drive my cock inside her, holding on to her hips while I bottom out. She cries out, the pain taking a little edge off her pleasure, enough to allow me to fuck her hard for a few minutes before she's teetering on that edge again.

I stop before we both come, easing my cock out of her trembling pussy. I give her another sharp smack before sinking back in. She moans, part ecstasy part she-hates-my-guts. Her pussy walls contract around my length, milking the precum from my crown. I collect some of her arousal with the tip of my pointer finger and circle her asshole. "I'm going to take you here when you're ready."

I inch the tip inside her, just enough for her to feel the burn. She cries out, throwing her head back and bucking her hips, chasing the orgasm I'm not going to allow her. Holding her still with my free hand, I drive my hips once more and empty my release inside her, roaring out my relief as I do.

She's trembling, filled with a desperate need to come. "I'm sorry, Lincoln," she whimpers. "Please?"

I slide my spent cock out of her and watch my cum drip from her pink pussy entrance. Then I lean over her, pressing her flat to the bed with my weight. "I know you are, baby, but we're only just getting started."

CHAPTER 35
IMOGEN

Every single cell in my being is screaming for relief. My body feels like it's trying to claw its way from my insides out. I'm trembling. Shaking. Crying. Delirious with need and frustration.

I beg him over and over and he refuses to take pity on me. Instead he sinks his fingers and then his cock into me, over and over and over again. Relentless and persistent. We're both covered in sweat. His cum is dripping out of me. I'm slick with my own arousal as he continues to bring me to the edge of oblivion time and time again without letting me fall. Keeping me dangling on the edge of that sweet precipice of release.

I try to touch myself but he bats my hands away. Tears squeeze from the corners of my eyes. This is torture. Actual torture. Worse than when I used to have to kneel on the gravel driveway for hours at a time. Worse even than the punishing strokes of my grandfather's belt. Worse, because I know the sweetness of the relief that's always a mere whisper away. And he withholds it from me. Brute!

"Fuck, angel," he grunts, spilling his seed in me once more. His hips still and I choke out a sob.

He nuzzles my neck softly, while gently unwrapping my legs from around his waist. Then he brushes his fingertips over my cheek, and it's so tender, so at odds with the way he keeps denying me what I need most that I want to bite off his hand.

"How are you doing there?" He's smirking. Asshole!

"I hate you," I pout, no longer caring about offending him. I don't want to be his perfect little anything anymore. I would kick him in the balls if my legs weren't currently made of rubber.

"That's okay. Will you ever disobey me again?"

"Just because you're old enough to be my father, doesn't mean you get to treat me like a child!" I snap, fraught with frustration and pent-up desire.

He lets out a dark laugh. "Oh, I like it when you're feisty, angel." He presses his lips to my ear. "And you are definitely all woman, Imogen, but you still haven't answered my question."

His gaze burns into mine while he waits for my answer. I can't lie. Hate it. I should though. For nothing if not self-preservation. "Maybe," I admit, bracing myself for his fury. Because if this was a test, then surely I just failed it.

But instead of a rebuke, he presses a soft kiss on my forehead. "That's my good girl."

I'm clearly too dazed and confused to understand what that was about. How does disobeying him make me a good girl? Maybe my brain is suffering from a dopamine shortage. Surely it can't do you good to have all that unleashed adrenaline and ecstasy charging around your system. Like a soda bottle that's shaken and the fizz has nowhere to go. What happens? Will it all just explode out of me? I wonder if anyone has ever actually died from orgasm denial.

Lincoln pushes himself up and heads to the restroom, emerging a little while later with a wet washcloth. I already suspect its warm and soothing, but I hate him all the same. "I don't need you to clean me up. I can do it myself," I huff.

"If that's what you want." He tosses it to me and it lands with a splat on my belly. And now I regret that, because I do want him to do it. I want his hands on me again, taking care of me, comforting me. But my stupid brain won't let me admit it. "I'll be right back."

He disappears from the room as I use the washcloth to clean the cum from between my legs. I'm done by the time he returns, carrying . . . what? Only a pair of fricking handcuffs!

"Wh-what are those for?" Surely he's not cuffing me as punishment for being a little bit stroppy after he's tortured me for the past god knows how long.

He sits on the bed beside me, a devious twinkle in his dark brown eyes. "On your front," he orders.

Anxiety knots in my stomach. I'm exhausted and sore and sad, and I just want to sleep. I don't tell him that. Instead I obediently roll onto my front. He takes my hands, brushing the pads of his fingertips over my wrists in a gentle caress before he fastens the cuffs on me. Then he pulls the duvet up over me and tucks me in.

"Why did you handcuff me?" I whisper. "Is it because I made the old-enough-to-be-my-father comment, or because I was a brat about you cleaning me up?"

He smirks. "Neither of those things. I enjoy the bratty side of you."

I suppose that's something at least, because I really like it too. "So why?"

"I wouldn't want you finishing the job I started. No telling what those hands of yours may get up to when I'm not here, is there?"

So don't go! Those words almost leave my mouth in a cry, but I rein them in just in time. He can go to hell. I hate him. Hate him and his stupid games.

"You want me to leave the lamp on?" he asks.

Tears clog my throat. He knows I like to sleep with the light on? "Yes, please."

He leans over me, dropping a tender kiss on the side of my cheek. "Good night, angel."

I don't reply, too worried my voice will betray me if I do, and I'll beg for his affection.

Begging is needy and emotional and beneath you, Imogen.

Larissa's words echo in my head. I wish that I could speak to her. I long to ask for her advice on what to do when the rules she set out for me don't seem to apply anymore. And whenever I follow them I seem to end up in trouble. And she would never want that. She would want me to thrive. She was the only person in the world to ever show me any kindness.

But now Pierre is kind to me. And Lincoln is too. When he's not being a brute. I wish I could understand what makes him tick a little more. Wish that I knew what he wanted from me, but every time I feel like I'm starting to understand him, he's cold again. And I shut down. And then he pushes me until I snap.

I need to break the cycle if I'm going to earn his trust and ever make it out of here. It's the only way I'll ever truly be free.

CHAPTER 36
IMOGEN

Everything hurts! Every single atom of my being is sore and scratchy. My shoulders are on fire from having to sleep with my arms cuffed behind my back. There's a deep dull aching in my core that feels like period cramps but definitely isn't. My eyelids hurt when I open them, blinking in the bright sunlight that creeps through the gap in the curtain.

With a groan, I push myself up and glance around the room. No sign of Lincoln, obviously. He emptied his cum in me and then left me to clean myself up. Which I know isn't entirely true; he did offer to clean me after. Doesn't negate the fact that he behaved like the spawn of Satan before that. My poor pussy throbs with the memory. My core aching with the need to climax. Maybe I shouldn't have pushed him to punish me, but it was still better than ignoring me. And he hasn't even come in here to let me out of these damn cuffs! How am I supposed to get dressed?

I ponder this question while using the bathroom, awkwardly managing to wipe myself with some tissue by squatting over the toilet bowl. I find no easy solution to my clothes dilemma though. If I owned a bathrobe, I could perhaps get it over my shoulders, but even so it would fall open. I could wriggle into a T-shirt or a tank top, but my arms wouldn't get through the holes. Perhaps I could at least slide my way into some panties. Except I'm not supposed to wear them. And after yesterday . . .

I groan with frustration and realize my only option is to go to the spawn of Satan himself and ask him nicely to uncuff me. I step gingerly outside of my room. Not that I expect anyone to be roaming the halls, but I still feel weird wandering around here naked. The door to Lincoln's bedroom is open so I figure he must have gone for breakfast. He's not in the kitchen though, and thankfully neither is Pierre, who I would be mortified to find me wandering the hallways naked and cuffed. A little further exploration leads me to the conclusion that Hellspawn is in his study in the library.

He simply lifts his head from his laptop when I enter, unsurprised to see me in my current predicament in his doorway. Well, of course he's not, seeing as how he's responsible for said state.

I summon all my good breeding and in as polite a tone as I can muster, I ask, "Could you please remove my cuffs, sir?"

He sucks on his top lip and stares at me, like he's considering my request. For a second, I'm worried he might actually refuse, but he gets up from his chair, pulls a key from the pocket of his pants and undoes the lock.

I shrug away from him, rubbing at my sore arms to try and encourage blood flow. They ache so much I want to cry. Although if I'm honest, it's not the physical pain that makes me want to cry, it's him. He left me all alone. Again. And that shouldn't hurt me, but it does. Tears burn behind my eyes.

"Do you have anything you'd like to say to me, Imogen?" he asks.

Fuck you! Obviously, I do not say that. Instead, I offer him as heartfelt an apology as I can muster, which for some reason makes him frown.

What the hell does he want from me? I don't know how to

THE AUCTION

be what he wants. I'm defiant and he punishes me. I'm obedient and he gets annoyed and pushes me away. Is he trying to break me? I want to hang my head in defeat, but I'm much better than that so I hold his glare with my own. I'm done playing his ridiculous games. I'm done trying to be who I was taught I had to be. I'm done being whoever Lincoln wants me to be.

I'm done. Lincoln Knight won't break me. Not now. Not ever.

CHAPTER 37
LINCOLN

She apologized. After I fucked her with no remorse and then left her alone in handcuffs, she *apologized* to me. I may have fucked this test of mine up. Except, *she's* there. Hiding beneath the veneer of obedience is the woman I'm searching for. The one full of fire and determination. The one desperate to tell me to go fuck myself.

Just a little more prodding and she'll come out to play.

It would be so easy to simply tell Imogen all of the things I'd like her to be and do. I could tell her that I'd like her to stop calling me sir because she thinks she has to, or that I don't want her to agree with everything I say. I don't want her to follow all my rules, and not only because I enjoy punishing her for any infractions far too much. I long for her disobedience. For her fire. And it pains me to see her so confused while she tries to figure out what I want from her, when all I want is whoever she truly is.

But I'm not sure she knows who that person is, and if I tell her who I think she is, then I risk her becoming the person I want her to be, and not her true self at all. Because as much as I *think* I see glimpses of the real Imogen, the one I love to touch and kiss and defile, perhaps that's simply another construction and not her at all. And if don't have the real her, then this is all meaningless. I cannot have a relationship with someone who believes she's my property and acts accordingly. I want a partner who has agency, one who isn't afraid to tell me no. Because if I don't have that, then I will never truly have her love or her respect.

"Is there anything else?" I ask.

Her face is unreadable once more and her armor is back in place, but she's fighting to keep it intact. The cracks are forming, spiderwebs appearing across her perfectly constructed veneer. "Should there be, sir?"

"You seem like you have something else you'd like to say to me. I'll remind you that you can speak freely in this house, Imogen. You're free to be yourself."

"Free to touch myself too, sir? Isn't that what you said?" The fury in her is desperate to spill out. But the way she maintains that calm steady tone to her voice is incredible. She's incredible.

I suppress a smile. "And you are, angel. But when you're being punished, I'm going to do everything in my power to see that punishment through. I didn't say you couldn't get yourself off. I simply made it more difficult for you to do so."

She elevates her chin ever so slightly but she doesn't press the point further. Instead, she raises another. "I don't like being made to walk around the house naked. It's degrading," she says, color saturating her cheeks.

I lean back in my chair, studying her face intently. Does she actually feel degraded or is she playing me? She's a mistress of manipulation. Like me, a product of her environment—raised to survive using whatever means at her disposal. While I don't hold that against her, it does make me much more cautious of her motives. There's the faintest tremble to her bottom lip before she schools her expression once more. She is either the most incredible actress I have ever encountered or she's telling me the truth.

"Why is it degrading?"

Her nostrils flare, but the rest of her body language remains unbothered—passive. "Why is it degrading to be forced to walk around this house naked?" There's only a hint of accusation in her tone. What comes out of her mouth is always more difficult for her to control than her body.

I sit forward, resting my forearms on my thighs. I'm close enough now to touch her, but she doesn't show any outward signs of discomfort. The only movement is the gentle rise and fall of her chest and the occasional flutter of her eyelashes against her cheeks.

"Yes, why? There's only Pierre and I here. As you are well aware, he cannot see you, clothed or otherwise, and I . . ." I reach out and slide the palm of my hand over her outer thigh. Her skin is cream silk, soft and yielding. So easily marked. "I have already committed every inch of your body to memory."

Her breath hitches almost imperceptibly. "Regardless, it's humiliating." Her dark green eyes hold mine captive.

If she is indeed humiliated, then it's not something I seek to prolong any further. I stand abruptly, and still she doesn't flinch. Still so well-behaved. Her pupils blow wider, and again I cannot tell whether it's from fear or desire. Her years of conditioning make it hard for even me to read her. In that way, we're perfectly matched.

I unbutton my shirt and her eyes wander, following the path of my fingers as I unhook each button. I slide it off and then slip it over her arms, the soft cotton gliding across her skin like silk over marble.

She stares into my eyes while I fasten the buttons and I find I'm unable to look away. I am captivated by her. Innocence and seduction. Strength and vulnerability. She's had to harden her heart to the cruel world she was raised in, but yet her capacity for compassion is unmatched. Despite how much I shouldn't want her, and how utterly wrong this is, I cannot stop whatever is unfolding between us.

Purposely, I leave the top few buttons open, enough to leave the valley between her breasts exposed. When I'm done, I slide my hands over her arms, kneading the muscles likely stiff and sore after last night, and feeling the warmth of her skin blooming beneath my hands.

"Thank you," she says, her breath dusting over my skin. The rosy-pink hue of her cheeks deepens to a cherry red—she couldn't control that if she tried. Her blushes are always real, even if nothing else is.

"Now that you have some clothes, will you join me for some breakfast?"

The faintest smile pulls at the corner of her mouth. "Yes, sir."

"What would you like to eat?" I ask her when we get to the kitchen.

She glances around. "Where is Pierre?"

"He's taken the day off."

"I didn't realize he took time off."

I know he's mentioned his family to her during one of their movie evenings, so I'm not breaking any confidence when I reveal where he is. "Today is the anniversary of his wife's and daughter's deaths and he always spends it alone, locked in his room with a bottle of French cognac."

Her eyes fill with tears. "Oh, that must be so hard for him."

I adore her compassion for others, and also that she doesn't assume she can help him or offer to go check on him. Pierre has dealt with his grief the same way on every anniversary since their death, and if he ever has the desire to change that, he knows I'm always here for him. I never travel on this day for that very reason. And I'm sure he knows that Imogen would be there for him too.

I wipe a stray tear from her cheek. "Breakfast?"

"Um." She presses her lips together. If she says oatmeal, I'll put the cuffs on her again and force feed her some pancakes and bacon. "How about waffles? I know how to make them if you don't. Pierre showed me."

Waffles? Not oatmeal. There's my good girl. Perhaps my test helped more than I realize. I would wrap her in my arms and kiss her right now, but that would likely lead to something other than breakfast. "I know how to make them. Can you brew some fresh coffee?"

"Uh-huh." She heads to the cupboard and hums to herself while she makes coffee and I gather up the ingredients for waffles.

"You like waffles too?" she asks.

"Not especially, but I eat them on occasion," I tell her.

"Oh." When I glance over at her, she's frowning into the coffeepot.

"Why does that surprise you?"

"It's just . . ." She purses her lips, and just like that she's clamming up again.

I suppress a sigh and I walk over to her, pulling her into my arms. I grip her chin and tilt her head up. "You don't have to think about your answer, Imogen. I want to hear the truth. Always."

"I don't lie," she whispers.

"Okay. But not lying is different from being truthful. Do you understand what I mean?"

"I guess so."

"So why are you surprised that I don't love waffles?"

"You just looked, I don't know, a little happy when I suggested them. I assumed you really liked them, is all."

Maybe I did let a little of my relief about the oatmeal slip out and onto my face. "I was happy with your choice, but not because I love waffles, because you hate oatmeal."

"I don't hate it," she protests. "It's edible."

"Only edible? So why do you eat it?"

"It's healthy and nutritious," she repeats that mantra that someone, probably Larissa, drilled into her head.

"So is fruit and yogurt, eggs, whole wheat toast. Even waffles."

She blinks at me. "I didn't realize my eating oatmeal was a big deal to you."

I shake my head. "It's not the oatmeal. It's that you do what is expected of you, Imogen, even when you don't want to. All the damn time."

"You don't think I should do what's expected of me?"

I pinch the bridge of my nose. How did waffles and oatmeal get this complicated? "Sometimes it's okay to say no. To push back when you don't like doing something. To tell someone to go fuck themselves if they make an absurd rule that makes you feel uncomfortable."

She bites down on her bottom lip, her green eyes widening as she stares up at me. She visibly steels herself before speaking. "I don't like not wearing panties. I like panties."

Despite not wanting to show her my reaction, I can't help the shit-eating grin that spreads across my face. "Then, you're free to wear panties whenever you like."

"Seriously?"

"Seriously."

Her brows pinch in a frown as she fails to hide her reaction, another layer of her armor slipping away. "So the no-panty thing was some kind of test?"

"Not exactly a test. An exercise designed to encourage you to speak up for yourself."

Her frown intensifies, and she appears deep in thought now. "But you punished me."

"Well, that was just for fun." I slide my arms around her waist, holding her close. "I'll still make you some rules to break, baby. I'll push you, especially when it comes to your body, and I'll enjoy punishing you, but I'll never hurt you."

A rough sigh escapes her as she takes a moment to consider what I just said. "I think I understand. But, if I can wear panties, what about your *access*, sir?"

"Do you really think a pair of panties will stop me?"

She wraps her arms around my neck and presses her beautiful tits against my bare chest. "No," she purrs. Her breath is warm on my face, her scent addictive and intoxicating. I fucked her three times last night and I still want her again.

"I'll make us waffles and then I'll reward you for telling me the truth about what you want. How does that sound?"

Her breath catches in her throat. Still so curious and naive, and that's something I hope she never loses. "Wh-what's my reward, sir?"

I nuzzle her neck, cock already aching for her. "As many orgasms as you can handle, angel."

CHAPTER 38
LINCOLN

I feel her eyes on me the entire time I'm clearing away the breakfast dishes, like a seductive caress on my skin.

"I would have been happy to do that," she says.

"I know that. But I'm perfectly capable of clearing some dishes." I enjoyed cooking for her, even though it's something I rarely do. Surprisingly, I enjoy taking care of her in the smallest of ways, especially as I'm sure she never had much of this in her life before.

When I'm done, she's still watching me, her eyes raking hungrily over my body. I crack my neck and smirk at her. "Was there something else I was supposed to do after breakfast?"

She squeals, her face lighting up with happiness. "My reward?"

Dammit, I feel things for her that go way beyond sex, beyond my need to protect her. She's unraveling me inch by inch and I have no desire to stop her. I scoop her up from her spot on the stool and bring her to her bed. I could have done what I had planned on the kitchen counter, or the table, but the bed will be more comfortable for her. And this will be all about her. I lay her down, spreading her legs wide open for me.

She bites down on her luscious lower lip, making me want to do the same.

Gently I swipe my finger through her pink swollen folds and she winces. "Are you sore, baby?"

"Yes, sir. But I'm okay." Her lower lip wobbles. I'm sure she's thinking she's going to miss out on her reward, but that's not going to happen. It's my reward too.

I press a reassuring kiss on her lower abdomen. "Relax. I'm not going to fuck you, but I'm still going to take care of you."

"But I want you to fuck me, sir," she whimpers.

I crawl over her and nuzzle her neck. "You're a good girl for telling me what you want and for admitting that you're sore, but right now, I'm going to ask you to trust me, angel. If I fuck you, it will hurt. Not like before. It will be worse. Even though you're wet. Even though I know you want me to."

My fingers work through the buttons of her shirt—my shirt—and I open it wide, exposing her beautiful body. The curve of her hips, her flat stomach, her luscious tits, begging to be bitten. Seeing her in my clothes spikes the possessive need in me. A contrast between the familiarity of it and the animalistic claiming of her by wrapping her in something that's mine. I trail kisses over her collarbone, down to her pert nipples. I lavish one with attention, flicking the peak until it hardens further in my mouth, before moving to the other.

She winds her fingers in my hair, pulling at the roots while she writhes beneath me. Desperate and eager. So fucking needy and sweet. "Lincoln," she whines.

Unable to deny her any longer, I move lower. The scent of her pussy already has my mouth watering, feral to taste her. I've thought about eating her cunt for so long, aware it's likely to be the final nail in my coffin. Fucking her senseless is one thing, but burying my face in the most intimate part of her, having her fall apart on my tongue . . . that's going to be my undoing. There's no going back once I do this. My ruin will be entirely complete.

THE AUCTION

She whimpers when my breath dusts over her clit. "Please. I need you inside me."

"I promise this will feel just as good, baby. Trust me."

I flick my tongue over her swollen bud and she cries out my name, her hips almost shooting off the bed. I suppress a laugh at her response, directing all my attention to the bundle of nerves controlling her entire body right now. I suck her clit into my mouth, letting her sweet taste overwhelm me. She tastes like salt and honey and sin.

She shrieks. "Wh-what was that? What are you doing?"

"I'm eating your pussy."

"That's a thing?"

This time I don't bother to hide the laugh that tumbles out of me, my lips still pressed against her flesh, sending vibrations through her that make her tremble in a whole new way that makes me even harder. Oh, it's a thing. A thing I plan on doing a lot of. I direct my attention to her entrance, lapping at the arousal already seeping out of her before slipping my tongue inside her.

"Oh, Linc!" she moans, bucking her hips and riding my face until I'm forced to hold her still with my hands on her waist before she gives herself chafe burns from my beard. "That feels so good."

Tastes so good too. I could spend hours eating this pussy, and I would if she weren't so tender. I move from her entrance to her clit, lavishing her cunt with careful attention. And she's so on edge, all her nerve endings still worked up from last night, that she climaxes easily—her cum rushing out of her and soaking my beard. I drink up every drop I can, wishing I could sink my aching cock into her but knowing I can't.

She protests that she's too sensitive to go again. I'd usually push her past that point until she comes on my face once more, but I really do want to fuck her tonight, so I acquiesce and move back to her nipples, sucking and biting on each one. She grinds herself against me, chasing another orgasm already.

"You're so needy, angel," I tell her.

"I'm sorry," she says, a tremor in her voice that stops me in my tracks.

I stare into her beautiful face. "That is absolutely nothing to be sorry about, baby. I fucking love it."

She gives me a faint smile. "You do?"

"You think I *don't* love you being desperate for my cock, or my fingers, or my mouth? Imogen, it's the biggest turn on ever."

"I was always told a woman being needy wasn't a good thing."

I brush back her hair and school my temper. "Forget everything you were ever told about sex and relationships, okay? Hearing you moaning my name is the sweetest sound I ever heard."

Her smile grows wider. "Can I do something for you?"

She does more for me than she will ever know. "Such as?"

She glances at my hard cock. "Take care of you the way you did for me?"

"No, baby. You don't have to do that. This was all about you."

"I want to do it though. You told me to ask for what I want, Lincoln." She sounds confident and self-assured. And I did tell her to ask for what she wants, but I can't be entirely sure I'm not simply blind to any alternative because the thought of what she's hinting at has me harder than titanium. And I can't quite get past the suspicion that pleasuring me is what she thinks I expect her to do.

She wraps her hand around the base of my shaft. "Will you show me what to do? Please?"

How the fuck can I deny her when she asks me so confidently. "You're sure?"

She nods, licking her lips. "I want to use my mouth on you."

Holy fuck! That line I just crossed seems in the distant past now that she's talking about sucking my cock. Imogen DeMotta on her knees sucking my cock. I can picture her lips stretched wide around my shaft and her bright green eyes filled with tears while spit drips down her chin. Her innocence being so beautifully defiled. I'm supposed to take care of her, and yet the thought of her taking care of me in that way is the sexiest thing in the whole fucking world. I shake the unwelcome thoughts that I'm a sick fucking monster who should be ashamed of himself out of my head, because it doesn't matter right now. All that matters is her. Her mouth. On me.

I sit up with my back against the headboard and direct her to kneel between my thighs. I pull back her hair and hold it in a ponytail and then fist my cock in my free hand. "You sure you want to do this, angel?"

She nods, her green eyes sparkling. Precum weeps from my crown. "Lick that off," I tell her.

She bends her head and sweeps her tongue over my head, making a soft satisfied murmuring sound as she tastes me while I'm desperate not to come too quickly. After the pleasure of eating her pussy, the merest flick of her tongue has my balls about ready to unload. No woman has ever made me unravel like this before. And I find myself wanting to fall apart for her. I want her to see what she does to me and fucking bask in her glory. Because she is glorious. I squeeze my shaft harder, staving off my release.

"When you're ready, take it into your mouth, baby. As far as you can go. You can suck or lick, whatever you prefer."

She does both. Wrapping those sinfully delicious lips around my cock and sucking me hard while her tongue flicks the underside of my shaft. Motherfucking fuck! I screw my eyes closed and try to think of unsexy thoughts, but her sucking noises are making it incredibly difficult. And when I open my eyes and see her spread out for me, ass up in the air accentuating the curve of her back while her head bobs up and down on my dick, I almost lose control.

Now her soft moans get louder and more desperate. "You

want to come too, baby?" I growl the words, overcome by the sight of her. She has no idea how much she undoes me.

She looks up at me, lashes wet with tears, and nods.

"Then rub your clit for me, the way I do. Pretend it's my fingers playing with your pretty little cunt."

Her hand slips between her thighs, and she keeps looking at me while she sucks my cock and plays with herself. I've never been so turned on in my whole entire life. I'm going to fucking explode.

And I do. Hot ribbons of cum spurting into her mouth and down her throat, and my good girl takes every last drop, drinking me down like I'm the only thing sustaining her. The appreciative little noises she makes have my eyes rolling back in my head.

When she releases me, spit and cum dribble from her mouth. It is the sexiest thing I have ever seen. She's goddamn perfect. She takes her hand from between her thighs but I know she didn't come yet. So, I pull her up to straddle me and take her fingers, guiding them over her sensitive flesh.

"Like this, baby." I press firmly against her fingertips, and push them against the swollen bundle of nerves.

"God, Linc," she whimpers. "That's so good."

I rest my lips against her hair, inhaling the scent of her mango-scented shampoo. My free hand cradles the back of her head while I go on guiding her fingers over her slick bud. Her breathing grows shallower, her body goes rigid, and then my girl falls apart. A cry rips from her throat and she buries her face into my neck, hot tears falling onto my skin. "You're okay. I've got you." I wrap her still-trembling body in my arms.

Only when she stops shaking, do I tip her chin up so I can look at her face. I swipe the remaining tears from her cheeks with the pad of my thumb. "You still with me?"

She nods, smiling. "Yes. Did I do good?"

THE AUCTION

It takes me a second to realize what she's referring to. "Baby, I just came so hard in your pretty little mouth I almost passed out. What do you think?"

Her grin grows wider. "I think I did good."

"You did incredible. You are incredible."

She sighs and snuggles against my chest, her fingertips lightly tracing over my scars in a way that surprisingly doesn't bother me at all. "Can we lie here for a little while?"

I kiss the top of her head. "If that's what you want."

We enjoy a few moments silence before she speaks again. "Thank you for teaching me so much about sex and my body, sir. You must have had a lot of practice."

"Imogen, if you're fishing for information, I would prefer you simply ask whatever is on your mind." This is a new dynamic for both of us, given that I've never allowed a woman to be this close to me before, either physically or emotionally. But I'm prepared to risk her asking questions I can't answer for the promise of her being more assertive and direct.

She hesitates and then asks, "How many sexual partners have you had?"

"Too many to count."

"Oh." I can't see her face, but she sounds saddened by that.

"I'm forty-two years old, angel. I have a past and it's not one I'm particularly proud of. Would you rather I lied about my sexual experience?"

"No. I was just . . . Were any of them serious?"

"No. Mostly women I hooked up with for one night."

She chews on her lip. "Have you ever bought a woman before?"

Anger burns hot and explosive in my chest. I hate that she thinks that I'd do that, even though she has every reason to. It's not like she knows why she's been such a brilliant, painful exception. I bought her, after all. "No."

"Lincoln," her voice is small and quiet. "Why did you buy me?"

Because I once promised someone I loved like a brother that I'd always protect you, no matter what the cost. That's the truth and she deserves to know that, but it would reveal the truth of my identity, and then she would know I am the monster everyone believes I am. I don't care what anyone else thinks of me, but I cannot bear for her to know what a sick piece of shit I truly am. So, I tell her another truth.

"Because I wanted you, angel."

CHAPTER 39
IMOGEN

I wake alone despite Lincoln being here when I fell asleep. It's been the same for the past seven nights. He holds me after sex, and sometimes we talk for a little while. He's always there when I drift off, but never here when I wake. A small wave of sadness washes over me, because it would be nice to wake up next to him. Perhaps curled up beside him, or with his chest at my back and his arms around me. I've spent most of my life on my own and I have always been perfectly content with my own company, but now there's Lincoln. And though I've never woken up with anyone before, I'm sure it would be wonderful.

I slip out of bed and turn on the shower, grabbing the new bottle of shower soap he bought me yesterday on his trip into town. He brought me a whole fresh supply of toiletries even though I still had plenty left of the others. This time, I noticed that he chose fragrances I've mentioned liking, such as jasmine and wildflower. And that he thought of me when making those choices, knowing that he listens when I speak, makes me feel cherished in a way I never have before.

Freshly showered, I make my way to the kitchen, meeting Lincoln in the upstairs hallway. Immediately he pulls me into his arms and runs his nose over my still-damp hair.

"Good morning, angel."

"Good morning, sir."

He growls, actually growls, then he takes my hand in his and leads me down the stairs to where Pierre is preparing some kind of pastry.

"What is it to be this morning?" Pierre asks with a smile. He was quiet for a couple of days after the anniversary of his wife's and daughter's deaths, and both Lincoln and I were there for him in all the ways he allowed us to be—if only with kind words or allowing him space when he seemed to need it. And on one occasion he even allowed me to give him a hug, which I cherished every second of. But he has been his usual pleasant, if bitingly sarcastic at times, self again since.

"My usual," Lincoln tells him.

"And for you, mademoiselle?"

"Can I try some eggs and toast too?"

Pierre declares his agreement and Lincoln goes to the counter, and as has become our new morning routine, he pours us each a coffee.

"Can you fetch me some eggs from the pantry, mademoiselle?"

"You know you should think about keeping chickens," I say, stepping into the pantry.

"Chickens?" Lincoln asks, an amused tone to his voice.

I pop my head out of the doorway. "Yes. You eat so many eggs and you have plenty of room." I've always wanted a pet, and chickens wouldn't *just* be pets; they'd be useful too.

"And who would look after the feathery little devils?" Pierre scoffs.

"I would! I'd love to look after chickens. I promise I'd take really good care of them. You wouldn't even know they were there."

Pierre hums softly, a rascally look on his face. "And we could roast them. They are delicious with the right sauce." He smacks his lips together.

THE AUCTION

"Pierre, no!" I shriek.

"Where do you think chicken comes from, mademoiselle? If not from a chicken?" He throws his hands in the air.

"But these would be different. I'd know them."

"Ah, you would name them all, wouldn't you? Silly *mon chou*." He chuckles and shakes his head.

Lincoln claps him on the back. "If Imogen gets some chickens, you cannot put them in a sauce, old friend."

Pierre grumbles but I can't help smiling so widely that my cheeks hurt. Lincoln didn't say no. In fact, he seemed totally open to the idea. Maybe one day, when I've cleared plenty of space in the garden, I'll officially ask him if we can get some—a chicken proposal. He's always telling me to ask for what I want, after all.

I head deeper into the pantry, searching for eggs when I notice the box on the shelf. A large box of Milky Way bars. It makes my throat clog up with emotion. As a child who was never allowed candy, I enjoyed the bars that Lincoln bought me a few weeks ago immensely. But I didn't dare ask for any to be added to the monthly grocery shop. I've never seen them in the pantry before, and to find them now and know that once again Lincoln has thought about my needs, makes me feel overwhelmed with happiness. I grab the eggs and make my way back to the kitchen.

Lincoln hands me my coffee and I smile at him. He gives me a half smile back, running a hand over his jaw. He never attempts to hide his scars now, and I don't notice them either. Well, not any more than I notice the rest of him. They remind me of how similar we are, that we've both endured and are still standing. And they're simply a part of his face—the most handsome face I've ever seen. "You bought Milky Ways?"

He blows on his coffee. "You said you liked them."

"Thank you, Lincoln." I feel the blush creep over my cheeks at the use of his name, which I usually only reserve for the bedroom.

He drops a soft kiss on the top of my head. "You don't have to thank me for food, angel."

"HOW WERE YOUR EGGS AND TOAST?" LINCOLN asks.

I glance at my almost-empty plate. I've been experimenting with different foods all week and trying to decide what I actually enjoy eating, which for some reason seems to have pleased both Lincoln and Pierre. "Very filling and quite tasty. Still not as good as waffles though."

He gives me that wonderful half smile.

"Maybe we could both have waffles tomorrow?"

"I have to leave tonight, angel."

I try my best not to look disappointed but obviously don't do a good enough job. I glance down at my plate so he doesn't see the tears burning in my eyes. I've never been a crier, and yet here I am welling up at him leaving. It's weak and against everything I was ever taught, but I can't help it. He cups my chin, tipping my head until I'm forced to look at him.

"What's with the sad face?"

"I'll miss you."

He leans across the table and dusts his lips over mine. "You have no idea how happy it makes me to hear you say that, angel. And I'll miss you too."

If missing him makes me weak, then that would mean he's weak too, and Lincoln Knight is definitely not weak. "Why do you have to go away so much?"

He grinds his jaw. "It's what I do."

"Like your job?"

"Kind of. It's hard to explain."

"I'm sure I'm smart enough to understand." I regret the sassy remark as soon as it leaves my mouth, but it only makes him give me that lazy grin of his. I've come to realize he likes my feisty side, which is a good thing, because I really like it too.

"You most definitely are, angel. One day I'll tell you, but for now . . . Let me just do what I do, okay?" His dark eyes burn into mine.

"You're not going to another auction are you?"

He pushes back his chair and walks around the table before dropping to his knees and taking both my hands in his. "I swear to you that you are the only person I have ever paid for, Imogen DeMotta. And believe it or not, I did that to protect you."

I brush away the tear that leaks from the corner of my eye. "I do believe that, Lincoln." That's true, even if I don't understand it.

He rubs the pad of his thumb over my lips. "I like when you call me Lincoln."

"I like calling you that too."

He smirks. "Like it even better when you call me Linc."

My skin flushes with heat. I only ever call him that when he's teasing me, or making me orgasm. "Can I still call you sir too?"

He kisses me softly. "Call me whatever you prefer, angel."

"I like when you call me angel."

He kisses me again. "You are my angel."

My entire body is singing with happiness and contentment. I love this feeling of being able to be so open with him. I adore being able to show my desire for some affection and him simply enjoying offering it with no agenda. "I love it when you call me baby too."

He growls when he kisses me one more time, and the sound rumbles through my bones. "I have to go prep for my trip, but I'll be done by this afternoon and I'll make you moan all the names you call me before I leave, baby. How does that sound?"

"That sounds perfect, sir."

CHAPTER 40
IMOGEN

I decided to take a long soak in the bath this afternoon, another luxury I've found I really enjoy, especially with the decadent bubble bath Lincoln found for me. When I've soaked long enough that my skin is wrinkled like a prune, I find Lincoln in my bedroom waiting for me. He's already dressed in the black cargo pants and tight black tee he always wears when he leaves on one of his expeditions, and he's sitting on the floor with his back to the wall. The huge antique mirror has been turned so it's facing him, which is odd as he doesn't usually like looking at himself. I also spy a black velvet-covered box on the floor beside him that piques my curiosity. He grabs the pillow from behind his back and places it between his spread thighs.

Then he pats it. "Come sit here, angel."

I do as he asks, excitement fluttering low in my belly.

He takes off my towel and hooks my legs over his own, spreading them wide while he drapes my damp hair over my shoulder. The two of us are reflected in the antique mirror and I marvel at how small my body looks against his and how my olive skin is pale against his midnight-black clothes. He rests his lips against my ear. "I have a gift for you."

"A gift?" More excitement. I can't recall the last time anyone ever gave me a gift for no reason before I arrived here and now this is my third in two months. More if I count the new bubble bath and the Milky Ways.

Lincoln hums, warm breath dancing over my skin and making goose bumps break out over my flesh. "Yes, but before I show you your gift, I want to teach you a little about this beautiful body." He spreads my legs wider with his own. "So you're going to watch in the mirror while I play with your sweet cunt, and we're both going to learn a little more about exactly what you like." Taking my hands, he places them behind my back and then wraps one arm around my waist.

Then he glides the pads of his fingers between my folds and spreads them open. It feels wicked and dirty to look at myself this way, and to enjoy watching his expert fingers manipulating my flesh, but I'm too transfixed to look away. "Look at this pretty pink pussy. Already wet for me."

"Linc," I whimper, watching every move he makes in the mirror, excitement shuttling through my veins.

"I know, baby." He circles his fingers, concentrating on the swollen bud of flesh. "You already know this is your clitoris, yes?"

I gasp, pleasure already coiling deep in my core. "Yeah."

I go on watching him in the mirror, hands moving methodically and skillfully over my sensitive center. "Did you also know it's not just this part here you can see, the nerve endings run deep, and even here . . ." He swirls a fingertip nearer to my entrance. "This is all part of your clit, baby. And you're particularly sensitive right here." He presses gently on a spot that makes my back arch in pleasure.

"Oh, god."

"Not god, angel. Say my name."

"Lincoln," I whine, writhing against his fingers as much as I can while he holds me firmly in place.

"I want you to touch yourself while I'm away. Discover all

the places that make you purr like that. Find out what it is that brings you the most pleasure."

"You," I gasp. "The way you touch me brings me the most pleasure."

He smiles against my neck. "That makes me so fucking happy, baby, and you're such a good girl for me. So watch my hands." One of his thick fingers slides inside me, making wetness rush between my thighs and warmth pool in my core. "And right here," he says, pressing firmly against a spot deep inside me and I almost climax right here and now. "This is your G-spot. But if you're fingers aren't long enough to find it, I got you a gift to help."

Oh, yes! The gift.

He opens the box beside us, the clasp making a soft click before he takes something out. In the reflection I can tell it's a glass object. Phallic-shaped with a golf ball–sized orb at the base and ridges in the shaft. He holds it up for me to see more clearly.

"What is it?" I whisper, my cheeks flushing with heat.

"It's a dildo. I want you to use it while I'm away. I want you to slide it inside yourself and pretend it's my fingers in your juicy little cunt."

I gasp in a breath as a wave of intense euphoria washes over me. The crude way he talks coupled with the way he's still teasing my G-spot has me trembling all over and on the edge of collapse. Before I crumble, he pulls his finger out of me and I watch in the mirror as he places it in his mouth and sucks it clean, making satisfied humming sounds while he does.

My attention is drawn to the dildo again. It's smaller than him, but it's still bigger than my fingers, and it's glass. Glass can break. Glass can cut. "Is it safe?"

"Yes, perfectly safe. I would never ask you to do anything that might harm you. I bought you some lube too. Be sure to use plenty of it if you're not wet enough."

"Do we need some now, sir?"

He laughs darkly and pulls my thighs even wider apart. "Look at yourself, baby. You're fucking soaked for me. You see that sweet creamy cum already dripping out of you?"

I do see, a pearl of white seeping from my entrance. Evidence of how much my body enjoys this, even if my conditioning sometimes tries to tell me that I shouldn't. I focus on my body, and on the pleasurable sensations swirling inside me. "Yeah."

He notches the head of the toy at my entrance. "So we won't be needing any lube. If you can take my fingers and my cock, you can take this." Then he pushes it inside me, and I gasp at the foreign sensation of the glass—cold and rigid. So different to the comforting heat of Lincoln. He sinks it all the way in, keeping a firm grip on the base and pleasure rockets up my spine. "Are you going to think of me when you use this on yourself?"

"Y-yes, sir."

"Will you think of me every time you make yourself come?"

"Yes!"

"Tell me what you're going to play with while I'm gone."

I stare at his reflection in the mirror, confused as to what exactly he's referring to.

He growls in my ear. "I want to hear you say the word, angel. What am I fucking right now?" He drives the dildo in deeper.

A blush creeps across my cheeks. "My p-pussy, sir."

He smiles at me in the mirror. "That's my good fucking girl."

"Linc!" I throw my head back.

"Eyes on me, baby. Watch me fuck you with your new toy."

I drag my eyes to the mirror and the sight of him working the glass dildo inside my pussy. The powerful muscles in his forearm flexing with each stroke, his free hand pressing down on my abdomen and the look of pure desire on his face, have me unraveling. It's erotic and beautiful and filthy all at the same time.

I cry out, ecstasy taking me under its heavy wave, pulling me under. Until Lincoln sinks his teeth into my neck, bringing me back to him. His hard length digs into my back and I rub myself against it, making him mutter a string of curses.

He begins rubbing my clit while driving the dildo inside me, deeper and harder each time. Until I'm on the edge once more, begging him to stop yet pleading with him to continue. It's the most delicious kind of torture there is, and watching it all unfold only makes it more special, more intense.

"You are the most beautiful creature I have ever seen, Imogen. And you look like fucking heaven when you come for me. So give me one more, baby. Give me a memory I can jerk off to when I'm not here with you."

My back bows. A cry is ripped from my chest. White-hot euphoria snakes through every vein and sinew of my body, until I'm sagging against him.

Gently, he slides the toy out of me and places it on the floor beside us. I meet his eyes in the mirror and smile. "Thank you for my gift, sir."

"You're welcome. I'm going to enjoy thinking about you using it, and then hearing all about it when I get back."

A wave of sadness washes over me. "When do you have to leave?"

He runs his nose up the back of my neck. "Soon, baby."

I wiggle my ass against his hard length. "I do love my gift, sir. But I'll miss the real thing."

He laughs once more. "My greedy little angel. Do you want my cock?"

"Yes please." More than I've ever wanted anything in my life before.

He growls and the sound sends a shiver down my spine. "Turn around."

I do as he asks while he unzips his pants and frees his huge cock. He fists it in his hand and I involuntarily lick my lips at the sight of the precum on the tip. He shakes his head. "Not your mouth today, baby. Slide yourself onto me."

THE AUCTION

With my hands on his powerful shoulders, I sink down onto his length, letting him fill me up completely. I smirk when his eyes roll back a little, enjoying the powerful feeling it gives me. He's so strong and fearsome in his black camo gear, but right now, I can unravel him with the right sway of my hips, or a squeeze of my inner walls.

"Fuck! That feels so fucking good."

It does feel good. Better than his fingers or the toy. It's incredible. I roll my hips over him, working him into a frenzy, until he grabs me and takes control, holding me still while he drives inside me over and over again. I see stars. He grunts out my name, and then his hips still as he climaxes, filling me with his release.

He pulls me close, pressing our foreheads together. "I have another gift for you." He pants for breath.

"Another?"

He hums in reply, then reaches for the black box again, flipping it open to reveal three cone-shaped metallic objects, each with a large round base set with a brightly colored jewel. There are three different sizes—ranging from the size of an egg to the size of a small apple. My eyes widen. They're so pretty. "What are those?"

His eyes darken and he brushes my hair back from my face. "They're butt plugs."

"Butt plugs. Like for your ass?"

He shakes his head, a devilish grin on his face. "No, for *your* ass." His tone is dark and serious, and laced with a little of the danger that makes me shiver. He takes the smallest one out of the box. "You'll definitely need lube for these."

"What are they for?" I whisper.

"They're to prepare your virgin ass for my cock. When you can take the biggest one comfortably, then I know I'll be able to fuck you as hard as I want to."

I take the plug from his hands and examine it closely. "I'm not sure this one will even fit."

He grins. "It will. I'd like you to wear them as much as possible while I'm away. Don't worry if you can only manage the small one for a while. I can wait."

I'm not sure I want him to wait. I want to be whatever he needs right now. And I'm even less certain about the plugs. As pretty as they are, the idea of walking around the house with one in feels naughty in a way I never anticipated. "Do I really need to use them, sir? Couldn't you just try anyway?"

"No. I know you enjoy it when I'm a little rough with you, but I won't be able to do that when I fuck your ass for the first time. And if you're not prepared properly, I could hurt you, and I would fucking hate myself for that." He takes the plug from between my fingertips. "So, will you try for me?"

I furrow my brow for a moment and nod. "Can you show me how to use one?"

His eyes flash with wicked intent. "Bend over my lap."

I climb off him and lie over his lap, my ass in the air and my face on the carpet. He tells me how sexy and incredible I am while he coats the smallest plug with a generous amount of lube from a squeeze tube that was also in the black box.

"Breathe, Imogen. I won't hurt you, okay? But tell me if it's too much."

I take a deep breath and he pushes the pointed tip of the plug at the entrance of my ass. Instinct makes me want to shuffle forward and away from the intrusion, but I remain in place, wanting to do this right for him.

"You're doing so well. You're such a good girl for me."

I lap up his praise, my entire body practically purring with contentment as he pushes the plug deeper. It feels strange. So very full. But I don't dislike it.

"Almost there, angel," he soothes, pushing deeper.

The stretch burns but I take another deep breath and the burning sensation stops. Leaving me with a deep ache in my core. The kind that I've come to love and the kind that makes my panties wet. I'm not sure how long I'll be able to wear a plug without him here to relieve me. He glides his hands over my ass. "How does that feel."

"Kind of nice actually."

He smiles. A real, genuine smile that makes his eyes crinkle at the corners. "You truly are my perfect little angel."

"Thank you, sir."

He pulls me to straddle him again, sliding his arms around my waist. "I wish I didn't have to leave you."

"I wish that too, sir."

He dusts his lips over mine. "I'll be back Sunday evening."

That's four nights without him. I let my mask slip for a moment, let him see the sadness in my eyes before I pull it back up, back to where it's comfortable. I was taught that emotions are weakness, but he's made me realize that they're not. They're beautiful and messy and wondrous and life-affirming. But old habits die hard.

CHAPTER 41
IMOGEN

My fingers tremble as I spread my legs wider, imagining Lincoln were here with his strong hands on my thighs, pushing them apart. The ache between them has grown impossible to ignore. Lincoln has unleashed a monster in me. If I close my eyes, I can hear the feral-sounding growl he makes when he does this, which is usually closely followed by him tasting me.

There's very little in this world that feels better than Lincoln's mouth on my pussy.

I whine, rubbing my fingertips over my sensitive clit and wishing he were here with me instead. My fingers never feel as good as his. There's no replacement for the scratch of his beard on my skin, of the way his thick length fills me so completely. And this is only my second night without him.

Heat blooms deep in my core. I fumble around on the bedclothes in the dark for my gift and quickly find the smallest plug. I discard it for later, and carry on the search until my fingers grasp the base of the glass dildo. Vivid images of Lincoln using it on me yesterday before he left, and the way he forced me to watch what he was doing to me, already have wetness seeping between my thighs. I notch the head of the dildo at my entrance, guided by instinct rather than any expertise, and increase the pressure on my clit, teasing around the edges the way Lincoln does.

My legs tremble, my body craving some kind of release. But I wait before pushing the toy inside myself, denying myself in the same way he does. Dipping it an inch before pulling it out again, imagining that it's him taunting me. I feel his breath on my skin, his hands, the silky strands of his hair tickling my inner thighs.

"Linc!" I whine his name into the darkness and then sink the dildo as deep as it will go. Pleasure floods my core. Wet heat slicks over the glass toy. I slide it in and out, and the loud slurping sounds fill the quiet room. My breathing grows heavy. My fingers cramp but I push through, chasing the sweet oblivion of release. And when it comes, it's quiet and devastating and wonderful. I whisper his name into the night, hoping that somehow he might hear me and wondering if wherever he is, he's thinking about me too.

CHAPTER 42
LINCOLN

Edgar hands me a small slip of paper, an address in his familiar handwriting. "This is his home, right?"

He nods.

"Where his fucking kids live?"

Another nod.

"Sick fuck."

Edgar snorts, like we didn't know that already.

I glance at the paper again, committing it to memory before handing it back to him. Adrian Farnham. Hedge fund manager, gun lobbyist and father-in-law to the governor of Ohio. Rich enough to have security, but not enough to have the kind that can stop people like me.

"How many guards does he have?"

Edgar holds up one finger. "One at the gate."

"Cameras?"

He nods. "I'll jam the feed and disable the alarm. Just tell me when."

"Three a.m.," I tell him. Three to four is the hour when people usually are in their deepest sleep. Adrian is a fifty-three-year-old man, and his two youngest daughters are nine and twelve, so no teething babies or night-owl teenagers to consider.

He has no live-in help. His wife died a year ago, and instead of getting himself a new one, he bought himself his very own slave at an auction. I'd love to slit his throat, but that would definitely draw a whole lot of attention, so for now, he gets to live. At least if everything goes to plan. Which is to get in, get the girl, and then get out again without anyone noticing—a far cry from my last rescue.

Edgar nods his agreement, then gives me a pat on the shoulder, as much affection as I imagine him showing for anyone. "Good luck."

THE GUARD ON THE GATE IS STARING AT THE camera screens, which Edgar is about to hack into so he won't see me climbing over the back wall. I land on the ground with a soft thud and skirt the edge of the property to avoid triggering any security lights. I studied the floor plan earlier, and it's a vast house, with east and west wings. I have no idea where Lot 23 is being kept, but I suspect the basement or somewhere as far away from the kids' bedrooms as possible, which would mean somewhere in the west wing of the house.

When I get to the back door, I'm relieved when no alarms go off. Not that Edgar has ever let me down before, but it's always a point where things could go wrong. I pick the lock and get inside, making my way along the downstairs hallway and looking for the door to the basement, until I see the door that's a little different from the rest. Its handle is less worn than the others, and more alarmingly, there's a lock. I bet he tells his kids it's to keep them out, but my guess would be it's more likely intended to keep someone in.

I press my ear to the door, my breathing slow and controlled as I listen for signs of life. I hear nothing but my own heartbeat. The bastard probably soundproofed it. I slip my backpack off and take out the small silent drill and remove the lock in less than a minute. Pushing open the door, I reveal a study. A neat and tidy desk. A desktop computer. Neatly arranged bookshelves. Why the fuck does he lock his study? Does he not trust his staff? Unless . . .

I step into the room, my instincts telling me he's hiding more in here than professional secrets. There's a rug on the floor, one of those artisan ones you might see in a café in Marrakech. Hours of quiet craftsmanship woven into the rich wool, dyed in shades of purple and mauve. Very out of place in this otherwise bland office. I kick the edge up and am unsurprised to uncover a wooden hatch, a trapdoor of sorts. In order to pull the rug all the way back, I'm forced to push the desk out of the way, and as I do I uncover the entire door. It's also fitted with a lock, a thick dead bolt ordinarily hidden from view beneath the rug and desk. I slide it open and it glides easily, like new metal often does. It takes two hands to pull open the heavy hatch, which is lined with some kind of metal too—something to make it soundproof, no doubt. I shine my flashlight into the space.

It's a small concrete room, maybe six by six feet. She's inside, her knees pulled up to her chest, wearing a dirty shirt with bare legs. An empty plastic cup lies on its side beside her.

She lifts her head, eyes wide and filled with fear. She's young. Maybe eighteen. I think of Imogen, and for some reason I pull my mask down a little, resting it beneath my jaw and revealing my mouth. "Don't scream, okay. I'm here to help you."

Her lower lip wobbles. "He said no one would come."

"He lied. What's your name, sweetheart?"

"Esme." Her voice cracks, and I expect she hasn't been asked her name for a long time.

I lie on the floor, sticking my arms through the hatch and holding out a hand to her. "You can trust me, Esme. You and I are going to get out of here, okay?"

Her eyes still wide with fear, she nods. I expect she has no idea whether she's about to trade one monster for another, but I also expect there can't be much worse than spending your life locked in a tiny windowless room. I wonder how many hours a day he lets his little pet out to play for, and whether she prefers being locked in here than being with him.

Gingerly, she pushes herself up into a standing position and raises her arms. I grab onto her forearms, and lift her up, pushing up onto my knees. There's no leverage for her to use and I'm conscious of hurting her stick-thin arms. "Can you wrap your arms around my neck, Esme?"

She does so, one arm and then the other. I pull her to safety, until she's standing with her tiny body pressed against me, arms still around my neck. She blinks up at me. I gently unwind her from me and she takes a step back, her eyes darting around the room. She's barefoot, but that won't matter. My car is nearby.

"We need to get out of here, Esme."

Her eyes are still scanning the room as she stays rooted to the spot. Is she waiting for him to come for her? Maybe she thinks this is some kind of test.

I grab the edge of the hatch, ready to close it.

"Wait," she whispers.

Then she sees something, something high on a shelf. She reaches and grabs it. It's an electric shock collar, the kind assholes use on dogs to stop them from barking. She spits on it and then throws it back through the open hatch. I close it and return the rug and desk to their previous position, wishing I could see his face when he finds the lock on his door removed and watch him scrabbling to open the hatch and find his little pet is gone.

I also can't help wondering who might end up in that hellhole instead of her, and make a silent vow to ensure that nobody will. It would be a fitting death for him to be locked down there, with no food or water—let him fucking starve to death.

As soon as I'm done, I head for the study door and that's when I see the piece of paper, a page torn from a notepad and a black pen beside it. They're just sitting on top of a sideboard—a note hastily scribbled before he left the room. Perhaps his kids were calling for him? Or his housekeeper? And he was keen to get out of the room before they got inside. I can picture him, cell phone pressed to his ear as he was given the name. I see him frantically searching for something to write it on—too important a detail to risk only committing to memory.

The name sends a shiver of excitement down my spine.

Fraser Lane—a ghost from my past.

Why is his name scribbled here on a piece of paper in Adrian Farnham's office? That can't be a coincidence.

Esme snaps me from my memories, curling her cold fingers around mine. I turn to face her and am about to tell her to let go, but she looks so fucking helpless and vulnerable that I allow it. We have to leave, and fast. The last thing I need is for this to go the way of Appalachia. I pull Esme behind me, along the hallway and out of the back door, into the gardens. She takes a deep breath of air, her head tilted up to the night sky.

"We're not out of here yet, Esme. We have to keep moving."

She nods once and then follows me. Maybe it's being out here free from her prison, but the change in her is profound. She glances around us, her eyes scanning for danger and her entire body language telling me she's on high-alert. Esme might be young and vulnerable but she's far from naive, and I fucking hate that she's experienced so much hurt already in her young life. The Brotherhood steals many things, but women like Esme and Imogen prove that they can't take everything.

ESME LOOKS FIDGETY AND NERVOUS WHEN WE get to my SUV, which is to be expected, given what she's endured these past few weeks. "You don't have to get in this car. I can give you some money and you can run. Or I can take you somewhere safe and have someone help you get back on your feet."

She stares at me and then at her bare feet. "Who are you?"

"A friend."

She tilts her head to the side. "I think I trust you."

"Then get in the car and let's go."

She climbs in and I proceed to drive out of town to the spot where I've agreed to meet Edgar. I talk to her along the way, reassuring her that there's a plan. I tell her we're going to meet my friend, who's going to give her the name of a place where she can go. A place where they help women recover from traumatic experiences. Leaving Leah alone the other week really played on my mind, and Edgar contacted the CEO of the charity in Chicago we use. She's going to have some of her volunteers on hand at the safe houses from now on. Keres Sideris is committed to this cause for reasons of her own, and she would have done this anyway. But her charity just got a hefty donation from their anonymous, reclusive billionaire patron.

Edgar is waiting for us when we get to the rendezvous point. Esme climbs out of the car and leans against it, fidgeting with her long shirt. He stares at her, a strange look on his face.

What the hell is he doing? It's not like him to stare at anyone, and he's risking making her nervous. I nudge him in the ribs to get his attention and when I do, there's so much sadness in his eyes that it makes me take a step back.

And then I see it. Esme reminded me of Imogen, purely because of her wide-eyed innocence, but actually, she looks a little like my sister, Olivia. Edgar's soulmate.

Fuck, the resemblance grows more startling the more I look at her.

I grab some fresh clothes and a pair of sneakers, probably a few sizes too big for her tiny feet, from his car and hand them to her. She dresses behind the SUV and there's a tentative smile on her face when she walks back around.

I introduce her to Edgar and he regains his composure, although he's still looking at her like he's seen a ghost. She doesn't seem to mind though, appearing at ease with him. She also doesn't seem at all fazed by the fact that he's deaf and even knows a little sign language. And that makes me feel like maybe this was fate, or at least a sign from the universe that we're doing something right.

"Edgar is going to take you to that place I told you about, okay?"

She nods. "Thank you. I don't know why you came for me, but I'm so grateful that you did."

"You're welcome."

Unexpectedly, she throws her arms around my neck and gives me a soft kiss on the cheek. "You're a hero, you know that?"

"Not even close, sweetheart. Now get out of here." I turn to Edgar. "I'd prefer you both to be in Chicago before that piece of shit even realizes she's gone."

"Consider it done."

I watch them drive away, feeling better about delivering Esme to people who'll take care of her, rather than the way I left Leah. I have no idea what the fuck's gotten into me. It used to be we left them in a safe house with enough cash to start over and then I rarely gave them a second thought afterward. Now, I see *her* in all their faces, and it's making me fucking soft.

Imogen is all I can think about. My entire body burns with hunger for her. I need to get home and have her in my arms. In my bed. Sometimes, I feel like I can hardly fucking breathe without her. She's everything. The other half of my heart and soul. And it terrifies me how much I need her when there's still so much about me she doesn't know, and still so much left for me to do. It's unfair of me to drag her any deeper into my life, but I don't know how to keep her at arm's length anymore. She's burrowed herself into my heart and I never want her to leave.

CHAPTER 43
IMOGEN

It's Sunday, which means Lincoln will be home today. I've had butterflies in my stomach all day thinking about his return. Pierre scolded me for singing very loudly, and badly, while we were tending to the garden today, and then for being fidgety and excitable at dinner, although there was no bark to his tone at all. I can tell he misses Lincoln while he's away too, and he's always a little extra when he's expecting him home. We did finally finish our Marvel universe marathon though and I am still holding firm in my opinion that Black Widow is the most kick-ass Avenger ever—*especially* after *Endgame*.

Pierre retired to his room shortly after dinner. I suspect he's well aware of the change in my and Lincoln's relationship and it's probably his way of giving us a little privacy, which I'm grateful for. I came to the library to read for a little while, or at least I'm trying to, but even my comfort read of Mary, Colin and Dickon can't hold my attention this evening.

The main doors open, vibrating through the walls of the house. My heart rate kicks up and the kaleidoscope of butterflies in my belly go from gentle flutterings to a frenzied flight. I jump up, placing my book on the reading table before running out into the hallway. He's heading toward me, looking dark and dangerous, yet delicious enough to eat. He drops his bag to the floor with a satisfying thunk and our eyes lock.

Wordlessly, he crosses the hallway in a few giant strides, his onyx eyes never leaving mine. Then he picks me up, wraps my legs around his waist and presses me flat to the wall, grinding his hard length against my aching pussy while he nuzzles my neck. "Missed you so much, baby."

I throw my head back and he cradles it in time to stop me from hitting the wall. But then he takes full advantage of the better access to my neck, trailing his teeth over the delicate skin there.

With his free hand, he pulls my panties aside before sinking a finger inside me with a deep guttural growl that rumbles all the way from his chest. "Why are you always so goddamn wet for me, angel?"

Pleasure builds in my core and I whine, curling my fingers in the thick hair at the nape of his neck. "I've been wearing my plug all day, sir."

"You have?" He twists his finger, working it deeper.

"Y-yes. I worked up to the biggest one."

"Imogen." My name leaves his lips on a pained groan. "You're going to be the ruin of me, baby."

Before I can ask him what he means, he crashes his mouth against mine and kisses me so hard I struggle for breath. He goes on kissing and finger-fucking me while he carries me upstairs to my bedroom and then lies me on the bed like a princess, before sliding his finger out of me. Quickly he removes all my clothes and then he climbs off the bed, leaving me panting from the loss of his touch.

He stands over me, eyes blazing with hellfire as they rake greedily over my skin. "Spread your legs for me, angel."

Obediently, I do as he asks, aware of the wet heat dripping from my center. He watches me while he undresses, his gaze never leaving my body.

"Jesus fuck, that jeweled plug looks beautiful in your ass."

"Thank you, sir."

"And you already worked up to the biggest one?" I nod as he crawls over me, spreading my legs wider with his knees. "You know that means I'm going to fuck your ass?"

A thrill of pleasure rockets through my body. "I know, sir."

He kisses my neck, sliding his hand between my thighs and pressing against the base of the plug. "You're such a good fucking girl for me. You're aching for me to fuck you aren't you?"

"Yes!" I gasp, because it's true.

"I'm aching for you too, angel. All I could think about while I was away was you playing with your pretty little cunt and stretching your ass for me with your plugs."

He sinks two fingers inside me now and I coat him in a rush of heat. My core ignites with pleasure.

"How many times did you make yourself come while I was away?"

"I don't know. I didn't count." I pause, relishing in the growing desire evident on his face. "Was I supposed to?"

He smirks. "Did my naughty angel make herself come so many times she lost count?"

Shame and guilt wash over me. "I'm sorry, I thought that—"

He silences me with a kiss, an all too brief one. "I'm teasing you, baby. Did the toy I bought you feel good? Did you think about me when you used it?"

He keeps working his fingers in and out of my pussy while he speaks, slowly stoking the fire inside of me.

"Y-yes, I always thought of you."

He hums appreciatively. "Good girl."

"It didn't feel as good as you though, sir." I purr the last word as seductively as I'm able to, my eyes locked on his, enjoying watching his gaze grow hungrier. "It never feels as good as you."

His eyes sparkle, letting me know he's pleased about that fact even if he doesn't say it. But then he stops what he's doing and pushes himself up until he's kneeling between my spread thighs. He grabs hold of his dick, squeezing it until a droplet of precum beads on the slit. "Show me what you learned, Imogen. Play with yourself for me."

"Linc, please?" I whimper. "I want you."

He rubs the pad of his thumb over my clit. "I know, baby. You're going to get all of me very soon. My fingers and my mouth. Then I'm going to fuck your beautiful cunt and your virgin ass. But first, I want to see what my girl learned while I was gone."

Heat warms my cheeks. I didn't expect him to want to watch. He tugs his dick and curses in a language I don't understand. It's exciting and thrilling, but it also reminds me that there's so much I don't know about him. However, I don't have time to think about that too much, because the way he's looking at me, like I'm the only thing that exists in the entire world, it's all the encouragement I need to do what he just asked me to.

I slide a trembling hand down over my stomach and between my thighs, pushing his thumb out of my way before rubbing my clit. Then I glide my fingers around the edges of the swollen bud, increasing the pressure.

"Fucking beautiful," he growls. "Show me what else you did while you were thinking of me."

Biting down on my lip to stifle a needy moan, I slide my free hand between my legs now too and push two fingers inside my pussy.

Lincoln's eyes are glued to my hands as he watches me. "That's it, baby. Make yourself come for me like my good girl."

"Linc," I whimper as I bring myself closer to the edge.

He trails his fingertips up the inside of my thigh. "So fucking hot to watch my perfect girl claiming my pretty little cunt."

His words are my undoing and he knows it. He smirks when my orgasm takes me under, making my back bow and my legs tremble. I'm still quivering when he gently removes my hands and pins them above my head. "Let me taste the mess you made, angel."

Oh, my god! He trails bites and kisses down my neck, over my breasts and stomach, his throat rumbling with feral pleasure.

"Keep your hands where they are," he orders before releasing me. And then he's pushing my thighs flat to the bed, dipping his head before he flattens his tongue against my pussy and licks the length of my wet slit.

My hips buck against his face as a lightning bolt of pleasure travels though my pussy, piercing deep into my core. Whatever pleasure I'm able to bring myself, Lincoln can multiply it tenfold. Every single touch is electrifying. From the firm grip of his fingertips digging into the soft flesh of my thighs, his teeth scraping my sensitive skin, to his skillful tongue coaxing wave after wave of pleasure from me. I grab onto the pillow and suck in a substantial calming breath, but it does nothing to stop the violent tremors from wracking through my body.

"You taste even sweeter than I remember, angel," he murmurs against my skin, the vibrations from his words sending tiny shock waves through my center.

"Linc!" I whine, needy and desperate.

His teeth graze my clit and fireworks explode behind my eyes. A deep aching warmth fills my core before bursting out of the spot where Lincoln has his mouth. He sucks and licks me through every tremor, until I melt into the mattress, feeling spent and almost boneless.

CHAPTER 44
LINCOLN

"On your front, angel," I command and she slithers obediently onto her belly, giving her juicy ass a seductive wiggle as she does.

I give it a quick slap, hard enough to leave a satisfying red handprint behind and cause a yelp to spill from her lips. Grabbing hold of her waist, I pull her up until she's on all fours before climbing between her legs and spreading them wide enough for me to enjoy the spectacular view. My girl stretched open for me, jeweled plug in her ass and her pretty pink pussy dripping with her creamy cum. I take a mental picture and store it away for safekeeping. One of the many images and memories that will get me through the nights without her. I run a fingertip over the base of the plug, pushing it a little deeper inside her until her soft needy moans fill the room.

"Linc," she whimpers and the sound of my name on her lips has me feral to fuck her. My cock has been aching to be inside her from the moment I walked through the door over a half hour ago, and eating her pussy has only made me hungrier for her.

"You ready to have your ass fucked?"

She turns her head, resting her cheek on the pillow. "Yes, sir."

"You must be, huh? Working up to this plug so quickly. My needy little angel."

She nods, screwing her eyes closed and letting out a gasp when I press down harder on the plug. "Soon, baby. Going to fuck my pretty cunt first though."

I grab hold of her hips and notch the crown of my cock at her dripping entrance until she mewls. And when I sink inside her a second later, I'm flooded with relief and bone-deep pleasure. She moans my name while I grunt my satisfaction. But I'm not deep enough. Never enough. I could crawl inside her and I wouldn't be as close as I need to be. With a growl of frustration, I spread her thighs wider with my knees, stretching her as much as possible before I bottom out inside her tight heat. Keeping a firm grip on her hips, I nail her like I might never get the chance to again. Driving into her over and over again until my shaft is slick with a thick coating of her cum. Watching her cunt swallow my cock whole has me on the edge of oblivion. And she goes on moaning and whimpering, taking everything I give her without resistance or complaint.

Before I lose control, I pull out of her, leaving us both panting for breath. She grumbles a protest, but stops when I grasp the base of the plug. Her body tenses.

"I'm going to take this out now. Okay?"

She nods, her cheek brushing against the pillow. Gently, I ease the plug from her ass, watching her puckered hole close around the tip when I do. The sight alone is almost enough to tip me over the edge.

She gasps when it's all the way out. "Linc!"

I grab the lube and slather my cock with it while rubbing my free hand over her ass. "You feeling empty? I'm going to fill you up again soon."

"Please!"

Gripping the base of my shaft, I squeeze, trying to stave off the release that feels like it's only a breath away. I inch the tip inside her, causing her to arch her back and groan. "That's my good girl," I praise her while rubbing her lower back. "You did such a good job prepping your tight ass with your plugs."

"It feels so big, Linc," she whines, pushing back like she wants more. I've created a different kind of monster.

"It's bigger than the plug, baby, but you can take me." I go on rubbing soothing circles around the base of her spine while I sink deeper.

Throwing her head back, she lets out a keening moan.

Fuck, she's so hot and snug, squeezing my shaft so tightly I don't know how much longer I can hold off from coming inside her. "Your ass looks phenomenal being stretched by my cock. I wish you could see how well you take me."

"I'm your good girl, sir."

"Yeah you are." I sink deeper and she cries out, her body starting to tremble.

"You gonna come with my cock in your ass, baby?" I pull out and sink back inside. The sound she makes is indistinguishable as human. More primal, animalistic. Suppressing a laugh, I slide a finger into her dripping cunt and then I fuck her ass and pussy at the same time.

She ripples around me. Her entire body bucking and shuddering. And when she comes she cries out my name, bringing me along right beside her. My cock pulses, balls tightening, as I empty myself inside her.

She falls flat to the bed, her eyes closed and a sleepy smile on her face. When I slide out of her, she winces and I'm flooded with guilt. I just fucked her ass. A woman who I shouldn't even look at that way, and I just defiled her in every single fucking way. But I brush the guilt aside and instead ride the high of the endorphins still racing around my nervous system. Tomorrow I can beat myself up and remember what a fucking monster I

THE AUCTION

am for what I just did, but tonight, my girl needs me to take care of her.

I press a kiss on her temple. "I'm going to get a cloth and clean you up. Okay?"

"Okay," she murmurs, eyes still closed and a contented smile on her face.

Yeah, I'm going to hell, but it will be worth it for all the moments I get of heaven right here.

IMOGEN IS ALMOST ASLEEP BY THE TIME I FINISH cleaning her with the soft washcloth. I toss it into the hamper and then lie on her bed beside her, pulling her into my arms. Not ready to let her go just yet.

She sighs contentedly and I drop a kiss on the top of her head. Her eyes snap open, a clearly automatic response, and I realize that gesture usually signals I'm leaving. Her green gaze finds mine and she stares at me for the longest time before she seems to summon the courage to speak. "W-will you stay with me tonight, sir? Not just while I fall asleep?"

I should, because I just fucked her the way I did. But if I spend the night with her . . . then I'm done for. There will be no going back from this. If I get used to waking up with her in my bed, then I might never be able to let her go. And she deserves so much more than me. She deserves everything, and especially a man who doesn't hide who he truly is from her. A man who doesn't lie to her every single day. Not letting her sleep in my bed is the last line of defense we have, and I feel it crumbling into dust as we speak. "I've been away for four nights, angel. I really want to sleep in my own bed."

As good as she is at hiding her feelings, she can't mask the disappointment. And I feel like shit. I know how much it cost her to ask me that—to let me see her vulnerability. But I do want to sleep in my own bed. I brush her hair back from her face. "So will you stay with me?"

The smile she gives me in return makes any doubt I had about asking her dissolve faster than salt in hot broth. And that's how I find myself carrying a naked Imogen to my bed, tucking her beneath the covers and then falling asleep with her in my arms.

CHAPTER 45
LINCOLN

Imogen is lying on her side, drinking me in when I wake up, her green eyes sparkling and a pink flush rosy on her cheeks.

"Good morning."

"Morning, sir," she purrs seductively.

I roll on top of her, pinning her flat to the mattress. "Why are you blushing, angel?"

She wrinkles her nose and looks even more adorable doing so. "I was watching you sleep, and I thought . . ."

"Thought what?"

"You've been hard since I woke up and I thought about how good it would be to take you into my mouth, or to slide myself onto you while you were still sleeping." Her blush spreads to her ears and nose.

"That would have been the best way to wake up ever, angel. It's nothing to feel embarrassed about."

She gives a single shake of her head. "No, I mean like I thought about how it would be to have you finish inside me, while you were still sleeping. Is that messed up?"

"No." I dust my lips over hers. "It's called somnophilia. Wanting to fuck someone while they're sleeping. And still, it's nothing to be embarrassed about."

"I didn't realize it had a name. So, do you think about that too, sir?"

I shake my head. "Not exactly that, but I would like to wake you up by sinking my cock into you, or burying my face between your thighs. I would very much like you to be awake when you come though, angel. But you have my consent to suck my cock, or sink your hot pussy onto me while I'm sleeping anytime you please. I can't promise I'll stay asleep once you do though."

That adorable, sexy flush races down her neck. She makes embarrassment look so hot. "Thank you, sir."

"And as we're discussing consent, do I have yours? Can I wake you up in the middle of the night by sinking my cock into you?"

She blinks, confused. "My consent?"

"Yes. Your permission to do that, Imogen."

"But, sir . . ." Her face is etched with confusion. "You own me."

Her words are the equivalent of being doused with a bucket of ice water, or a kick to the balls. Either of those options would be more appealing right now than facing down the truth of her words. And I know she hasn't said them out of spite or malice. There was no intention to hurt, just the mere stating of a fact. Her truth. Her life. And as much as I can tell myself that she wants this, what other fucking choice have I given her? The princess locked away in this tower with only a monster and a butler for company.

I rest my lips against her forehead, drinking in her scent for the final time. This is wrong, no matter how right it feels. I have taken away her free will and the power imbalance between us will always be there. No matter how confident or assertive she becomes, to her, I will always be the man who holds her life in his hands.

And that's why this has to stop. I'm no better than the men who sold her, or her grandfather who willingly handed her over to those sick fucks. She deserves better.

Reluctantly, I push myself off and climb out of bed.

"Lincoln, is everything okay?" I can hear the pain in her voice and that only makes this harder.

I nod, avoiding her gaze while I pull a pair of sweatpants from the dresser drawer and yank them on. "You'll stay in your own room from now on, Imogen."

"What? But why? You just said—"

"I know what I said, but trust me. This is for the best. I'll leave you to get dressed."

"Sir?" She calls after me, but I've already left. Already headed down the stairs and away from the temptation of her lying naked in my bed.

I'm a sick piece of shit. Telling myself that I brought her here for her protection when I'm taking horrible advantage of her naive nature. Jesus Christ, I robbed her of her fucking innocence. I picture her blood rubbing down my palm that night in my office. That should have been enough to shock me into stopping, but no, then I took her virginity too. My own fucking . . .

"Would you like some breakfast, sir?" Pierre's voice interrupts my self-flagellation . . . for now, at least.

"Why do you insist on calling me sir?" It comes out in a snarl.

He falls into step beside me and we make our way to the kitchen. "Because I know it pisses you off."

At least he's honest.

"Anyway, which name would I use?" His voice has dropped to a whisper. "Sir is easier. Less likely to get any of us killed." He offers me a wry smile and I can't deny the truth of that. Unfortunately.

We step into the kitchen and I take a seat at the table while he makes a start on breakfast. Inevitably my thoughts drift to Imogen making her way back to her room naked. Or maybe she'll have taken one of my shirts, and maybe it will smell of her scent and therefore I'll never wash it again.

Recalling the pain and confusion in her voice when I walked

out of the room has guilt burning in my chest. She did nothing wrong and I should assure her of that fact, but it's more important for my sanity and her well-being that I just stay the hell away from her.

With that goal in mind, I ask Pierre to serve me my breakfast in my study. Making a start on the research for my next trip will be the perfect distraction. Perhaps one day I'll redeem myself enough to give Imogen the truth about our pasts. But until then, she's much better off without me.

CHAPTER 46
IMOGEN

I eat breakfast alone. Well, Pierre is nearby, but he's buttering in the pantry and stores, doing an inventory before Lincoln's next visit to town. But I feel very alone. This is my fifth day eating breakfast without him, yet today his absence is even more acute. Because the past four days he was away, but this morning he's here somewhere in this house, yet he's choosing to purposely avoid me. And that hurts me so much that it causes an actual physical ache in my heart.

Leaving me alone in his bed was so abrupt, and so unlike him to be that cruel. One minute he was lying on top of me, all fire and yearning. And then he was cold and distant. I know it was something to do with what I said about him owning me, but I didn't intend to hurt him. I was simply stating a fact, at least in that moment I was. It was only afterward that I realized to a man like Lincoln, the fact that he bought me doesn't mean the same thing as him owning my body. He's not like those other men who go to those auctions. I can understand now how hurt he would be by my assumption. He didn't bring me here to his house to use me for his own pleasure. He says he did that for my protection, and while I still don't understand the why of that, I do believe him.

"Have you eaten enough, *mon chou*?" Pierre's comforting voice washes over me. I've barely eaten anything, but I can't face food. I feel lost and desperately sad. That's what's filling me up right now.

"Yes. *Merci*, Pierre."

He busies himself clearing my plates away and I watch him for a few moments. He always seems so content, locked away here in this mansion with so little company. I used to be content that way too, in my grandfather's house, having learned to be so happy with small comforts in life from as early as I can remember. But do I want to keep doing that for the rest of my life? I used to dream that if I ever did get my freedom, I would use it to see as much of the world as I could. But for now, my world is right here, and the most vibrant part of it is refusing to talk to me.

Sliding off my stool, I bid farewell to Pierre and then I go in search of Lincoln. As expected, I find him in his study in the library, his head bent over his desk, the light from his laptop illuminating his handsome features. He doesn't look up when I walk in, nor when I wait patiently in front of his desk, as I imagine a naughty student would wait in their principal's office.

"Sir?"

He finally looks up. "What is it, Imogen? I'm busy."

Imogen? He very rarely calls me that. Usually angel or baby, the latter being my favorite. I'm sure it means something that he uses my name now instead of one of those sweet nicknames. "I'd like to know what I did wrong, sir?"

His right eye twitches. "Nothing."

I hold his gaze and summon all my courage to ask, "So why are you ignoring me? Why did you leave your bed so quickly this morning?"

His throat works. "You did nothing wrong, Imogen. I, on the other hand, have done all manner of things wrong."

"Like what, sir?"

His dark brown eyes seem to flash with anger. "Too many things to count, but most of all the things I have done to you."

What does that even mean? "Do you mean buying me from the auction?"

He shakes his head. "I don't regret that. It was necessary."

"How did you even know about that auction? I was led to believe the only men invited to such events were affiliated with the Brotherhood in some way, or at least they hoped to be."

He snarls. "I have no links with the Brotherhood. I despise them."

"I guess we have that in common, then." I fold my arms across my chest and glare at him. He seems to be growing more annoyed with my questions, but he was the one who taught me to ask instead of assuming, so I persist. "I still don't understand what you mean by what you've done wrong. What things have you done to me?"

"All of the things, Imogen. Kissing you. Touching you. Fucking you!"

His breathing is fast and hard, his eyes wild with both anger and desire, and I know exactly how he feels. Those same emotions rage through me. Lincoln looks like he might leap over his desk and fuck me right here where I stand, and I would welcome it. This push and pull between us drives me crazy with confusion sometimes, but at the same time I live for it. It makes me feel vibrant and necessary. It makes me feel alive.

"I resent the idea that those things were *done to* me, sir, and I was merely an unsuspecting participant." My tone is filled with defiance, so much of it that even I'm startled.

His jaw works, like he's visibly struggling to contain his emotions. "Regardless, they won't happen again."

His words crack open my heart, leaving me reeling. "What if I want them to happen again?" I hear the desperation in my voice now and I hate it, but I'm powerless to stop it.

"How can either of us truly know that's true, Imogen. Like

you said, I own you. There's a power imbalance here that we can never get past."

"I'm sorry I said that. I'm sorry . . ." My lips and my voice tremble.

Instantly, he pushes back his chair and stalks around the desk. Cupping my jaw in his powerful hand, he gently rubs the pad of his thumb over my lip. "You have nothing to be sorry for."

"Then why does this feel like a punishment, sir?"

His dark eyes narrow. "I can assure you that it's not. One day, you'll realize that what I'm doing is the best thing for both of us."

"I don't believe you."

His tongue darts out and he looks like he wants to argue with me. That, or kiss me, but he does neither. Instead he returns to his seat. "See yourself out and close the door behind you. I don't want to be disturbed for the rest of the day."

Anger and injustice burn through my veins. How dare he! I want to cuss at him, call him out for being a hypocritical asshole, but I clamp my lips together instead, and do as he asks. Like the obedient little pet he bought.

I DON'T SEE LINCOLN AGAIN ALL DAY, NOT EVEN for dinner, when I'm sure I'd get at least a glimpse of him. I thought about going into the library to read, but the door remained closed, and I took that as a sign he didn't want me in there.

With all of that, I'm lying in bed and it's after midnight. I heard him coming to bed about a half hour ago, hoping that he would stop by my room, if only just to say good-night. I closed my eyes and imagined him peeking inside and thinking I was sleeping, then silently tiptoeing across the room to kiss my forehead.

THE AUCTION

Of course he didn't though and I'm still lying here, wondering how things went so badly so quickly. I go over and over our last conversations in my head. How his entire demeanor changed this morning when I reminded him that he'd bought me.

And before that . . . before that we were talking about somnophilia, and consent. He asked for mine, and I made an assumption that my consent didn't matter. But I understand now that it does, to Lincoln at least. Today in his study, when I asked what he'd done wrong, he said *all the things I have done to you.* I found it odd at the time but was too caught up in feelings to really unpack that with him.

But it *was* an odd choice of words—done *to* me, not *with* me. As though I had no say in the matter? And now I realize how poorly I handled the consent conversation. Since I arrived here, he's never touched me without my permission. Never taken advantage of me. Never pushed me too far. Not once have I ever felt afraid of him. I've been mad as hell at him, like when he cuffed me and left me alone all night, but never afraid. I can't recall a time in my life before living here when I wasn't afraid.

I hurt him when I assumed my consent wasn't even on the table, because if I think about how he's behaved toward me, of course it is. And I should go tell him that, shouldn't I? Right now in fact.

I pull back the covers and jump out of bed. Then I pace up and down the room for another twenty minutes, debating the pros and cons of marching into Lincoln's room and telling him that I made a mistake. Offering him my consent of my own free will and not because of the fucked-up auction that brought us together.

I chew on a hangnail. It was Lincoln who told me to speak up for myself. He rewards me for telling him what I want. So surely, he would want me to do that now? Instead of pacing up and down my room and driving myself sick with worry. I can do this. What's the worst that can happen? He'll tell me I'm crazy and send me back to my own room again. That will hurt, but it won't be any worse than this.

With my mind made up, I leave the sanctuary of my bedroom and cross the dim hallway to his. My fingers tremble on the handle, but I summon all my courage and push the door open. He's asleep in the middle of his bed, the covers pulled up to his waist, the contours of his muscular body highlighted by the slivers of moonlight.

Not a monster at all. He looks more like an angel to me. With the exception of my father, whom I remember so little of, Lincoln is the best man I've ever known.

I tiptoe silently across the room, my eyes never leaving his sleeping form. He looks so peaceful. So beautiful. The pale light from the moon shimmers on his olive skin, making him look like he's been carved from the finest marble. He has his right arm thrown above his head, revealing the full extent of his scars. White mottled flesh covered by dark tattoos.

I'm driven by the same desire I had this morning, to sink myself onto his rigid length while he's sleeping. To unravel him using only my mouth or my body. To have him powerless beneath my touch. I peel my T-shirt over my head and drop it to the floor. Then I inch the cover down slowly, revealing his nakedness and the tip of his length. He's already semihard. Is he dreaming about me? Wishing that I'd wake him the way I told him I'd like to?

I edge closer. He did give me his consent. Anytime and anywhere were his exact words. Does that still stand now after he ignored me all day? But he didn't revoke it. And what better way to show him how much I truly want him than by initiating sex. If he's worried that I'm not able to consent, then I'll show him that I can.

My mouth waters at the memory of his taste. The salty velvet of his skin. How his length thickened in my mouth. His warm cum coating my throat.

I crawl onto the bed, careful not to wake him yet. With the flat of my tongue, I lick a path from the base of his shaft all the way to the crown. He groans. I do it again, until his cock stiffens further. Then I take him into my mouth and he bucks his hips, sinking deep into me, just like I hoped.

CHAPTER 47
LINCOLN

My cock throbs, suddenly encased in soft wet warmth, the kind that makes me let out a loud groan. If this is a wet dream, it's the most vivid one I've ever experienced.

Except I'm not dreaming. My eyes fly open, panic engulfing my entire body . . . until I see her—her dark locks tumbling over her shoulders and her head bobbing up and down on my cock. And fuck me, it feels good.

Feels incredible actually, but it's still all kinds of fucked-up.

"Imogen! What are you doing?" My voice is thick with both desire and sleep, but it's still sharp enough to make her flinch.

Slowly, she lets me slip out of her mouth, the moonlight highlighting a string of saliva connecting her pouty lips to the crown of my cock, stretching and thinning until it eventually breaks. "Tasting you, sir."

I flick on the lamp on the nightstand and immediately regret it because she's naked, and I'm not sure I'm a good enough man to resist. But even worse, her eyes are filled with so much hope, and I'm about to snuff it out. "You can't just come in here and—"

"You gave me your permission, remember?" she cuts me off, and the sudden fire in her makes my cock twitch in response. "You said I could wake you like this whenever I wanted to."

I scrub a hand over my face and try to get a handle on my frustration, while also trying to ignore my cock screaming at me to shut the fuck up and let her get back to what she was doing. "But you can't . . ." I trail off when she plants her hands on my chest.

"*This* . . ." she straddles me, sliding her pussy over my shaft and coating me with her slick arousal, and my deviant fuck dick almost slips inside her of his own accord " . . . is what I want, Lincoln. What I need." Her lower lip trembles. Her eyes are pleading. My hands fist in the sheets in an effort not to touch her. My entire body is screaming for her. "Please?" she begs.

How the hell can I deny her. Just this once. Just tonight and then I'll put a lock on my goddamn door. She's right that I did tell her she could do this. And she's wet. And needy. And so damn fuckable. "Then take whatever you want, angel."

Her eyes sparkle. She grasps my shaft and lowers herself onto it. So fucking slowly. Her tight heat hugging my cock inch by torturous inch, until I'm groaning her fucking name. With a satisfied smile, she sinks all the way down and I bottom out inside her.

"Like this, sir?" she asks, her voice dripping with sin and seduction.

"Yeah. Exactly like that, baby."

She rolls her hips over me and pleasure rockets up my spine. I grab onto her waist, guiding her, making sure her swollen clit makes contact with my pelvic bone.

She gasps and her eyes roll back. "Oh, god. That feels so good."

It feels fucking incredible. Sliding my hands over her rib cage, I cup her perfectly round tits in my palms, her supple flesh spilling between my spread fingers as I squeeze just enough to make her moan. I toy with her pebbled nipples while she rides me. When her pussy walls start to ripple around my shaft, I rock my hips into her, hitting her G-spot and making her tremble.

"Lincoln," she whines.

"I know, baby. You're so good at that. You're gonna make us both come the way you're riding my cock."

She nods, bottom lip trapped between her teeth, her eyes fluttering closed. Searing heat coils at the base of my spine and I grab onto her waist once more as she takes us both over the edge. A contented grin spreads over her face and she lies down on top of me, my cock still inside her.

I allow her a moment to stop shaking, my fingers trailing up and down her spine. "You should go back to your own room now, Imogen."

She burrows her face into the crook of my neck. "No."

"No?"

"I can't. No, I won't."

Her outright refusal would be amusing if it weren't so infuriating. "You can and you will."

With a heavy sigh, she peels herself off me, but instead of getting out of bed, she rolls onto her side, her body still pressed against mine. "I understand why you got upset with me yesterday and—"

"I didn't get upset with you." I pinch the bridge of my nose. "Although I know it may have appeared that way. I was angry with myself, because you were right, Imogen. You can't give me your consent. Not while I'm keeping you here against your will. So this . . ." my eyes rake over her sinful curves of their own volition " . . . all of this is wrong."

"No," she says again, all fire and defiance.

I roll onto my side, trying to keep a lid on my temper. "Yes."

"I thought a lot about it all day and I can give my consent. And I do. You can do whatever you want to my body. Anytime and anywhere. If I'm awake or sleeping, or—"

"Imogen!" I growl. She has no idea what she's saying. But I need to get a handle on my temper before I say something I regret. "It doesn't matter. This is wrong. So very fucking wrong, no matter how good it feels."

Her beautiful face twists in a scowl. "No!" she snaps, and before I can reprimand her for her attitude, she pushes herself up onto her elbow, her free hand on her hip. "*You* told me that I need to ask for what I want. And I want this, Lincoln. I do *not* consent to sleeping alone when I could be in here with you. I do not consent to being pushed away because of some kind of code you think you're breaking that you won't even explain to me. I do not consent to you withholding affection from me because of your guilt."

Her eyes are shining with indignation, and she's never looked more beautiful to me than in this moment. I'm both thrilled and proud that she's standing up for herself, but if I use that to justify what I'm doing, then I'm still a monster like the rest of them. "I don't mean to withhold affection, but it's hard to be close to you and not touch you, Imogen."

"So touch me!" she pleads. "I trust you with my body, Lincoln. All of it."

That stops me in my tracks. She trusts me? Her revelation fills me with equal parts shame and pride. "You shouldn't trust me."

"You've never given me any reason not to. You've never touched me against my will. Never pushed me further than I could handle." She places her hand on my chest, tracing her fingertip over my scars. "I know you think you're a monster but you're the furthest thing from one I've ever known. Even when you punished me, and even when you're rough, you're still always patient and kind. You always make me feel cherished and protected. You make me feel . . ." Her lower lip wobbles again. "You make me feel safe, Linc."

Safe? Me? The man who has spilled more blood than an entire army. The man who enjoys breaking bones and watching his enemies bleed far too much for it to be explained by a healthy desire for revenge. The same man who broke the most important promise he ever made—to protect her no matter what the cost. My throat constricts with all the words I should say. All the truths I should tell her but can't. Instead I focus on her truth, the one thing that makes all of this worth it—I make her feel safe.

"And so now I think I truly understand what consent means. I was taught that mine didn't matter because it wasn't mine to give, but I realize now how very wrong that is. You were right about there being a power imbalance between us, but now I understand that dynamic makes my consent even more important, not less so. And this is me, giving you mine of my own free will. Please don't refuse it."

Fuck, how could I? That was quite the speech, and I'm so damn proud of her. Grabbing her leg, I hook it over my hip before palming the back of her head, so I can pull her as close to me as humanly possible. "I won't refuse it, angel. But trust goes both ways. I need to trust that you feel safe enough to tell me no if I ever push you too far, if I ever hurt you or do something you don't want. Can you promise to always do that for me?"

She nods eagerly. "Yes."

I want to believe her so much that I do.

CHAPTER 48
IMOGEN

We are eating lunch when I feel the telltale cramps indicating my period has arrived. I excuse myself from the table and head upstairs to my bedroom. Taking the tampon from the wrapper, I study it closely. I've read the instructions and think I understand how they work. And they have to be more comfortable than pads, because, well . . . they have to be. Pads make me feel sticky and uncomfortable and tampons seem so much less messy.

"Are you feeling okay, angel?" His voice sends shivers through my entire body. I should have known he'd follow me.

"Yes, I'm just figuring out how to use a tampon."

He hums, taking the blue plastic tube from my hand. "Would you like me to show you?"

I arch an eyebrow. "You've used tampons before?"

One side of his mouth lifts in a smirk. "No, but I'm very willing to learn. How hard can it be?"

He pulls out the end of the plastic applicator and holds it up. "The white part goes inside you, correct?"

Why does that sound sexy the way he says it? I nod.

"And the string stays out?"

"Yes."

"Then I got it." He drops to his knees before I can protest further. Then he grabs my foot and plants a sweet kiss on the inside of my ankle before placing it on his shoulder. He pulls the tampon out of its applicator.

"We need that! That's what pushes it inside."

He looks up at me, his dark eyes sparkling with wicked intent. "I think I have that part covered, baby. Relax."

Relax? I'm trembling like a leaf in a hurricane. And the sight of him on his knees is doing all kinds of things to my insides, like melting them. He trails kisses up the inside of my thigh.

"Linc, I'm bleeding," I whisper.

"I know, baby." Then his hand is between my thighs and I'm incredibly conscious that I'm about to drip blood all over him. He pushes the tampon inside me with his finger. It slides in easily and the sensation is unfamiliar but not in any way unpleasant . . . and then he twists his finger sending a wave of pleasure pulsing right through me. That's not supposed to feel like that, is it? "That feel okay?"

His finger is still inside me. I clamp my lips together and nod.

With a husky laugh he kisses my lower abdomen and then slides his blood-soaked finger out, leaving the tampon in place. "Still okay, baby?"

"Yes. I can barely feel it."

"Good. And I'll be available later for removal if you need me." He winks.

I roll my eyes, even though the thought has me feeling all kinds of ways I probably shouldn't. I hide it well though, at least I try. "I think I have it covered, sir."

"We'll see." He pushes himself to his feet and then he . . .

"Lincoln, don't you dare!"

Too late.

He keeps his eyes locked on mine while he sucks his finger clean. I'm part grossed out, and part turned on, so much that I feel like I'm about to combust. I snort a giggle. "That is gross, sir."

He releases his finger with a wet pop. "Actually, much like any part of you, angel, fucking delicious. And just so you know, I'm available for all manner of tampon insertion or extraction. Whenever you need me."

I slip my arms around his shoulders. "That's very sweet of you, but like I said, I think I can manage." While I adore him taking care of me, I also want to learn how to do all these things for myself.

He nuzzles my neck. "I'll be pulling it out later to fuck you though."

"What?" I can't help the gasp that comes out with that word.

He frowns. "Can't fuck you with a tampon in, angel."

"I know, but . . ." I chew on my lip. "Is that . . . can we do that when I'm on my period?"

He laughs softly and it's a wonderful sound. "Baby, we can do anything you want. Did you know orgasms are good for cramps?"

I gasp even louder. "That can't be true."

"It is, but we can test the theory later if you like."

"Why didn't you tell me that before?"

He trails kisses over my neck. "Because the last time you had your period, I wasn't here, and the time before, I was trying to stop myself from touching you." He lifts me onto the vanity and wraps my legs around his waist. "But trust me, I would have loved to have slipped my hand into your panties and made you come. I thought about it for the entire movie."

"Me too," I admit, heat creeping over my cheeks.

"I have to go do some work, but if you have cramps that you need help with, come find me. Or you need your tampon changing. Or just want to be fucked . . ." He bites down on his lip and groans.

"Won't that be very messy, sir."

He nods. "Really fucking messy, angel. But that's why we have this wonderful invention called soap and water. And showers. And baths."

"Actually, I've thought about what it would be like to have sex in a bath. Or in the shower." Specifically, I have imagined his massive hands soaping me all over, and how good they would feel gliding over my wet skin.

He kisses me softly. "Then that's what we'll do. I'll get you fucking filthy and then I'll clean you up."

Pleasure snakes in my core. "I can't wait, sir."

With a final kiss, he leaves me alone to get dressed and I spend the rest of the day daydreaming about sex in the bath and shower while I make a start on clearing a fresh patch of garden for some extra vegetables, having finally defeated the chaotic web of knotted vines that were strangling the wild roses.

By the time I finish for the evening, I'm dirty and streaked with sweat and mud. And when I get to the bathroom, he's already waiting for me, along with a bath full of hot bubbly water and a wicked grin on his face.

CHAPTER 49
LINCOLN

The smudge of dirt on her nose is absolutely fucking adorable. I truly have never seen anything more beautiful in my entire life.

I help her out of her T-shirt. "Did you enjoy working in the garden, angel?"

She nods. "I think by next year we'll be able to plant a whole range of new vegetables. We could easily grow enough for the three of us."

The way she talks about the three of us like we're a family, and her plans for next year make me happier than I could ever have imagined. I try in vain to keep the smug grin from my face while I undress her. I toss her top into the laundry hamper and press a kiss on the tip of her nose while I take off her bra. Then I crouch down to take off her leggings. As I peel them off her perspiration-covered skin, she chatters away excitedly about her plans for next spring and her enthusiasm for this place she now calls home lights me up from the inside. When I've removed all her clothes and she's spectacularly naked, I take her hand and help her into the bath.

She sinks beneath the water, disappearing beneath the bubbles for a few seconds before she pops back up again, like a seal breaking through the arctic water. A soft laugh tumbles from her lips and I just sit on the edge of the bath, smiling at her.

"Are you getting in, sir?" she asks with a sultry purr.

I shake my head. "I wasn't planning to, angel."

"What? Why?"

"Because you've worked hard all day and you deserve a little taking care of. And if I get into that bath with you . . ." I grab the bottle of shampoo from the side. "Then I'm certain all we'll end up doing is fucking."

She bites into her bottom lip and flutters her eyelashes. "But I like fucking, sir."

I love hearing her use words like that with such confidence. As a reward, I lean down and give her a lingering kiss. I suspect she's tired after her busy day, and I want her to know that us spending time together doesn't always have to be about sex, as much as I'd like to climb into the hot water with her and fuck her senseless. "I know, angel. Bath first though. Okay?"

I squeeze a generous amount of shampoo into my palm and begin washing her long locks, working my fingers firmly over her skin. She moans softly when I gently massage her scalp, letting her head hang back between her shoulder blades and closing her eyes.

"That feels so good, sir. I might never want to wash my own hair ever again."

I drop a kiss on her forehead. "I'll wash your hair whenever you need."

She smiles. "Hair washing. Tampon insertion and removal. You'd better be careful, sir. I might just make you my personal serv-vant." She stutters on the last word like she regretted using it midway through saying it, and I suspect I know why.

With a soapy hand, I cup her jaw. "Imogen?"

She keeps her eyes tightly closed.

"Imogen. Look at me, baby."

Her eyes flit open, and she worries her lip again, appearing anxious.

"There is no act of service that I wouldn't gladly do for you. In fact, I would worship you on my knees if that's what you wanted. I may have bought you, but you own me."

She blinks, her eyes shining with tears. I dust my lips over hers and give her the briefest of kisses before I go back to washing her hair.

"Nobody has ever washed my hair before," she whispers. "At least not that I remember. I'm sure my mom must have."

Your mom did, and your dad, because they loved you with all their fucking hearts. That's what I should tell her, but I'm too much of a coward to do that, so instead I tell her how beautiful and special she is to me. She blossoms under my praise, like the roses do under her tender care.

When she's clean all over, I help her out of the bath and wrap her in a warm purple fluffy towel before diligently drying her skin, making sure I tend to every inch, which is just another reason to have my hands on her. Then as promised, I change her tampon before I help her into a clean T-shirt. When we're done I carry her to bed and tuck her in.

"Lincoln, we haven't eaten dinner yet," she protests.

"I know, baby. Pierre is fixing us something we can eat here in bed." I check my watch. "It will be ready in about five minutes."

Her eyes sparkle with delight. "We're eating dinner in bed?"

I nod. "I thought dinner and some movies."

She claps her hands together. "That sounds perfect."

WE ATE DINNER AND WATCHED ONE MOVIE, AND then Imogen fell asleep before the second one was even halfway done. I turned off the TV and then I just watched her sleeping for hours. Mesmerized by the gentle rise and fall of her chest, and the occasional twitch of her nose. She looks so different now. So unguarded and peaceful. Stripped of her armor while she sleeps. I suppose we have both peeled away our layers for the other.

But I must have fallen asleep because I'm being woken by her squirming, which has her wriggling her perfect ass over my rapidly hardening cock. "What's wrong, baby?"

"Cramps," she groans.

"You want me to get some Advil and the hot water bottle?"

"No," she breathes out the word. "I want to try your other method, sir."

My sleep-addled brain takes a few seconds to register what she means. "Oh? You want to try my orgasm method?"

"It seems only right to test it out after you made such a bold claim."

I nip her shoulder blade. "You're such a brat." I delicately slip two fingers into her mouth. "Suck, baby. Give me plenty of spit, because we're going to need a little lubricant."

She sucks, covering my fingers with saliva before I pull them out. I slide my hand into her panties and find her clit, already swollen.

She moans softly. "But why do we need lube? I feel . . ." She doesn't finish what she was saying.

I rest my lips at her ear, working my fingers over her sensitive flesh. "You feel what?"

"Wet," she whispers.

"I'm sure you are, but that tampon you're wearing is soaking up all your lovely cum, along with your period. And you're going to need to change it in an hour." I set an alarm on my watch for myself so I could do that for her. I read it's dangerous to leave them in for more than eight hours and I have no intention of letting any harm come to her.

"Oh, god, I'm so naive."

"Not naive, baby. Just learning new things." I press more firmly and she gasps. "And I love being your teacher."

She throws her head back in pleasure and I take advantage of the expanse of skin on her neck, kissing and licking while I play with her needy clit. "Y-you're such a good teacher, Linc."

"It's not hard when I have such a bright, enthusiastic pupil."

I sink my teeth into her throat, biting gently while I work her over, and it doesn't take long to push her over the edge. She moans my name when she comes, whispering her thanks for helping with her cramps.

She's already drifting back to sleep when she confirms that my theory is indeed true. With a smile, I wrap her tightly in my arms, ignoring the ache in my dick as it's still pressed against her ass. Tomorrow, I'll take my fill of her, but tonight, all I want to do is hold her while she sleeps.

CHAPTER 50
LINCOLN

It's September, and the nights are getting longer and the days shorter and milder, which means Imogen spends much less time in the garden tending to her vegetables and flowers, and more time in the library with me. I enjoy watching her work in the garden every morning and I spend far too much time doing that and not enough time working, but seeing her happy and making the overgrown garden her own is a much more pleasant way to pass the time. Selfishly, though I'm enjoying the fall, I can't wait for winter when she will be inside much more frequently, and we can spend nights curled beneath a blanket in front of a log fire.

She saunters across the room, hips swaying like a pendulum, hypnotizing and distracting. Her eyes drop to the chessboard in the center of the table.

"Do you play?"

She wrinkles her nose. "A little. Not very well."

"Would you like a game?"

She smiles, and there's something wicked and inherently sexy about it. The transformation in her these past few months is astonishing, and I'm enjoying every facet of this new Imogen. "I'd love one, sir."

"I'm always black."

She sinks into the seat opposite me, her tongue darting out to wet her bottom lip. "Of course you are."

It soon becomes obvious that Imogen is much better at chess than she led me to believe. She takes my bishop. "Are you trying to hustle me, angel?"

"No, sir. I have no idea what you mean."

"You said you don't play very well, but I think you're lying."

Her green eyes sparkle. "I don't lie, sir."

I take one of her pawns. "But you are good at chess."

"I suppose that's a matter of opinion. My grandfather was very good at chess. He taught me the game, but I never won a single match against him." She makes another move. "I used to beat his drivers a lot though."

"Drivers?"

"Yeah, he had six."

"Your grandfather had six drivers?" She hasn't spoken of her past or her grandfather much recently, and I've been too wrapped up in this blossoming relationship between us to push her on it.

She nods. "He's a very rich man."

So, why didn't he pay the Brotherhood off instead of handing you over to them? Piece of shit! I keep that thought to myself. Six drivers are excessive, no matter how rich a person is. "Six drivers? Did they all take a day each and have a Sunday off?"

Her eyebrows pinch together, making her frown look adorable, but she's focused on the board now, concentrating on her next move instead of me. Still, she answers my question. "No, they all worked full-time. They were pretty much always around. I never really liked chess all that much, but my grandfather said it was good for me to practice, so he used to make them play me sometimes."

So they weren't drivers at all. Bodyguards. Security. For her or her grandfather, or both? "Did they drive you often?"

She glances up for a half second before focusing on the board again. "What do you mean?"

The hairs on the back of my neck stand on end. These drivers were obviously an accepted part of her life and it strikes me as odd that they were referred to as drivers when they clearly weren't. "It sounded like you spent time with them. Was it because they drove you places?"

"No. I never left the estate." She makes her move.

I knew she was sheltered and I suspected that they tried to keep her from me, at least in the beginning when they knew I was still alive, but I had no idea her isolation was so complete. "Never?"

Her green eyes are wide when they meet mine. "No."

I've researched her grandfather's estate, which consists of forty acres of land in Nebraska. A big enough area for a child to grow of course, but that she never left it at all is unusual. "Didn't that ever bother you?"

"I can't leave here, can I? And that doesn't bother me."

I don't know if that's an accusation or her natural ability to speak plain, uncomfortable truths without any emotion. "But you've been here for five months. You were there for eighteen years. And you were a teenager. Teenagers are supposed to rebel and do crazy shit. You didn't get to do any of that."

"I wasn't allowed to watch TV, eat candy, or even wear a tampon, Lincoln. What on earth makes you think I was ever allowed to rebel in any way?"

The skin at the base of her neck turns a light shade of pink, as her frustration starts to spill out. Until now, she's done a great job of convincing Pierre and me, and probably herself, that her childhood wasn't all that bad, that it was good enough. I've long suspected that wasn't actually the case, even if she believed it was. "I'm not accusing you of anything, angel. I'm just trying to understand you, that's all."

She swallows, her slender neck working. "I didn't know any

THE AUCTION

different. And I knew it was for my own protection. The Brotherhood were supposed to kill me when they killed my parents. My grandfather saved me. So it was either live on his estate, or don't live, Mr. Knight. Those were my choices. Survive or die."

I reach for her hand, squeezing it gently in mine. "I'm not trying to piss you off, angel."

"Who said you pissed me off?" She shrugs, trying to wrench her hand away but I hold firm.

"You only call me Mr. Knight when you're really annoyed with me." Her eyes spark with defiance. "Because you know I fucking hate it."

"I feel like you're accusing me of being untruthful, and I'm not a liar."

I lift her fingers to my lips and kiss the tips. "I know. And I'm not accusing you of anything, I promise."

Her green eyes rake over my face, like she's scrutinizing me to determine if I'm telling the truth. After a moment, her face softens.

"How did your parents die?" I know the question is a difficult one, not to mention a potential minefield for me, but I need to know what she believes. What that bastard told her.

"How did yours die, sir?"

Okay. An eye for an eye. I can live with that. "My dad was a junkie who OD'd before my first birthday. And my mom was murdered by her pimp when I was two. Thankfully, I was with a neighbor at the time."

Her green eyes fill with tears. "I'm sorry."

"I don't even remember them, so . . ." I shrug. "Now tell me about yours."

"You don't know about the traitor's daughter?" she gasps, feigning outrage to mask her true feelings.

"Do you remember them?"

She nods. "I remember their faces. Their laughter. Their smiles. I remember being happy."

"Was he a traitor, your father?"

"Do you think he was?"

"I don't know him, angel." I lie with ease. "That's why I'm asking you."

"No, he wasn't. He was a good man. He didn't betray the Brotherhood. I think he tried to expose them for what they were and it got him killed." So despite any lies her grandfather would have told her, she still believes her father was a good man, probably because she remembers enough of him to know that it's true. I'm filled with pride at the way she's so quick to leap to his defense and I wish I could tell her more about the kind of man he was. I wish I could tell her about both her parents. "I suppose if he did try to expose them, then the Brotherhood would call him a traitor."

She bristles. "Well, I would call him a hero."

So would I, but I obviously don't tell her that. "How did they die?"

"They were murdered, by my godfather."

There it is. It takes every single shred of willpower and strength not to react, but she may have just as well punched a hole right through my chest.

"Your godfather?"

She nods, angrily swiping a tear from her cheek. "Killian Wolfe. He murdered my father and my mom took me and hid, but he found us too. And he killed her. He would have killed me if my grandfather hadn't saved me."

Lies! All fucking lies! I want to roar that declaration at the top of my lungs, but I maintain my calm. It's not her fault she was brainwashed. I let them brainwash me too—let them convince me she was dead. Left her all alone when I should have taken care of her. None of this is on her. "Is your godfather still alive?"

I hold my breath waiting for her answer. "No. He died in an explosion a few months later. They found his body burned to near ash, indistinguishable except for a stupid tattoo."

Instinctively, I want to rub at the patch of skin on my wrist. That tattoo has been long covered, but it's still there beneath, in my blood and memory.

"Anyway, that's it. I'm a sad lonely orphan, just like you, I guess."

I cup her chin and rub my thumb over her pouty lips. "Well, right now, I'm neither sad or lonely. You?"

She shakes her head. "No."

"But you are very good at chess. And you should never underestimate your abilities."

"Thank you, sir." She blinks, her eyelashes dusting against her cheeks.

"Shall we resume our game?"

She nods and I release her. We continue our game, but the air is charged with tension now. Sparks of electricity crackling between us whenever our eyes meet or our fingers brush—like a really long incredibly sexy form of foreplay.

Imogen's chess game is calculated and ruthless. I've always known how smart she is, but she's as sharp as a needlepoint. She almost has me on the ropes, when she makes a move that surprises me, moving her knight from its position defending the king, stopping me from taking her queen but leaving herself open to checkmate in two more moves. Is she letting me win? "Why did you do that when you left your king wide open?"

Her green eyes sparkle with mischief and she catches her bottom lip between her teeth. "A good knight always protects his queen, sir. She's the most powerful piece in the game."

Check-fucking-mate!

God, she's fucking incredible. And now I'm hyperaware of my breathing, faster and heavier than before. My heart is beating in my throat. Without taking my eyes off hers, I tip over my king and admit defeat.

Imogen DeMotta has defeated me in all things.

"Come here," I growl the words, red-hot aching need for

her pulsing through my entire body. Impossible to ignore and too intense to even try.

Obediently, she stands, walking around the desk until she's standing between my spread thighs. With a sweep of my hand, I clear the board from the center of my desk, sending most of the pieces scattering to the floor, and then I lift her onto it, inching my chair forward and spreading her legs apart with my body. She rests her bare feet beside my thighs on my chair. Wordlessly, I pull off her dress, and she lifts her arms in compliance. When that's done, I unhook her bra, allowing her beautiful tits to bounce out right in front of my face. Her nipples stiff and begging for my attention.

I oblige them with my tongue, sucking one pebbled peak into my mouth. I bite gently, causing her to moan and run her hands through my hair. I lavish the other with the same attention, until the scent of her wet pussy becomes too irresistible to ignore.

"Lie back for me, angel." I press a hand between her breasts, gently encouraging her, until she's flat on my desk with her sweet-smelling pussy right there for the taking.

I run my hands up the insides of her thighs and she trembles.

"Linc!"

I hook my fingers into the waistband of her panties and slowly slide them over her hips, making her gasp. "You won our game, and this is your prize. You want your prize, don't you?"

"Y-yes, please."

I love making her beg. Love making her come on my tongue. I love every damn thing about her. I love her.

When I pull her panties off her pussy, they remain attached by a thick string of her creamy arousal for a second, and it might be the sexiest thing I've ever seen.

"Soaked already, baby." I press a quick kiss on her slick clit that makes her whine. "You're going to be dripping down your legs when I'm done. My needy little angel."

I pull her panties all the way off and instead of returning her feet to their former position on my chair, I spread her wider and place them on the edge of my desk, and now her beautiful cunt is right there, glistening and begging for my mouth. "So flexible too. Look at you all spread open and dripping for me."

I swipe two fingers through her wet center and her hips lift off the desk as she lets out a series of soft desperate moans. Her scent is intoxicating and addictive, the greatest high a man could ever have, and it's mine. She's mine. Only ever mine.

I grab hold of her waist, keeping her still so that I can devour her. My tongue flattens over her swollen clit first, and I lap it the way that she likes, until she's moaning and bucking her hips. I graze my teeth over the swollen bud before moving lower, letting my mouth taste every inch of her juicy cunt. My tongue dips inside her, over and over, teasing and taunting while I work her over, savoring every drop of her.

I sink my middle finger into her pussy, coating it in her silky cum before I slide it into her ass.

"Linc!" she squeals. "I can't . . . I'm gonna . . ."

I growl, keeping her teetering on the edge even while I'm desperate for her to fall apart for me. Her entire body is trembling now, needy for some release. "Come on my tongue while I fuck your ass, baby."

"Oh, fuck, Linc!" she screams as her orgasm takes her under, her breathing harsh and raspy while her hips buck against my face and I drink her cum like it's the nectar of the gods.

My cock is feral for her now, desperate to be hugged by the silky wet velvet of her cunt. I stand up and quickly free my aching shaft. Gently, I wrap her still-trembling legs around my waist before I drive balls-deep into her in one thrust. My eyes roll back and, fuck, nothing in the world feels better than this. Feels more right than this.

She tugs at my T-shirt, and I help her to pull it off me. She seems to prefer skin against skin when we're fucking, and I always want to give my girl what she wants. I crush her to me, arms wrapped around her while I sink in and out of her. I want to nail her, but I want to savor the feeling of her snug cunt, still tight from her orgasm, milking me. I want to revel in her needy little whines as she claws at my skin for more.

Her hot mouth is at my ear. "I didn't mean to piss you off, sir."

"Angel, you can piss me off whenever you want, intentionally or otherwise, and I will still always give you what you need. You know that, don't you?"

"Yes, sir."

"You are my queen, Imogen. And I would fucking die before I let anyone take you."

She throws her head back and I sink my teeth into the soft skin at the base of her throat, hard enough to leave a mark. I'm driven with a possessive need to claim her, to make her my own. Not because I bought her, but because she wants to belong to me, just as surely as I belong to her.

Forever and always, she is my queen. My heart. My entire soul.

CHAPTER 51
IMOGEN

Lincoln drops a soft kiss on the top of my head, the kind that makes me feel all warm and fuzzy inside. "Enjoy your book, angel. I'll be back up in a few hours."

"Are you going to your lair?" I flash him a smile.

"It's not my lair, vixen."

I flutter my eyelashes. "That's what Pierre says it is."

He grips my jaw in his hand, squeezing firmly—it's possessive and commanding and I love it. "It's just the place where I work. I adore this bratty side you're developing, by the way."

"So do I, sir."

He growls, pressing a kiss on my lips. "I'll be back soon. Be good while I'm gone."

When he lets me go, I already feel bereft from the loss of his touch. "Will you ever allow me down there? I'd like to see where you work."

That makes him stop in his tracks and he turns back around to face me, his face unreadable. "There's nothing much of interest down there, baby. Just some security monitors and computers running programs." Feeling emboldened, I stand and walk toward him, deliberately swaying my hips as I do. His eyes narrow to thin slits, raking over my body. "I know what you're trying to do, angel."

I reach him, draping my arms around his neck. "Is it working, sir?" I purr, rubbing my breasts against his chest.

He mutters a curse, and then his hand is on my ass, squeezing it tightly. "I should put you across my knee and spank your ass red for being such a distraction."

I'm pretty sure my cheeks turn red at his words. "I think I'd like that, sir." *No, I would definitely like that.*

He brushes his knuckles over my cheek. "My wicked little temptress."

"I just don't like being apart from you. Is that a bad thing?"

"No, baby. I don't like being apart from you either." He runs his nose over my throat, inhaling deeply, rumbling like a tiger about to pounce on its prey. "I like being as close to you as humanly possible as frequently as possible."

"So let me come to your lair with you. I'll bring a book. I won't bother you."

He stares at me for a few seconds, considering my request. I'm sure he's going to say no. "If I let you see it, will you stop calling it my lair?"

I almost squeak with excitement. "Yes."

"Fine. But don't touch anything, okay?"

I flash him a wicked grin. "You mean I can't touch anything at all?" I run my hand over his chest.

He does that sexy half smile. "You can always touch me, angel."

Pushing up onto my tiptoes, I press my lips over his and he slips his arms around my waist, pulling me tight to him. This may be the first kiss I've ever initiated, and from the way his cock is growing stiffer by the second, I think he's enjoying it. It's also me who pulls back first, leaving him gasping and staring into my eyes. He grips my jaw again, squeezing until my mouth opens. "Brat," he mutters.

THE AUCTION

Then he grabs my hand and leads me to his basement lair. He unlocks the door and it opens into a spiral staircase that descends into the shadows below. This feels so much like the mansions in the gothic novels I've been reading, while also serving as a reminder that there is still so much about this house, and about Lincoln, that I don't know. He walks down the stairs, not speaking, but looking back just once to check I'm still behind him. I hesitate at the doorway, fingertips brushing the cold stone walls. A deep breath fills my nose with the scent of cold metal and damp earth, laced with a hint of the cologne that Lincoln wears. The space smells so much of him. I take another deep breath, grip the iron railing and descend the staircase after him. The door behind me closes with an almost imperceptible click, and now the stairwell is bathed in a soft blue glow.

At the bottom of the steps, the space opens up into a cavernous room. A bank of computer screens fills one wall, responsible for the eerie blue light. Each of them display different moving and flickering images. A worn leather desk chair sits idle, like it's awaiting his return. The floor is concrete. The walls bare brick. A steel door leads to another room at the far end of the space. It, too, has a lock.

"Where does that lead?"

Lincoln reaches for my hand and squeezes it in his. "My armory."

I don't know what I was expecting, but it wasn't that. I've seen the knife he wears strapped to his thigh when he leaves, but this is something much more intense. "Your armory?"

"Yes."

"Exactly what kind of work do you do, Lincoln?"

He dusts his lips over my temple. "All kinds of work, angel. Nothing for you to worry about."

Easy for him to say when he feels the need to have an entire armory locked in his basement. "Are we safe here?"

He presses a soft kiss on my knuckles. "Always."

The one-word answers tell me to stop asking questions, but I can't. "Then why do you have an armory?"

"Because the people I run into aren't always nice people, angel."

A shiver runs down my spine. "Like the Brotherhood."

"Exactly."

Another shiver. Is there something about Lincoln that I've been missing? Something underneath his kindness that's genuinely dangerous? "Do you work with them?"

"No."

This is growing even more confusing. "So, how do you *run into* them, then?"

His tongue darts out and he licks his bottom lip. "Do you trust me?"

I take a moment to consider my answer before I reply. "Yes."

"Then don't ask me questions I can't answer. I promise you I don't work for the Brotherhood. I abhor what they do. And I would never ever put you in danger, and that is all you need to concern yourself with."

I trust him but that doesn't mean I want to be kept in the dark. I reach up and trace my fingertips over his scars. "You keep so much of yourself hidden from me, Lincoln."

His eyes fill with pain and he pulls me into a hug, pressing my face to his chest and stroking my hair. "Only the dark parts, angel. But I show you the deepest and most vulnerable parts of myself. Nobody else gets that part of me but you."

"I want to see your darkness too, Linc," I whisper. "I want to see all of you. Will you ever trust me enough to show me who you really are?"

He kisses the top of my head. "One day, angel. I promise."

I let myself melt into his embrace, trusting that he would tell me if he could. Whatever secrets he hides, they seem to torture him, and I know how that feels. So I trust what I can see and feel. His care. His protection. His love. And for a girl like me, that should be more than enough.

CHAPTER 52
LINCOLN

A text from Edgar flashes up on my watch.

That lead you had me look into seems promising. Maybe even what we've been looking for all along. Sent you some info.

My pulse spikes. What we've been looking for? That means we may have just found ourselves a Rook. I had him research Fraser Lane after seeing his name in Farnham's study, and it seems like it's paid off.

I type out a quick thanks to him, itching to get to my basement and assess what he's sent me. Imogen is reading, her head on my lap as we cuddle together on the sofa in the library. I run my hand over the soft skin of her arm. Although I trust her enough to allow her into my basement, whatever Edgar has uncovered isn't the kind of thing I want to dive into while she's there with me, until I at least have an idea of what it is he's sent me. There could be a link to her father for all I know, and while I know I need to tell her about our connection, I just have no fucking idea how to go about that. Especially now that I know what she was told about her parents' murders. The fallout could be disastrous, and the only thing more painful than keeping secrets from her is the thought of losing her. "I have to go check something, angel. I won't be long."

She sits up, gives me a soft smile and nods. "Okay. I'll finish my book."

I rest my lips on the top of her head, inhaling the sweet scent of her hair. How can I ever tell her the truth and risk losing this? I didn't intend to tell her about my armory, but when she asked, it seemed natural to give her the truth. To give her something in return for her trust. Her reaction was as positive as I could have hoped for. She sat in my basement with me for an hour afterward, reading her book. But then I saw her shivering and forgot how cold it is down there for someone not used to it, so we came back up to the main house. At least showing her the room seems to have satisfied her curiosity somewhat, and for that I'm grateful.

I slip out of the room and head down to my basement. I've been there only a few minutes when I hear Pierre's distinctive footfall on the stairs.

"Are you spying on me, old friend?"

He scoffs. "Heard you coming down here and anything that tears you away from the sofa this late in the evening lately must be important."

I pull up Edgar's email on one of my screens, and my encryption decoding program quickly gets to work. "He said he had some interesting information on a lead I gave him."

Pierre pulls up his usual chair and sits beside me. "A lead on a woman, or . . ."

"Not quite. A lead on a Rook."

"A Rook?" His excitement is palpable.

Not wanting to get his hopes up before I see what it is Edgar has sent me, I say, "Maybe. I need to check. It was just a hunch."

He waits impatiently, drumming his fingers on his thigh.

THE AUCTION

"A Rook, a Rook, my kingdom for a Rook," he murmurs to himself.

I stare at the screen, waiting for the text to be deciphered. I spent a lot of time here in the early days teaching Edgar everything I know about computers, coding, encryptions, hacking, and he's put it all to good use over the years. His encryptions are as complex as my own. When the text finally forms on the screen, I read through it quickly.

"Well? Anything yet? Don't keep an old blind man in suspense."

I peer at the screen, making sure I have all the information before I relay it to Pierre. "You're not old, you just like to act it."

He huffs.

I see the name I've been hoping to read—a man I assumed was dead until recently. Adrenaline thunders through my veins and I feel the smile spreading across my face. Finally, after all these years. "I think we've got one, Pierre."

He grabs hold of my forearm, squeezing tightly. "Lincoln?"

I pat his hand, my own excitement bubbling over as my eyes still scan over the text.

"Who?" he demands.

"Fraser Lane."

Pierre shakes his head. "Don't recognize his name."

"He's a Knight. At least he was eighteen years ago. But he's obviously risen through the ranks since I last saw him."

"You knew him? But I thought you already dispensed with all of the Knights you remembered?"

I did. Methodically and ruthlessly, over the course of eighteen years, I hunted down and killed every single Knight I knew. Some were already dead by the time I got around to them, no doubt a few would have been killed at the hands of the Brotherhood themselves, but the rest met with unfortunate, untraceable-to-me ends. Heart attacks. Car wrecks. A few suicides. It took a lot of willpower to do it that way, because for those where I can get up close and personal, there's nothing like the recognition on their face when they realize who's responsible for taking their lives.

I have many names within the Brotherhood. The Freak. The Ghost. Traitor. But whatever one they knew me by, they always know my real name at the very end.

Killian Wolfe—the man the Brotherhood couldn't kill.

"Did this one slip under your radar?" Pierre asks.

"I thought he was dead. I even went to his funeral." I stood amidst the trees on a rainy day, in a gray cemetery just outside London, and watched as they lowered a casket into the ground. It seems Fraser Lane wasn't inside it. "It looks like the Brotherhood gave him a new identity along with his promotion. Now he's Francis Davies. And he lives in Surrey."

"Surrey, England?"

I murmur my agreement, doing an internet search on Francis Davies. A Conservative MP with a questionable voting record on human rights issues and the ability to come through numerous scandals unscathed while still holding on to his position.

I send a quick text to Edgar.

Contact my broker and have him set up a meeting in London. Tell him I'm looking for a UK company to invest in. Lincoln Knight needs a legitimate reason to fly to the UK.

He replies immediately.

You'll need the jet?

I tap out my reply. Yes.

"So you're traveling to England, then, sir?" Pierre dons his best British accent, which is as appalling as my French one.

"Looks like."

"As Lincoln, or covertly?"

"As Lincoln."

"Won't that draw attention? If you're in the UK when a Rook is murdered, then it could bring suspicion?"

I know that it will, and maybe that's why I'm doing it. It's taken me eighteen years to get this far, and I can't wait another eighteen to find another one. Rooks are given high-level access for a reason. They are chosen because they would die before they'd betray the Brotherhood, so this might be my only chance to send a message that I can get to their elite. It might be the only chance I get. Playing the long game and picking them off one by one was viable when I had nothing but time and nothing else to live for, but now I have Imogen. And she's made me realize that this all needs to fucking end. Maybe another King will take this one's place and maybe the Brotherhood will go on forever, or another organization will rise to power in its stead. But I want the opportunity to look *him* in the eye. The one who established the auctions, the one who gave the orders for the murder of Luca and Carmen DeMotta, and who framed me for the crime. I want him to know that it's me taking his life.

Then, I can walk away.

"I think maybe it's time to stop playing so safe and up the stakes, Pierre."

He smiles. "And not before time, sir."

CHAPTER 53
LINCOLN

After spending the day in a suit and tie meeting with dozens of CEOs from start-ups that are looking for funding, and then dodging paparazzi getting to and from the office building to my car, it's a relief to remove all the vestiges of Lincoln Knight and put my usual uniform back on.

When I slip out of the hotel again, dressed all in black, with a surgical mask and the hood of my sweatshirt pulled up over my head, nobody notices me. One of the things I love about London is that nobody notices anybody. People are too busy in their own lives to even look up from their cell phones.

I take the Tube to the train that will take me to Surrey, the small part of the English countryside where Fraser Lane, or Francis Davies as he's currently known, lives. Here in the pretty village of Shere, I'm much more conspicuous, so I don a regular face mask you can buy in any drugstore, and swap out my black hoodie for a Barbour coat, stuffing the former into my backpack.

As luck would have it, a few minutes after I situate myself in a prime position hidden amongst some trees opposite Francis's house, he ventures out for an evening stroll.

He's changed a lot since I last knew him. Gone are the camo gear and shaved head, and in their place are some slacks and a cashmere jumper, along with a thick perfectly styled head of sandy-colored hair. The arrogant fuck heads straight toward me, stopping a few meters ahead, where he walks in circles while chatting on his cell phone. From the creepy laugh and the low timbre of his voice, not to mention the use of the words *naughty little sugar muffin*, I'll wager he's not on the phone to his wife, Agnes, and is instead speaking to one of his mistresses. Even the most calculating and intelligent of men can make mistakes when blinded by the promise of some good pussy. The irony of that is also not lost on me, even though Imogen is much more to me than that.

I take the syringe from my backpack and wait for him to end the call before I step out of the trees and into his path. He regards me with suspicion upon seeing me, but continues walking, turning back in the direction of his house.

"Fraser, that you?"

He stops in his tracks and spins around, teeth bared like a rabid dog now. The country gent act has been dropped, revealing the Fraser I remember. "Who the fuck are you?"

"An old friend." I take a few steps toward him.

He pulls a knife, like the good soldier he is deep down inside. Never go anywhere unprepared.

"Who sent you?" he growls.

"The King himself."

His eyes narrow in suspicion. "I have no idea what you're talking about, or who you're referring to. But back the fuck off, or I'll slit your throat and bury you so deep nobody will ever find you."

"You can try, but the King wouldn't be very happy about that, now would he? Not after he asked me to give you a message."

He jerks his chin in an arrogant challenge. "What message?"

"He wants to know about the traitor's daughter. You know where she is?"

He frowns, still assessing me. "I have no idea what you're referring to."

"Oh, come on, Fraser. You don't remember Imogen De-Motta? Luca's kid? He was a Rook too, you know?"

I keep inching closer and closer.

I see the flicker of surprise, but he's too shrewd to give anything up willingly. It's why he got to where he is, and why I have the syringe discreetly tucked behind my palm.

He shakes his head. "You're batshit, fella. And I will give you one last warning." He holds the knife aloft and I take my moment to strike. Back when we were Knights together, he took a bullet to his left knee, it tore the ligaments to shreds, and nobody ever fully recovers from an injury like that. I crouch low and barrel into it, hearing the satisfying crunch of bone as he drops to the ground. He swipes the knife through the air at me, but I dodge it easily and snap his arm in half, causing the blade to fall to the ground.

Before he can take a swing at me with his good arm, I stick the needle into his neck and inject the entire contents into him. He grabs at the fresh entry wound. "What the fuck did you just give me?"

I stamp on his good kneecap, crushing that one too. "Snake venom."

That's a lie. I just injected him with what's colloquially known as truth serum. My Japanese chemists have been working on this one for a while, and it's better than any other on the market, but it still takes an annoying two to three minutes to take effect. If Fraser realizes what it is, he'll pop that little cyanide capsule all Bishops and Rooks have hidden in one of their upper molars, and I won't get anything from him.

I crouch down and pick up his knife, turning it over in my hand, buying some time. "Who the fuck are you?" he growls.

"I already told you. I'm a messenger for the King. Now tell

THE AUCTION

me what you know about the girl?" I need to save my questions about who the King is for when the serum takes hold. For now, I'll keep up my pretense that we're on the same side, even if he isn't entirely buying it.

He grunts, a sound full of pain and frustration, but he can handle a lot more pain than a couple of busted knees. "Same as everyone knows. She was bought by some weird billionaire recluse."

I grind my jaw. So they don't know who I am? Of course, Fraser could be lying.

It's been two minutes and the serum should be working now. He'll bite on his capsule as soon as I ask him who the King is, and then I only have one to two minutes before he dies. I hope that's enough.

I remove my mask. "Who is the King?"

He blinks rapidly and his eyes blow wide as he recognizes me. It's always the scars that do it. They never saw my face after, but they all heard the horror stories of the road tearing through the skin on my right side. The Brotherhood sent one of their fiercest Knights, Diego Madden, after me when I left. He failed, but he did scar me for life.

As I suspected, Fraser dislodges his capsule and bites into it. I grab his jaw, but's he's already swallowed the lethal dose of cyanide.

"Killian Wolfe?" he snarls.

"That's me."

"You're dead."

"You know people keep telling me that, but I don't feel dead. Who is the King?"

He clamps his lips together, fighting the serum. Then his body starts convulsing. Fucker! I bet he hasn't eaten dinner yet, and cyanide works faster on an empty stomach. I knew this was always going to be the problem when dealing with a Rook and it burns my insides up with frustration that I might have waited eighteen long years to find one of these bastards and still walk away with nothing. I can't let that happen.

I kick him in the face, shattering his jaw and splitting open his lips and gums. "Who is the King, Fraser?"

He grins at me, the blood pouring from his mouth. Smeared around his lips, it gives him the appearance of some kind of Halloween clown. Then his eyes roll back in his head. Piece of shit is going to die before I get any truth out of him. *Fuck! Fuck! Fuck!*

I straddle him, grabbing him by the shoulders and shaking him so hard his teeth rattle. "Who is he? Where do I find the King?"

He laughs until blood bubbles up in his throat. "You're looking in the wrong place, Killian." He chokes.

"What the fuck do you mean?"

His grin widens, psychotic and unhinged. "The Queen is the most powerful piece in the game." His words are stuttered and broken, but I hear him perfectly, and they hit me right in the chest. I've heard those words before.

She said the exact same thing to me.

Fraser convulses again and then his head lolls to the side. He's already gone, but his words are still here with us. Was he speaking the truth, and I should be looking for a Queen instead of a King? Or were they the ramblings of a man who was about to take his last breath in service to the Brotherhood, designed to throw me off?

Regardless, the similarity to what Imogen said to me only a week or so ago is too startling to ignore. And there's a cold heavy feeling of dread already settling in the pit of my stomach. Have I been totally blinded by her all this time? Has she been playing me, or are they using her to get to me? Either way, I need to get home as fast as possible.

CHAPTER 54
LINCOLN

I got back from England yesterday, and Fraser Lane's words have haunted me since I watched him die in that field. Whenever I look at Imogen's beautiful face, I hear her saying those same words too. Only now here in the basement with Pierre, while she's upstairs tending to the garden, do I dare to voice any of the thoughts tumbling through my head.

"Do you think it's strange that the Brotherhood kept her alive all these years only to then try and sell her at one of their auctions?"

Pierre frowns. "Evil. Vile. Disgusting. All of those things, but I'm not sure what you mean about strange. They've always found new ways to assert their power and punish their enemies."

"But why do that? If they wanted her dead, why not just kill her?"

"I thought you said the grandfather brokered some kind of deal for her life? Well, at least her childhood?"

"Yeah, but still. The Brotherhood aren't exactly known for their mercy. What if it was something more, Pierre?" The information I have is not adding up, and the longer I'm in the dark, the more dangerous it is for everyone in this house.

"You're going to have to give me more to go on, Lincoln."

I tell him about what Fraser said, and he agrees that it could as easily be a way to throw me off the scent as the truth. And then I tell him that Imogen said almost exactly the same thing to me a week ago.

He hums softly, thinking. "It's definitely a hell of a coincidence if it is one. So you're thinking what? That she knows who you actually are? And that she's some kind of spy? The Brotherhood think Killian is dead, or they would never have stopped looking for him."

"What if they don't, Pierre? What if they know the truth?"

He shakes his head. "There's no way they know. They may suspect, but they can't know. Lincoln Knight is a ghost with no connection to Killian Wolfe." He nods, still humming softly to himself. "But if they do have doubts about Killian's death . . ."

Anger at my own stupidity rages inside me. Just like Fraser, I'm taking too many risks, blinded by her. "Then what better way to draw me out."

Realization dawns on his face. "Than putting your goddaughter up for sale."

"So what is she, Pierre? Is Imogen in on all this, or is she an innocent fucking victim they're using to get to me?"

"I supposed you'll have to find out."

"And how do I do that exactly?"

He tilts his head to the side. "Have you heard of the phrase give someone enough rope . . . ?"

Of course I have, but I don't want Imogen to hang herself. I don't want to trick her, manipulate her, or lie to her. She's been here for almost five months already. If she was some kind of spy for the Brotherhood, or she had any kind of revenge planned, she would have acted on it by now . . . right? She could have easily killed me in my sleep at least a hundred times. Then killed Pierre.

But then she'd be trapped, wouldn't she? She knows the fingerprint and retina scan are sensitive enough to only work on living tissue with a blood supply, and she's not strong enough to knock me out and drag me to the door. She can't even lift me up.

"I can hear your cogs turning, Lincoln, and you can think it over and try to rationalize it all you want, but the cold hard truth is if she's one of them, and she was raised as one of them, she would cut out your heart and smile while she did it. You will never know unless you test her."

"Nobody can be that good of an actress, Pierre," I insist, despite knowing that he's right. My heart is splintering in my chest, fragmenting even at the thought that she may have betrayed me—betrayed us. I can't fathom how she could be so cruel. No, she's not. The woman I've fallen so deeply in love with is not that cruel. She is kind and pure and good. Everything that I am not.

"Unfortunately, we know this is not the case." He places a hand on my forearm. "For what it's worth, I sincerely hope she's not one of them. But even if she is, Lincoln, then she's only being what she was raised to be. She was three years old when her parents were killed."

"I know, Pierre." I almost choke on my own words. Whatever she is, it's my own doing. I should have found her. Should have protected her the way I promised to.

Pierre is right, the only way to know for sure is to test her. Give her enough rope, as he so crudely put it.

Is Imogen DeMotta a Pawn in the Brotherhood's game, or is she the Queen?

CHAPTER 55
IMOGEN

Lincoln takes my hand, his warm fingers curling around mine in a tight grip. It's possessive and reassuring and I've come to love it. "I have a surprise for you, angel."

I don't know yet if I like surprises, but I can't imagine Lincoln's are unpleasant in any way. "What is it?"

He guides me toward the room next to the library, the one that's barely used and contains only a couple of huge sofas gathering dust. Not anymore though. Now it also has a shiny new TV on the wall above the fireplace. "You got a TV for in here?" I squeal excitedly.

He slides his arms around my waist, his chest against my back as he nuzzles my neck. "I know you've been watching the TV in your old room sometimes, and I thought it would be nice to have one down here. Where you can watch in the evenings while I do some work."

I spin in his arms. "You know it wouldn't hurt for you to watch a little TV sometimes too, sir. It's very relaxing. You work far too much."

He kisses the tip of my nose. "Because there is much to do."

And now I feel guilty because I do so little. I've even stopped exploring the house, looking for ways to escape. Like an adopted feral cat grown too used to comfort and affection, I have become far too domesticated. "Can I help with anything?"

"You do enough," he assures me.

"I barely do anything but a little laundry."

"And the garden. You've already freed the roses from their vine prison, and cleared a patch big enough to grow dozens of vegetables," he reminds me.

It's true I have cleared a lot of space, and I'm proud of the progress I've made in such a short time. I've also enjoyed every second of it. "That doesn't feel like work though."

"Nevertheless, it's enough, baby. Now are you going to come sit and watch some TV with me while I work?"

I nod, too eagerly probably, but I'm learning to stop trying to hide my feelings from him. He seems to like it when I don't and I want to be totally honest with him. With the kind of support and care he offers me, I believe I can truly uncover my real self.

LINCOLN TRAILS HIS FINGERTIPS LAZILY UP AND down my arm while I watch a movie with my head on his lap. He has his laptop perched on the arm of the sofa and continues to work while still making me feel wanted.

It's heaven sitting here with him like this. So normal and comfortable, which is odd, given how we came to be in each other's lives. Never in my wildest dreams did I ever imagine a future like this. It feels too impossibly good to be true.

The movie ends and I sit up, which gets me his full attention. "Did you enjoy your movie, baby?"

"Yes. And now I'm all done with TV for the night."

He arches an eyebrow. "And what would my little angel like to do now?"

I straddle him, wrapping my arms around his neck. "Umm!" I press my lips together, pretending to think.

He closes his laptop and circles my waist with his arms. "Have I told you how much I adore how bold you're becoming?"

"No, sir."

He runs his nose over my throat and growls. "Well, I do."

Butterflies are swirling in my stomach, but I've been thinking about this for a while now, and the books I read about love and romance don't seem to give me a clear answer on it. "Can I ask you something, sir?"

"Anything." He goes on nuzzling my neck.

"How do you know if you're in love?"

He stops kissing me and stares into my eyes.

"I've never been in love before, and I don't know what it's supposed to feel like. I was never taught about that kind of thing. Of course I've read about it in books, but in real life . . ."

His Adam's apple bobs as he swallows. "Being in love with someone is hard to describe. It's so many things all at once."

"Can you help me understand?" I plead.

"It's wanting to be near that person all of the time. Not being able to stop thinking about them. Needing to see them and touch them and know that they're okay. That feeling that you would die if they weren't in your life. That's a lot of what it feels like."

Warmth and contentment bloom fierce in my chest. That's exactly how I feel about him and up until now I wasn't sure if those feelings were deep enough to be love, or if they were more akin to infatuation.

He brushes my hair back from my face. "But those feelings can also just be lust and attraction. And that can wax and wane like the phases of the moon. Truly loving someone means that you would want their happiness above all else, even at the expense of your own. Love is being able to hold someone at their worst and yet still know that they're the very best part of you."

It's like he's reached inside my mind and put into words everything I feel about him. Tears are stinging behind my eyes. I want to tell him that I love him, but what if this is just infatuation or lust for him? He dusts his lips over mine. "Does that answer your question, angel?"

"Perfectly. It was a beautiful answer."

He hums, lips still close to mine. "I simply explained the way I feel about you."

I let the tears fall. Tears of happiness and an overwhelming rush of what I now know is love. "I love you too, Lincoln."

His mouth finally presses against mine and he flicks his tongue over the seam of my lips, gently easing them open until I allow him inside. His arms tighten around me, crushing me to his chest. I curl my fingers in the thick hair at the nape of his neck, and for a long time, we do nothing but kiss. It's both tender and rough. Passionate and steadfast. Possessive and liberating. My body melts into his, pouring all my depth of feeling into this single snapshot of time.

This must be love. And if it's not, then it must be something deeper and more profound. Because it is everything. He is everything. My safe space. My home. My heart.

CHAPTER 56
LINCOLN

"So you're actually leaving the house with her? Entering the civilized world?" Pierre asks after I told him about my plans for the day.

I rummage in the pantry for the antique picnic basket that was here when I bought the place sixteen years ago. "Not exactly. Just a picnic while the weather is still mild enough for us to enjoy it." I won't risk anyone seeing either of us, so yes, we're leaving the house, but mingling with the civilized world is a definite no.

"Does she know?"

"Not yet, but she will when she gets out of her bath and sees the new clothes on the bed." Along with the note I left her. It's been a week since she asked me what being in love felt like, when we told each other how we feel. And since that time, I've fallen in love with her more every single second. I cannot imagine a world where she doesn't sleep in my arms, and I believe she loves me too, but still Fraser's words continue to plague me. *The Queen is the most powerful piece in the game.*

"Are you letting her off her leash to see if she'll run?" he asks, his voice barely a whisper.

I snarl. "She's not a dog, Pierre."

"True. But are you doing that, knowing what you now do?"

"Weren't you the one who told me I couldn't keep her locked in here forever? You know she was never allowed to leave her grandfather's estate, right?"

"Also true, but you still haven't answered my question."

Spotting the hamper I'm looking for buried deep at the back of a cupboard, I pull it out and brush off the surface dust. "I actually want to do something a little special for her, even if it is only a picnic," I tell him truthfully. "But, while we won't be venturing anywhere close to town, we will be in walking distance of the road. Close enough that she'll be able to hear any passing vehicles."

"And you're thinking she might run?"

"I'm thinking I'd like to see what she'll do when presented with the opportunity to escape."

He frowns. "That's exactly what I said."

"Lincoln!" she calls from the kitchen, and when I stick my head out of the pantry, she's wrapped in a towel with her hair soaking wet, clutching the new white dress I gave her to her chest. She obviously left the matching underwear on the bed. "Are we really going out somewhere?"

I hold up the picnic hamper. "Just for a drive and then a picnic, angel. If you want to?"

She's practically vibrating with excitement. "Yes, I want to."

"Then go get ready while Pierre and I make our picnic."

She squeaks, actually squeaks, and then runs out of the room.

"She seems very excited," Pierre says dryly.

"She's about to leave the house for the first time in almost half a year, of course she's excited," I snap defensively.

"Just an observation, sir."

An observation we shared. Because I also felt a fleeting wave of panic at her excitement too. What if she does run? And what if that means none of this is real? I'm not sure how I will react if I were to find that everything between us were a lie. I'm sure my blackened heart would be destroyed forever. I swallow down my doubt and leave it there for now.

"I'M SO EXCITED TO SEE WHERE WE'RE GOING." She cranes her neck, peering out the window and trying to see past the forest of trees. My eyes stray to her legs. The new dress with the violet lace trim that sits perfectly against her olive skin has ridden high enough to expose almost all the soft skin of her thighs, hinting at the sweet temptation beneath, currently encased in the new purple lace underwear set I also bought for her. I know that because I lifted her dress to get a glimpse when she came running down the stairs earlier. And when she purred at my attention, I almost slipped my hand into her panties right there and finger-fucked her in the hallway. But my girl wants a picnic, and a promise is a promise.

I grab hold of her hand and lift it to my mouth before pressing a kiss on her knuckles. "It's just a nice spot I know, angel. Nothing special."

"It will be special to me," she says, eyes shining with happiness.

Yeah, there's no way she's one of them. She's too fucking sweet and innocent to be a member of the Brotherhood. Pierre's words come back to haunt me. *If she's one of them, and she was raised as one of them, she would cut out your heart and smile while she did it.* I push his words away, not needing him in my head right now. Besides, she chose to wear a pair of flimsy sandals with her new dress. If she were going to run, she'd have made an excuse to wear her sneakers, surely?

"Yeah, it will be special to me too."

She beams widely. "I'm glad to see you're not wearing your mask, sir."

"Why would I?"

"You usually do when you go out in public, don't you?"

Maybe it's Pierre's suspicions getting in my head, but for some reason that rankles me. "We're unlikely to see anyone where we're going, angel. And if we did, it would be a hiker. Nobody likely to come close enough to see my face. Or yours."

That doesn't seem to faze her at all and she goes back to staring out the window with all the excitement of a child on Christmas morning. I spent two Christmases with her as a child, although she was much too young to understand what it was. I push those memories away too, because they're a reminder of how I'm betraying her father. *Protect her for me*, he said. One hundred percent sure he didn't mean like this.

But we are where we are, and I'm in far too deep to stop this now.

"THAT WAS ALL DELICIOUS." SHE LIES DOWN ON the blanket, her hands resting on her stomach. "That was my first picnic ever."

I lie next to her on my side and link my fingers with hers. "Mine too, angel."

"Really?"

"Yes."

"You never went on any as a kid? Or you know took anyone else special for a picnic?" She blushes at the last few words.

"I already told you I never had relationships before. Just casual sex. Definitely never anyone I wanted to take on a picnic."

"I'm happy to be your first, Linc," she giggles and I fall in love with the sound. This is how she should be all the time. Carefree and happy. "And you never went as a child either?"

"My childhood wasn't exactly about picnics, baby. It was about survival."

She traces her fingertips over the scars on my cheek. "I guess we have that in common."

"I guess we do."

"Will you tell me about your childhood, Linc?"

"Why?"

"Because I want to know something about you. You know so much about my past, but I know nothing about yours."

"There's not a lot to know. I grew up in foster homes. I got into a lot of trouble. But I figured my shit out eventually. Realized I could read computer code the way that other people can read a book, and I never looked back."

I don't tell her I was recruited by the Brotherhood at the age of fourteen and brainwashed into believing they were the good guys until I was twenty-four. And then when I found out they weren't, it was too late to save the one person I should have protected. And they hurt her. Maybe even worse than that are the decisions I made afterward, which destroyed the only people who were ever a real family to me.

"So you have no family?"

I cup her jaw, my grip possessive. "I have you." She has no idea how honest I'm being. Her smile makes my heart race, and I'm in danger of revealing too much about my past. I roll on top of her and silence any follow-up question with a kiss.

When I let her up for air, she traces her fingertips over my scars. "How old were you when you got these?"

"In my twenties."

Her eyes narrow and she studies them intently. "How did you get them? They're very . . ." she chews on her lip " . . . unique."

I was shackled to the back of a motorcycle by my neck and driven a few hundred yards down a gravel road before I somehow managed to pull the fucker off and beat him to death with his own chain. Obviously, I don't tell her that, and simply say. "A motorcycle accident."

THE AUCTION

She doesn't reply, goes on trailing her fingertips over the damaged skin. Down my neck, dipping beneath the collar of my T-shirt. "Did they hurt a lot?"

"Not as much as you'd expect. I think I was used to pain by then."

She nods, like she knows how that feels.

I want to change the subject from our pasts, before I say too much. Before I'm confronted with so much of mine that I feel compelled to tell her the truth. I know I'll have to one day, but not yet. Not when she's looking at me the way she is. I run my nose over her jawline, drinking her in. "Do you like the new underwear I got for you, angel?"

Her cheeks flush an adorable shade of pink. "Yes, sir."

"Good girl."

"Would you like to see it all now, or wait until we get home?"

I don't miss that she just called my house her home, and I fucking love that she did. "That depends on whether you'd like to be fucked in this field before we go home."

"Yes please, sir."

"Yeah?"

Sinking her teeth into her juicy bottom lip, she nods. I slide my hand beneath her dress, over the soft supple skin of her thigh and a possessive growl rolls out of me. She arches her back, pressing herself into my touch.

"This dress is beautiful on you, baby, but I think it will look much better off you."

"Yes," she pants.

She helps me to pull it off over her head and lies back, her hair spread around her head like a dark halo. I let my eyes rake greedily over her body. The bright purple underwear looks stunning against her olive skin. Her pert brown nipples peeking through the sheer fabric of her bra, begging for attention. And don't get me started on the panties and the strawberry-shaped wet spot currently staining the material at the apex of her thighs. "Fuck, you are perfect, baby."

Her cheeks flush a delicious shade of pink. "Thank you, sir."

I slip my hand into her panties and she spreads her legs to accommodate me. "And you're such a good fucking girl for me."

She grins mischievously. "Not always, sir. I wore something else today too, something you didn't tell me to wear."

As far as I can see, she's wearing nothing right now but the underwear. Unless . . .

I slide my hand to the seam of her ass and feel the jeweled base of one of her plugs. "Wearing your plug makes you a very good girl. Did you want me to fuck your ass today, or are you just experimenting?"

"Yes, I want you to fuck me there, Linc."

My cock throbs with the need to be inside her. Quickly, I free it from the confines of my pants. "When we get home, okay?" I tug her new panties aside, too impatient to take them off. "I want to fuck my pretty cunt first."

I sink inside her in one smooth thrust, all the way to the hilt. Thanks to her plug, she's fucking soaked already.

"Linc!" she gasps, wrapping her legs around my waist and pulling me deeper.

I drive inside her, trying to get as deep as I can, but it's not enough. Never enough. With a grunt of frustration, I flip her over until she's on all fours. She squeals a half protest, but then she wiggles that delicious ass in my face. It looks goddamn edible under any circumstance, but in her tiny panties and with the plug visible through the fabric, it takes all my willpower not to bite into it like a juicy peach. I spank her instead. Once on each cheek.

I growl before pulling the panties down, leaving them midway up her thighs. Then I sink inside her and she feels so fucking good my eyes roll back. "I can get so much deeper like this, baby."

She whines her agreement.

I spank her ass again. "Do you like being bent over and fucked out here in the open?"

"Yes, sir."

"Like teasing me with your plug when you know I have no lube out here?"

"I don't need lube, sir."

I grab onto her hips and drive in harder. "Yes, you do."

She glances over her shoulder at me, her lips parted in an O and her breathing coming in desperate pants. I ease up a little. "Don't we have something from the picnic we could use? The salad dressing?" she asks.

I lean over her, resting my lips against her ear. "As much as I admire your creativity, it has lemon and vinegar in it. And I'm not a sadist." I slide my hand between her thighs and rub her swollen clit. Her pussy walls ripple around me until she moans my name.

I brush my fingertips over the plug. "Wearing this made you all wet and needy, huh, baby?"

"Yes, sir." Her lip trembles. My greedy girl still needs more. I want more. The sight of that plug filling her ass instead of me has a feral kind of possessiveness burning in my veins. I close my eyes and recall the first time I fucked her tight ass, how hard she came for me and how soft and tired she was afterward when she curled up in my arms.

I draw in a breath. As much as I'm sure she'd let me, I can't fuck her with no lube. I'd hurt her and that would kill me.

I slide my cock almost all the way out of her, and it's coated in her thick creamy cum. Would that be enough?

"Linc, please," she whines at the loss of fullness.

I glance at the picnic basket. We do have a little butter left too. That and her cum would be enough.

She whimpers when I pull out of her, but it takes me two seconds to lean over and grab the basket. Then I'm back behind her, one hand on her hip while I rummage around for the butter with the other. "Hang on, baby. I think I have something for you."

I find the small plastic tub containing what I'm looking for and flip the top off. There's enough left for what I need. Gently, I pull the plug out of her ass first, making her moan.

"You want my cock in you instead, angel?"

She nods, her cheek rubbing against the blanket. "Please, Linc."

I scoop out the butter and smear it over my cock, and it melts quickly in my hand. Then I push two fingers inside her ass, using the butter and the residue of the lube from her plug to prep her for me.

Her groan is sexy as fuck. "What is that?"

"Butter, angel."

She purrs like a kitten. "Oh, it feels nice."

Satisfied she's prepped enough, I slide my cock inside her. It feels better than fucking nice and I will never ever look at butter the same way again. "Because your ass is fucking perfect. You take my cock so well."

She arches her back. I gather her hair into my fist, using it to pull her up until her back is pressed against my chest, and then I rut into her like the animal she brings out in me while I play with her swollen clit. And my good girl takes it all from me, whimpering and moaning while she rides my cock until we both come.

WHEN WE'RE DONE, I PUT HER DRESS BACK ON and she curls up on my lap while I wrap her in my arms.

She yawns and buries her cheek against my chest. "I'm sorry I think I ruined my new panties, sir."

I kiss the top of her head. We both smell of butter and sex

THE AUCTION

and there's a lake nearby we could clean up in, but I can't be bothered to move. "I'd be happy to ruin every pair of panties you own doing that, baby."

She giggles and I hug her tighter. The sound of a truck horn in the distance disturbs some birds in a tree nearby, but Imogen doesn't react. All of the residual tension left over from my earlier conversation with Pierre slips away. She shows absolutely no sign that she wants to be anywhere but here in my arms. And I'm certain it's the only place I want her to be—ever.

CHAPTER 57
LINCOLN

"How was the picnic?" Pierre asks.

I close my eyes and suppress a groan. The picnic was fucking incredible, and then after was just as incredible when I washed us both clean in the shower and I fucked her again. After, we moved the TV into my room and lay in bed for the rest of the night eating snacks and watching movies. I know that's not the kind of answer Pierre is looking for though, which is why he's waited until the privacy of the basement to ask.

"It was good. She didn't seem on edge at all. Didn't ask any questions about where we were. I did tell her the road we turned off led into town and we heard some traffic while we were out there, but she showed no sign of wanting to run."

He does that humming thing when he's thinking. "Per'aps she realized it would be futile to run? I mean you would surely catch her, and she is a smart girl."

I had considered that. "I know, but it was her whole body language. She just seemed happy to be outdoors, and to . . ." I swallow the knot of happiness and perhaps disbelief that clogs up my throat.

"And to what?"

"To be with me."

He smiles.

"Am I fucking insane, Pierre? I feel like a fucking teenage boy."

"You are in love, *mon ami*. It happens to the best of us, and yes of course it feels like you are going crazy."

"I'm twice her age," I remind him. I've never fucked a woman young enough to be my daughter before, let alone take her for a picnic and discover a new and incredibly satisfying use for butter.

He shrugs. "Only for one more year, and then you will simply be twenty-one years older."

"I'm her godfather," I add.

"In name alone. You have not known her for almost her entire life."

Guy has an answer for everything.

"She thinks I murdered her parents."

He throws his hands into the air. "Then tell her the truth. Tell her you did not!" He says that like it's easy.

"She spent eighteen years of her life being convinced otherwise, Pierre. We know her grandfather is a piece of shit, but she loves the guy. She's still loyal to him, and I'm not sure yet whether she'd believe me over him."

"Not yet, but one day. Maybe you should look into her grandfather a little more, *non*?"

I'm already looking into him after the whole chess quote, but he's frustratingly difficult to get information on. Like me, he has very little online presence. Despite being incredibly wealthy, he has very few expenses or social interaction. He's a shut-in—even more of a recluse than I am.

I did entertain the notion that he may be the King I've been looking for, but that makes no sense. He's just too . . . bland. The King, while his identity is protected, would live the kind of decadent lifestyle his wealth afforded him. Despite Imogen telling me Saul has six drivers, he rarely leaves his estate except for an annual board meeting once a year. He's a born-again Christian, devout advocate of *traditional family values*, yet he doesn't even leave his estate to attend church. His expenses are minimal. He doesn't fit the profile of a King.

"Find proof that he is a bad man, and then maybe she will believe you instead?" Pierre adds.

"I'm a bad man too," I remind him.

He laughs. "Not bad to her though. Never bad to her. To her you are a teddy bear."

Definitely wasn't a teddy bear yesterday when I fucked her ass out in the open with only butter for lube. The memory makes my cock twitch in my pants.

I shake the image from my head. I came down here because I got an alert from one of my tracking software programs, and I need to focus on that. Not the siren currently sitting in the garden, looking innocent and far too fuckable for my mental health.

I drop into my chair and pull up the tracking program. "Bingo."

"You have found something?" Pierre asks.

"One of the girls from the auction. She's only a little over a hundred miles away too." I check my watch. It's a little after ten, meaning I could be there and back in a day if I leave this afternoon.

"You are leaving today?"

"Yeah."

"You have not been home long. *Mon chou* will be very sad."

I know she will, and I hate leaving her, but if she knew why I was, she'd want me to go. She'd probably insist on coming with me. Now there's a thought, but one for another day, one day in the future. "I'll be back tomorrow. Maybe you and she could watch a movie or something? Explore a new universe now you've finished showing her the wonders of Marvel?"

He shakes his head. "You know I like to spend my evenings alone, *mon ami*."

THE AUCTION

I rest a hand on his shoulder. "I also know you enjoy her company."

He snorts. "Says the man who likes to be alone even more than I do, at least until the girl arrived." Then without another word, he heads for the staircase, leaving me to prep for my trip.

He's right. Before her, I preferred my own company, even where Pierre was concerned. We've lived in this house together for sixteen years, and we've spent most of that time alone, coming together only for work, or the occasional game of chess. But yeah, that was before her. Before I truly knew what it felt like to be alive. And being locked away in this mausoleum is no life for any of us.

CHAPTER 58
IMOGEN

Is it snooping if the drawers aren't locked? If there's something he doesn't want me to find, then he'd lock it away, wouldn't he? Not that he has a safe I'm aware of—the entire house feels more secure than Fort Knox. But if this was the right thing to be doing, I wouldn't be feeling so guilty about it.

Yet I want, no, I need to know more about Lincoln Knight. He's so evasive about his past, about how he became the man he is today, his scars, his family. Why he paid ten million dollars for a traitor's daughter. And these past few weeks, I've felt him pulling away from me. Not physically. He's still attentive and kind and loving, but he's definitely more guarded than he was before. And I've spent so much time here being lulled into this domestic, if highly erotic, bliss we've created for ourselves that I suppressed my innate curiosity about him.

Or perhaps I'm simply inherently suspicious rather than curious. Perhaps I was simply raised by awful people, who taught me to question kindness and love while blindly accepting cruelty and pain. Either way, this must be wrong or I wouldn't be sneaking around doing it while he's not here. Yet I don't find myself stopping. Because I know that Lincoln Knight has a secret and I know in my gut that it has something to do with the reason he bought me from that vile auction.

I go through his desk drawers methodically, making sure that I put everything back in its rightful place. There isn't a lot in here. Stationery. Deeds to a property in Vermont. The spare key to his SUV. A half empty packet of gum. Nothing that gives me any clues to the man.

I suppose everything is digitalized now and he'd have no need for masses of paperwork. And in the five months I've lived here, he's never received any mail to my knowledge. Nor a single visitor. My grandfather was a private man, but there were always visitors to the house. Every day people would arrive, and I would be shunted away to my room by Larissa, or one of the drivers, until the visitors left. I've been so wrapped up in Lincoln and finding my own happiness that I stopped noticing what was around me.

I run my fingertips absentmindedly over the carved ebony. This is an antique desk, made before a time when computers and access codes and fingerprint technology was even a thing. I crouch down and crawl beneath it, looking for a hidden drawer or some kind of lever or something, but find nothing. With a sigh of frustration, I crawl out from under it and sit cross-legged on the floor, staring at the ornately carved corners and the filigree work on the silver handles. So much craftmanship into one piece of furniture.

I pull the bottom drawer open again, all the way to the end. It doesn't slide all the way out, stopped by one of those pieces of wood that are designed to do that very job. Reaching inside, I twist it aside and pull the drawer all the way out before peering inside the empty space I left behind.

Nothing.

I do the same to the other three on that side. Still nothing. With little else but time, I move to the other side of the desk and do the same, not even sure what it is I'm looking for. Even if something were hidden behind these drawers. When I pull the middle drawer all the way out, I see the corner of a faded brown envelope peeking out from the space above and my heart leaps into my throat. It can't be much bigger than a greeting card, probably something that simply fell down the back of the drawer and was forgotten about. Still, my heart is racing when I pull out the final drawer. And that's when I see the envelope is taped to the wood.

My fingers are trembling as I gently peel back the yellowed Scotch tape. It looks like it's been stuck there for years. I'm careful not to tear the tape from the envelope and damage it, so it seems to take forever for me to remove it. The envelope is unsealed and it's so thin it doesn't contain much at all. I peer inside and find a photograph. A polaroid-style one that prints immediately. Why does Lincoln have an old photograph taped to the back of his desk?

My hand is shaking as I reach inside, my fingers gripping the edge of the glossy paper. I'm filled with anticipation and excitement and a healthy dose of dread. What if I don't like what I find? He clearly hid this for a reason. Perhaps it's a photograph of him before his accident. One that he can neither bear to look at nor throw away.

I pull it out, expecting to see his face. And I do. His face before the accident that left him scarred. He's smiling for the camera.

But it's not his face that makes me feel like I've been punched right in my solar plexus. Not his smile that makes time stand still. I recognize the two adults he's standing beside who also smile widely for the camera. My parents. My father has his arm around Lincoln. My mother stands between them both, holding a small child in her arms. A little girl of about two with a shock of dark curly hair.

THE AUCTION

Me.

I struggle to breathe as all the oxygen is siphoned from the room. My heart races erratically, thundering like a bass drum in my ears, making my head spin with confusion and fear.

Lincoln knew my parents. Lincoln knew me before the auction.

I peer at his face more closely, eyes narrowed in concentration. How did I not recognize him immediately? Even through the fog of confusion, it's clear as day to me now, as I stare at his younger self. He doesn't have the beard or the scars, and his hair is cut much shorter, but how could I have not remembered those eyes?

I experience an entire lifetime of pain in a single moment. My poor heart, which only just discovered how to beat, stops. Then it disintegrates into nothing but dust, leaving a gaping, sucking hole in my chest where it used to be.

Lincoln isn't Lincoln Knight at all. He's not the man I've spent the last few months falling in love with. He's Killian Wolfe. The man who betrayed and killed my parents.

My godfather.

I HAVE NO IDEA HOW LONG I STARE AT THE PHOtograph for, but time starts to lose all meaning. My life as I know it has lost all meaning. Everything I've come to believe, everything I've learned about myself these past five months is all a lie.

None of it was true. Lincoln lied to me. *Killian* lied to me. The man who betrayed my parents. The man who slaughtered them and would have done the same to me had my grandfather not intervened. So is that why he bought me? To finish the job? Was making me fall in love with him always part of his plan, or a sickening by-product? Has he been laughing at me all this time? Making me dependent on him? Making me care about him? Love him?

A river of silent tears runs down my cheeks, dripping onto my T-shirt and soaking into the fabric. I can't believe he would be so cruel. Not the man who is capable of such tenderness. I refuse to believe that everything between us has been a lie. My soul would surely disintegrate into particles of dust along with my heart if that's true.

But why would he do this? Why seek me out if not for some revenge? Surely it's not for redemption, because there is no redemption for a man who took my parents and left me to a life of anguish and humiliation. An entire childhood of believing my only fate was to be sold by the Brotherhood into a life of pain. Or is that exactly why he chose me? His final sick twisted revenge against my father? The Brotherhood's ultimate vengeance. Fuck her before you kill her.

Did he always intend to make me need him before he eviscerates me? Was that part of the plan? Although none of that hurts more than what he made me believe. He made me believe I was loved. He made me believe I was worthy.

Sick, twisted bastard!

I want to tear the photograph in half, remove him from the image and keep the rest of it somewhere safe with me. I want to run from this house. Far away into a world without this kind of bone-deep betrayal. But there's no escape from here. Not unless I'm smart. Not unless I stick to my original game plan. I have to let Killian believe what he wants to believe. Let him use me in whatever way he needs while I figure a way out.

It will be more difficult now that he's broken down my walls. He's too shrewd. If I put the same ones back up, he'll notice there's something wrong, and I can't allow that to happen.

I gather myself back together, mentally collect all the broken fragments of who I was and piece them back together into a form that resembles me, if not the same me from this morning.

Now I'm more like the one who first arrived here. A safer version of myself.

Then I scrub the tears from my cheeks and press a kiss on each of my parent's faces. With steady hands, I carefully return the photograph and the envelope to its previous hiding place. I'll build new walls—stronger than before. Impenetrable. Lincoln Knight is dead to me. And Killian Wolfe can go to hell.

CHAPTER 59
LINCOLN/ KILLIAN

The closer I get to home, the faster I drive. Gas pedal to the floor as I wind through the lanes cutting through the forest. Although it's not home I'm anxious to get to, it's her. Imogen DeMotta is home.

She's in the library when I finally arrive, flicking through a book. Her eyes scanning the pages so intently that she mustn't hear me come in, because she doesn't look up.

The sound of my shoes on the polished wood makes her head snap up, and there it is. The smile that could bring a man to his knees. I drop to mine at her feet and spread her knees apart with my body. "I missed you, angel."

She puts her book down and curls a lock of hair at my temple between her fingertips. "I missed you too."

Her smile stays in place, but there's a hint of sadness in her eyes. I glance at her book. *Watership Down*. It's not her usual kind of reading material but it explains the melancholy. I read that book once as a boy and vowed never to read it again. "Are you ready for bed, baby?"

"Yeah." Still that smile, but everything else about her is . . . It's just fucking sad.

Worry gnaws in my gut. "Are you okay?"

"Yeah. That book just hit me in all my feels." Her vernacular is another change in her these last five months—one that I enjoy seeing blossom—influenced by her love of movies and the songs she likes to sing along to when she's working in the garden. She laughs off her comment and then leans forward, snaking her arms around my neck. "But I am *definitely* ready for bed, sir."

My cock twitches in my pants. He's missed her too.

I waste no time scooping her into my arms and carrying her to bed, where I lay her down and slowly peel off her clothes, kissing each inch of skin I expose.

She winds her fingers through my hair, and she makes all the soft moaning sounds she usually makes but something's still off. There's still an unidentifiable sadness about her.

I crawl over her, brushing all her hair back from her face and staring into her deep green eyes. "Are you okay, baby?"

"Yeah. I'm just . . . That book was sad, and I . . . I love you, Linc. I hate it when you go away and leave me."

I nudge her thighs apart and settle between them, the crown of my cock nudging at her wet heat. "I know, but I'm here now."

She bites down on her lip and nods.

"You want this, angel?"

She wraps her legs around my waist, sinking her heels into my ass. "Yes, sir."

I sink inside her, bone-deep relief surging through my entire body. "I love you. I'm sorry I have to leave you sometimes." I really wish I didn't have to, but I can't see a time when that won't be the case. Or a time when I don't have to keep her locked away in this prison for her own protection, and selfishly, for my own. She deserves a much better future than the one I'm offering her, but I'm not sure I'm a good enough man to ever let her go.

"I know," she whispers.

Maybe her sadness is merely a reflection of my own. Maybe

she understands that this thing between us is toxic and unnatural, no matter how good it feels.

I kiss her softly, parting her lips so that I can slide my tongue into her mouth while I fuck her slowly. We don't come up for air until she climaxes, wrenching her lips from mine as she moans my name. I would live in these moments if I could, where no one else can touch us. Perhaps that's the key to our future. Both of us disappearing forever and forgetting that the Brotherhood even exist. But doing that would feel like a betrayal to the man whom I loved like a brother. The man who sacrificed everything for me. And I'm already betraying him enough by corrupting his innocent daughter, aren't I?

I push thoughts of him and the Brotherhood aside, and I focus only on Imogen. On her tight heat rippling around my cock. On the heavy cadence of her breathing, the scent of her, the feel of her skin against mine. There's no redemption for a man like me, but I'll take whatever salvation I can find, and that's only in her.

CHAPTER 60
IMOGEN

I remember lying here like this less than twenty-four hours ago, but somehow in another lifetime, staring at him while he sleeps. I distinctly remember thinking that if I could permit myself to believe in true, real happiness—the kind that lasts—then it would be waking with his arms wrapped around me and my cheek pressed against his chest, my muscles aching from all the pleasure our bodies took from each other in the night.

But yesterday was a lifetime ago, when he was Lincoln Knight and not Killian Wolfe.

I trace my fingertips over the mottled scars on the right side of his chest. I know he thinks they make him monstrous, but not to me. They were always a beautiful part of the beautiful whole of him. Until I realized how he must have got them in the first place.

So how? How can he touch me like he does, kiss me the way he does, make my body sing the way he does if it's not real?

I lie on my side and go on watching him sleep, his hand gripping my hip possessively even in his slumber. Is that because he can't bear to let me go? Or because he doesn't want me to escape? It feels like the former. When I'm with him, everything feels right in a way that it never has in my life. He makes me feel like I can be me. Doesn't he? Because the truth is I don't know who I am. I was the person I was trained to be for eighteen years, and then for the last six months . . . who knows. Maybe I became the woman Killian wanted me to be.

And what really happened to my parents? Do I believe my grandfather—a man who taught me loyalty, who saved my life, yet only ever showed me cruelty at worst and indifference at best? Or do I believe in Killian? My godfather. A man who murdered my parents. A man who should have protected me when I was a child instead of allowing the Brotherhood to make a deal with my grandfather. A man who has lied to me from the moment we met. The same man who tells me he loves me and has shown me more kindness and compassion in a few months than I've ever known in my whole life.

I refuse to believe that everything between us has been a lie, and I do believe that in his own way, he loves me. But I live in a world where truth and lies can't be so easily distinguished from the other, and more importantly, a world where I no longer trust my own judgment.

What I do know as fact is that man in the photograph is the man lying next to me. My godfather. And whatever his motives, he's lied to me from the moment we met. For that reason alone, I need to discover my own truth, and the only way to do that is alone.

Thunder rolls in the sky outside and I shiver. Instinctively, he pulls me into his arms, wrapping me in his warmth and pressing his lips to the top of my head. "I've got you, angel," he murmurs sleepily.

Tears sting my eyes. That his instinctive response is to protect me makes me falter, but only for a second. He lied to me. Fact. He's not who he says he is. Fact. And that is all I truly know to be real.

I may have been raised by wolves, but they taught me well. How to do whatever is necessary for survival.

CHAPTER 61
LINCOLN/ KILLIAN

"Do you think she's acting strangely?" I ask Pierre while he prepares dinner and I watch her from the kitchen window. Ever since I got back from my trip a few days ago, she's seemed a little . . . off. She's polite and responsive and she smiles at the right times, moans at all the right times, but she's lost some of that feistiness she was developing. All in all, there's just an overall air of fucking sadness about her.

"She seems a little quiet today. But then she is often quiet, *non*? Has she found a new and all-consuming book, per'aps?"

"I don't know. But it's more than that. I can't put my finger on it, but she's different, Pierre. At least with me."

"Per'aps she is growing bored of being locked in this prison? You gave her a glimpse of the outside world taking her on that picnic and now she wants more, *non*?"

He could be right. This all started after the picnic. He sidles up next to me and pops a slice of raw carrot into his mouth. "Or are you thinking about what the Rook said? About her saying the same thing?"

Guilt washes over me. She's never given me any reason to doubt her, and yet . . . My name might be Wolfe, but she really was fucking raised by them. I don't doubt that she cares for me, loves me even, but maybe that's why she's so conflicted.

"I don't think the picnic was enough of a test, Pierre. There was never any real chance of escaping."

He chews his carrot loudly. "Okay. So what would be enough of a test?"

"She needs an opportunity to actually be able to escape, Pierre. A viable chance to get out of here and get to her grandfather." I hate even saying the words aloud, not only because the thought of losing her terrifies me, but if she does try, then it will crush my heart to fucking dust.

"Isn't that dangerous, sir? What if she succeeds?"

I stuff my hands into my pockets, watching her as she tilts her face toward the sun and smiles. I'd pay a billion dollars to know what was going through her head. "She won't."

He scoffs. "Do not let your arrogance misguide you, Lincoln."

He goes back to preparing dinner and I keep watching her. "I'm going to schedule a trip for next week. And we're going to leave a trail of breadcrumbs for her to follow."

"And where will those breadcrumbs lead, sir?"

Hopefully, to the truth. "To the trunk of my car."

"Then let's make some breadcrumbs."

Yes, let's.

I go out into the garden and take a seat beside her. She offers me a smile, but it lacks her usual warmth. Still, there's that sadness in her eyes that I can't seem to unsee. Is it something that I did? Or is it something unshakable from the life she's had to live.

I take her hand in mine and she allows me to curl my fingers around hers, even giving mine a gentle squeeze.

"You doing okay, angel?"

She nods. "Yeah. It's so nice out today, isn't it?"

I hum my agreement, watching her intently. "I need to go on another trip next week."

"Again? But you only just got back?"

THE AUCTION

I rub the pad of my thumb over the back of her hand. "I know. But it will be a short one. I have a meeting in New York I need to attend next Thursday."

Her slender throat works as she swallows. "I'll miss you."

Will she really?

"Come here, baby." I tug her onto my lap and she comes willingly, letting me wrap my arms around her while she buries her head against my chest. For whatever reason, my girl is sad. Maybe it is because she had a taste of freedom and she wants more. And if that's the case, I'm going to have to figure out a way to give her some so I don't lose her.

I rest my chin on the top of her head. "You know we never did get those chickens."

She laughs softly. "Because Pierre would probably cook them for dinner."

I laugh too, gripping her tightly against me. "I love you, Imogen."

She snuggles closer. "I love you too, Linc."

Jesus, my heart just fucking shattered. Why the hell am I testing her again? Because I'm a suspicious fuck who can't trust that someone as incredible as her could love someone as fucked-up as me. I should say fuck the breadcrumbs. Tell her I won't go on my fake trip next week. Because I want to do nothing but lie in bed, and sit in the garden, or the library or on the sofa, with her. Talking with her. Kissing her. Fucking her. Loving her.

But I don't. The wheels are in motion, and I have to see this through.

CHAPTER 62
LINCOLN/ KILLIAN

18 years earlier

Wind rushes against my ears and the driving rain blurs my vision, but I gun the throttle anyway, pushing the Kawasaki to its limits. Adrenaline and fear race like lightning through my veins.

When I get to the place I lost his signal, my tires screech to a halt and I jump off the motorcycle, letting it topple to the ground. The door to the safe house is ajar, hanging from one hinge. A gust of wind causes it to smash violently against the interior wall.

And already I know I'm too late.

My racing heart tries to clamor out of my throat while my blood thunders loudly in my ears. I run down the hallway, my wet boots slipping on the linoleum floor. There's a body in the hallway, his eye protruding from his socket and half his head blown off—another one with a knife in his neck.

Pawns no doubt, sent to kill a Rook. They failed, but I have a sinking feeling that whoever else was with them didn't.

Another body is slumped against the basement door, blood oozing from his eye sockets. I make my way to the kitchen and my racing heart stops beating. More bodies, and in the midst of them all, the man responsible for killing them all—the man I call my brother.

Luca DeMotta is sitting up against a cupboard. Deep red blood streaked across the floor and white plywood doors paints the macabre picture of his effort to get to the medicine cabinet. Bandages and rubbing alcohol are strewn around him, bloody handprints marring all the packets although none are open.

He holds his hand to his throat, thick ribbons of blood trickling through his fingers.

I crouch down beside him. "Luca!"

He opens his mouth to speak but chokes on his own blood. "We need to get you out of here."

"No!" He croaks out the word and then coughs up a clot of blood, spitting it onto the floor beside him. "It's too late for me."

An intense wave of guilt almost knocks me off my feet. Guilt and despair. I know he speaks the truth. His carotid artery has been severed, and he likely has only a few minutes left. There's no way to stop the bleeding. No way to save him. I push down the overwhelming tornado of feelings because they don't help us here. Logic and quick thinking are our only recourse now.

"Where are Carmen and Imogen?" I ask, praying they're not in this house. If they've met the same fate as him, then I might as well just sit on the floor beside him and stick a knife in my own throat.

"They're . . . Vermont safe house. She's not . . . I need you to . . ." He coughs up another mass of blood as he grasps for my hand, struggling to find a grip.

I slide my palm against his and squeeze reassuringly. "I'll protect them, Luca."

He screws his eyes closed. "P-please, Kill. Take care of . . ."

Tears leak from my eyes and I'm powerless to stop them. I rest my forehead against his. This is all because of me, because of what I learned and told him. He's dead because I chose to leave the Brotherhood, and he wouldn't let me leave without him.

"I'm sorry, Luca. If I hadn't—"

"No!" He sucks in a breath. "Couldn't let her . . ." Every word from his mouth sounds pained. "Protect my baby."

I give his hand another squeeze. "I promise I'll protect her, Luca. Always. No matter what the cost."

He doesn't reply. He's already gone.

My brother and best friend.

CHAPTER 63
IMOGEN

Where are my best salt and pepper pots? Pierre throws his hands in the air and then turns to face Lincoln and me with a scowl.

I shrug. I have no idea.

Lincoln winces. "Shit! I took them on our picnic. Were they not in the basket?"

"If they were in the basket, then I would not be asking where they are, would I?"

"Can't you just use a different set of pots?" Lincoln asks, shooting me a conspiratorial eye roll.

Pierre places his hands on his hips. "*Non!* I cannot just use a different set. They are my lucky salt and pepper."

Lincoln shakes his head but Pierre is seething. He's always been a little temperamental but cooking brings out the passion in him. It's one of the things I adore about him, and one of the things I will miss.

"Maybe we left them in the trunk or something?" I suggest.

Lincoln shakes his head. "I don't think so. I checked the trunk."

Pierre huffs. "Oh, really? Because you both seemed a little distracted to me."

The memory of that day has heat searing between my thighs. It was a perfect day. The last one before I found out Lincoln was a lying, murdering piece of shit.

"So, go. Go check!"

Lincoln winks at me, and I remind my treacherous lady parts that we hate him. "You want to come help me, angel?"

"Sure." I slide off my stool and let him take my hand, following him to the garage. He lets us inside, using the retina scan.

I didn't pay much attention the last time I was in here, too excited for my surprise. But I do this time, taking in the time delay on the door closing behind us. I count in my head and it takes a full thirty seconds to swing fully closed. That's enough for me to sneak in here behind him if he's ever distracted enough.

I stand by the SUV and study how Lincoln opens the locked key cabinet on the wall, also controlled by a retina scan. He takes a key and then presses the fob to pop the trunk as he walks over to me. I peer inside the open trunk and see the small salt and pepper shakers nestled in the corner.

"There they are," I exclaim, reaching in to grab them. "Pierre will be pleased."

Lincoln murmurs his agreement and then glances inside the trunk. "I'd better check that there's nothing else in here." He pokes his head inside and feels around. "No nothing else. Oh, shit!"

"What is it?"

He holds up his hand and his finger is bleeding. Not a lot, but enough for blood to be dripping down into his palm. He takes the salt and pepper cellars from me with his good hand and then presses the car key into my palm. "Can you put this back for me, angel. It goes on the top row. If I take these to Pierre, he might show me where the first aid kit is."

Then with a kiss on my forehead, he leaves me alone in the garage. I glance around. What if I jumped in the car and made a getaway attempt right now?

Shoot! The giant steel doors can only be opened by Lincoln and I'm not sure even his armored SUV could get through those things.

Is this a test? It feels like a test. What if he's watching me on the cameras right now? Not wanting to give him any reason to be suspicious of me, I head straight to the key cabinet. On the top row, there's a sign, in both braille and handwritten pen, saying SUV. There's another key hanging below it, which looks exactly the same, with the BMW logo right there in enamel.

Is it a spare key? And if it went missing, would he notice? It's not on the same hook and there are other keys in here, so he might not. It's worth a shot, and I have no other means of getting out of here. I don't even know what I'd do with a spare key, but I have time to think.

Unless it's not a spare key at all, meant for something else. I press the small fob and the SUV clicks open.

Yes! It is a spare! Quickly I lock it again and then hang the key Lincoln gave me in its rightful place, while discreetly palming the other one.

I leave the garage and close the door behind me. I don't know exactly how yet, but I think I just found my way out.

CHAPTER 64
IMOGEN

Every day this week, I've waited with bated breath for the moment Lincoln realizes the extra key to his SUV is missing, yet he doesn't seem to notice. He even went to town to get supplies yesterday and I was sure I was done for, but he bought me some Milky Ways and fucked me like a demon when he got back, so I guess he didn't.

Today is the day he leaves for his trip to New York, and I've figured that's how I get out of here—with him.

It's late when he's leaving and I feign a headache, kiss him goodbye and tell him I'm going to bed. "I think maybe it's my period coming, or I'm getting a cold. But, I feel really tired too." I wrinkle my nose and create a sad face.

Lincoln's eyes narrow in concern and he rests his cool palm on my forehead, like he's checking my temperature "Do you want me to postpone my trip, baby?"

I plaster on a smile. "There's no need. I'm sure I'll be fine after a good night's sleep."

He nods, although he doesn't look entirely convinced. So I push up onto my tiptoes and kiss him. "I'll miss you."

That makes him grin. "I'll be back as soon as I can."

"I know."

He wraps me in a hug and then insists on bringing me to bed and tucking me in. With a final kiss on my forehead and a promise of love, he leaves.

As soon as his footsteps have faded, I climb out of bed and quickly get dressed in a pair of leggings and a sweatshirt before grabbing the spare car key from the pocket of my jeans where I stashed it last week. If he doesn't close the door behind him manually, which he has no reason to, I have thirty seconds to get inside the garage. It's going to be close, and he could catch me, but if he does, I'll tell him I needed one more hug goodbye.

I have no idea how the hell I'm going to get myself into the car, ideally the trunk, without him seeing, but I have to think of something. And if I can't, I'll simply slip out the doors after he's driven out. Not that I relish finding my way out of these woods, but I have options and that's what matters.

My heart is racing so hard I'm worried both Pierre and Lincoln will hear it as I tiptoe down the staircase. I hold on to the spare key tightly. My lifeline. I hear the muffled voices of the two men as they chat in his study and I quietly make my way to the other side of the house. The garage door is already open. Is this a trick? No. he's definitely done that before. He's left the garage open while he's gone to grab his bag or speak to Pierre. *You're spiraling, Imogen. There's no way he'd risk you escaping, now get it together!*

The lights in the garage are on. The SUV already unlocked.

I open the trunk, wincing at the clicking sound, which reverberates around the otherwise empty garage. It seems so loud. Almost as loud as my heartbeat ringing in my ears. But this feels far too easy. My escape can't be this easy, can it? *Yes, it can, Imogen. Because he trusts you. He believes you're in love with him, because you were.*

Maybe I still am.

I pull the trunk closed and get into a comfortable position. And now every scenario where this could go tragically wrong starts playing through my head. What if he doesn't put his bag on the back seat as normal? What if he goes back upstairs to check on me? What if he hears me breathing?

The car door opens. I hold my breath. Something, I assume his bag, is tossed onto the back seat. And then he climbs into the car and starts the engine. I breathe again now that there's some ambient background noise. He puts some music on. Sleep Token, if I'm not mistaken. Unsurprising. We've never really discussed our taste in music, but this is the kind I thought he'd enjoy. Imagine if he was a secret Swiftie. I could tease him about that relentlessly.

Except there will be no more teasing. No more Lincoln—or Killian, or whoever the hell he is. If my plan works like it's supposed to, I'll be free and clear in a matter of hours. It doesn't matter that I have no idea where I'll go or what I'll do for money or food, but I won't be in prison. Freedom is so close—I can almost taste it.

I close my eyes and mentally sing along to the songs that I know. It's calming and gives me something to focus on.

And I wait.

CHAPTER 65
IMOGEN

The car comes to a stop. The engine cuts off. I hold my breath, waiting for him to get out and leave. I listen intently. His seat belt is unclipped. The door opens and then slams closed. Next, he'll take his bag from the back seat.

I wait.

He doesn't open the door to the back seat of the car. Instead there's noise. Screeching tires. Shouting. A gunshot. Now another. And voices. Familiar voices.

My heart is racing. Adrenaline thundering around my body. I cover my head with my arms. What's happening?

The trunk opens.

My heart stops beating and I blink as a bright flashlight shines in my eyes, obscuring my view of whoever is holding it. It's not Lincoln though. The silhouette of the frame is too small to be him.

And then I hear that familiar voice again. "There she is. My darling girl."

Grandfather?

The light is gone and a hand is reaching for me, pulling me out of the trunk. My head is spinning with confusion and so many questions. Why is my grandfather here? Where is Killian?

Was he aware of my plan all along? Does he know I stole the key? What if they're all in on this sick twisted scheme together.

I spin around, straining to see in the darkness. We're at a deserted car lot. There are two other cars here. And there is Lincoln, on his knees with his hands behind his head. A gun is pointed at his temple by a man dressed head to toe in black military gear, similar to the kind Lincoln wears. Blood runs down his face.

In addition to the man who pulled me out of the trunk, there are another four men here surrounding the small lot, dressed in a similar getup as the man beside Lincoln. And of course there's my grandfather, staring at me with what looks like pride. He runs a hand over his thin gray beard and winks at me before directing his attention to Lincoln.

But Lincoln is only focused on me. His scowl murderous and his eyes burning into my skin with laser focus.

My grandfather slips an arm around my shoulder, and like the good granddaughter I was trained to be, I resist the urge to shrug him off. "She did such a good job for me, Killian. Don't you think? Weeding out our traitor."

Wait! What? He knows this is Killian? And what the hell does he mean by a *good job*?

Lincoln growls. "I should have fucking known, Saul."

Thoughts and questions are tumbling over themselves in my head, none of them making any sense. What should Killian have known?

"I thought you were onto me when her delightful little tracker stopped working," my grandfather cackles. "But, imagine my surprise when it popped up on my screen last week. I knew then it was only a matter of time before we found you."

Her tracker? I have a tracker? Where, and how? This is getting more bizarre by the second. I keep my mouth closed, trying to figure out what the hell is going on. Who it is I'm supposed to be most afraid of. Lincoln might not be the man he said he was,

THE AUCTION

but then it's clear my grandfather has been keeping plenty of secrets from me too. I want to escape them both. Them and every other man who has ever lied to and manipulated me.

My grandfather runs a fingertip over my cheekbone, then hugs me closer, smiling at me, his eyes full of admiration as he looks at me in a way he never did when I was a child. "I knew my good little princess would bring you back to me, Killian. She always does exactly as she's told."

"What? No!" I shout my protest. My grandfather's fingernails dig into the muscles of my shoulder, a warning designed to silence me.

But I'm focused on Lincoln, and the indescribable pain on his face. Not physical pain because I'm sure he could stand a lot more of that, but the deep pain of betrayal. A pain I recognize all too well. At this moment, I have no idea what I feel for him. Everything is too mixed up and confused—my love for him bleeding into my anger and confusion. But I know that I can't let him believe I betrayed him. "Linc, I didn't—"

"Now, now, Imogen. Let's not get ourselves worked up into a tizzy." Her voice cuts me off, and it's so achingly warm and familiar that it makes my legs almost buckle.

"Larissa?"

She steps out from behind the parked SUV beside us and smiles. "Welcome home, my darling girl."

I shake my head, trying to make sense of anything that's going on. "What's happening? I don't understand."

She cups my face in her hand. "You did it, Imogen. You did exactly what you promised you would. You delivered us the traitor."

The traitor? Do they mean Killian? So they both knew who he was? They used me as bait? "No," I murmur. Not her too. What are they doing? Why are they saying this?

"Imogen!" Killian's roar shatters through the fog in my brain and I turn to face him. We stare at each other across the fifty feet of distance that separates us. His scowl is dark and dangerous and it sends a shiver down my spine. "I'm coming for you." His tone is no less menacing than the look he's giving me, and I realize he's making a threat, not a promise of rescue.

What happens next takes place so fast that it's a chaotic blur. A shot is fired and the man with the gun pointed at Lincoln's head drops to his knees. Then Lincoln quickly disarms him and shoots him in the face. He fires another two shots in quick succession, dropping two more of my grandfather's soldiers. Shots are fired back and my grandfather dives behind the SUV while Larissa drags me with them.

I crouch low, covering my ears, praying that we don't die. More gunshots ring out. And then there's the unmistakable sound of car tires screeching. I peer out from behind the car. Five dead soldiers lie on the ground as Killian climbs into the black car that just pulled up. And despite everything he's done, the messed-up part of me that is stupid enough to still care for him is relieved he's not dead.

My grandfather curses his fallen men for "not doing their fucking jobs" and I'm reminded of the cruelty of the man who raised me. While I was away, I thought of him fondly because I had no one else in the world to compare him to. Another thing that's changed.

I stand to my full height. Wind whips my hair around my face and I roughly push it out of my eyes. But it's too late. Lincoln Knight has gone. Killian Wolfe has gone.

And his last threat rings in my ears, sending a shiver of pure unadulterated fear up the length of my spine.

I'm coming for you.

★★★★★

For the sizzling, heart-pounding conclusion to Imogen and Lincoln/Killian's love story, preorder a copy of *The Game*, the second book in the Wages of Sin duology. Available November 2026 in print, ebook and audio wherever books are sold, from Sadie Kincaid and HarperCollins.

And if you want more of Sadie's deliciously dark romances, check out her Chicago Ruthless series, set in the same universe as *The Auction*. This complete series is available now in ebook and audiobook, as well as in print with exclusive endmatter from Sadie Kincaid and HarperCollins.

Read on for an excerpt of *Dante*, book one in the Chicago Ruthless series, a spicy dark mafia romance with kidnapping, forced proximity, accidental pregnancy and touch-her-and-die energy.

EXCERPT FROM *DANTE*

DANTE

Katerina's arms and legs are crossed as she hugs her body and tries to make herself as small as possible, nestled against the corner of the car so she's as far from me as she can physically be. I decided to accompany her in the back in case she tried to pull any kind of escape attempt. Given how feisty she was in her house earlier, I'm pretty sure we got ourselves a live wire. There aren't many people who would have the balls to try and shoot Max.

Speaking of my best friend, I can sense his eyes on me in the rearview mirror every few minutes, probably wondering what the hell I'm even thinking, bringing her to my house instead of making an example of her.

Unfortunately I have no answer to that question for him. No reasonable explanation as to why I'm taking her as payment for her brother's debt. Instead I should be doing whatever is necessary to get any information out of her that might lead me to the slippery little fuck. But, I believed her when she said she had no idea where he was, and besides that, there's something about her that intrigues me. I did a background check on her when we were trying to find Leo. She trained to be a nurse, and she worked as one in Northwestern Memorial for three years. Seems she was good at it too. I read all her performance reviews. Incredible with patients and respected by her colleagues.

Then two years ago, she quit, and nobody from the hospital ever heard from her again. She left her nice apartment block and moved to one of the poorest neighborhoods in the city. She took a night shift, cleaning empty office blocks. Besides that, she rarely leaves the house.

She's a mystery. A puzzle I want to solve. I've always been good at reading people. Usually, within a few minutes, I can figure out their story, but not her. That's what intrigues me about her. It has nothing to do with her bright blue eyes and the fire in them when she stood up to Maximo and me. Nothing to do with her perky tits straining against that cleaning uniform she has on beneath her coat, or her full pink lips and how good they would look if I was fucking her smart mouth. And absolutely nothing to do with the way her blatant defiance and disregard for who I am made me harder than I've ever been in my life.

No. Not that at all.

WHEN WE PULL UP TO MY HOUSE, KATERINA cranes her neck to get a full view of the place. It's huge, with two wings, one for me, and one for my brother and his wife. But he's not living here right now. No doubt, she's already looking for ways to escape. She won't find any.

Once Max has stopped the car, I climb out and walk around to her side. When I pull the door open, she scowls at me. I suppress a smile. Feisty little kitten.

I hold out my hand to her. "You can walk into the house, or I will carry you in. And you can kick and scream for help and not one single person here will stop me or come to your rescue."

She glares at me as she weighs her options, and a few seconds later, she steps out of the car, ignoring my proffered hand. Her jaw is set in defiance as she walks the few steps to the house beside me. Max grabs her small suitcase from the trunk. She didn't bring much, just a few clothes and toiletries and a photo album.

My housekeeper, Sophia, opens the door as we reach it, having been informed of our expected arrival by Max.

"Mr. Moretti," she says with a polite nod.

"Sophia, this is Katerina. Can you show her to her room?"

She doesn't show any hint of surprise on her face, despite the strangeness of this situation. It's not like me to introduce my female houseguests to my housekeeper, and even more so for me to offer them their own room. "Of course, sir," she replies, opening the door and ushering Katerina inside.

Katerina turns to me, her eyes wide and full of anxiety. A shiver of excitement runs up my spine. I like the way she looks at me. Here, I am the man with all the answers she needs. I'm the man who holds the key to her future. She is dependent on me, and for reasons I'm not entirely sure of yet, I definitely like that.

"I'll bring your bag up in a moment," I tell her, and she nods, although her face is still understandably clouded in confusion and uncertainty.

She obediently follows Sophia along the hallway and up the stairs and I watch her, drawn to the sight of her round ass swaying in her skintight uniform. I'm not sure which side of her I like best yet—feisty or obedient. But I'm determined to acquaint myself with both. I sink my teeth into my bottom lip to stop a groan from escaping.

A few seconds later, Max joins me.

"You sure you know what you're doing, D?" he asks, giving me a look that suggests he knows my motives aren't entirely driven by my need to recoup the money that Leo Evanson stole from us.

As I always do, I answer him honestly. "No fucking clue, Max."

He rolls his eyes. "So, what exactly is she gonna be doing while she's here?"

"I'll think of something."

His lips twitch in the hint of a smirk. "I'm sure you will."

I ignore his innuendo, not wanting to talk about her like that with him. And the truth is, I don't *only* want her here because the thought of breaking down her walls and fucking her until she screams my name is so appealing. "She was a nurse, right?" I remind him. "Surely, she has skills that will be useful to us?"

"Sure," he says, but he's still looking at me like he knows I'm thinking about another set of skills she might have. "You haven't forgotten your pop is coming for dinner later, have you?"

"Fuck!"

He chuckles. "You did forget?"

I screw my eyes closed and pinch the bridge of my nose, trying to stave off the headache that's already building. "You know I do my best to forget anything related to him."

"Good thing one of us is on the ball though?" He nudges my arm, and I roll my eyes at him.

Anyone else tried to ride my ass like he does and I'd put a bullet in them. But Max is like a brother to me. He's a year older than I am and we grew up together. Our fathers were best friends until his was murdered when he was fourteen. He lived with us after that. There was no official adoption—it just was. I would die for him and he'd do the same for me in a heartbeat. Loyalty like that is hard to come by, especially in this life.

"Why do you think I keep you around here?" I say as I take Katerina's bag from him.

"Because you couldn't fucking function without me." He heads off down the hallway to my study, whistling as he goes, while I head upstairs to welcome our guest.

SOPHIA IS LEAVING THE ROOM WHEN I REACH IT, and when I walk inside, Katerina is staring out the window, looking at the courtyard below. She's taken off her coat at least, so I figure she's accepted she won't be leaving anytime soon.

"How is the room?"

The sound of my voice makes her spin on her heel. She glares at me, eyes full of fury. "Kind of nice for a prison cell," she says, brimming with snark.

Goddammit, I want nothing more than to throw her on the bed and fuck that attitude out of her. *Perhaps later.*

"Well, it does have a very robust lock," I tell her. "Not that you'll need it."

She folds her arms across her chest. "I wouldn't be too sure of that."

I take a step closer and she doesn't flinch. "Well, nobody lives here, except me. And Sophia of course, but she lives downstairs."

She arches an eyebrow at me and I would dearly fucking love to fuck that defiant look off her face. "It would take more than a lock to keep me out if I wanted in here, kitten."

She averts her eyes for a second, then hugs her arms to her chest, shivering as she rubs her bare arms as though she's cold despite the warm room. Is that from fear or something else? A few seconds later, her eyes are on me once more. "What exactly do you want with me? Are you planning on just keeping me here forever, or am I only supposed to stay here until I pay off this debt?"

"Yes."

The spot between her brows pinches in a frown. "Yes what? You're keeping me here forever or until I work off Leo's debt?"

How about both? I roll my neck and take a breath. Something about this woman has gotten under my goddamn skin. She challenges me, and I should hate that, but I really fucking don't. "You'll work off your brother's substantial debt and then you can leave," I say instead.

"And just how do I do that? And how long will it take? What about my actual job? My house?" She fires off the questions, arms still crossed over her chest.

"Your employer will be informed of your new circumstances. Your house will be maintained until you're ready to return to it. And as for how long that will take, that all depends on how good you are," I say, crossing the room until I'm standing so close to her I can smell her scent. It's not a perfume. It's sweet like chocolate. The cocoa butter lotion I saw her throwing in her bag earlier.

"Good at what?" she whispers, and her lip trembles slightly.

I don't know what makes me harder—feisty Katerina or trembling-with-fear Katerina. I'm going to have plenty of fun with both of them. But not today. Not yet.

I could pin her down on this bed and fuck her senseless and there wouldn't be a single thing she could do about it. No matter how hard she fought me or how loud she screamed, nobody would come to her aid. But as much as I want her, and despite the kind of man I am, I'm not in the habit of forcing myself on women.

"Whatever it is I tell you to do."

Her lip wobbles again and I step closer until I'm invading every inch of her personal space. She sucks in a deep breath, making those goddamn tits strain against the snaps on her uniform even more. One flick of my wrist and that damn uniform would be open and her chest would be completely exposed. I ram my hands into my pockets to stop myself from touching her. I can tell that she wants to step back and give herself a little space, but she's too stubborn to back down. And that only makes me want her more.

"I am not having sex with you," she snarls.

"I don't force women into having sex with me. I certainly don't have to pay them for the privilege."

Relief shines in her eyes momentarily, and because I'm a twisted fuck who likes to see how far I can push her, I say, "My men, on the other hand . . . Well, they are a different matter."

"I—I'm not having sex with anyone," she stammers, and tears well in her eyes as she steps away from me, pressing her back against the window. "I'd rather you kill me than keep me here like some paid whore to entertain your men."

DANTE

There's a terror in her eyes that wasn't there a moment ago. Something deeper and more primal than anything I've seen from her already. She's hiding a secret and it's shimmering just beneath the surface now. I can almost feel it, but she keeps it well hidden. And I find myself doing something completely out of character—giving her some reassurance. "You were a nurse, right? So I'm sure you have other talents that will come in useful instead, Katerina."

Without waiting for her reply, I walk toward the door. I don't want to give her any further indication that I am anything but the monster she believes I am. It's better for both of us if she goes on believing that.

"My name is Kat. I hate Katerina," she calls after me.

Is this what déjà vu feels like? Because I've heard those words before. It stops me in my tracks and I turn around and face her once more. And suddenly it's six years ago and I'm looking at someone else's face. We stood here in this room, just like this, and she said almost those exact same words. Except Nicole preferred Nicci, and she was never my prisoner. She was here through choice. Until she wasn't.

My chest tightens as five years of rage and guilt surges up from my gut, threatening to spill out until I push it all back down where it belongs.

"Are you okay?" Kat's voice snaps me from the past, reminding me that that time in my life has long gone. "You look like you've just seen a ghost."

"Maybe," I mumble, and she blinks at me in confusion. "Anyway, make yourself at home until I figure out what to do with you."

Something unreadable flickers in her expression.

"Except for my study, you're free to explore the house. But you try and escape and I will hand you over to my men to do with as they please. You understand me?"

She offers a single obedient nod. "Yes."

Fuck! My cock is twitching with the idea of pushing her and seeing exactly how submissive I could force her to be. I blow out a breath and try to clear my mind of images of her on her knees. "Sophia makes dinner around eight. You can eat wherever you like, but my father is coming this evening, so I'd prefer you eat in your room."

"I'd rather eat in here anyway," she snipes.

From docile to full of sass in a heartbeat. Kat Evanson fascinates me. "Of course you would. Not much of a people person, are you?"

She rests her hands on her hips. "Well, you tell me since you seem to know a hell of a lot about me, Mr. Moretti."

Whatever glimpse of vulnerability she allowed me to see a moment ago has vanished, and her armor is firmly back in place. I remind myself that's a good thing; she'll need that armor while she's living here. "I make it my business to know everything there is to know about my enemies, Ms. Evanson."

I walk out the door and close it behind me. I need to do something to take my mind off the fiery wildcat because walking around my house with a semipermanent hard-on isn't my idea of a good time.

Maybe I should just fuck her and get it over with. Get her out of my head so I can focus. Except that I don't want to simply take Kat; I want to own every single part of her. And the worst of it is, I have absolutely no idea why.

★ ★ ★ ★ ★

Continue Sadie Kincaid's bestselling Chicago Ruthless series with *Dante*, available now in ebook, audio and print wherever books are sold.

ACKNOWLEDGMENTS

I always start these by thanking my incredible readers, and that is because without you, none of this would be possible!

I owe a huge thanks to my wonderful agent, Lesley Sabga, for believing in me and helping to make this dream come true. To the entire team at MIRA Books, it is so incredibly wonderful to work with you all. The enthusiasm and support you have shown for me and this book is both humbling and awe-inspiring. Thank you for believing in this story the way that you do! And a very extra special thanks to my amazing editor, John Jacobson, whose insight and editorial eye has made this story so much richer than it originally was. I adore the passion you have for these characters and I can't wait for us to work on the next part of their adventure.

A special thanks to my beta readers, Kate, Katie and Dani, and their ability to read at lightning speed. And I can't not do a shout-out to the members of Sadie's Ladies and Sizzling Alphas. You are all superstars and I value your support and encouragement more than you can ever know. Thank you to my group mods, Connie and Sydney, for helping keep that amazing group running smoothly.

A huge thanks to my author friends, both near and far, who

help make this journey all that more special. And a special mention to Jenny Madore and the authors in her sprint room for giving me a kick in the pants when I most need it.

To my lovely PAs, Kate, Katie and Andrea, for their support and everything they do to make my life easier.

And last, but definitely not least, to my three incredible boys, who inspire me to be better every single day. And Mr. Kincaid—you are still all my book boyfriends rolled into one and I never want to do this without you!

Sadie x